CRUK
1-50
9/4

THE SUMMER ISLAND SWAP

ALSO BY SAMANTHA TONGE

The Christmas Calendar Girls

THE SUMMER ISLAND SWAP

Samantha Tonge

Dear Catherine,

Happy Reading!

Best wishes

Sam Tonge ♡

HEAD
of ZEUS

An Aria Book

This edition first published in the United Kingdom in 2020 by Aria,
an imprint of Head of Zeus Ltd

A CIP catalogue record for this book is available from the
British Library.

ISBN: 9781838930783

Typeset by Siliconchips Services Ltd UK

Cover design: Cherie Chapman

Aria
c/o Head of Zeus
First Floor East
5–8 Hardwick Street
London EC1R 4RG

www.ariafiction.com

For dearest Jay - I wouldn't swap you for the world.

I

'I still think it's madness,' I said, getting up from the faux-leather sofa to peer over Amy's shoulder. 'To come into five thousand pounds, only to blow it all on a single holiday…'

Amy turned around from the circular dining table and folded her arms. 'No. Madness would be turning down a month of luxury, all expenses paid. I've spotted a great deal. Even my winnings wouldn't normally cover four weeks at this particular destination. Our break must be written in the stars.'

'Written in platinum, more like. And who on earth goes away for that long?'

'Someone who hasn't been on holiday – not a proper one – for nine years, because she's been so busy building a home and a future for her amazing younger sister. That's me, by the way.' She smiled.

My cheeks felt hot.

'And I'll be left with a bit of my winnings. Perhaps I'll finally get to enjoy all the musicals I've been longing to see, like Hamilton.'

Over the years Amy had developed an obsession with West End musical shows. Perhaps it was an obvious outcome after being addicted to Disney films as a child. I'd never believed in the whole 'prince and princess' story. Being older, observing my parents' relationship, I always knew that grown-up life was different.

'But you could use your windfall to go one step further with your career. It would boost your finances to start studying full-on veterinary science and probably pay for the first year's accommodation. What with student loans and...'

I talked for a few minutes. After years of scraping money together to keep up the payments on our modest London flat, it wouldn't feel right splashing out on private sunbeds and cocktails. It went against all the instincts I'd honed since leaving the house I'd grown up in, to set up on my own.

Amy's face darkened and she turned back to the screen. 'I've told you a hundred times, Sarah, university... that's one of the few things Dad was right about. I... I would have loved to be a vet. It was my life's dream for such a long time. I'm not grateful to Dad for much, but he did at least stop me making a fool of myself by applying to study such a challenging subject. He was right – I just haven't got what it takes.'

'How can you say that, Amy? Your grades alone—'

'Being a veterinary nurse is more challenging than I ever imagined,' she continued, ignoring my comment. 'Look, Sarah – two other members of the lottery syndicate are also taking holidays. One of the surgeons is going on a cruise... I wish you would trust me on this.'

I opened my mouth to protest but the stiffness that had taken hold of her shoulders stopped me. We shouldn't argue. It was rare that we both had a Saturday off. Tonight we were going to the cinema. My chest glowed at the prospect of Amy's usual excitement over a blue slush drink and ketchup slathered hot dog. Sometimes it was hard to believe she was twenty-three.

But then I was twenty-seven and hadn't even been kissed. Not properly. One-night stands and short relationships didn't count. I meant proper kissing like you saw in the romantic movies I loved watching, where it was savoured on a bench or under a lamppost. I should have had that with Callum but looking back, the spark wasn't there; I never got the sense of wanting a kiss with him to last forever.

'A trip away is exactly what we both need,' continued Amy as tentative rays of sunshine that had snuck through the blinds retreated behind assembling April clouds. 'Especially you.' Her voice sounded thick. 'You've worked your guts out all these years, giving me a roof over my head and so much more – like funding my training to become a nurse at Paws & Claws. Words can't explain how much it meant to me, having this flat, your home to move into when I turned eighteen and could finally get away from *him*.'

'This has always been *our* home – even when you weren't here.'

Her eyes shone. 'Well, this is my small way of paying you back.'

'There's no debt.' I rubbed her arm and crouched down by her side.

She closed the screen of her laptop and turned around, face flushed as I stood up. 'Let me do this on my own. For a change let me take charge.'

But had she checked the reviews on TripAdvisor? And I'd have to find a way to subtly remind her about holiday insurance. The last year or two she never seemed to understand when I was simply trying to help.

I loved Amy more than anything in the world but she'd always be the younger sister who'd run to me when Dad had been mean; the sister who needed me.

'Or are you trying to sneak a peek at exactly where we're going?' Her sharp tone couldn't disguise the twinkle in her eyes. 'There are several islands to choose from and I've finally made a decision. Now go and make those chocolate cookies you promised, whilst I book this surprise.'

'Ooh, an *island*? Thanks for letting that slip.' I chuckled. 'And, um, I might have already seen a few other clues,' I said sheepishly. 'Like photos of a lush hotel with Roman pillars. Waterbeds. An indigo ocean. White sand beaches. Something about tropical massages and Aqua Dancing and all-day buffets offering pyramids of pastries and colourful seafood platters.'

'Sarah! The details are supposed to be top secret.'

'But I'm excited!' I bent down and gave her a tight hug.

'Get off,' she protested and pushed me away. She peered up from under her fringe. 'So, did it look okay? I want everything to be perfect.' She curled a section of hair between her fingers. It was short. Gamine. Brown like mine was without the highlights. It suited her petite figure currently dressed in dungarees over a high-necked jumper. I was taller, like Dad. Her whole look shouted practical.

'Okay? Amy, it looked idyllic. But are you sure about this? I work in the hotel business. My day is spent in hospitality, even though Best Travel doesn't exactly offer five-star accommodation. But you work with animals. You love the outdoors. Hiking. Getting down and dirty with our window box. Spa treatments and fine dining aren't exactly your thing.'

'They could be,' she said in a bright voice.

I raised an eyebrow.

'All right… we both know manicured nails would chip within an hour on me and I'd rather climb rocks than have hot stones placed on my Chakra points. And I'm a little concerned I might get bored. But who knows? I might enjoy the pampering and it wouldn't be a selfless break. Feeling that I was finally doing something for you – that would give me a sense of wellbeing that no fancy massage could ever match…'

Whistling – out-of-tune, as Amy never ceased to remind me – I went into the kitchen. It was only the size of Dad's and my stepmother's en-suite bathroom. Fondly, I ran a hand over the scratched units and gazed at a couple of cracked tiles. I loved every inch of this flat because it belonged to me and Amy.

And Nelly, our much-loved Burmese cat. She was ten now and became more regal as years passed. She padded into the kitchen, sat by her bowl and tidied her tail into a circle around her body.

I took out flour, butter and sugar. 'I can't help worrying about Nelly, if we're away for that long,' I called through to the living room. It was cluttered with Amy's animal ornaments and my beauty magazines, framed photos of the two of us, and several shelves of novels – romance for me, thrillers for Amy. But I didn't mind the lack of space in what was already a cramped room. Those objects were proof of the new, happier life we had now.

'Sarah, I'm a veterinary nurse. I told you, I've a queue of great people offering to look after her. Or don't you believe me?' There was an edge to her voice.

Of course I did. It was just my habit to worry about Amy and Nelly, my little family.

They were all I needed. Having seen the life Mum led, I'd decided long ago I was never going to get married. The only weddings I wanted to be a part of were the fictional ones in my favourite movies and books.

'I'll still have to clear it at work. I'm not sure how Prue will feel about me taking a month off.'

Just the mention of my boss's name made my stomach knot.

'No one's indispensable. Not even wonderful you,' she called back.

My chest felt warm. Over recent years, Amy had matured and started to look out for me, cooking dinner and mowing the lawn. However, I'd never lose my maternal feelings towards her. When we were ten and six ours was quite an age gap. As was eighteen and fourteen when I'd had to leave her behind with Dad but promised we'd live together again. I beat the sugar and butter, remembering her tears and his folded arms as I dragged my suitcase past the fountain and out of the huge driveway, into the street. I'd finally realised I had to leave after… I swallowed. No. I wasn't going to think about that now.

I let Nelly into the back garden, busied myself with ingredients and cleaned up whilst the cookies baked. Their sweet aroma wafted through the air as I carried them into the lounge, on a tray, with two coffees.

'Good timing,' said Amy and turned off her screen, looking pleased with herself. I put the tray on the table and joined her.

'Is it all booked?'

She nodded. 'A modest deposit paid. The rest is due in the middle of June, two weeks before we leave.'

'Can't you at least share which part of the world we're visiting?'

'That would be telling,' she replied airily and took the largest cookie.

I jumped up and held her right arm firm whilst tickling the armpit. 'I won't stop until I find out, Amy Sterling.'

However, she was as strong as me these days and, giggling, held the cookie in her mouth and forced both of my hands away. I sat down once more. I recognised that expression. She was determined to keep her secret. Sometimes, with my impulsive sister, that could be a dangerous thing, like when she'd agreed to do a charity skydive with colleagues at work. She didn't tell me until the morning of the jump.

'Just a clue. A teeny one,' I said. 'Please...'

'I've never seen you this excited before. Well, not since you were made assistant manager. Oh, and the time you found that fancy moisturiser for half price.'

'It wasn't just *any* moisturiser. The Duchess of Cambridge uses it.' I pressed my palms together. 'At least let me guess... the Canary Islands? Barbados? Australia's an island, right? I mean, you and me – we share most things, don't we?'

'Best buddies, always,' she said solemnly.

It was a promise we'd made to each other, the day after Mum's funeral. And sure enough, we confided in each other about our latest celebrity crushes, about our dreams for the future; we put the world to rights over Chardonnay and Pringles. I knew her favourite colour, favourite food, favourite band. She could always tell when I'd had a stressful day at work and, without prying, would make me a hot chocolate, fetch a blanket and switch on my current Netflix obsession.

Amy laughed and put down the cookie. 'I can't face this interrogation for the next three months. All right – but no more questions after this, agreed?'

'Promise,' I said, beaming.

Her chest puffed out. 'I've booked us the *best* break ever. It's exotic. Luxurious. Our holiday destination is… one of the British Virgin Islands.'

I stared.

'What's the matter?'

'Nothing… it's just…' A lump rose in my throat. 'That really is high-end.'

'And no less than you deserve,' she said quietly. 'But don't ask me which one. You'd never guess, anyway. There are over fifty.' She pretended to zip her lips shut.

My stomach fluttered as I imagined the celebrity treatment and Michelin-starred food awaiting us. I'd have to get my nails done, especially themed for somewhere so grand, perhaps with tiny aeroplanes painted on them. My highlights would need re-touching. I'd treat myself to a new bikini.

'What are you thinking?' Amy asked.

'I'm imagining what it would be like, living in a part of the world like that forever. Away from the grind and dust of London… Only mingling with jolly tourists seeking a good time…'

'I'd prefer to mix with the locals – otherwise it would feel false… manufactured… like moving to Disneyland.'

'Reality is overrated, if you ask me. The ultimate getaway must be working and living on a cruise ship.'

Amy pulled a face. 'I can't think of anything worse.'

I smiled. 'You'd miss saving animals. Doing good. You're not as shallow as me.'

Her voice softened. 'Perhaps my perspective is different because I've had it easier. You had a brutal introduction to reality on your own, aged eighteen. Whereas I've always had you to rely on, looking out for me...'

I'd tried to act as a mum to Amy all these years because I knew how hard life was without that maternal presence.

I shook myself, sipped my coffee and pictured myself on a beach, a daiquiri by my side, wearing large sunglasses and an Audrey Hepburn *Breakfast at Tiffany's* hat. Amy and I clinked mugs.

This was going to be the most perfect holiday ever.

2

Finally the showery spring had passed, yet it was June and still the sky was threatening. I'd been hoping for a few weekends to gain a tan in the local park, before my imminent trip to *the British Virgin Islands*...

I still couldn't believe I was going. My anticipation was building.

Despite the bad feeling it had caused with Prue.

Despite her making it clear I'd have to work all hours when I got back, to make it good.

I unclenched my teeth. It had felt like a long early morning shift. These weeks running up to my break should have been filled with excitement about the trip of a lifetime. Instead Prue had done her best to wear me down. It was true – I should have consulted her before Amy booked it, but it all happened so fast. However, I'd rather her have said no, if I'd known she was going to continually make me suffer for it, with her frequent comments about how I'd have a mountain of paperwork to catch up on when I got back; that I owed her big time for letting me go off during one of our busiest months.

I sat in the poky staff room at Best Travel and gazed at the half-eaten egg and cress sandwich. It used to be a favourite of Mum's. Very occasionally, she put herself first with Dad and served them, even though his nose would wrinkle. I wiped my mouth and finished my bottle of water. A reusable one, of course – Amy made sure of that. For a moment I wished I'd swigged something stronger, ahead of the chat I wanted to have with Prue before I left to meet Amy for holiday shopping. I'd had another of my ideas on how to improve Best Travel and wanted to run it past my boss. It had kept me awake last night and I couldn't wait to share it, optimistic that this would be the one that inspired her to finally embrace change and would make up for me taking four weeks off.

I tried to ignore the niggling voice in my head, telling me that Prue was being unfair. That I'd never taken more than one week off at a time, in all the years I'd worked at Best Travel. That I was the first to muck in if a member of housekeeping rang up ill. That I'd worked hours and hours of unpaid overtime since I'd become assistant manager.

But it was no good. The frustration within me swelled. My fists formed balls.

I never let on to Amy just how tough it was working for that woman; never wanted to risk my sister feeling guilty about all the years I'd had to suffer condescending put-downs in order to put food on the table. To be fair, Prue had eventually promoted me from receptionist and in my new role I'd learnt loads about the financial side. However, Prue wasn't a dreamer and always knocked back any fresh ideas I had to grow our reputation and make more money.

I felt like a clipped bird.

Please let things be different today.

But if they weren't… I sat up straighter. A month in a luxury hotel was going be an opportunity to find out what it would take to reach the top of my profession. I felt as if I'd put in enough years now, as assistant manager, to take the next step forwards in my career. I'd been researching for several months. It was fascinating. For example, the walls of The Dorchester contained compressed seaweed and cork for soundproofing. Apparently Hitchcock said it would be the perfect place to commit a murder.

I was so used to working all hours but there was no chance this trip would make me feel guilty because I'd be taking notes on the way things were run and still focusing on work. This five-star holiday might set me in a good position to seek a more personally rewarding – and better paid – job once I got home.

'You still here?' asked Prue. She made herself a black coffee and sat down next to me, bringing an atmosphere as sour as the vinegar on her crisps. 'Then I've just got one last job for you, before you knock off for the day – the new family with those bawling twins want to know if we have blackout curtains for tonight. I don't trust myself to give them the bad news, so you'll have to.' She rolled her eyes. 'Honestly. Some people truly believe a hotel should be a home from home.'

That's where Prue and I were fundamentally different – I longed to work somewhere that went that extra mile to fulfil a guest's every need. There was no better feeling than when some little difference you made brightened their stay. In spite of my critical boss, I enjoyed the hands-on aspects of my job so much. I was lucky seeing as I'd only applied to work here, all those years ago, because the position came with accommodation – a perk I was grateful for until I could afford a proper place of my own.

'I'll sort it. No problem, Prue. Perhaps I can find some black bin liners to put up instead.' I closed my Tupperware lunch box. I pressed down firmly on the lid, clutching the sides as I spoke. 'Could I just run an idea past you that I've been working on – on how we could make the Best Travel experience even more... special?' I couldn't help smiling. 'It kept me awake until the early hours.'

With her hair scraped back into a ponytail, there was nothing to hide the bored expression that crossed her face. Only last month she'd rejected my suggestion that we extend the basic complimentary toiletries range to include a plastic shower cap and sachet of hand cream. Not having much money to spare myself, I knew that for our average customer the small things like that meant a lot. But 'Don't fix what isn't broke' Prue was a fan of the status quo.

Still. I had to give it a go. One thing I'd learnt, since leaving home, was to never give up. Like the way I'd taught myself to hang wallpaper. There'd been tears. Rolls of discarded paper that had gone on wonky. I'd felt so proud when I finished one wall.

I took a deep breath. 'The rooms on the top floor that are slightly bigger... Why don't we trial stocking them with better quality linen, curtains that match duvets, small mini bars and trouser presses? We could charge more and might snag customers wanting a bigger slice of luxury at a lower price.' I leant forward. 'We'd be more competitive against that posh hotel down the road and—'

'What... this break will remind you of the nine 'til five?'

'Well, I do work in a hotel,' I said and shot her a humorous glance. 'Just imagine the clientele you could attract at that sort of place. I'd offer butlers and personal masseuses and waitressing staff on the beach. This holiday is going to give me a fantastic inside view of high-end hospitality. Don't get me wrong, I... I love my assistant manager position at Best Travel, the job is great... but you know I've been researching working at top-notch hotels. This trip is going to provide me with brilliant insight for interviews. I shall take a notebook and write down everything we experience, from start to finish.'

She gave me a sideways glance. 'This holiday is supposed to be a getaway – a getaway from the usual routine.'

'And it will be.'

'No, it won't. By the sounds of it you're going to spend every hour thinking about the hotel business – namely work.'

'But I'll be experiencing hospitality from the other side of the fence – that's completely new. This is the perfect opportunity to make up for my lack of experience of actually working in a luxury setting. I think I'll write a personal statement, based on this trip, to attach to my CV, explaining what I've learnt from living for a month as a five-star guest.'

Amy raised an eyebrow and gave an exasperated sigh.

'What?'

'Nothing.' She glanced away. 'I've put the oven on for those pizzas we bought.'

'I'll chop up some peppers and mushrooms for the top. We can kid ourselves it's healthy, then.'

Half an hour later we both sat on the sofa again, in our

pyjamas, eating pizza and drinking squash. The day's cloudy sky flirted with dusk. I didn't mind. Whilst I loved eating ice cream and favoured my summer wardrobe, the best season was winter and evenings holed up in the flat. We'd drink hot chocolate and watch Netflix in our dressing gowns with a plateful of biscuits whilst diplomatic Nelly would stretch herself across both our laps.

Amy finished her last mouthful, crusts and all. It had been a busy day – although the calorie hit didn't perk her up. Her mood had been more subdued than usual since we got back.

'Good morning at work?' I asked.

Amy's lips upturned. 'The best. You should have seen this owner's face when she came to pick up her dog, Brutus – he's a feisty Chihuahua…' Her eyes twinkled. 'He's been so ill after eating a large bar of chocolate. He almost didn't make it, but turned a corner after a night on an intravenous drip. Mrs Smith couldn't stop crying when he swiped her with his paw like he always used to.' Amy picked up some strands of melted cheese from her plate. 'She's a really interesting woman and works for a company that makes jewellery out of recycled household objects such as knitting needles, cutlery and vinyl records. I'm going to buy something small out of what's left of my winnings. I think it's fantastic, the difference businesses like that are trying to make.' Amy stuffed the gooey splodge of cheese into her mouth and then looked at me, embarrassed.

'I'd better take that plate off you before you lick the pattern off it,' I said and grinned as she pretended to hide it.

'Do you remember when you got back from guide camp, pizza was the first meal you craved?' she said. 'You declared you could never face eating another marshmallow or barbecued sausage again. I was so jealous. Roughing it was – and still is – my idea of heaven.'

'Yes, I had fun on that trip.'

'Did you? Honestly? Ten days in the outdoors, away from your bubble baths and neatly ironed clothes?' Amy stared.

'We slept outside, under the stars one night. I've never forgotten how dark the sky is, away from city lights. So pretty.' I leant back into the cushions. 'It was great, not having to bath every night and keep my hair tidy. Building dens. Learning about orienteering. The sense of freedom was brilliant.'

Amy gave me a curious look.

'But you wouldn't want to go on that camp now, would you?'

I shrugged. 'Grown-up life can become complacent. I need to be more adventurous. That's why it's time for me to really go for a new job. Not that I'm desperate to leave Best Travel. It's not awful,' I said and forced a laugh. 'I'm just ambitious, that's all...' I picked up our plates and hurried into the kitchen before Amy could ask any more questions. I fed Nelly her evening snack and relished the lingering smell of cheese, tomato and oregano. When I returned to the living room, Amy was sitting at the table in front of her laptop. I headed over and she snapped it shut.

'Holiday secrets,' she said and beamed.

I smiled and went into my bedroom to unpack my new clothes. When I came back Amy was still in front of her screen.

'I've just paid the full amount. There's no room for second thoughts now.'

'Good! Although there's no worry on that score – why *wouldn't* I want to go?'

'No reason. I… I just hope I've done the right thing; chosen the best holiday.'

She bit a fingernail. A habit from childhood. She didn't do it often now.

'How could you not have?' I said and squeezed her shoulder. 'Like I said earlier – you're older now… it's time I took some adventures. I'll have fun whatever this exotic stay brings.'

She caught my eye, thought for a moment and gave a thumbs-up.

'And you've put so much thought into next month. It's not as if you've made a spontaneous, last-minute booking.'

Amy's cheeks reddened and she grinned. Looking more like her usual cheerful self, she stood up and gave me a hug.

3

'Please tell me you're joking,' I said, my mouth feeling as if it were lined with beach sand. I'd just woken up with a crick in my neck, due to falling asleep against the aeroplane's window. 'What sort of name is Beef Island Airport, anyway?' I yawned and snuggled down again, this time on Amy's shoulder. 'The island we're landing on is actually called Tortola.'

Twenty-two hours – that's how long we'd been in the air, to get to one of the few Virgin Islands with a main airport. And now I'd just found out we still had to take a trip across the ocean when we landed, to get to our particular destination that Amy was still keeping secret.

Twenty-two hours of lying to my sister about what happened yesterday at work. Well, not lying exactly. I just hadn't found the right moment to share the bad news.

'I know, exciting isn't it?' said Amy and flicked through a travel guide. She was looking at photos of geckos and pelicans. I watched how she chewed on the inside of her cheek as she concentrated, like she'd used to as a little girl. It was me who'd read her a bedtime story after Mum passed away.

'Strictly speaking it's called the Terrance B Lettsome

Airport now,' she said. 'I believe the name Beef Island came from the fact that a nearby bay was where people stocked up with food for long voyages, in the eighteenth century – smoked beef being a staple.' Amy smiled at the air steward who came past to make sure everyone was wearing their seat belt, in preparation to land. Not that there was any need as I'd already subtly checked my sister's. I rubbed my neck and gazed out of the window. My stomach fluttered as the aeroplane decreased its height.

It began to sink in.

We were really doing this.

I was on the cusp of enjoying the holiday of a lifetime. I hadn't been on an aeroplane or sailed since my last holiday with Dad. I'd been sixteen and had run out of excuses to stay at home, despite having applied for a summer camp. Dad had a business meeting at a potential client's villa in Monaco and wanted to showcase his picture-perfect family to help close the deal. It was Amy who finally persuaded me – or rather begged. Teenage hormones had just hit and she'd become even more sensitive to his hurtful comments.

Picture-perfect.

Imperfect where it counted.

I forced my mind back to the present. It was my fault this journey had taken forever. Once Amy had made the final payment for our accommodation, I'd said the least we could do was be economical with the flights, despite her concerns about the carbon footprint of a longer journey. Her voice had a defeatist tone as she'd agreed, but later in the year, when she needed money, she'd realise I'd been right.

So instead of flying here in just thirteen hours, with one stop in Antigua, we'd flown to Miami and then on to San Juan airport in Puerto Rico. There we'd grabbed a lunch of chicken, rice and beans. And coffee, with these cute little pastries filled with guava paste. After those, I felt almost human again and my body finally decided it was relaxed enough to sleep – unless I'd just sunk into a carbohydrate coma.

'Have we already got tickets for the last leg of our journey?' I asked and yawned again before pulling out my hairbrush and compact mirror.

'Sarah. Stop worrying. It's all in hand.'

I swallowed several times as my ears popped whilst the aeroplane continued to descend. My spirits, in contrast, soared as I studied the clearest, most turquoise seas that appeared as the white cloud thinned and disappeared. I gazed across the cluster of islands, with their vibrant forest greens and sandy golden outlines.

There had been nothing pretty about yesterday and the thing I hadn't told Amy yet because the worry would ruin her holiday. We'd gained a large group booking at Best Travel. A group of salespeople who were holding a conference in a newly built local office building. It was one they'd be holding each month. Prue was off work – thank goodness. The atmosphere since I'd confronted her had been unbearable and for the first time in my working life I'd been tempted to ring in ill. Without her to consult, I took what I thought was the best decision and offered the sales team a discount if they booked with us again. It was a way of securing their business, even throughout the quieter autumn and spring months.

Prue phoned later in the day and when she found out about the discount came straight in. She didn't say much at first. Her silence unnerved me. Eventually, she said I shouldn't have authorised that without asking her first. I tried to explain my position – I told her I felt Best Travel needed to broaden its vision to stay afloat, especially as the local airport was being closed down. We could no longer rely on the bookings that brought in.

Using that word *vision* again was a mistake. She sacked me. On the spot. Declared it had been coming a long time. Announced I was too flighty for Best Travel. That her nephew who'd worked in housekeeping for a year wanted to go into hotel management – that he understood how things worked there and deserved promotion. She'd been planning to train him to help, whilst I was away, but now thought it was best if she offered him my position permanently.

The smug look on her face suggested she'd been planning this all along.

So I didn't have a job to go back to. That's the other reason I didn't tell Amy – I... felt ashamed. I'd always prided myself on being independent and always paying my own way.

A tear trickled down my cheek as I stared down at the ocean. Quickly I wiped it away.

Therefore this hotel holiday was more important to me than ever. I couldn't face returning to a job like the one I'd had. My disagreements with Prue proved I needed more responsibility – and freedom. During these four weeks I'd learn what it took to work for a more dynamic company and arm myself with that knowledge for interviews. I'd already compiled a list of the specialised recruitment agencies I would send my revised CV to. The quicker I got a new job and salary, the less likely it was I'd have to bother Amy with financial concerns.

'Do you think the ferry will have a shop on board?' I asked, pushing away thoughts of my unemployment. 'You know how Cheryl opposite loves perfume. I'm hoping to see some different brands.'

'We won't be taking the ferry.' A grin crossed Amy's face. 'It's a boat. Our island is only thirty minutes away. You see, it's private.'

My heart raced. 'Does that mean…?'

I could hardly stop myself from standing up to disembark, as the aeroplane bumped up and down on the runway. Necker Island. It had to be. The one owned by Richard Branson. I'd watched a documentary about it. Celebrities… world leaders… they all stayed there, spending tranquil days on the beach and sunsets at mouth-watering dinner parties.

Oh. My. God. Perhaps we'd become friends and he'd give me a great reference for my CV. Business tycoon, Richard Branson, had built his business empire from nothing. What an inspiration. That was one of the rare things Dad and I had in common – a respect for people who worked hard for what they wanted.

But not *so* hard that you hardly saw your daughters or thought family time meant attending a work barbecue to schmooze the latest client. Richard Branson seemed to have found the right balance. I'd watched footage of him kitesurfing and relaxing with loved ones next to pools with fairy lights. Impatience tightened my stomach as other passengers took their time, reaching up for their luggage. The thought of living on Necker for a whole month had reenergised me.

As we got off the aeroplane I wondered what our room's welcome package would consist of. No doubt champagne and a basket of exotic fruit. I pictured myself, just for once, being the guest and someone looking after *me*. I'd be able to catch up on Netflix shows at night and have the permanent knots in my shoulders massaged away. I could wallow in hot tubs and sleep between Egyptian cotton sheets.

'There's our luggage,' said Amy, pointing at the conveyor belt. My suitcase was twice the size of Amy's and I managed to get to it before her, even though, despite her small frame, she could deftly handle the feistiest cat or biggest dog. I didn't want Amy to hurt her back. She'd reckoned we should travel light but I'd bought lovely new sandals, a choice of handbags and jewellery… I'd probably brought my entire summer wardrobe but it wasn't as if I owned loads of clothes and we *were* away from home for a whole month. Ever practical Amy had tried – and failed – to get me to pack practical items like walking boots and long-sleeved shirts to protect against sunburn. Whereas I'd secretly packed the pineapple bikini she wasn't so keen on wearing.

I wanted to look my best. That had become a habit. Right from my first week in work, all those years ago, it was drilled into me that the first impression given by a hotel's staff was as crucial as a vacuumed welcome mat or polished glass. I'd become used to keeping my nail varnish crack-free. My foundation flawless. My clothes pristinely ironed.

I hated the tiny bit of me that thought at least how I presented myself would make Dad proud.

He'd sneered at Amy's academic ability. My flaw apparently was my weight. Was that why I dressed myself each morning with military precision? A deep-rooted fear of being looked down on, because of my appearance? Just the thought that his sly comments could still be affecting my life, today, made me feel sick. But if your own dad mocked how you looked, you grew up believing any stranger wouldn't hesitate to think the worst.

I followed Amy and relished stretching my legs as we went through customs and entered the airport. Her style was completely different to mine. She'd quickly run a brush through her hair in the morning, whereas mine had been clamped between straighteners and then sprayed to within an inch of its life.

Airline workers announced flight departures and people hurried past, speaking into their phones. A janitor pushed his trolley. A group of chattering schoolchildren congregated around a stressed-looking teacher. Amy's eyes narrowed as she looked for a sign presumably bearing the word Necker. I searched too, for greying blond curls. Okay. Perhaps it was too much to expect a multi-millionaire to meet us personally. I couldn't help grinning at how quickly I'd acquired airs of grandeur. How different my days would be here, compared to the stuffy commute to work and hours spent mucking in with housekeeping and any other department, to make sure our guests enjoyed nothing but comfort.

Not that I disliked the more basic aspects of my job. I enjoyed feeling self-sufficient. Like the time the bathroom sink got blocked in the bed and breakfast, that first month I left home. I asked the landlord to look at it. A day passed. At eighteen I soon realised life was easier if you could help yourself. So I searched on the internet and with the help of baking soda, vinegar and boiling water, unblocked it on my own.

Suddenly Amy waved at a tall, solid-looking man with a confident manner. I studied the black spiked short hair, the warmth of his deeply tanned skin that matched the warmth of his laugh that boomed across the airport. The gorgeous smile.

My stomach flipped.

Then my default position returned and mentally I rolled my eyes. Jeez, I really did need a holiday if my inner narrative read like a soppy movie. I was too old for crushes. In fact, I tried to remember the last time a man had caused that reaction.

I couldn't.

In one hand he held a sign saying... *Seagrass Island*. Oh. So I wouldn't be picking the brains of a global entrepreneur.

Still.

Private was private.

And something about this man made it hard to look away.

As we got nearer, I studied him and his friendly, open manner. Those mocha eyes told a different story and suggested an air of... dissatisfaction.

Call it a sixth sense. I'd always had that about Dad as a child.

It started when I began going to friends' houses to play. Watched how their dads would hug them when they got in from work. They'd ask about their day at school. Talk about taking them swimming at the weekend.

I'd been brought up to think only mums did that stuff.

And I'd become accustomed to analysing someone within seconds of meeting, after the years I'd spent working as a hotel receptionist. By the time someone had checked in I'd usually surmised exactly what sort of guest they would be. Take the businessman who smelt of alcohol and straightaway asked to be upgraded to a bigger room for free. He'd be ringing the desk throughout his stay with an impolite manner.

However, this man seemed courteous. I watched him interact with the people gathering around him. He was a listener. Friendly. Focused. Patient. Organised as he ticked names off his list. If he'd booked a room at Best Travel there would be no last-minute requests. He'd have double-checked everything in advance. He'd still charm the staff but with no ulterior reason.

There was no avoiding him, with his stature and appealing looks. That square jaw. The assured gestures. A group of young women in shorts and high heels teetered past and stared at him before chatting amongst themselves and giggling.

If he noticed, he didn't show it.

We joined the group. The word seagrass did at least sound lush and luxurious. Amy gave him our names. I raised my eyebrows. Most of the others carried big rucksacks instead of cases and were dressed more like interrailing students. We were in one of the wealthiest corners of the world. I'd expected fellow guests to have smart sets of luggage and designer sunglasses.

'Are you sure we're in the right place?' I asked Amy, as she came back.

'Absolutely.'

I fiddled with my watch, feeling nervous, not knowing why. Something didn't add up.

'Good to meet you… Sarah,' said the man loudly, consulting his list. He strode over. 'I'm Rick Crowley.' He held out his hand. Long fingers pressed against my palm that suddenly felt sweaty, as his eyes met mine. They made me simultaneously want to both turn away and never break contact. 'Thanks for booking your stay and helping us continue our mission.'

Mission?

What exactly had Amy signed me up for?

4

'A friend of mine stayed here last year and said it was excellent, with amazing local food and staff who couldn't have been friendlier,' said a young woman next to us, crisply. She wore a plain white T-shirt and cotton trousers. Her hair was neatly tied back and her nails were filed short and polish free. I tried to place her accent. German perhaps. 'This trip is a dream come true,' she added.

My shoulders relaxed. I was tired. Hungry. Thirsty. That was making me paranoid. I smiled to myself. Honestly! What was there not to like about this corner of the planet?

'I hope we meet your expectations,' said Rick laughingly and bowed before moving away.

No doubt his *mission* was simply to deliver excellent customer service. 'It's a dream for me too. I think I'll have a cocktail first. Then a dip in the pool.'

The woman rolled her eyes. 'I know. Who on earth would waste money on a holiday like that?'

I grinned, having always been a fan of a healthy dose of irony. Not that I'd always been good at understanding indirect humour. Like when I was young, before I plucked my untamed eyebrows. Dad would hold leaves above his eyes and say I looked like that. I didn't understand why it was funny. It wasn't until I got older I realised it wasn't.

Rick waited until all the names were ticked off his list. Nine in total.

'Follow me guys. Let the adventure start.'

'Adventure. That's what you wanted, right?' said Amy and she beamed.

That nervous feeling washed over me again, like years ago when I'd sense Amy was pulling a practical joke. On my seventeenth birthday Dad and our stepmother, Anabelle, were out. As a surprise Amy had baked me a large muffin and covered in squirty cream and sugar sprinkles. She watched me take a big bite. Turned out she'd decorated a bath sponge. I couldn't help giggling with her for hours afterwards.

Rick's style was more casual than I'd expected for Very Important guests like all of us. Not that I saw myself like that, but in view of how little was left of Amy's five thousand pounds, now that she'd paid in full. Perhaps the hotel I worked for was behind the times, with its staff's formal, detached manner. Rick led us out of the bustling building, in his well-fitting chinos and army beige shirt that complimented his long legs and broad back. We walked towards the exit opposite the customs area we'd just come through.

'I've hired a small taxi van,' he said and ran a hand over his stubble beard, 'although it wouldn't take long to walk down to Trellis Bay where our boat's waiting.'

As we left the airport sunshine wrapped itself around me, tropical wind teased my hair. The air smelt of vanilla.

'Thanks for this, Amy,' I said. 'You've done a great job of booking this holiday. I can tell it's going to be fantastic. I'm so impressed.'

'I hope it will be,' she said.

We piled into the bus and sat down. Amy took out her guide again. I leant forward and looked around, trying to remember the names and information I'd overheard. There was me and Amy. Two young couples, one from England, one from France. The neat woman was Helga, from the Black Forest in Germany it turned out, here with her brother Jonas. I wondered how long his dreadlocks took to plait. With the large guitar tattoo on his left forearm and beaded bracelet he looked like the antithesis of his minimalist sister. Unlike serious-looking Jonas, there was Benedikt, from Hamburg, who had a permanent smile on his face, as if his mouth were drawn upwards by the fashionable man bun at the back of his head.

Where were the older people or young families with children? Why did everyone look as if they were about to spend the week with Bear Grylls? I looked around, feeling conspicuous. We were talking jeans with holes, worn trainers and T-shirts with save the planet logos. My sixth sense revved up and went into overdrive.

Amy glanced my way. 'Sarah – sit back and relax. Just enjoy the view.'

A quirky trinket market came into sight as we approached the bay, the land curving around and rising green and dense on the far side. I almost gasped at the shades of blue. The ocean looked even more radiant this close, with warm hues near the shore and darker blueberry ripples the further you looked out.

'This is stunning,' I murmured, enjoying the sensation of being cocooned in the island's heat. Perhaps I was the odd one out, clothes-wise, because I wasn't used to worldwide travel. I looked down at my knee-high skirt and bejewelled sandals. A small red lump had appeared below my right knee. It itched. What a good thing we'd brought repellent although no doubt every corner of the hotel would have one of those special mosquito lamps.

The bus stopped at the dock and I could hardly wait to get off. Rick waited whilst we unloaded our luggage and then strode down to the shore, chatting to Helga and Jonas. Rick tried speaking German. Helga politely complimented his accent and that made him laugh. Yet still his voice still didn't sound completely relaxed, as if words he really wanted to speak were locked up and just waiting for someone to release the catch.

I forced my attention away from his neck and unexpected thoughts of wanting to stroke it.

I hadn't been with a man I'd cared about for two years.

I thought that last one had cared back until I discovered he was cheating.

Apparently it was my fault. I put up barriers. Six months in and Callum still didn't feel I needed him.

Anyway, I hadn't come all the way to the Caribbean for romance and a relationship – the only R&R I was interested in was rest and recreation (and research). I concentrated on my surroundings. The soundtrack was so different to the one I was used to back home, with the rumble of the underground and impatient London traffic. Here it was the screech of seabirds and slosh of waves against the beach, the rustling of leaves in the wind and sailors good-naturedly shouting.

I breathed in and could almost taste saltwater. A sense of freedom enveloped me that I hadn't experienced since… memories rewound, a long way, to primary school, before Mum died. Me running as fast as I could, across school fields… climbing high in a tree, both terrified and thrilled by the prospect of suffering a fall… and then there was guide camp. There I'd felt like a free spirit.

'Here we go,' said Rick and people started to clamber onto… Oh. A fisherman's boat? I'd expected a catamaran or a yacht at the very least, with a polished hull and spotless white sail. I almost gagged at the smell of fish guts. Algae had crocheted itself through nets hanging over the sides.

'Blue marlin are local to the Virgin Islands, aren't they?' asked Amy cautiously and peered into the water. 'I… I believe they can grow up to five metres long.'

'Yes. Amateurs confuse them with swordfish but—'

'The bill growing out of their head is pointed instead of blunt.'

Rick nodded. 'I'm impressed. Someone's done their homework.'

A smile lit up Amy's face.

Jonas stepped onto the boat after me and ran a hand over his tattoo. His sister, Helga, chatted with Amy. He shot me an uncertain look.

'I don't like boats,' he said. 'When I was nine I fell off one during a school trip to a water sports centre, near Munich. I've never forgotten the taste of the water. It was worse than my university friends' home-brewed beer.'

I asked him about the Black Forest. He chatted about growing up there. I said it sounded so picturesque. He said it was but at heart he was more of a city dweller. I told him about my life in London. The conversation flowed. Jonas was so easy to talk to.

'At least there will be delicious food and drink waiting to revive us after the boat trip,' I said.

'Yeah, right,' he snorted, clearly not a fan of Michelin-starred cooking. 'It's no secret that I only came along to keep Helga company. She's wanted to do this for ages but none of her friends had the money. Mum and Dad insisted on contributing.' He sighed. 'That's twins' love, for you. I was all set to say no but my instincts took over.'

'Amy and I are sisters. I get that sense of loyalty.'

His face relaxed.

'But what's not to like about a month in the Virgin Islands?' I asked.

'I'd rather be at home for the summer with my vinyls and guitar. Helga's always been the outdoorsy type, like my parents, and naturally suited to our childhood Black Forest home – whereas I'd have been happier in a high-rise apartment in a city like Hamburg where I studied. I was just talking to Benedikt – he's so lucky to have grown up there.'

'Have you finished university now?'

'Yes. We've both just completed the final year. Helga did Environmental Studies in Munich. Me, Computer Science. I scraped through.'

'Your parents must have been tempted to join you here,' I said and laughed as we climbed aboard, imagining that there couldn't have been a worse scenario idea than that for two twenty-one-year-olds abroad.

I would have hated it – but only because of Dad. If

Mum had still been alive, I'd have loved to go somewhere glamorous with her, like this place or the south of France. We'd have bought exotic ice creams and gone shopping.

Shallow water swished across the floor of the boat. Jonas clasped his hands and looked warily out to sea. I patted his shoulder. 'I'm out of my comfort zone too. My sister bought this break as a surprise present. I haven't been on holiday for ten years.'

'She got you this? And I thought I was out of luck,' he said and grinned.

I rolled my eyes and nodded but didn't really understand what he meant, sensing again that something was off.

A woman with bobbed curly caramel hair stood in the bow cockpit. She and Rick chatted for a moment before he donned a brown jungle fedora hat and took the steering wheel. With ease he guided the boat away from the jetty. Noisily it chugged. A bird with a white belly and dark head and wings flew overhead. Someone called it a Brown Booby. I thought that called for a joke but none of the native English obliged. With serious expressions everyone else took photos.

The boat hugged the ocean's swell and the horizon bobbed up and down. Up and down. Deep and high. A wave of nausea lapped against the back of my throat. I even stopped whistling. That was a habit. I used to whistle as a child, when I got nervous. It helped me cope with the atmosphere when Dad was in one of his moods.

As I'd grown older, I whistled for other reasons too, when I was on my own. A good day at work. A fun evening cooking with Amy. But old habits died hard and if I was out of my comfort zone my lips rolled into an 'o' shape and – unfortunately for everyone else – a not very pleasant sound came out. Amy was the musical one.

I'd forgotten that I used to get seasickness. Dad would tell me to get a grip. I started to pray for the journey to end and closed my eyes…

'Wake up sleepy head, we're almost there,' said Amy. I squinted and relief flushed through me as the boat aimed for an island ahead. It was oval-shaped and covered with foliage that became mountainous on the right-hand side. I felt as if I were in one of those movies where we'd land and dinosaurs from another era would appear. Perhaps there would be a Caribbean band playing to welcome us, and coconut and pineapple cocktails. Not that I'd be able to drink one. I staggered to stern. Helga called after me that seasickness could be defeated by visualising calm waters.

It didn't work.

As we approached the island there was no calypso music. No aroma of rum. In fact, a wrecked boat lay on the beach, amongst unkempt bushes. In parts, fallen-down trees lay across the sand, along with strewn seaweed and shells. The jetty looked worn. The woman steered now and Rick cleared his throat loudly. He took off his hat, ran fingers through his spiked hair, and put it back on.

'Almost there, folks. Thanks again for booking with us. We'll disembark and then I'll run you through a few basics about your stay. As you'll know from the website, my family own Seagrass Island and I've been in charge of restoring it since Hurricane Irma in 2017.'

'I remember seeing that storm on the news,' I said to Amy and gave a low burp. 'Richard Branson's place was trashed. That international luxury hotelier magazine I subscribe to featured it recently. He was back in business a year later, everything fully restored.' Despite the nausea, I managed a smile. 'If Rick's family have had enough money to own an island then they'll have been able to afford an opulent rebuild. Our rooms should look even more immaculate than they ever did before.'

'No. You're wrong. It must have been a real struggle because...' She rubbed her hands together. 'Surprise! I've been dying to tell you, these last couple of weeks... I swapped plans at the last minute, a few days before the full payment was due for the other luxury stay. I swapped islands. Swapped holidays. Instead of paying the full amount for the high-end hotel trip when I went online, I booked and paid for four weeks living as part of a community, camping out and contributing to conservation. That's the only stay available here.'

The feeling of sickness swelled.

'That day we went clothes shopping for this holiday... how you talked about using these four weeks to draw together a personal statement for your CV – I realised the break I'd planned was too much like your everyday routine at work. So instead I looked for a true escape from your daily life. No one should be doing career research when they are taking a break. The way you spoke so fondly of guide camp... how you felt grown-ups became complacent... I promise you, Sarah, there's nothing about the next four weeks that is going to remind you of Best Travel or the hotel industry or any of your responsibilities there.' She clapped her hands together. 'It's been really hard to keep this secret as I knew you'd be so excited at the prospect of such an adventure.'

I stared at Amy.

No pastry pyramids? No hot tub or opulent beach huts? No evening entertainment or Netflix?

I blinked several times before leaning overboard and throwing up.

5

Jonas rummaged in the pockets of his trousers. He handed me some tissues. I wiped my mouth.

'Happens every time,' said Rick as he came over. 'I must put a reminder on the website for people to bring travel sickness pills. The waters around Seagrass Island can get pretty choppy. It's because we lie in the belt of the Trade Winds. They are at their strongest in July. It's why the Virgin Islands are great for sailing.'

He draped an arm around my shoulders and steered me off the boat and onto the jetty. He let go as soon as we were on solid land.

Rick felt solid. I couldn't remember the last time I'd been held in arms like that. Helga shot me a piteous look and delved into her rucksack. She offered me her bottle of water.

The drink revived my spirits and brought back my sister's words. Living in a tent? My face broke into a wide smile. Honestly. Amy had really chosen her moment to pull such a joke. She got her audacious sense of humour from Mum who was always trying to fool us. Like when she served our favourite fried eggs with toast on April Fools'. They were actually peach halves in circles of yoghurt. The three of us cried with laughter.

I missed that.

Feeling nostalgic, I decided to go along with the charade for now.

'What do you think?' asked Amy, eyebrows raised. 'It's going to be just like when Mum took us camping to Cornwall. Remember how much fun we had? She'd tumble dry our wellies because it rained so hard on the beach, but we didn't care. Remember those bags of doughnuts? And how she let us stay up late?'

Dad had been too tied up at work to go. It was the best holiday ever, exploring rock pools and running away half-screaming from the cold tide.

However, that was over twenty years ago. My tastes had changed.

'This whole idea is so thoughtful,' I said, deserving an Oscar. 'It's just a shame I've brought all my handbags and high heels.'

Amy linked arms as we headed to Rick who was beckoning us over. 'I nearly said something, but didn't want to give away any clues. That's why I encouraged you to bring those walking boots. At least, underneath your fancy clothes, I've hidden a practical cap and...'

Oh, she was good. I swigged more water before wiping the bottle's top with my palm and passing it back to Helga. 'Imagine how boring it would have become, doing nothing for four weeks but sunbathing and sipping Cosmopolitans?' I'd get Amy worried now. We'd laugh about it later. I'd tease her about not being able to get one over her older, clearly much wiser sister.

'I'm so glad you feel the same as me. I was prepared to stay somewhere high-end for your sake, but secretly that's my idea of hell. All that posh interior decor with its artificial smells and plants... instead, we'll be waking up in the outdoors...' she said, dreamily.

Mosquitoes? Spiders? Soil instead of carpet? Sticky heat instead of aircon?

No thanks.

Inwardly I chuckled at her believing I'd actually prefer a month roughing it.

The curly-haired woman stood next to Rick, her short, slight frame emphasising his height. She passed him a clipboard. He read it and nodded. I smacked my arm as a fly landed near my elbow. Once we'd checked in, I'd take a long bubble bath and apply a thick layer of insect repellent – after insisting that Amy chose her bedroom first. It's the least she deserved. I'd carefully unpack. Knowing Amy, she'd just grab her costume and head straight for the pool. Then I'd check the location of fire exits and ring home to make sure Nelly was okay.

'Welcome to Seagrass Island,' Rick said. 'It's a pleasure to introduce you all to my family's Caribbean home. My grandmother, Margot Crocker, bought it in the early Eighties when she was CEO and head designer of Crocker & Crowley.'

'The shoe shop?' I said. Mum had always taken us there as small children to get our feet measured. I hadn't seen a high street branch for a few years.

'Yes. She set up the company, having studied fashion design at university. Her dad soled shoes for a living and that's where Gran got her interest from. My late granddad, Dave Crowley, took care of the business side. They started off small, selling her designs from a stall on Carnaby Street.

Parents loved the friendly service their children received and she soon worked out offering a personal service for families would succeed.' Pride shone through his voice. 'My mum and dad run the company now with my brother, Lee, although she still attends board meetings. Gran wanted to create a getaway destination for her family – an escape from the hustle bustle of London. She did an ancestry test once. Apparently, way back, our family has Latin American blood.'

That explained his sexy dark looks.

'She said that must be why she'd always longed for an island home. I suspect she might have bought one in say Costa Rica or Haiti if it weren't for my dear grandfather's belief that he should be able to sail through life only ever speaking English.'

Everyone smiled.

'The build was complete by 1985. There have been eleven family weddings here since. A couple of big birthdays. Many Christmases. Even a divorce celebration. I've spent most summers here for as long as I can remember. That's how I developed a love of the natural world and ended up studying Geology at university. As a child I'd spend long summer days studying all sorts landscapes and creatures – collecting rocks and wildlife. I'll never forget Mum's shriek when she discovered a garden snake in my bedside drawer.'

I wondered why he'd share such private information. Best Travel guests knew nothing personal about me.

'Sadly the bricks and mortar were wrecked by Hurricane Irma three years ago, along with parts of the forest and the coastline. Since then we've been working hard to restore the island to its former glory. At this point I'd like to introduce Jackie.' He nodded at his friend. 'Twelve years ago, we were freshers together, at university. Jackie studied Zoology and has been working in an animal rescue centre in Colombia. I was thrilled when she jumped at the chance to help me here. It makes up for the time she couldn't jump back quick enough when I made a freshman's attempt to date her.'

Playfully she punched his arm.

My heartbeat skippity jumped. This was probably one of the most cutting-edge hotels in the world. I imagined trips diving for pearls and swim-up bars.

'Hurricane Irma had a devastating effect on parts of the animal, marine and bird populations.' He became serious for a moment and went into detail.

I loved our cat Nelly and was fond of next door's dog, but didn't watch David Attenborough documentaries and wished Rick would focus more on describing the spa treatments or cordon bleu food. Yet everyone else was rapt with his wildlife chat and Helga filmed him, on her phone. Apart from Jonas. He looked at me and pulled a face.

'The days straight after the hurricane dolphins and manatees found themselves stranded on our beach. Birds were blown out of nests. Trees and foliage destroyed. One of the island's butterfly species is now even more endangered than before and...'

I couldn't help zoning out. Oh, I'd contribute to a conservation charity box or sign a petition. I did my best to recycle and had stopped using plastic water bottles. It's just that I wasn't nearly as passionate as my sister. Her vision focused on the future. Mine concentrated on the day-to-day. Amy worried about the longevity of our planet and that was good – we needed people to do that. But I was more concerned with the longevity of my pay packet and whether it would pay bills and the mortgage.

I was tired. Hot. I needed a shower. Something to drink. But then Amy's enamoured face brought my attention back to what Rick was saying.

Because I never wanted to be like Dad.

Whenever Amy talked about animals as a child, he'd change the conversation, somehow always ending up on a subject where he was king. 'It's all very well enjoying Biology, Amy, but never forget, Maths is the most important subject. I was the high-flyer of my class for five years running at high school. You need to push yourself and start getting top marks instead of your usual seven or eight out of ten.'

I never dared zone out of Dad's chats. Not until my late teens hit and I saw him for who he really was.

Therefore, I re-focused again and found myself becoming invested in what Rick said, genuinely joining Amy with a sad face when he talked about turtles' nests having been ruined by the hurricane. I felt relief alongside her when we heard that tree frogs and iguanas did okay. Jonas also seemed moved. I understood sibling love. How he'd solider on and enjoy the holiday for Helga's sake. Once settled perhaps I'd speak with the resort's entertainment manager. Maybe there was a group of musicians who could lend Jonas a guitar. That might perk him up.

I'd watched a television series last year about top hotels around the world. One featured was Giraffe Manor in Kenya. Giraffes stuck their long necks through windows in the dining area, to be fed treats. It looked amazing. My pulse quickened. What if this was a luxury resort specifically for animal lovers or those who wanted a holiday with a difference?

I couldn't wait to find out!

As if the universe had heard me, Amy nudged my arm. Rick said something about seeing our living quarters and we walked upwards, away from the beach and through forest. The path wasn't well established and I struggled to pull my unwieldy case. I jumped as a nettle batted my leg. I couldn't wait to see mown lawns and symmetrical borders bursting with colourful flowers. Up ahead a building came into view with scaffolding blurring its outline. Our home for the next month was no doubt beyond that.

Except we turned a sharp left.

'This way,' said Rick and undid a button of his shirt. I tried not to stare at the toned pecs. 'Would you like me to take your luggage?'

'No thanks,' I said and immediately regretted it. It's just I was used to managing on my own.

Downwards we walked now, along a narrow path lined by prickly looking plants.

'You'll love our accommodation,' said Amy. 'It's far better than any stuffy hotel.' She swang her arms and sang 'Be My Guest' from *Beauty and the Beast*.

Benedikt caught up and joined in. 'That musical is almost as good as *Mamma Mia!*' he said when they finished the song. 'But nothing will ever beat *Hamilton*, don't you think?'

Amy groaned. 'I haven't been able to afford to see that yet.'

He shot her a sympathetic look. 'I was lucky. My friend

works in the theatre and got me a discounted ticket. It meant travelling all the way to Frankfurt but was worth it.'

Rick called out that the prickly plants were called Christmas bushes and we should avoid them as contact with skin could cause a rash. Under my arms felt increasingly damp as our descent continued. The dazzling sunshine made me squint. If only I was wearing the wide-rimmed Audrey Hepburn hat I'd packed.

Rick and Jackie turned around as we finally came to the beach, lined by palm trees near the forest. For a moment I forgot my discomfort. Waters clearer than micellar cleanser rippled over golden sands. The sharp white sales of distant yachts broke up the horizon. Sun rays lit up waves, making the ocean look as if it were made up of liquid jewels. A cackling noise broke my concentration and I looked up to see a bird with a white chest and black head. Its call was sharp and made up of a series of loud notes.

'Is that a… laughing gull?' asked Amy tentatively.

'Well spotted,' said Rick.

'There are over two hundred species of birds on the British Virgin Islands, and whilst some are endangered, during your stay you'll see a glorious array of ones that feed from the sea, shore or forest,' said Jackie. She was softly spoken.

'It would be brilliant to spot a West Indian whistling duck,' said Helga.

'Yes. They're under threat,' said Amy and pride filled my chest at my knowledgeable sister.

'You might just do that, on the far side of the island,' said Jackie. Members of the group took off their shoes and ecstatic expressions crossed their faces as their toes wriggled in the sand.

'Perhaps we will be lucky enough to see the wunderbar yellow-billed cuckoo,' said Benedikt.

'To spot a parrot would be amazing,' I chipped in, hoping that breed frequented this place.

'Or a flamingo,' piped up Jonas.

'They aren't indigenous to this island, Dummkopf,' said Helga and rolled her eyes.

I sent Jonas a sympathetic look.

I was used to being the one in the know. As assistant manager my day was spent fielding questions from staff and customers. But on this trip, so far, I felt like a pub quiz loser.

Rick readjusted his hat. 'Let's get you to your home for the next month. There'll be time to freshen up and then I'll take you on an introductory walk around the island before dinner.'

No chance, I thought, and scratched my arm. Amy and I could explore in our own time tomorrow. I dragged my case along a bumpy dried mud path, past the palm trees and once again through forest. I struggled when we came to rough ground. Before I could protest, Jonas took my case and easily lifted it over a tree stump. He'd tied back his dreadlocks and wiped his perspiring brow with his arm. Soon we came into a clearing where the treetops parted. Rays of sunshine beamed down, like giant torches leading the way to…

… a cluster of shacks on stilts, made out of wood, with pointed triangular roofs.

They were small, with mosquito blinds for windows and a short ladder going up to the front door. Hammocks hung in between trees. Dotted about were benches carved out of thick trunks. Rick had fallen back from the rest and suddenly put out his arm in front of me. I stopped. He bent down and gently picked up a shiny striped brown millipede. I flinched and stepped back as it crawled across his hand. He encouraged the others to take photos. Amy explained how she'd read that they could emit a foul-smelling liquid if under threat. Rick nodded and carefully put the insect down, onto soil, out of the way of my feet.

'Off you go, little chap,' he said. Defiantly those many legs marched off.

I felt like joining them.

6

I gazed at my comrades – that's what they felt like, in the face of the battle ahead of us to insist that this was *not* the accommodation we'd booked. Despite being younger than everyone else, Helga seemed like a sturdy sort. Between us I was sure we could arrange a full refund or transfer to more suitable premises.

Yet why was everyone else smiling, including Amy?

'This is hardly the British Virgin Island experience I signed up for,' I said, brightly.

'My fault,' said Amy and looked around at the others. 'I'd just told my sister we'd be camping – you know, in tents.'

Rick's frown disappeared. 'Ah. Agreed, and I feel for you – there's nothing quite like the fresh smell of damp polyester in the morning. But you'll get to camp on the beach when it's your turn to go on the night-time turtle nest excursion. We run those daily in July and August and go out in small groups.'

What was he talking about?

Rick started allocating shacks. He directed the two couples over to one on the left and Jonas and Benedikt straight ahead.

'Each shack has two bunks, so sleeps four. You two men

will be joining a father and son from Scotland who've already been here for a week. They are helping to mend a rope bridge, at the moment, with one of our most enthusiastic volunteers, Carlotta, who comes from Italy. Everyone is always out at this hour, Monday to Friday, completing the day's tasks. This is the third summer Seagrass Conservation has been running. It started off very small but now we have around fifty volunteers here at any one time, with people coming and going from May to October. Around ten are staying for the whole season and some of those have become task leaders, alongside our small team of permanent staff. There are two other clusters of shacks further along the beach.'

Huh?

'They will all be back for dinner in an hour or so which gives you time to settle in and then we'll take a tour before meeting them. We eat together in the canteen block, every night. That's at the far end of the beach, next door to a games room. Malik's the chef and a genius at making use of local ingredients for meals.' He consulted his list. 'Helga, Amy and Sarah, you're here.' He pointed to the shack nearest, on the right.

'I don't understand. Where's our hotel?' I said to Amy in a low voice.

She grinned. I didn't grin back.

'The Roman pillars and waterbeds, the Aqua Dancing… everything I saw on that website back in the spring…'

'Sarah…' Her cheeks pinked up. 'I thought you agreed that this was a great idea?'

I shook my head vigorously.

'But that pampered kind of break wouldn't have felt like a break from the everyday. I didn't want you to be in a work environment whilst you were supposed to be on holiday. So… as I told you, I… I swapped the holiday a couple of weeks ago.'

'You aren't serious?'

She stared.

My hand flew to my chest. 'We're actually sleeping *here*?'

Slowly she nodded.

'As part of a volunteering community, with no mod cons – no bath or air-conditioning…?'

'Exciting, isn't it?' interrupted Helga who overheard. She picked up her rucksack and headed towards… *our* shack?

Rick held up a hand. 'Before you settle in… Jackie, could you introduce everyone to the toilet and washing facilities.' He winked. 'May as well get that over with and then we'll explain everything else when we show you around later.'

I didn't like his tone. What could be wrong with the bathroom facilities?

Amy pointed at the hammocks. 'It's just like that jungle celebrity programme you love.'

'That's on the telly. I get to watch it in my pyjamas, on a comfy sofa, with my cosy water bottle and mug of hot chocolate,' I hissed.

No wonder Jonas had reservations. He'd known what was coming. Numbly I followed Jackie, further back into the forest. She pointed to two unisex cubicles, their walls made from sheets of hemp. Their roofs were made from corrugated metal. To the right stood a basic sink and bar of soap.

Please. No.

'*Compost* toilets?' said Benedikt and his face lit up as he took out his phone. 'My Instagram followers won't believe it.' He started singing 'Circle of Life' from *The Lion King*.

Jackie pulled aside the front sheet of hemp of one cubicle to reveal what looked like a plastic-rimmed bucket in the middle of a square box. 'You sit on the seat and do your business, then...' She pointed to a bowl of sawdust next to a roll of toilet paper. 'Sprinkle a handful of that on top. Once the bucket is full someone must empty it – your name will be put on a rota for that. All the rotas are in the canteen. Each cluster of shacks has its own toilets.'

Amy kept shooting me nervous looks.

About ten metres further into the forest we stopped and Jackie pointed to something called the compost bay that was a shallowly fenced off area of ground, about two metres square and in two halves. 'You pour the bucket's contents into this half and then fork the hay from the other half on top. Everything is left then, to compost down. You just keep repeating this process until the bay is full. This lovely compost is perfect for growing vegetables.'

'Every household in Europe should be made to have one and eat homegrown produce,' said Helga.

'I don't think there would be many vegans, if they did,' I said weakly to Jonas.

We walked back towards the camp and veered right. There was a white shower block. It didn't have a roof. We opened individual doors behind each of which was a plughole and shower head.

Amy had mentioned my favourite reality show. Perhaps that's what this was. I looked around hopefully for cameras but enthusiastic television presenters didn't jump out of the bushes. I rubbed my eyes and opened them again… this had to be a bad dream. Perhaps I was still on the aeroplane and would wake up to some charming air steward offering me a glass of Prosecco and a packet of nuts.

It reminded me of how I felt, the day I left home, all those years ago – like I didn't belong. I remembered giving my stepmother a small smile and ignoring Dad's glare as I walked down the drive… I'd never forget the surreal prospect of coping alone as an adult. I'd missed Mum even more than usual at that particular moment – especially after his cruel accusation that followed me into the taxi like a slow-moving poison dart. I didn't have a family. Or a home. All I had was the dream of, one day, being able to build a life with Amy.

I looked up at the treetops. All my creature comforts were back in England. My familiar life. The certainty of routine.

None of the creatures here would be comforting.

'Eventually you'll get used to all the bugs, attracted by the water,' said Jackie, 'but if you find a tarantula Malik is more than happy to move it with a bucket and brush. He grew up over on Tortola. We're very lucky to have him. His brother is a marine biologist who runs a conservation project there and Malik has picked up a lot of his knowledge. His wife, Zina, lives on Tortola, working in a beauty salon, but Malik spends many nights here during the summer as he's up early to cook breakfast and—'

'Did she say tarantula?' I glared at my sister.

'They're not much different to anything back in England, really,' said Amy brightly. 'Just think of them as house spiders with glamorous fur coats.'

'Nothing is glamorous about this place,' said Jonas.

He already felt like a best friend.

Why would anyone spend thousands of pounds on a break like this? It didn't make sense. This Rick bloke was taking advantage of well-meaning people by charging that much.

'It's cold water, of course, but you'll probably be grateful for that after a day out in the heat,' said Jackie. 'The sea is only a five-minute walk away, if you fancy a dip there instead.'

'I'm so excited,' said Helga and calmly swatted away a wasp.

I didn't like wasps but at least it was an insect I'd seen before.

'It reminds me of summers spent roaming the Black Forest as a small child,' Helga continued and turned to her brother. 'They were such fun, *nicht wahr?*'

'I could never wait to get back to my books and drawing pencils.'

She clapped him on the back. 'Always you protest too much. Fresh air like this for one month – think how healthy and clear-minded we will be on our return home in August.'

'Just imagine what a sense of achievement we'll feel after our stay,' said Benedikt. 'I'm betting it will feel even more intense than the rush I got after climbing Everest last year with my colleagues at the bank – or when I saw the number of likes I got on Instagram when I posted a photo of me at the peak.'

Clearly this was a holiday for adrenaline junkies.

'Are spiders very common around here?' asked Jonas.

Instinctively he and I edged nearer to each other – safety in numbers. Even if there were only two of us who had sense enough to realise this place was a death zone. Tropical insects? In my job I was used to dealing with bedbugs. Sometimes scabies mites. Or woodworm. Occasionally fleas if someone had smuggled a pet in. But anything bigger than those creatures...

'We are lucky enough to have several types of tarantulas,' said Jackie.

'I can't wait to spot one,' said Helga.

'Lucky?' I said, folding my arms as if to protect myself.

'They are actually reclusive little things...' Jackie shot me a smile. 'There are scorpions too, but you don't need to worry. In all my years working here I've never heard of anyone getting stung.'

A lump formed in my throat at her soft tones. Apart from Jonas, Jackie was the only person who suspected this island was my idea of hell. She announced she'd be back in five with some complimentary reusable drinking water containers. It was hardly the champagne welcome I'd expected. Everyone made their way into their shacks.

But to unpack? Not likely. Firstly, my suitcase would remain zipped tightly shut to keep out any creepy crawlies. Secondly, there was no point. I wouldn't be staying. This was all a terrible mistake. And I'd been so looking forward to being pampered. Tears welled but I blinked them back.

'You didn't know exactly what kind of holiday this was going to be?' said Jonas as we walked back to our shacks. 'That's tough.'

'That's a generous use of the word holiday,' I said, trying to keep my voice steady.

He shook his head. 'The only bugs I am used to are the ones I come across in my computer. What if we get bitten? A bite might paralyse my arm. I've got my music to think of.'

'You're serious about your guitar?'

His eyes lit up. 'Yes. I was in a band at uni and—'

'Sarah! Let's get settled in our shack,' called Helga and she waved. She was already on the steps, Amy not far behind her.

'Why did I agree to this?' muttered Jonas. 'I've no idea how I'll get to sleep, tonight. What if a snake gets in?'

I hadn't thought about that.

'At least you and I can moan to each other about those sorts of things, right?' he said. 'Helga doesn't understand. She thinks I'm weak.' Jonas sighed. 'See you later,' he mumbled and headed over to Benedikt.

I reached our shack and went in. Helga took the upper bunk on the left. Amy asked me if I wanted top or bottom on the right.

I stared at the sleeping bags. There was no pretty throw, nor carefully placed array of plump cushions. Instead of a centimetre of plush carpet beneath my feet there was hard, unpolished wood. I wasn't a diva. Goodness knows I'd made do with the basics when I'd first left home, living at the grotty bed and breakfast. There had been hairs in the bedding and mould in the shower.

I pursed my lips and focused on the situation in hand. The narrow bed. The suffocating atmosphere. The thing was, I'd worked hard for a better standard of living. A rest from work wouldn't be found in turning time backwards.

I spun around and hotfooted it outside.

Amy followed. 'Sarah? Where are you going?'

'I'm sorry. I can't do this.'

7

'Look at me,' I said to Amy. 'I paint my nails. And eyebrows. I even iron my socks. I'm just not cut out living in the wilds. I played along when you first told me – thought it was one of your practical jokes.' Deep breaths. 'You stay. Enjoy yourself. It'll be more fun without my complaints about bugs and humid nights.' I kissed Amy on the cheek, already feeling better. 'Why not ring Holly at work? Perhaps she'd like to join you here for a couple of weeks and take my place. She'd only have to buy an air ticket.'

Her cheeks turned blotchy. 'But I booked this place especially for you. For us. Quality time away from our London lives. You and me, together, making a difference.'

'You really booked it for *me*?'

'What's that supposed to mean?'

'Nothing.' I sighed. 'Ignore me. I'm just feeling out of sorts.'

Amy folded her arms and tilted her head. She'd done that as long as I could remember. It was her way of extracting an answer to a difficult question. Like when I was about ten and once scoffed the last piece of her Easter chocolate, thinking it wouldn't be missed, telling myself that *me* eating it would be better for *her* teeth.

'It's just... I'm not the David Attenborough fan who works with animals.' I tried to keep my voice sunny.

'You really think I'm that selfish – to put my desires first?' Her voice wavered.

Amy was the most selfless person I knew. She'd offer up the last slice of pizza and was always bringing home waifs and strays from the surgery that had been handed in and couldn't be homed for a few days. 'Of course not,' I said and exhaled. 'It's been amazing of you to spend thousands of pounds on me... but honestly... what were you thinking?'

'That holiday with Mum we talked about, in Cornwall...' She spoke in a small voice. 'You loved camping... and I thought this would be an adventure.'

'At the time I also loved the Spice Girls and banana and jam sandwiches.'

'But what about the fun you had at guide camp?'

'Yes, the night under the stars was brill, but Amy... I was a child. It was exciting, staying up late all night – whereas these days getting a good shut-eye is one of my priorities.'

'But a luxury getaway... you'd have spent this holiday studying how the hotel was being run. I wanted you to forget work for once. After all these years...'

Yes. That too. After all these years of working my guts out, for once I wanted to be the one people waited on. A sob rose in my throat. I was bone tired. The last decade had worn me out. Shift work. Worrying about Amy as if she were my own child. Taking on responsibilities at eighteen that some people didn't shoulder until they were into their late twenties or thirties – and me without the support of a family or partner.

I swiped away a fly. More than anything I hated seeing Amy upset. Her current expression reminded me of every time Dad put her down. Like when he told her short hair made her look like a boy. Over the years he'd been equally critical of me, but for some reason I remembered the times he'd hurt Amy more vividly.

'For anyone else this would be an amazing trip,' I said and couldn't help raising my voice. 'But I knew I should have got more involved and checked the details.'

'Don't speak to me as if I'm a child.' She turned away.

'And almost five thousand pounds? For the two of us to stay here? Rick must be having a laugh. It's criminal, charging that much. Everyone here is a right mug for paying that amount.'

'Does that include me?' she asked in a tight voice and span around.

'I didn't mean…' I sighed. 'But you've got to admit – it's a ridiculous price for living in huts.'

'I've done my research. Our food and board is covered. Admin costs. And Rick explained his mission when I emailed him a couple of times about details. This conservation project is about preserving the wildlife that was under threat before the hurricane hit, as well as re-building a habitable environment for those creatures whose lives were devastated by the storm. Then there are ongoing veterinary bills and specialist animal food. And he's done what he can to create employment for locals who lost their businesses when Hurricane Irma hit. So yes, it's thousands of pounds – but I checked beforehand to make sure that every penny of it was being well spent. Any profits are ploughed straight back into—'

'But his family are loaded,' I said. 'Why can't he dip into the business to support his scheme?'

A muscle flinched in her cheek. 'You don't trust me to have spent my winnings wisely, do you?'

'Perhaps we should discuss some house – or rather shack – rules, guys,' called Helga, interrupting.

'Go on, back in,' I said to Amy and shook my head. 'I need a few minutes – some fresh air.'

She paced up and down. 'What, to get over the fact that your younger sister always messes up unless you're hovering over her? Even though she is twenty-three,' she snapped.

I stepped back, shocked. 'No, of course not.'

Amy stood still, chin held high. 'Is it always going to be like this, Sarah?'

'It's just... I guess I... because of Dad... the way he was... I just want to make sure—'

'Are we never going to be able to leave him and our childhood behind? I love you, Sarah. So much. You know that. You've been brilliant bringing me up when Dad and Anabelle were doing such a crap job. It's more than anyone should expect from an older sibling. But I'm grown up now.' An exasperated tone cut through the humid air and her speech sped up. 'If you were my mother, I'd have politely told you to butt out a long time ago. And that's normal. Gaining independence, isn't that parenting's ultimate goal? Instead you still change my sheets even though I tell you I will. I've offered countless times to help you run the practical side of our flat, in terms of being the one to make sure the gas and electric bills, the insurance, mortgage and council tax are being paid every month – but you steadfastly refuse. When I wanted my last boyfriend to stay over for the night I gave up, you made so many excuses.'

'I didn't think he was right for you,' I protested.

'That's not your decision to make. I'm a grown woman.' She threw her hands in the air. 'I can't take it much longer. Living with you... it's been great. I love our little flat. But I'm older now... perhaps it's time I got a place of my own.'

Amy move out?

I hurried into the forest and leant up against a tree. I covered my face with my hands. Hot tears trickled down my face. Annoyed at myself, I wiped my eyes on my arm and sniffed. Amy mustn't see me like this. I stayed there until my cheeks dried, digesting everything my sister had said.

Those angry words made my mind up. Four weeks apart would give Amy the independence she craved and maybe she'd miss all the little things I did. Then when she returned to England life would just carry on as it always had. She'd love being back at our cosy place and would forget all this nonsense about setting up on her own. Our London flat wasn't in the most desirable area. We'd need a new boiler soon. The main road we lived on was noisy. But it was home. We had Nelly. And our friendly neighbours.

We had each other.

Once more I thought about the trip I'd been expecting. My holiday weeks off work were so precious. I didn't get time to relax properly all year round as I never had even two days off straight.

I wanted to collapse in a heap and wail at the injustice.

Yes, I loved my career. That didn't mean I wasn't in need of chill time. My chin trembled. I'd dreamt of daily massages and sunning myself by a pool… but now I imagined this break would consist of getting up at the crack of dawn and using muscles I never even knew I had, despite helping housekeeping make beds and guests move suitcases that felt as if they'd been filled with lead.

I scratched my neck and ants covered my hand. I yelped and leapt away from the tree trunk, brushing myself down as if I were on fire.

That was it. I strode back to camp and went straight up to Rick.

'Can you tell me the time of the next boat back to Tortola, please?'

His lifted the front rim of his hat and smiled. 'I'll put a list up of day trips, for the weekend. And just let me know if there's anything else you want to know. I'm always here to help.'

'No. I mean, for before then.'

He looked puzzled. 'There isn't one until tomorrow morning.'

'But there must be. This is a holiday destination.'

'No. This is a conservation project.'

Suddenly his voice sounded almost as tired as I felt. I didn't blame him, permanently living in a place like this. Although I wasn't blind to its natural appeal, like the relaxing sound of waves breaking instead of car engines or a computer's whirr, the pollution-free air and trees greener than AstroTurf.

'That we're nevertheless paying handsomely to visit,'

I said, assuming the voice I used at work if a guest was being unreasonable. 'What if I had an emergency back in England? There must be some sort of shuttle service. I don't mind how long I have to wait on the beach. Just give me a time and I'll sort myself out. I know you're busy.'

'Is it urgent?'

'Yes,' I said, trying to work out, in my head, exactly how long my meagre savings would last whilst I wasn't employed.

Rick rubbed the stubble beard that left me wondering what it would feel like against my skin, if we kissed.

A purely hypothetical question. We were hardly a match. All the men in my line of work wore suits and full-beards or were clean shaven. Management didn't approve of the nine o'clock shadow look.

'Or more a matter of cold feet?' he asked. His hand, with the clipboard, dropped to his side. Jackie appeared, carrying a bag of water bottles.

'No. Because that implies I knew about—'

He gave a small sigh and muttered to Jackie, 'Another one.'

'Another what?' I interrupted.

He looked back at me. 'Pardon?' His mouth upturned but the smile didn't reach his eyes. 'Nothing. Look, get down to the shoreline for ten o'clock tomorrow morning. Jackie will sail you back.' He looked at her. She shrugged and nodded. 'But I'm afraid there's no refund. If you've read them, you'll know that is stated in the terms and conditions.'

'Another *what*?' I repeated.

He hesitated. 'Just occasionally people turn up who've either watched too many YouTube videos of Richard Branson's island...'

Heat crept up my neck.

'Or who think conservation is a fashion and means of building their Instagram feed. I call it Green Bragging. Needless to say, in both cases, they haven't studied Seagrass Conservation's website in detail so our way of life comes as a shock.'

'Now just a minute, I—'

'Rick. Why don't you leave this to me,' said Jackie and shot me a sympathetic glance.

Who did this Rick bloke think he was, talking to me like that?

'I can assure you, that's not the case with me. I didn't even know that—'

'You aren't the first and probably won't be the last person apprehensive about hard manual graft. I don't blame you,' he said in a kinder tone. 'What with technology, man's life has evolved to rely on easier options. Look, if you want to take some photos of the animals and birds we have, before leaving, I'm happy to take you over to the enclosures first thing and—'

'Hard graft? Since I was eighteen I've worked as hard as anyone I know. I could easily—'

He raised an eyebrow. 'Tolerate cold showers and toilets that don't flush? Patiently search for turtle nests or count birds? Of course, I partly blame celebrity jungle shows. Fans watch them believing that behind the scenes participants are secretly allowed luxury baths and MasterChef meals.'

Heat moved from my neck and into the tips of my ears.

Jackie passed him the bag. 'Do you want to hand those out, Rick?' she said, smoothly. 'I'll sort out... Sarah, wasn't it? It doesn't surprise me that, now and again, a guest changes their mind when they actually get here, however well-intended their booking has been,' she said to Rick and shot him a pointed look. Jackie handed the bag to him when her phone rang. She answered. Frowned.

'Change of plan, I'm afraid. Apparently one of the parrots is looking ill.'

Rick took the bag as she shot me a smile and headed off. So there *were* parrots here. At least I'd got that right. He stared down at me for a moment. Took off his hat and rubbed his forehead.

'Look… sorry. I didn't mean to be rude. Things have been stressful what with the rebuild of the family estate and running this venture… you're more than welcome to sleep in the main house for one night.'

I shifted uncomfortably. 'That wouldn't be fair on everyone else.'

'Your travelling companions seem happy enough. I think you'll find they'd feel *you* were the one missing out.'

Rick stared over my shoulder. I turned around. Benedikt and one of the other men from our group were good-naturedly arguing over the best way to start a fire. Helga looked impossibly cheerful as she came from the direction of the toilets. One of the couples was smooching near the trees. The sound of running water indicated that someone was taking a quick arctic shower – and wasn't even screaming.

That weighty sense of not belonging washed over me again.

Although Amy didn't look cheerful… she sat dismally on the ladder leading up to our room, knees up, chin resting on folded arms.

'Fetch your luggage,' he said. 'It's no problem. I'll take you up to the house. The last one to jump ship left behind a couple of novels he'd brought. I've read one – a detective story. It's not bad. You can stay there, if you prefer, until you leave tomorrow.'

8

'Your friend can bring your dinner over to the house,' continued Rick. 'Despite the scaffolding I think you'll find it quite comfortable just for one night.'

'She's my sister.'

He consulted his list again. 'Ah yes, I remember. Amy emailed far more than any volunteer ever has. I got the impression she wanted this stay to be perfect. She reminds me of my older brother, Lee. He likes to cover every angle.' Briefly a cloud crossed his features. 'Almost too much so, if you ask me. Anyway, Amy's certainly a nature buff. Her enthusiasm is infectious.'

An unpleasant sensation gnawed at my stomach. She'd gone to so much trouble and had genuinely thought this kind of break would relax me. Plus how could I leave after an argument? I didn't want to ruin Amy's dream holiday, even if it was my idea of hell.

And *jumping ship*? Is that how Rick Crowley saw me? His phone rang and I stared at trees that were doing a merengue with the wind. Is that what I'd done all that time ago, as soon as I'd turned eighteen? Abandoned Amy? The thought had haunted me ever since. But I'd had to. I couldn't live any longer with Dad. I had to keep myself safe and strong, otherwise I'd have been no good for my sister at all. I visited as often as I could during those four last years she'd had to live with him, until she could legally do what she wanted and move into the flat. She'd bought me a box of chocolates when I'd finally scraped together enough money for a deposit. The amount Mum had left me from her private savings helped. And I'd made sure Amy had a say in how I decorated it, choosing the wallpaper and colour of carpet.

However, the feeling that I'd somehow let her down had never left, so I'd tried to make up for it by always trying to keep her happy and safe.

Jonas stood nearby, at the edge of the forest, jabbing his finger at the screen of his mobile. I went over.

'I can't get a signal,' he muttered.

'Trying to contact a friend?'

'Maxi. I had wanted to spend the summer with her,' he muttered. 'Just when we'd become friends again, after our breakup. Things were going well but then I had to travel here.' He looked up. 'Sorry. Too much information.'

'It's okay,' I said and gave a wry smile. 'I'm the queen of broken romances. I've got the T-shirt and the hat.'

He put his phone away and opened his mouth but then seemed to have second thoughts and swiftly closed it.

'What?' I asked.

'I couldn't help hearing you and Rick – is it true? You're leaving?' He sighed. 'Don't abandon me, Sarah. You being here might just save my insanity. I should never have agreed to do this but Mum and Dad persuaded me and said it would look good on my Lebenslauf – I mean, CV – and show I was adventurous as well as a team player.' He looked around. 'Now I'm here, it's even worse than I expected.'

I rested my hand on his arm. 'It's very hard to say no to those you love.'

He met my eyes. 'Guess I've just got to get on with it.'

'You can do this,' I said. 'At your age I was discovering I was stronger than I'd ever imagined. I found myself in a tough situation and looking back… it taught me a lot.'

I *was* strong. I'd had to be. No one had been around to pick me up.

But was I strong enough to live in a jungle?

'I know that doesn't help how you feel right now, though.' I smiled. 'But anyone who can withstand a needle long enough to get a tattoo that size…'

'It's a myth that tattoos hurt,' he whispered, 'but don't tell anyone. I like people thinking I'm tough.'

Me too. It acted as armour. People thought twice about messing you around. After a couple of years on my own Dad just rolled his eyes at me instead of hurling an insult or putting me down.

'I know you're right. But still – it'd be good to have someone here to share the horrors with… The thought of having to be bright and cheery with *everyone* for four weeks…'

'Well, seeing as you make it sound so appealing…' Hold on. No. Don't say it.

'What? You're not leaving after all?'

Don't be silly. Of course I am. 'I've decided to stick it out,' I heard myself say. 'I can't have you take all the glory.' Aargh! Where did that come from?

His face split into a smile and he lunged forward, slipped his arms around my waist and lifted me into the air.

I couldn't help laughing and struggled. 'Jonas! Put me down this instant!'

Gently he did and cheekily grinned before running off towards the sound of Helga calling his name.

I smoothed down my top and walked back to Rick. 'Hi again. Um… change of plan. I'll stay.'

'Really?' He frowned. Not the reaction I'd expected.

'I was just being silly. How hard can it be?'

'You might feel differently in the morning, after one night in the shack. For a start it's up at six tomorrow morning, if you're on the trail clearing team.'

I bristled. 'It's fine. That's the usual time my alarm clock goes off.'

'It's important work we do here – as a team. We all rely on each other. People can't turn up late or duck out of a task at the eleventh hour – or not pull their weight.'

'I manage my own staff back in England,' I said abruptly. I thought he'd be pleased!

'I'm saying all of this because I've also got your interests at heart. I won't lie, Sarah. It's a challenge volunteering here. If you haven't got a passion for conservation then the tasks might seem too daunting.'

'It won't be the first time in my life I've had to do something I didn't want to. Although it's never cost this much before…' I muttered.

'What?'

'Well, you could have at least made the shacks a bit better and connected hot water to the showers. We're paying thousands of pounds – or rather, my sister is. I don't like seeing her ripped off.' I snorted. 'Your family must be laughing all the way to the bank.'

His face reddened. 'You couldn't be more wrong,' he said quietly. 'And every spare penny is invested long-term. My dream is to make Seagrass Island a hub of environmental expertise for the whole region. I'm working not only to save species here but across the whole of the British Virgin Islands – *and* play my part in educating people about climate change.'

'If you say so,' I said and folded my arms.

'Ultimately it's your decision about staying,' he said and shrugged before striding away.

I'd show him. Changing his pompous view of me was a good enough reason not to leave. However mainly, this was about my sister. She'd be concerned enough when we got home and she found out I'd been sacked. Amy deserved these carefree four weeks and I'd try to back off and give her more independence.

I'd do anything to make her smile.

Walk over coals.

Swim the Channel.

Spend a whole month here without a comfy mattress and Pringles.

Amy was still sitting on the steps to our shack. I went over. She stood up. We both hesitated. I rushed forwards and pulled her towards me in a tight embrace.

'I'm so sorry for being an ungrateful cow.'

'I'm sorry, too. For everything I said. I'm just tired too.' A pained expression crossed her face. 'You've an absolute right to feel miffed. I should never have booked a holiday like this without consulting you first.' She looked sheepish. 'Typical me. I didn't think about anything like the insects or the dirt.' She shook her head. 'All these years we've lived together and I've teased you about your obsession with dusting and vacuuming. I should have realised this trip wouldn't tick any of your boxes.'

'Obsession? Amy. I hate to tell you this, but you're the abnormal one, being happy to live with crumbs everywhere.'

She didn't smile but instead peered up at me, from under her fringe. 'This trip was meant to thank you for being the best sister ever, but instead...' She bit one of her nails. 'I've messed up, haven't I? By being spontaneous?'

Heart thumping, I took her by the shoulders. *Messed up*? I hated hearing those words that Dad so often used to say.

I recalled one time she got seven out of ten in an important maths test at primary school. The teacher had given her a special certificate. Mum and I were so proud, especially as that had been the highest mark in her class. But Dad...

'Sevens won't get you a great job like mine, Missy,' he'd said.

He was the reason she'd never had the confidence to become an actual vet. Mum would give her a cuddle, and sweets, say that Dad was just ambitious, but over time his words engraved themselves in her mind.

Sweets became Mum's way of making up for the harsh tones of the man she nevertheless loved. Amy wasn't a fan of them but I was. When hormones and the teenage years hit, along with my love of baking, I continued to fill out and Dad started to pick on me for my shape. Thankfully I'd reached an age where I was starting to see him with fresh eyes and realise that curves where nothing to be ashamed of.

Although that realisation didn't stop me working hard to always look well-groomed. Just like Mum and Anabelle I looked after my hair and wore makeup.

My last boyfriend said I needed to learn to chill. We'd gone swimming. I swam with my head above the water so that my mascara didn't run.

How stupid was that? Still trying to impress a man I didn't see and thought so little of?

I squeezed Amy's shoulders. 'No. Ungrateful me is the one in the wrong. It was just a shock. This is going to be the best break ever. One I'll never forget. Just imagine, Amy – we'll actually be helping this troubled planet dogged by melting ice caps and extreme weather. You can't put a price on that.'

'You're just saying that,' she mumbled.

I put my hands on my hips, steeling myself not to squeal as a long-bodied insect landed on my skirt. 'I'm not.' I thought about Jonas. 'Apart from anything else, it's going to look fantastic on my CV, now that I... I mean... if I ever change jobs. You've done brilliantly to book this trip. It must have taken a lot of organisation. And I don't know how you managed to keep the exact details secret. I could never do that. I'd have accidentally blurted them out by now. I'm so impressed.'

Her words echoed through me – about how she felt I still treated her like a child. Was I really that bad?

'Impressed? Honestly?'

Resigning myself to four weeks in this hellhole, I nodded vigorously.

9

I didn't enjoy lying – especially to Amy – about me actually being excited about staying. However now and then I honestly believed it was the kindest thing. I'd worked that out by the time I was eleven when Mum died and I promised my little sister that everything would be all right, that we would be okay.

'This month will prove that I'm up for any challenge. I can already picture myself now, in an interview room, talking about the compost toilets. Rick described some of the tasks ahead of us – I can't wait!'

I didn't want her to think I was pretending to want to stay. She'd only put herself last and insist we both went back to London immediately. Rick passed by at that moment, with the water bottle bag Jackie had been carrying. I swept the insect off my skirt.

'Rick?'

He stopped.

'I was just telling my sister how I've changed my mind about leaving because that chat with you about the four weeks' activities really inspired me.' I gave him a hard stare.

He paused and I held his gaze. Eventually a smile crossed his lips. 'Sure... Amy... I've seen a lot of volunteers over the last three years and it's clear to me Sarah is *totally* up for roughing it. Getting last-minute nerves after arriving is totally normal. I've seen it time after time. I think both of you are going to be great assets to the project. Thanks again for booking.'

Amy stood more upright.

'In fact,' he said, warming to his subject, 'Sarah insists on being the first to empty the compost toilet. Isn't she a star? Anyone who genuinely wanted to go home would never do that.' He gave the brightest white smile.

'Oh, that's a shame. I was going to volunteer,' said Amy. 'My dream, one day, is to own a house with a huge garden where I can have a compost toilet of my own – along with a bee hive, a hedgehog house, feeders for birds and a large house for the battery hens I'll adopt…'

'Sounds great,' said Rick. 'You'll learn a lot here, such as how to choose plants to attract butterflies.'

They chatted for a moment and I zoned out, wondering how bad the meals here would be.

My eyes followed his tall frame when he headed off humming. Suddenly Rick spun around and fished two water bottles out of the bag.

'I forgot to give you these,' he called.

'I'll go,' I said and hurried over to where he was standing. 'There was no reason to go quite that far,' I said in a low voice. 'You heard my sister – she'd much prefer to clean out the toilets.'

'I'm all for throwing people in at the deep end and there's no avoiding any tasks here. We all muck in – literally.' His eyes flickered with amusement. 'I get it, you not wanting to lose face in front of Amy. And you might be thanking me by the end of this week. Doing this first will make the rest of the tasks seem easy in comparison.'

I took the two bottles.

'Although… it's none of my business, but don't you think it might be better just to be honest? Tell her that it's not really your cup of tea but you're prepared to give it a go? In my experience lying never ends well.' His face darkened and he stared past my shoulder for a moment.

'No. Amy mustn't get a whiff of the fact I want to leave. She deserves to enjoy this month without worrying about me. It's best this way.'

'She may not think that. Being lied to always brings hurt.' His face flushed. He gave a small bow and walked off.

I made my way back to Amy. 'Can we get on with our unpacking?'

'Everything all right? Between you and Rick?' she countered.

'Of course. He… he seems like a great bloke.' For some reason I blushed.

Amy took my hand and pulled me into the forest. Birds called overhead. Tree canopies threw shade. Twigs snapped beneath our feet.

'Amy? What are we doing? The toilets are the other way if you—'

Finally she stopped and placed her hands on my arms. 'Are you absolutely sure, Sarah? About not going home? Look… I can see how lots of women would find Rick attractive – I could understand if he managed to sway your opinion with some smooth talking.'

'He hasn't—'

But we're here for four weeks. I… I would understand

if you wanted to book the first plane out of here. Granted, Rick's charming...'

Is he?

'... and Jonas is funny. Jackie's so nice. Helga is interesting. But the novelty of a new crowd might wear off after a few days. When reality sets in about the kind of holiday this is... the physical work... the lack of mod cons... I don't want you to regret committing to it.'

'You think my opinion has been swayed by Rick? That I find him good-looking? I think you've had too much sun.'

She gave me a curious look. 'You don't think he's fit? Remember, I'm the person who once worked out you had the hots – no pun intended – for candlestick Lumière from *Beauty and the Beast*.'

'It was a long time ago. Please never repeat that to anyone.'

'Rick's not my type,' she continued. 'We've too much in common. Unlike you, I believe in opposites attracting. It's more exciting...'

'Hmm. I remember the butcher you briefly dated.'

'Don't remind me! But I totally get why you'd go for his humorous, whole Indiana Jones take-me-to-bed vibe. In fact, he's nothing like the recent guys you've dated. Perhaps you are coming around to my point of view, about *un*common ground being sexy.'

Amy was right about my previous boyfriends. They weren't remotely flirtatious. In each case our relationship had started off as a friendship. They were sensible. Liked routine. Weren't especially sociable. Trying to be funny wasn't part of their agenda. But this was no accident. As an adult I'd eventually grown to avoid men of a certain type.

Those who were deemed handsome. Who were charismatic. Who were difficult to ignore, like Rick.

I had very good reason.

I shuddered, glad she'd reminded me of this.

'No. Honestly, Amy, I'm not looking for love. I'm here for adventure in terms of… of learning new skills and broadening my mind. Then back in England I'll be focusing on pushing my career forwards so whilst this might be tough, it'll also be a good break – a complete change of scenery.'

'Fair enough,' she said and her shoulders relaxed. 'As long as you are staying for *you*.'

No. I'm staying for you.

'Come on,' I said. 'Helga will be making all the shack rules without us.'

She gave me the tightest hug. 'I'm so glad we're doing this together, sis. It's going to be the best four weeks ever.'

10

I stared over at Rick, having reluctantly joined the tour of my home for the next month. My heart started to melt. I wanted to tickle him under the chin and behind those adorable ears. Chatty, that was – the Capuchin monkey, sitting on Rick's shoulder, a lead around its neck, the other end of which had a handle and was wrapped around Rick's wrist.

The little creature kept pulling off his hat and throwing it onto the ground. Everyone chuckled. Rick encouraged people to take photos on their phones. I batted away thoughts suggesting that he looked even more attractive wearing his caring side for this adorable animal.

'This is the star of our zoo – or so he thinks,' said Rick. 'Chatty came to us six months ago. I was getting in supplies, on Tortola island, and overheard a tourist describing a monkey she'd seen being used as street entertainment. It's rare in the British Virgin Islands. Jackie gained a lot of experience in Colombia, working with animals that had been kept by circuses or caught up in the illegal exotic pet trade. She'd dealt with monkeys coming from similar circumstances and that's why I thought we'd be able to give him a good home.'

'Doesn't he need to mix with his own kind?' asked Benedikt. Chatty was talking in a series of whistles and squeaks. I admired the gloriously blond face and bib that contrasted the dark fur elsewhere.

Rick turned to Chatty and tickled his cheek. The monkey swiped him and stuck out his tongue. Jonas and I caught each other's eyes. Even we had to laugh. I'd changed into comfortable yet stylish shorts, spurning the long trousers Amy had secretly packed, despite an increasing number of mosquito bites. I was determined to enjoy as much of this stay as I could, and wearing my new, fashionable wardrobe was part of that. I compromised by wearing the only pair of trainers I'd brought, bearing rose gold stars.

'It's not going to be a straightforward rescue, rehabilitate and rehome story,' he said. 'Otherwise it would have been better for him to go somewhere where his species is indigenous. You see, this little fella's blind. That's one reason we think he's particularly vocal – one sense making up for another. His lack of sight probably made him easy to catch in the first place. Funnily enough it might have been a blessing in disguise. He wouldn't have lasted long at all, in the wild, with predators such as snakes or eagles, and finding food and defending himself against other monkeys would have proved nigh on impossible.'

My heart melted further into a messy, emotional puddle.

'For those reasons we can't ever release him or house him with fellow monkeys.'

'Why don't you make him a real pet, then, and keep him in your living quarters?' I asked. I bet Rick didn't live in one of the shacks. No doubt his evenings and nights were luxurious, up at the house he'd spoken of.

'Won't he become sexually mature when he's five?' said Amy. 'That could introduce a whole set of problems.'

Rick looked surprised. 'Yes… that's it, Amy. Spot on.'

Her cheeks glowed.

'Chatty is currently about two years old. At five his behaviour could really change. He might become more aggressive. So we'll see… but for now he seems happy enough with positive human contact during the day and his swinging ropes and trees at night. His confidence has grown since arriving here and now he's a cheeky little guy.' He smiled. 'Someone give me their phone.'

Benedikt darted forward. Rick switched the camera to selfie mode. He reached out, holding the phone.

'Chatty. Selfieee,' he said.

The monkey wrapped his arms around Rick's head. Everyone looked rapt as Rick took the photo.

'Preparing the food for our animals is a messy but important daily task. It has to be fresh and healthy. Chatty was in a terrible state when he first arrived. He'd been fed nothing but junk food. Patches of his fur had fallen out with the stress.'

'I hope his captor was flung in jail,' said Amy and screwed up her face. I'd seen that expression before when she'd brought home an animal that needed twenty-four hour love and attention.

'The authorities never caught him,' said Rick. 'By the time I got to his patch he'd done a runner and left a whimpering Chatty tied to a lamppost, right by the edge of a road. He could have been killed. It's taken a lot of time day in, day out, and gentle care to get him to trust humans again. In fact…' He laughed. 'I think Jackie and I went too far. He has absolutely no respect for us now.'

Everyone laughed.

'Let me show you the rest of the animal quarters. There's a large aviary.'

'For parrots and parakeets?' asked Amy. 'Didn't some need their wings amputating after the hurricane?'

Rick smiled. 'Nice to see someone has been reading the website.'

Was that aimed at me?

'Yes. And others are from the rescue centre south from here, in Colombia, where Jackie worked. They were overrun last year and couldn't cope. Most of those had their wings clipped by poachers. Others were injured after being stuffed in lead pipes, to smuggle them out of the country on boats.'

Clearly this work was Rick's passion. His eyes shone and his hands moved in a lively fashion as he talked about the animals.

'Some birds have been well enough to be released here,' he said. 'But most of these ones will be permanent residents. We also have an owl from Colombia. Over there they are associated with witchcraft.' He pointed to a tawny speckled owl. 'Wink is a screech owl. She was stoned. A passer-by intervened but not before her wing was irreversibly fractured. And across the Virgin Islands this species is now endangered due to deforestation. Funds allowing, it would be great to find her a partner and start a breeding programme to benefit the whole region.'

There was a large flight cage for fruit bats covered in plywood sheets to keep the inside dark.

'It's not advisable to house different species of bat together – or even ones of the same species but from different roosts,' said Rick. 'In here we house the ones we found injured in the same area – it looked like they'd come from a single roost in one of the large trees that had been blown over. They've bred since we rescued them in 2017 and we're hoping to release this lot soon. Then we'll turn this cage into another aviary.'

The next enclosure had a large pool and was home to seabirds that had been swept into trees and buildings during the hurricane and lost limbs. On from that was the lizards' enclosure. Survivors of the hurricane had managed to cling to trees but numbers had been badly affected so Rick and Jackie were running a breeding programme, away from predators. They were doing the same with tree boas. Apparently they were endangered across the whole of the British Virgin Island region due to deforestation. We were also taken past a pair of iguanas who'd been permanently injured by the storm.

This was an expensive break but I was beginning to see how the money was needed and would be used.

'And lastly,' said Rick, as Chatty threw his hat on the ground again, 'here is the butterfly enclosure. Volunteers have almost finished building it. By this time next year, we're hoping it will be buzzing with endangered species.'

'I thought there would be more animals,' said Benedikt.

'You mean the furry kind?' asked Rick. 'It is something we are working on – but only from a financial point to raise funds to restore the whole island. We know cuter looking residents will make the place more attractive as a destination and give us a wider reach when it comes to attracting volunteers – and educating people about conservation. So we're putting feelers out to other rescue centres in the Caribbean that are getting overcrowded. The most important thing is that any animal is suited to our specific habitat and that we can provide all the necessary nutrients from plants growing here.

'Colombia has a real problem with sloth smuggling, for example, but they are incredibly sensitive animals. Jackie isn't convinced they would thrive here. Their diet has to be one hundred per cent accurate and we aren't like a national zoo – our money for importing animal feed and growing foreign species of plants is limited.' He consulted his watch. 'Right, we've been here longer than I planned. I'll show you the beach and trail clearing areas tomorrow.' He glanced at his shoulder. 'How about we head straight to the canteen, Chatty? The other volunteers should be back and washed now, and ready for something to eat. Malik might even have one of your favourite hard-boiled eggs.'

Chatty cocked his head and squeaked and whistled.

'That means yes,' said Rick with confidence. 'It's a great food for him as long as he doesn't smell and try to swipe any mayonnaise.'

Rick told everyone to go back along the path we'd come along, and then instead of going straight into our camp we were to veer right, past the shower block and the two other clusters of shacks. At a fast pace it should take about twenty minutes to reach the canteen. Helga and Amy strode off, in a deep conversation. Benedikt and Jonas followed.

My shoelace was undone. I bent over to do it up, wishing I'd tied my long hair back in a ponytail. I started whistling 'Daydream Believer' by the Sixties pop group, the Monkees, inspired by Chatty. It had been Mum's favourite song. When I straightened up Rick was waiting for me. He'd locked up Chatty's cage to make sure snakes didn't get in whilst the monkey was away. Chatty had stopped moving and squeaking.

'Blimey. He must like that song. He's so rarely quiet.'

I stopped whistling and reached out to touch the animal's back. He jumped.

'Don't ever forget that he's blind,' said Rick. 'If you are going to touch him then talk first in a reassuring tone. If those false nails are detachable, I'd take them off – or he will. Same for your hair extensions.'

'Excuse me… both are my own.'

'Your long earrings will have to go too. They could get caught in foliage.' He started walking. 'There is intermittent Wi-Fi at the canteen. Perhaps you should try to download our website and read it. I did set all these things out in the guidelines. I assume you haven't made time to study them, but you really ought to now.'

'Clearly, you've got me sussed,' I said in a tight voice.

'I'm not very good at sussing people,' he continued.

Silence fell for a moment. I sensed a story that he didn't want to tell.

'Believe me, Sarah, I'm only trying to be helpful and get you up to speed with everyone else. There's a lot of work to do this summer. One less team member is better than one who isn't fully invested in our cause – for their sake and ours. Right. We'd better catch up with the rest.'

I stopped and pretended to tie my hair, waiting for him and Chatty to disappear. Chatty was an utter delight but I'd rather walk back on my own than have to spend a single second more with that Rick.

II

I made my way along the path, with random stems growing across it. Sooner than I expected, it veered to the right. Rick had said that would happen when we reached our shacks but I wasn't near them yet. However all the paths had to lead in the same direction. Perhaps this would even be a short cut and I'd beat Mr Know-It-All back.

So what if I took my chances? I'd learnt not to be risk-adverse with Dad. During my teenage years I'd started to call him out. Pressured him to compliment a new dress of Anabelle's. Comforted Amy in front of him, to make him realise he'd done wrong. Of course, it often resulted in me being grounded or missing pocket money but that was better than living a lie and letting him think he was the perfect father.

This had increasingly been the problem at Best Travel. Prue was against the slightest, best calculated risk but my nature told me that veering from the straight line, sometimes, was the only way to make progress.

Out of breath, I stopped. I'd been walking upwards for fifteen minutes. My whole body dripped with perspiration. I'd tripped over a rock and scratched my arms on bushes. I pushed myself up. My knee was bleeding. I ignored the voice in my head telling me I should have worn long trousers.

Around the corner, I came to a fork and turned left. Down I went, following a path. Nothing seemed familiar – no, scrub that, the problem was it did. The mish-mash of plants with gleaming leaves all looked the same. The sprawling canopy of trees meant only chinks of sunlight got through. I almost shrieked as I walked straight into a huge sticky spider's web.

I brushed the silky strands away and decided to climb straight down, through vegetation. I pushed straggling foliage out of the way. My hair got tangled. A nail broke. What if I got stuck in the rainforest overnight? I might rub up against some venomous frog. Maybe there would be a bout of tropical rainfall and I'd catch hypothermia. Did wolves or bears live here? There was nothing for it. I was just about to yell for help when I heard laughing. I hurried further down, slipping every now and again in the soil underfoot. Eventually the trees began to clear.

I emerged at the back of a building and peered inside. The canteen. The chef had a round smiley face and looked as hot and discomposed as me. Smoothing down my hair, I walked around the side. Rick stood with his hands on his hips.

'Where on earth have you been? I was just about to instruct staff to search, what with evening approaching...'

'I decided to take a look around,' I said. 'I didn't realise I had to inform anyone of my whereabouts.'

'Well, you do – until you are more familiar with the place. With due care Seagrass Island is a perfectly safe place to explore, but newcomers need to be aware of the risks – plants that cause bad reactions on the skin, marshy areas of ground that mean you might fall and sprain your ankle and be unable to get back.'

'I did look out for snakes,' I said, trying not to sound totally naive.

'You'd actually be lucky to spot one. The vibration of footsteps normally scares them off. You're more likely to come across blood-sucking leeches and...wait a minute...' His voice sounded strained. 'Please tell me you've had your jabs.'

'Of course,' I said, irritated. 'Sorry for the inconvenience.' I wasn't used to feeling like a nuisance. 'I would have climbed a tree if wolves had come or—'

Was that amusement or irritation that flickered across his face?

He pulled a twig out of my hair, passed me a tissue and looked down. I followed his gaze and wiped my bleeding knee.

'Weren't you worried about trekking through the vegetation on your own? Anyone else might have just waited and looked around the zoo until someone returned to guide them back.'

I shrugged. 'I'd rather give things a go myself. You don't get anywhere in life by relying on a hand up.'

His frown softened. 'Right... yep... okay, well, we'd better get you something to eat before chef stops serving. Your sister's inside. The smaller building, to the left of this canteen, is the Games Room with a snooker table, darts and board games. Most people pile in there after dinner and...'

Without saying a word I went in, politely listening to him.

Amy hurried over and stared at my knee. 'Sarah! What's happened? Are you all right?'

'Nothing to worry about,' I said breezily. 'I got lost for a while, but it... it was fun, although I've reassured Rick I won't go AWOL again.'

Jonas waved and pointed to a seat next to him. I went over and sat down. Amy sat opposite. I swigged back a glass of water.

'Rick tells me that all the electricity comes off at nine to save costs,' I said. 'Apparently it sets a good routine. Many volunteers are up very early if they are trail clearing or doing a bird count. He said there are torches for everyone.'

'Living the high life, eh?' muttered Jonas.

I couldn't help laughing at his expression. 'It's funny,' I said, gazing right, at Helga, with her starched top tucked into her trousers and scraped back hair, and then back to Jonas's dreadlocks and flowing cotton shirt. 'Going by appearances you look far more laidback than your sister. Yet none of this seems to faze her. She's happily unpacked in our shack and said she couldn't wait to see her first tarantula.'

'I *am* laidback,' he said indignantly. 'Just in more of a... a bohemian, find-me-in-the-bar-jamming-with-musicians kind of way.'

I pushed his shoulder. Amy took me up to the serving hatch. There were flaky-looking burrito style wraps called roti, stuffed with curried meat or vegetables, with peas on the side.

'They are delicious,' she said, when it was my turn.

Malik's smile widened further and he reached for my plate. 'You must have two, after such a high recommendation.'

I went back to the table where Benedikt was also sitting and a couple of long-term volunteers. It was basic with hard chairs and reminded me of eating lunch at high school. I took several bites. The roti was delicious.

'Curried goat,' said someone.

I gagged. In the supermarket I liked my well-known brands. I was all for taking risks, but not when it came to food and that meant not trying other labels, let alone eating something like goat. Jonas went up to the serving area and game back with two mangos.

'You okay?' asked Amy and stared at my plate.

I bit into the fruit to prove I was. 'Just a little jet lagged.'

'Yet you sound really keen about getting started – seems like you had quite a chat with Rick.'

'It's going to be an experience of a lifetime.' I avoided Jonas's eye.

'And there's no time to waste, as you've already proven. *Rick,*' she called and waved her hand across the room.

He was sitting with Jackie and an attractive woman with an infectious laugh – the Italian Carlotta he'd mentioned before. Rick had fed Chatty a hard-boiled egg and fruit. The monkey had seemed especially taken with Carlotta's glossy black curls and they'd all grinned every time he grabbed a handful. Every ounce of me was longing to give him a cuddle. Carlotta had been here since the beginning of June. I'd spoken to her briefly whilst queuing for my roti. She'd asked if it was true that English people looked like lobsters when their skin burnt. Then she'd given one of her joyous laughs that attracted attention wherever she went. I couldn't decide if she'd meant to insult me – until she'd said that when she burnt she looked like she'd eaten nothing but tomatoes for a week.

Rick strode over. 'Everything all right?'

Amy scraped a chair across the floor and positioned it in between the two of us.

'We've all got so many questions and I know I, for one, am too excited to wait until tomorrow to find out more. Can you just tell us a little about how the next days are going to pan out? My sister, Sarah, is especially impatient.' She squeezed my hand.

'That's lovely to hear,' said Rick and sat down, a twinkle in his eye.

Jonas choked on his water and Helga came over and clapped him on the back. I glared at my friend, hoping he'd not make me laugh.

'Er, yes... seeing the zoo has really inspired me,' I said. 'So... lots of questions, like... do we get any days off?'

A muscle flinched in his cheek. 'I can see that you're really keen.'

'Sarah covers all aspects. She's always told me success is in the detail,' said Amy.

Rick raised an eyebrow my way. 'That's exactly what I've always thought.'

I felt uncomfortable with him so close and couldn't help scanning his long legs... the broad shoulders... the determined jaw and soft lips.

An image flashed through my mind of the two of us strolling hand in hand along the beach. Where did that come from? Questions popped into my head. Had he ever been in love? Why did his last relationship break up?

Why did I care?

None of this would have intrigued me if he was simply a regular, friendly guy. But there was a story behind that professional exterior and a bit of mystery. It was undeniably sexy.

I'd still rather have been met at the airport by Richard Branson.

Definitely.

No question about it.

He pointed to a large white board on the wall behind us.

'That's the rota. It gets updated every couple of days. The main tasks are preparing the animal food and feeding them twice a day. And lots of trail clearing. Then overnight we set nets in the forest and a team will get up early, at six, to count the different birds caught and release them. This is done in various different locations – on the beach and in the forest, to monitor various species. Bird counting is also done with binoculars.'

'I heard someone talking about rope bridges leading up to the tree canopies,' said Benedikt.

'Yes. There are observation points up there. Also, every night between midnight and four a.m. a group look for turtle nests on the beach, on the other side of the island. It's quite a trek to get there. We collect the eggs, bring them back and bury them in a protected sandpit. Other tasks will include butterfly catching when the enclosure is ready and...'

He spoke of rotas to clean the shower blocks and toilets, and sessions spent helping the chef.

'But in answer to your question,' he said to me, 'you have every weekend off from the work – apart from animal feeding.'

My brow relaxed. That was better than back home. Two consecutive days free every single week?

'What is there to do in free time?' asked Jonas and sat more upright.

'Head over to Tortola for shopping or there's a great selection of bars with local bands and dancing. I've spent many happy a night over there, unwinding to the best Caribbean beats.'

Jonas surprised everyone by pulling a harmonica out of his shorts pocket although the notes he played sounded nothing like calypso.

'There are sailing trips,' continued Rick. 'Plus we run fun events – a sports day is coming up. There's the beach here, of course. Swimming. Cricket and boules. On Sunday mornings Chef lays on a special brunch.'

There was hope.

Rick got to his feet again and yawned. 'Tomorrow morning I'll break you all in with a trail clearing session. We need to meet here at six. It gets too hot otherwise, as it's hard physical work. Bring your water bottles. You can fill them up in the kitchen and take a piece of fruit and bread roll. Chef won't have made breakfast but you'll need something to fill you up. Make sure you wear trousers and long-sleeve tops along with insect repellent on visible skin. We'll work until ten – as a team. And we stick together.'

He gave me a pointed look.

'Then come back here for a proper late breakfast. Right. Time for me to take Chatty back to his bed.' He pointed to a table by the door. 'Help yourself to one of those torches each. The electricity will be going off in about an hour. People are starting to head off to the Games Room. I'd highly recommend that.'

'Just don't play cards when Rick does. He's very competitive,' said Jackie as she walked past.

Rick went over to get the monkey. He said hello and touched its head. Chatty sniffed and immediately climbed up Rick's arm and sat on his shoulder, showing total trust. Jonas stacked our plates and took them over to the trolleys, which were brimming with dirty crockery. Amy went over to see the monkey. Rick encouraged her to talk to him. She stroked Chatty and told him about her job at the vet's. Rick asked her a few questions and her voice bolder, she explained about Paws & Claws. He listened intently. She looked as happy as a child on Christmas morning.

If only Dad had paid that much attention, she might have had more confidence when it came to her abilities.

I sank into thoughts about how my time here couldn't have had a worse start. At least the weekends sounded… normal. So what if I'd got lost? I found my way to the others, in the end. That was probably the worst experience I was going to have during this month.

'It's not all doom and gloom,' I said to Jonas as we both picked up torches. 'There's shopping.'

'And music,' he said.

'And moonlight. Don't forget romance.'

He grinned. 'Love that song by Nat King Cole song about there being trouble ahead.'

'Hmm, well let's hope not. I do like the sound of Sunday brunch.'

Jonas switched his torch on, lifted it up and cast a spotlight on his face. 'You heard it here first, viewers,' he said in a TV presenter's voice. 'Maybe one month on Seagrass Island isn't going to be so bad after all.'

12

I'd set my alarm for half past five, just as the sun was beginning to rise. That would give us time to throw on clothes before getting to the meeting point for trail clearing. Helga was already awake and sat crossed-legged in her bed, meditating. Amy snored from the bunk below. I'd opted for the top one, away from any insects but last night questioned my decision due to hot air rising.

Optimistically I'd collapsed into bed after phoning home to check up on Nelly. However, I hadn't slept a wink. Every inch of my skin had never been so hot and sticky. The humidity had felt like an overzealous lover wrapped around me all night. I'd worn my skimpiest nightie but that made no difference so I'd pushed my mosquito net to one side, seeing as the windows were protected anyway.

A cacophony of humming, buzzing and chirping from afar and near didn't help my restlessness. I worried moths had found their way into the shack due to the close sound of fluttering wings. The most I heard back in London was the occasional car driving past or plane overhead, or the whirr of the central heating and fridge – identifiable sounds that felt safe.

I scratched my legs and got out from under the covers.

I climbed down the bunk bed ladder. The sun hadn't risen enough for me to be able to spot spiders on the floor and so I landed on my tiptoes. I crouched down, pulled away Amy's mosquito net and gently pushed her shoulder. The sweaty hair and dribble running from her mouth reminded me of childhood sleepovers. She'd creep into my bed whenever Dad had upset her.

'Where am I?' muttered Amy.

'In a five-star hotel, waking up to waiter service,' I said with longing.

'Very funny,' she said. Helga's eyes were open now. She'd already made her bed. I scratched my legs again and went over to the front door to examine them under better light. It had been left ajar. I'd need to have a word with the others about that. I'd suffered dubious bed partners in the past but never a snake or scorpion.

'Oh my God – look at this rash,' I said. My legs were covered in itchy red mounds. 'I must be allergic to something. Or perhaps I've caught a tropical disease…' Helga marched over, took my elbow and nudged me down the outside ladder. We stood on the grass. Hurriedly Amy followed.

'No wonder I couldn't sleep,' I said and moaned.

Helga bent over. 'Didn't you use your mosquito net?'

I frowned. 'No. The windows are so protected. Why, are these all bites?'

Her cheeks flushed. 'It looks like it. Sorry, Sarah – I left the door open a bit, to allow in cool air. I didn't think to mention it.'

I pursed my lips tight, like I did when I was trying to stop myself snapping back at Prue.

'I've got some cream to help with the itching,' said Helga.

'That will ease them. We'll be too busy this morning for you to notice the discomfort.'

I slathered on the cream, got changed and applied insect repellent to any exposed areas. I checked Amy had done the same and she rolled her eyes as a reply. I didn't have time to clean my teeth or wash. I quickly applied deodorant and scraped my hair back into a scrunchie. I pulled on my Audrey Hepburn hat, ignoring the practical cap Amy had secretly packed for me. This, at least, would give me a degree of style. Yawning, I followed the others along the path to the canteen, Amy singing songs from *The Jungle Book*.

'Sleep okay?' I asked Jonas as we lagged behind the others. He tied back his dreadlocks.

'*Nein*. I was hungry and lay awake thinking about strudel and sausage.'

'What I wouldn't do for a pizza takeaway…'

'Apparently they sometimes serve fish soup for breakfast.' He pretended to vomit.

I opened my mouth to join in but his shoulders drooped, his feet dragged. The face that had been laughing under the spotlight of a torch yesterday now had dark shadows and had lost its sparkle.

'I know, it sucks, but honestly, I'm sure we'll soon laugh about this. Remember, it's Thursday – in two days we go shopping and can treat ourselves to a beer and ice cream. And just think of all the inspiration this holiday will give you for songwriting. This initial misery will help you create heartbreaking ballads.'

'What? Call a tune "Miss Apple Cake, oh how I'm missing you"?'

Trying to ignore the waves of itching across my legs, I smiled.

'The prospect of four weeks here wouldn't seem nearly so bad if I had my guitar. Benedikt plays the piano, you know. His dad's a piano tuner.' Momentarily his face brightened.

I kept him talking about music. Jonas didn't have ten years of adult experience on his side to let him realise that life *was* a series of ups and downs and that somehow people got through the troughs. It was human nature to grit your teeth and soldier on.

Rick was waiting at the canteen. As we filled our water bottles and ate aromatic starfruit and passionfruit, he discussed afternoon rotas with Jackie. Chatty stood perched on her shoulder. Rick kept teasingly holding the end of his tail.

I whistled 'Daydream Believer' and went over to join them. The monkey stopped moving, just like yesterday. With a nod from Jackie and still whistling, I tickled his head. He didn't jump this time. Perhaps he remembered the song.

Amy came up behind me. 'I can't believe he likes that,' she said and pulled a pained expression, cupping her hands over her ears.

'Clearly he's got great taste,' I said airily, momentarily forgetting the tough morning ahead.

'Right, let's go. Everyone stay together,' said Rick. 'We don't want any of you getting lost on your first proper day.' He glanced my way and handed us each a machete and pair of gloves and demonstrated the best way to swing it from side to side and hack up and down.

'The rainforest grows back incredibly quickly,' he said, 'so trail clearing is an on-going challenge. The bits you cut off, just throw them into nearby undergrowth. You'll need to wear the gloves for handling the foliage as some is prickly or can sting. There are considerable distances between the different areas of Seagrass Island such as the animal enclosures and beach, so it saves time if we are able to walk as quickly as possible, along the manmade pathways.'

'We must be careful, in case we risk cutting each other?' said Benedikt in his crisp High German accent. Like everyone else, he was dressed in long trousers and a long-sleeve top. I stood out having quickly thrown on my three-quarter-length floral crop pants and flamingo-print T-shirt.

'Yes,' said Rick. 'Although none of you should be in danger. This morning we'll work on a fifty-metre strip and you'll be spaced out so that you have about five metres each to work on.'

'That doesn't seem like much,' said Jonas in a hopeful tone.

'It's not a ready established path,' said Rick. 'This is a new trail I want to create access to a marshy area near the top where we can observe a whole new range of amphibians and reptiles.' He adjusted his Indiana Jones hat. 'Right. Are we ready? Be careful and gentle with any wildlife you need to clear, such as beetles, spiders, frogs or grass snakes…'

Everyone apart from Jonas and me looked excited. I already felt tired by the time we'd hiked up to the marshy area and my feet were hurting. Not even Benedikt and Amy's rhythmic rendition of 'The Bare Necessities' could distract me. My fashionable trainers were far from supportive for uneven terrain but there was no way I was going to wear those clunky walking boots Amy had secretly packed.

I was usually the queen of practicality but this would be my only holiday for months. I'd carefully chosen gorgeous new pieces for my summer wardrobe and couldn't bear to leave them unworn.

Also… it sounded ridiculous but I thought I'd look stupid in such cumbersome boots. They suited Amy and her more unisex dress sense. She could carry anything off – frills or straight lines, dresses or jump suits. But me? I needed clothes that were tailored to suit my figure.

Memories flashed into my head of Dad criticising the appearance of a female weather forecaster or actress on the telly.

Rick allotted us each a strip. I was the furthest away from the top with Amy in front of me. Slash. Swipe. Hack. Brush to one side. Throw. Scrape. This was a full workout. I went to swig from my water bottle. It was empty. Of course. I'd downed it all after that fruit and forgotten to refill. My mouth felt dry. I wanted to ask Amy for a swig of hers but didn't want to draw attention to my mistake. It would only confirm what Rick already thought of me. I grabbed a handful of leaves and squealed as they revealed one of those big shiny millipedes. Feeling shaky, I dropped it to one side. A wave of dizziness washed over me as I cleared the ground of stones. Something felt strange inside my left glove. I took it off. Great. Two of my long nails had broken. I jumped as I noticed Rick by my side, looking at my hands.

'How's it going?' he asked. 'You aren't quite keeping up with everyone else. In fact, your sister's made fantastic headway. Perhaps it might be easier if you took off that unwieldy hat.'

It wasn't much bigger than his. Well, only a bit. The rim was really wide and it did keep slipping forward. I swayed, for some reason finding it hard to stand.

'There's something you should know. My sister, Amy, she booked this trip without—'

'The two of you are very different, aren't you? She's almost finished her strip,' he said. 'Shall I ask her to help you?'

'No thanks.'

What I needed was a long drink. A fragrant bath. A massage. A plateful of pastries and shade.

My eyes welled up but I squeezed tears away. For Amy's – and Jonas's – sake I had to be strong.

'Are you okay?' Rick said and took my arm.

His voice was hard to hear. The rainforest went in and out of focus. I tried to shake him off. 'If you could just leave me to get on, I'll… I'll…'

My knees felt like jelly and as they buckled my hat fell off and everything went black.

13

Tropical warmth wrapped around me like a winter duvet. I opened my eyes. Or did I? Perhaps this was a dream – me, lying in the arms of an indecently handsome man. Fingers gently brushed hair out of my eyes.

The good thing about dreams was that you could do whatever you wanted. There was no point in wasting them. At the very least I could bag a swoonworthy kiss, without the baggage of real-life insecurities and limitations. I lifted a hand and tucked it behind his neck, gently pulling his face towards mine.

'Sarah? How are you feeling?' asked an English voice.

There was something about the line of the jaw and the way those eyebrows pinched together into quizzical frown that I recognised.

I was lying down. A strong arm around my shoulders. In the middle of the rainforest.

Oh crap!

I sat bolt upright.

'Ow!' He rubbed his chin.

'Sorry, Rick,' I said, feeling myself blush furiously. 'I… was just grabbing onto you to pull myself up.'

'You fainted,' he said. 'Unless you fell over.' He glanced at my pink trainers. I should have put on the boots. 'Did you not even read the kit list before packing?'

'No, because—'

'Right. You'll have to buy some proper footwear over on Tortola at the weekend. Have some water.' He picked up my bottle, shook it and looked further puzzled.

'I forgot to refill it,' I said lamely.

'Then you'd better have some of mine.'

'That won't be—'

'No arguments,' he said firmly. 'You need to rehydrate. I'll get your sister to take you back to the camp and take you off the turtle trip tonight. I was going to roster you on with Amy.'

'No way. I was just thirsty and tired. See?' I knocked back some water and stretched my arms. 'I'm perfectly capable of carrying on.'

'That's all very stoical but I don't want a health and safety issue on my hands. And you need a hat that stays on in this heat.' He picked his up off the ground and put it on my head.

'There's no need to make a fuss,' I said, in an urgent tone.

Rick glanced at me. I stared back rebelliously. He rubbed his forehead, stood back and studied me as if I were a new species of insect he'd spotted.

'Sarah? What's going on?'

Too late. Running footsteps. Amy appeared by my side.

'What happened?' she asked as Rick took his bottle. Gratitude washed over me as he walked away without saying anything.

'Nothing. I just wasn't drinking enough.' I stood up and swiped with my machete. 'See. I'm stronger than ever.'

She shook her finger at me playfully.

'Sarah Sterling. You really are a sly one, pretending to faint, to get Rick's attention. To be honest, I wasn't ever convinced you'd suddenly become converted to the cause of conservation. But a crush on Rick? You know I've had my suspicions. And who could blame you? A holiday romance? That's just what you need after some of the losers you've dated.'

'No!'

Her face dropped.

I *did* want Amy to believe I wanted to stay – and that I was really able to cope with the outdoors challenges. I sighed to myself. Perhaps this was the only way. 'Oh... okay... rumbled – I was hiding the truth. But that's because it's just a silly crush – so there's no need to tell anyone else.'

'Oh Sarah, I'm so happy for you. He seems lovely – and genuinely concerned about your welfare. He's even given you his hat!'

'Well, he's very impressed with how *you* are doing.'

'He is?'

'Oh, definitely.'

'I know this is only the second day but this trip is already everything I dreamed of. I've spotted birds and insects I recognise and Jackie's been talking to me about some of the problems the zoo animals have. I was able to make a few suggestions, based on things I've picked up at the vet's.'

'You've always had a natural ability when it comes to understanding and helping animals. Like that time you thought Nelly was off colour and it turned out she had a urinary tract infection. You just sensed it.'

'Anyone could have,' she mumbled.

I held her arm. 'No. I didn't. Your talent is obvious. Since we arrived Rick has clearly been impressed by your knowledgeable comments.'

Her face shone as she went back to her strip.

I started to cut the bushes and long grass again, determined to show I was just as capable as anyone else. Rick came back over, didn't say a word and passed me his bottle. I glugged from it again, before carrying on. I almost decapitated a frog and managed not to scream when a beetle with scarily long antennae scuttled over my wrist. I scratched my arms on prickly branches and my lovely new trainers became covered in mud.

All of that was nothing compared to the headache that banged and the painful blisters now covering my hands to match the ones forming on my feet. In a daze I walked back to camp with Jonas. He was exhausted too, his damp T-shirt sticking to his chest.

Gratefully we headed into the canteen and downed large glasses of cold water. I couldn't wait for breakfast except that when the Malik appeared at the serving hatch to announce it was served, the meal turned out to be the awful fish soup we'd heard about.

'This is a joke, *nein?*' muttered Jonas who sat next to me.

'If it is, I don't think much to Caribbean humour.' Reluctantly I got up to fetch a bowlful and did my best to sound sincere as I thanked Malik. Everyone else tucked in, talking about how great it was to try indigenous dishes. Jonas and I swapped looks that said we'd rather be eaten alive by midges. I stared at the slosh – the slimy white lumps and small black bean spheres that resembled fish eyes. A cat wandered into the canteen. Without anyone else seeing

I put our two bowls on the floor. The contents disappeared in minutes.

My only sustenance until lunchtime would be another piece of fruit. Amy and Helga were too busy comparing the best machete techniques, to chastise their siblings' pickiness. Not that I'd agree that we were being fussy. Soup for breakfast? What sort of parallel universe was this? Maybe lunch would be muesli.

Rick stood up and knocked a spoon against his mug. 'Great work this morning. Clearly the universe has sent a fantastic bunch of people to Seagrass Island.'

Smiles spread around the room.

'You've a couple of hours to relax now, before lunch. Once you feel reinvigorated, I suggest you check out the laundry area that's at the far end, by the last cluster of shacks. You'll find large sinks with running cold water, detergent, a mangle and lines to hang your clothes on. Before you leave here, take a look at the blue rota on the wall.' He pointed to the back of the room. 'Some of you are rostered in for the turtle egg collection trip tonight.'

'You and me are going. And Benedikt,' said Amy, eyes shining.

Phew. Rick had kept me on. It was a matter of self-pride now. I was surprised that Jonas seemed genuinely disappointed – although he wasn't happy to see that he and I had been rostered on as the first to clean out the compost toilets.

I went to leave and passed Rick.

'I've done as you said and kept you on the turtle trip,' he said. 'But if you're feeling at all woozy before then, please do yourself and the team a favour and pull out. Cleaning the toilets will give you a good idea of exactly how well you are.'

Feeling utterly exhausted and longing for a dip in a lagoon, with iced lattes on tap, I simply nodded and went back to my shack where I could pull the bed covers over my face and…

I mustn't cry.

I'd stopped doing that a long time ago.

When Mum died I needed to be there for Amy. She'd wanted to pass away at home but Dad said hospital was best. It was less work for him. I may have only been eleven but saw how Mum had been too tired to argue. I'd felt angry about that for such a long time but even managed to keep those tears of rage in. Hard as it was, I stopped them at the funeral as well. I'd sat in the church, sucking in my cheeks, trying not to think about Mum, lying cold, in the wooden box, all alone. Holding Amy's hand as her sobs burst out during the hymns. Braving relatives' piteous stares. Ignoring the whispers talking about 'those poor girls'.

Oh, I had shed tears, but alone at night, my head under my pillow so that there was no way Amy would hear.

Getting through all of that made it easier to deal with anything afterwards. Dad's cruel jibes could no longer hurt. I didn't cry my first night alone in that terrible bed and breakfast. And I only had one sobbing fit after my last boyfriend dumped me for being too independent.

So I'd do my best not to weep over blisters and bites and having to clean out a prehistoric toilet. I went back to the shack but only for a rest and to reluctantly swap my hat for the practical cap. Well, sort of rested. I'd come out in another rash – prickly heat. I'd stopped smearing on Helga's cream because I didn't want to use it all up. Amy had brought anti-histamine tablets but they hadn't kicked in yet.

'Come on, let's get it over with,' I said to Jonas, after we'd picked at rice for lunch. 'At least you don't have to go on the turtle trip tonight.'

Jonas glanced at me. 'Me and Benedikt get on really well. I was actually hoping to be part of it. Honestly, he takes the stupidest selfies for his Instagram feed. Last night he managed to attract the biggest moth onto his head and snap it before it flew away.' Jonas looked the most cheerful I'd ever seen him. Noses wrinkling, he and I stood in front of the toilet cubicles. The sawdust covered the waste but the smell still stole through because of the humidity.

'You first,' I said.

'No chance,' he replied.

'Okay. Both together.'

We moved forwards and after counting to three, each lifted out a bucket. The contents shifted from side to side. I gagged.

'Quick as we can,' I spluttered. Without looking down I led the way to the compost bays, praying that neither of us would trip and fall over. As if they'd been waiting, flies ambushed the slop. We set down our buckets. Jonas picked up the fork and dug into the hay.

Over the years I'd had to do many dirty tasks on my own, at home and at work, so I braced myself and poured the buckets' contents into the left-hand side. Jonas lifted up the hay, let it drop and forked it over. My throat contracted and for a second I almost vomited. But the feeling passed. The smell dissipated. We picked up our empty buckets and returned them to the cubicles.

When I got back to the shack I noticed a splash of waste on my T-shirt. My limbs felt heavy after the early start and lack of sleep, but I trekked as fast as I could over to the laundry area. Vigorously I hand-washed the top, pounding out my frustration.

Surely the day couldn't get any worse?

14

We left for the turtle nesting site at five to set up camp as the sun went down at seven. Before arriving in the British Virgin Islands I'd imagined long sunny, summer evenings with very late sunsets. In so many ways I'd been unprepared for this trip.

We packed large rucksacks and carried plastic buckets to bring the turtle eggs back in. Malik had provided individual plastic boxes generously filled with rice and chicken. Rick gave us each an extra water bottle. He carried one of the two-man tents and Amy offered to take the other. So I insisted we'd swap rucksacks halfway there. Benedikt said the same to Rick. We waved goodbye to the others.

Jonas gave Benedikt one of his treasured chocolate bars he'd brought over from Germany. He lent me one of his long-sleeve shirts. For once comfort took precedence over appearance. Amy hadn't managed to pack me enough sensible clothing, hidden under my other clothes, and my curves didn't fit into hers. We climbed uphill at first, past the animal enclosures. As twilight sneaked in the humidity increased. For the only time in my life I wished I had a thigh gap as my legs rubbed together at the top.

'The flame trees have almost finished flowering,' he said and pointed to the right.

I admired the clusters of bright red, leaf-like petals. I didn't know much about nature. I could recognise a sparrow. Could name daisies and dandelions and the flowers Dad used to give Mum after an argument. However I was more familiar with brands of clothes than wildlife species.

'What are those? They are so delicate,' I said and pointed to a tree bearing delicate, fluffy pink blooms, trying my best to look enthusiastic for Amy; to make her holiday memorable. The last time she'd been abroad was with Dad and Anabelle in Spain, just before she'd come to stay with me. Her A level results had come through whilst she was there. She'd got three As. I couldn't have been more proud but Dad said the lack of A*s just proved she wasn't clever enough to do veterinary science. He'd been going to take her out for paella and sangria but cancelled the celebration. I'd never felt so angry when she told me. His ego couldn't cope with the notion that one of his daughters was brighter than him.

Apparently, Anabelle had done her best to change his mind with the usual compliments and platitudes.

They never worked. So instead, over the years, she'd try to make things good by doing the things with us Dad should have. She hugged. Asked questions about our school day. Watched television with us. Attempted to get to know our friends. But it wasn't the same as with Mum. Anabelle was too worried about her figure to have cake out and I could tell her interest was just ticking boxes. I didn't blame her. She'd never wanted kids.

'Powder puff trees,' he said. 'They are all over the Virgin

Islands. Nothing to do with the *Powerpuff Girls*, so don't go thinking eating them will give you superhuman powers.'

I couldn't help smiling. An extra power boost would have come in handy as the trail became more overgrown.

'They look difficult to eat,' I said as we passed small lime, nobbled fruits hanging from a group of trees.

'Their outside is deceptive,' he said. 'Fleshy and white inside, those sugar apples taste like custard.'

It was a relief to hit the top of the hill. For a moment we stopped and stared, pointed at other islands and admired the crisp cleanliness of the greens of the forest and turquoise of the sea. Then we make our way down the other side. We descended for a few minutes before Rick stopped abruptly and pointed to a low-hanging branch of a tree.

'An iguana?' said Amy clapped her hands. 'It's an adult right, because it's brown? The young are fluorescent green?'

'Well done! These ones can grow up to six feet long if you include the length of the tail.'

He and Amy chatted about the other species of lizard that lived on Seagrass Island. I had to admit the animal's unusual appearance gave it a certain beauty. The pointed scales on the back of the neck, standing to attention. The perfectly pointed, streamlined shape of that tail. The widely spread toes..

'What an honour to see this creature in the wild,' mumbled Benedikt. 'It's a luxury future generations may be without.'

My knees hurt as we went down the steep decline.

'*Mein Gott*, this place is a photographer's idea of heaven,' he added a few minutes later, stopping every now and again to take shots. 'So far, I have taken fifty photos of different plants and insects and ten of that iguana. The setting sun adds a touch of atmosphere.'

'Make sure you add #SeagrassIsland when you post your shots on social media,' said Rick. 'We need all the publicity we can get.' He stopped dead for a moment. 'Listen.'

The buzz of insects and evening calls of birds continued but there was an added element. Relaxing. Reassuring... a constant, rhythmic splashing.

'The sea,' said Amy and punched the air.

The ground had levelled out and we managed to run, leaving behind the towering tree canopies. Sea. Space. Fresh air. A cooling breeze. We emerged from the forest and onto the beach. After hesitating for a moment, I dropped the rucksack and like the others, I slipped off my shoes and socks and carried them, my toes playing piano notes in the warm sand. I admired the tangerine sun, its head almost ducked under the horizon, its last rays appearing dappled across the undulating water.

I could do this. We were on the flat now, away from the claustrophobic, sweaty, insect-filled forest. Although thinking about it, claustrophobic wasn't the right word. I hadn't felt hemmed in. The beach simply provided a contrasting environment and the breeze was most welcoming. The forest was just... crowded, in a good way, like a diverse neighbourhood where people led their lives side by side. During just this short walk I'd seen how plants and animals helped each other. Mutualism, I think it was called, a term someone had jokingly used once during a training session at Best Travel. Like the termite mounds built through team work to create a home for all the workers. Or the bees collecting honey and thereby getting pollen stuck to their legs and consequently pollinating flowers. One species of frog Rick pointed out carried its tadpoles from plant to plant, letting them grow in the pools of water offered by various large cupped leaves that collected rainwater.

The rainforest felt like a carefully attuned community where everybody had an important part to play. Everyone belonged. Like a big family. I wondered what that felt like. For so long it had been me, Amy and Nelly. Even when I'd lived at home with Mum and Dad, there had never been that sense of us all being part of the same bigger thing. We were just individuals, Dad the centre of attention, the rest of us skirting around the edges, Mum always looking to calm him and me protecting Amy from his cruel comments.

Benedikt and I swapped rucksacks with the others. He didn't speak much to me and that was fine. We couldn't get on with everyone equally. He seemed to have hit it off with Amy whereas I'd bonded with Jonas. I let him go ahead and dropped back. For the first time since arriving I appreciated the tranquillity. I'd quickly realised that on this kind of break personal space was a luxury.

Eventually Rick slowed his pace and I caught him up. I jumped as something swooped overhead.

'Bats,' he said. 'They can't harm you. Well, not unless they pass on a disease. I take it you've had the relevant jab? It was optional but on the website I said—'

'Yes… the bat one…'

He shot me a curious glance. 'So which one was it?'

All you could hear was the sea.

'Do you know which jabs you've had?'

'Amy did all the research. I just turned up for the appointment, it was a busy week and—'

'Ah, right,' he said dismissively. 'It was the rabies one in case you are interested.'

I wished the sand would swallow me up. It was clear my lack of know-how irritated him, much as he tried to hide that with humour.

Amy linked her arm with mine and talked about the sunset, flashing her torch as we passed stranded jellyfish, her wishing she could save every one. Eventually the beach veered around to the right and came to a long, wide cove with boulders either side. They cut off the wind making it the perfect, secluded nesting site.

'Why do the turtle eggs need our intervention here?' I asked.

'Not even these huge stones could protect their eggs from the hurricane,' said Rick. 'In 2017 nests across all the islands were affected and the population is still recovering, so we carry the eggs back to our specially protected sand pits to protect them from predators such as lizards and crabs.'

'This conservation work is also about trying to compensate for the problems caused for turtles on other islands, isn't it?' asked Amy – though it sounded more like a statement. I could sense her confidence growing.

'Yes. Poachers operate where the land isn't private and tourists bring a different set of challenges. The curious want to look at eggs and their noise disturbs nesting patterns, plus beach front lights disorientate hatchlings. Their instincts tell them to crawl towards light as soon as they are born, because that is moonlight on the waves and gets them into the water – but in very commercial areas they head for the street lights by accident and end up getting run over. I'm hoping our project helps to support the turtle population of the whole region.' Rick dropped his rucksack and bucket at the top of the beach. 'Let's set up the two tents here before the sun disappears. Then we can eat and get to bed. We should manage a few hours' sleep before getting up at midnight.

Amy smiled at me and took Rick to one side. I felt uneasy as she chatted to him for a minute. He looked puzzled and then shrugged. She came back.

'All sorted,' she whispered. 'You'll be sharing a tent with Rick, not me.'

15

'What?'

'I told him you felt nervous about camping out in the wilds; that I knew you'd rather sleep close to someone who knew the ropes here – either him or Jackie and seeing as she isn't on this excursion... Benedikt doesn't mind at all.'

'Amy. For God's sake. He must think I'm a complete wuss. Of course I'm not that worried and when it comes to wildlife, you work for a vet and I'd be fine sharing with—'

She gave a sheepish smile. 'Couldn't help myself. You haven't been in a relationship for forever.'

'I'm not a charity,' I said and threw my hands in the air.

'But you won't help yourself! I've tried to get you to register with an online dating site, but it's work, work, work with you. So I intend to make it my job to bring the two of you together.'

'Amy. We aren't at school. This is worse than leaving a note in a locker.'

'You'll thank me, just you see,' she said, firmly. 'Time's ticking. We're only here for a month. I bet he's a great kisser. And you've seen how gentle he is with Chatty, mark my words, he—'

'If I agree to share a tent with him will you stop talking?'
She grinned.

I was still cringing half an hour later, once the small tents
had been erected. We sat in a circle, lit up by our torches,
eating the chicken and rice. The others chatted. I put on
more insect repellent and passed it to Amy. She shook her
head and gave a small sigh, saying not to fuss over her, she'd
already reapplied it.

Day two. I had blisters. The pink trainers I'd been
determined to wear were ruined. I had a bed mate I didn't
want and felt numb with tiredness.

I shook myself. *Come on, Sarah. You're made of stronger
stuff than this. Remember that first day at Best Travel?* I'd had
no one that morning to tell me everything would go okay and
wish me well. My send-off had been a simple glare from the
landlady whom, I'd quickly learnt, saw tenants as necessary
intruders. The bathroom tap had dripped loudly all night and
I'd woken to find a cockroach on the bathroom wall. Yet I'd
got through that first day. That first week. That first month.

I went to the loo in the bushes, crouching down, terrified
ants in your pants was an actual thing. Then I headed back
to the beach. Hugged Amy goodnight. Rick was already
inside our tent. A mound of sand had formed in the corner.
One of us must have accidentally kicked it on top of the
ground sheet. Rick wanted to keep the tent unzipped so that
we could enjoy the cooling sea breeze but I was too worried
about mosquitoes. The result was I'd never run a higher
temperature in my life.

'Maybe we could just unzip it a tiny bit,' I said to Rick.

A snore replied. I couldn't even see his face as the Indiana
Jones hat lay over it.

I heard Amy and Benedikt laughing but that was nothing compared to the sudden shriek that emanated from my mouth. Something had jumped up against the roof of the tent. Then again. I sat upright, clumsily turned on my torch, tore Rick's hat off his face and shook his shoulder.

'Sarah…? What's the matter?' He rubbed his eyes.

I jumped again. 'What the hell is that?' I went to crawl out of the tent but Rick held my shoulder and chuckled.

'Don't worry. We call them sand crickets. I haven't been able to identify their exact species yet. The pesky little things only come out at night and are hard to catch.'

I directed the torch onto the mound of sand as he called to the others that everything was all right. It moved. A small creature's head appeared and then it launched itself out and landed on top of my sleeping bag. Vigorously I shook my bedding.

'What if it lands in my mouth?'

'That's never happened to me and I lead a couple of turtle excursions a week. Just chill.'

'But—'

'We need to rest and can't do that if your torch is turned on.'

I paused. Perhaps it would be better if I just walked the beach for the next couple of hours. However, my head was thumping. What if they got into my ears? Or crawled into my sleeping bag? I tried to cheer myself up by imagining the horror on Jonas's face when I told him all about it. This really was like my favourite celebrity jungle show, except there was no reward for enduring the challenge.

Somehow I got through the next few hours. We got up at midnight. Packed away the tents. Despite all the discomfort

I took a moment to gaze into the night sky. Without the city glow or cloud, the sky looked like a pool of spilt black ink. We followed Rick with our buckets. He walked near to the water's edge, looking for the turtle trails. Eventually he found some and followed them across the beach, up towards the forest area. They stopped at one point and Rick told us to gently dig down with our hands. My fingers curled around something smooth out of view.

I didn't even worry about sand crickets as an unexpected wave of emotion washed over me. Gently I dug out the egg and held it in my hands. Inside it was the makings of an endangered animal. For a fleeting moment I understood what might appeal about volunteering here. You couldn't put a price on this work. I'd thought Amy should invest her lottery win so that she'd reap the benefits of it in the future – but now I was starting to realise that's exactly what she *had* done, looking at the bigger picture.

She and Benedikt also pulled out eggs in silence. We placed them in our buckets. Rick noted how many we'd collected. We drank water. Listened to lapping waves. Watched bats swoop across the sand. Felt the more intense warmth of sunrise approaching. Amy and Benedikt talked musicals. Rick said he wasn't a fan but said how his brother, Lee, loved the theatre and when he worked back in England was always buying tickets for the two of them. Apparently, he thought Rick needed to get more culture into his life. With a sparkle in his eyes Rick grimaced at Amy and Benedikt who almost started a sand fight with him when he confessed to hating *Wicked*.

It was time to begin the long trek back to the site. I was careful not to trip, aware of just how precious the contents of the bucket were. I gripped the handle tightly even though it aggravated the angry blisters on my hands from the morning's machete swiping. I winced.

'What's the matter?' Rick took the bucket. 'Ooh. They look nasty.'

'I'm okay. I've just run out of plasters. I can manage until I get back.'

'No way,' he said and reached into his pocket. Swiftly he prepared a couple of plasters and placed them over the blisters.

I reached for the bucket. He shook his head but I didn't withdraw my arm. He tilted his head, stared at me and then slowly passed it back to me.

'What are they?' I asked after we'd reached the top of the hill again and made our way down the other side. I hadn't noticed this stretch of about twenty trees before, with large glossy leaves and huge red-yellow pods attached to the trunks.

'Cacao trees,' said Rick.

Benedikt put down his bucket and pulled out his camera.

'Wow,' said Amy.

Rick pointed. 'Those big pods contain the beans.'

'You've got *chocolate* trees growing here?' I said, feeling a genuine flicker of excitement. Jonas was going to be so annoyed to have missed this.

'A traveller from the Ivory Coast brought one to the island before my grandmother bought this place. The rainforest is the perfect place for them to grow. They need tropical heat but also the shade that the taller trees provide. I must get around to pulling some down, though. I do that now and again. I don't want them getting out of control and pushing out the indigenous plant species that serve this environment.'

That confirmed it. Rick and I could never be a good match if he destroyed a plant that grew my all-time favourite food.

Thoughts about those pods and their contents distracted me enough to get me back to the site where an early morning team took the buckets from us, to bury the eggs. We were instructed to go to bed until lunch time. I could hardly bend my sore hands. I stumbled into the canteen to pick up some fruit. Jackie was in there with Chatty and the sight of his cheeky blond face revived me. I whistled 'Daydream Believer'. His head raised. Jackie smiled and nodded. He'd started to squeak louder. I let him smell my hand and he cocked his head towards me. I obliged and tickled just the right spot.

Reluctantly I left him and went over to the rota. Rick had rostered me in for early bird counting on Monday followed by another turtle excursion that evening. The hard work had only just begun. Not even the prospect of shopping tomorrow cheered me up as it would be for practical items.

Covered in sweat and grime, I desperately needed to wash. I dragged my feet to the shower block. In a daze of exhaustion, I stripped off and draped my clothes and towel over the top of the door. I turned on the water and flinched. Of course. It was stone cold. I shut my eyes and washed my hair. Leaves must have swept in under the door because something gently brushed the top of my foot.

Whatever it was stayed there. I rinsed my hair, turned off the water and opened my eyes. I looked down at the biggest, hairiest spider lounging on top of my toes. I suppressed a scream and shook my foot. It tumbled onto the floor. Instead of crawling off under the door it held me there, hostage. Without my clothes I couldn't make a run for it.

I reached forward to grab my towel. The creature reacted by raising a front leg. When I was little, Mum had drilled into me never to kill spiders. So after she'd passed I'd always been the one to put them out as Anabelle was too scared. At least Amy helped when she got older. But this one was huge and I'd read somewhere that tarantulas could jump. With one swift movement I grabbed my towel and my clothes promptly disappeared down the outside of the door.

I wrapped the towel around me and slid down, sitting on the wet floor whilst the spider played dead.

'Sarah? Are you in there? Amy's looking for you,' said a voice outside the door.

Fantastic. Just the person I wanted to see me in this state.

'Are you all right?' Rick continued. 'Your clothes are out here.'

I covered my eyes, unsure as to whether it was the shower water or tears running down my cheeks.

'Sarah. Open the door.'

Please. Just go away.

The cubicle jiggled. 'Look. I'm coming in. I've the knack of opening these doors. I really ought to get the locks changed. They aren't the best.'

Still my hands hid my face. If I didn't open my eyes perhaps it was possible that this was all just a bad dream. That's what I used to imagine as a girl when I lay in bed hearing Mum crying in her room after an argument with Dad who'd be watching TV downstairs.

The door swung open.

'What the…?'

I heard a small movement.

'The spider's gone,' he said.

Losing my job at Best Travel. The last twenty-four hours from hell. The prospect of four weeks of this torture. It was all too much. A sob escaped my lips.

I heard him kneel down. Large hands covered mine. Carefully he prised my fingers away from my face.

16

'What's wrong?'

'I must look a wreck,' I muttered and sniffed.

'Not at all. You should see me first thing after too many rum cocktails.'

A sense of failure overwhelmed me as I thought about those memes that went around social media about stepping out of your comfort zone in order to achieve great things…

For the last nine years I'd controlled everything about my environment. My life with Amy and Nelly felt steady, reliable. This was the first time I'd left the safety net I'd created. And how had I managed? By throwing a big pity party. By only seeing the negatives. And that made me even more disappointed in myself.

We looked at each other. He passed me my clothes. 'I've got something to show you up at the house. I'll wait for you outside and tell someone to find your sister and tell her you are fine – that you and I just have a bit of business to attend to.'

I was too tired to argue. Five minutes later I stood next to him.

'This way,' he said and put an arm around my shoulders. 'We can cut through the forest, behind the toilets.' Up we climbed, towards the scaffolding that I'd noticed on my arrival. Rick steered me out of the way of dragonflies and beetles. It felt good to be looked after. Not that I'd ever admit that.

The large house looked almost complete. Builders were removing the poles and wooden planks from the outside. The front and far side of the house had no walls or windows. Simple upright wooden frames held shutters at the top that were presumably pulled down at night or if it rained. So you could walk into the house on the ground floor and out of the other side without having to open a door. I'd never seen such an accessible building but then break-ins wouldn't be a problem on a private island.

Rick and I went inside. His arm slid away. This huge living room had a long unit in the middle, made out of a patchwork of grey stone tiles. On top of it was a ceramic vase filled with the powder puff and flame tree blooms, along with various colourful handmade clay bowls and a marble chess set. The roof was made of mahogany beams going up into a pyramid shape in the centre. The walls at either end were whitewashed, decorated with green tropical leaf prints in each corner. Various pictures – mainly modern art versions of rainforest scenes, insects and animals – had been hung across each white expanse.

A wonderful black grand piano stood to one side, at the rear, with a guitar leant up against it and a wooden carving of a parrot on top. Two long magnolia sofas contrasted the warm, dark laminate floor. At either end of them were nests of mahogany tables, the feet carved into animals' paws. Tall glossy plants filled the room's four corners. A winding staircase led upstairs and I counted eight doors up there for bedrooms and bathrooms, I supposed, spread around the central beamed pyramid. A door to the far right on the ground floor was open and inside I could just make out kitchen equipment. That part of the building wasn't quite complete.

'I love the natural feel of this place,' I said, my horrendous day forgotten for a second. 'It totally fits in with the surroundings and is so bright, as if you are just walking into another part of the island.'

'It's an exact replica of what was here before the hurricane. My grandmother is a huge nature fan and loves down-to-earth furnishings. She wanted this place built the same because it brings back memories of my granddad and the time they spent here. He died five years ago.'

'I'm not surprised she could buy an island. Crocker & Crowley has done so well.'

Considering this was his family home, Rick was very modest.

I walked across to look at the back garden and gasped. 'This is beautiful...' I gazed at a wide area of decking. On it was a long wooden dining table. Beyond that was a turquoise swimming pool, surrounded by more decking and plant pots. In the right-hand corner was what looked like a bar built out of bamboo, under a palm leaf parasol. Swaying palm trees punctuated the surrounding grounds made up of the greenest mown grass and several had hammocks hanging in between them, along with five well-spaced out Tiki-style two-storey beach huts, on stilts like the shacks.

This was the luxury accommodation I'd expected to be staying in. Rick indicated to one of the sofas. We sat down next to each other on it, facing the pool, enjoying the breeze. I wondered about the money again. Rick seemed genuine but a generous slice of what the volunteers paid must have gone into building this personal space for his family.

'I've been living in one of the shacks until a few days before you arrived. It's been quite a job to restore Seagrass Island, to be honest.' He ran a hand through his hair. 'After the hurricane several of the local insurance companies went bust. Gran got about two thirds of her money. The rest of the build we have to fund ourselves.'

'At least, I guess, you've got the shoe business to fall back on.'

He didn't answer.

'You've run the renovations by yourself? That must have been quite a task.'

'The family business has been... demanding of late so there's no practical way my parents could be on hand here. Nor Lee – although despite being thousands of miles away, sometimes, via phone, he acts like an on-site manager.' He gave a wry smile. It sounded as if he and his brother didn't get on. 'Gran has flown over a few times since the hurricane and stayed on Tortola. Me being in charge of the rebuild made most sense. Malik and his brother have been great. Having lived on Tortola all their lives they put me in touch with a great team to do the work. I was lucky to get them, after so many properties were damaged, but the building company is owned by a family friend of theirs.

'Anyway...' He turned back to me and concern cast a shadow over his face. 'How do you feel?'

'I'm okay. Sorry for the inconvenience.'

'Come on. I had something to show you.' Gently he took my hand and led me up the spiral staircase and into the second bedroom from the right.

It should have felt uncomfortable, him holding my hand like that, but it didn't.

The bedroom was not like one I'd ever seen before with the mahogany ceiling and open windows like downstairs, and a balcony. Whitewashed walls contrasted the warm wooden features. Tropical paintings and lush plants circled the huge bed in the middle.

Amy would have practically died from excitement at the thought of Rick and me being near a mattress, alone.

He let go of my fingers, extended his arm and swooped it through the air. 'Stay here tonight. This room is finished. Catch up a bit. Think about whether or not you should really go home.'

Oh, I felt tempted. But that would mean I'd failed. 'Is there much more left to do to the house as a whole?'

'The kitchen and utility room are nearly ready, and the indoor dining room on the other side of them. However, work hasn't started on the downstairs office we had before, nor the downstairs toilet. But the cinema room is finished and the gym. Also the room looking out to the sea where my grandmother liked to paint and design shoes.'

'Margot is still very active.'

'At seventy-nine she's an inspiration.'

'Aren't you worried about another hurricane striking?'

'No. The occasional hurricanes in the past have only caused slight to moderate damage across the islands. The problem with Hurricane Irma was that we got stuck in the eye of it. I know climate change might alter the frequency and intensity of these events but...' He shrugged. 'These days extreme weather might happen anywhere around the world.'

'True. Even in England.'

He pointed to a shelf. 'There's a load of novels there left by the previous person who left early, only last week. I think I mentioned them to you. He couldn't take the early starts or heat. Before him was a woman called Judy. She'd thought the shacks were only for show and that really we'd have set up some kind of glamping facilities. There was Jean-Paul. He came with his girlfriend. It was tougher than they both thought. It ended badly. They split up. The trip had been her idea. He went back to France after a week.' Rick looked sheepish. 'This room has kind of become a haven for those who want to leave.'

I raised my eyebrows. 'I thought you said only a couple of people had ever changed their minds?'

I wasn't the only one knocked sideways by this experience? That made me feel so much better.

Rick sighed and sat on the bed by the pillows. He stretched out his legs. My eyes scanned his long frame. I hesitated before sitting next to him.

'I didn't want to give a negative impression. However, the last couple of days – seeing how you've struggled – it's made me realise that perhaps I need to be clearer on the website. I'm sorry if, at times, I've come across as a bit… touchy. Seagrass Conservation means the world to me and it's hard to acknowledge that it's still not stable with a guaranteed future.'

An apology? His shoulders slumped and out of nowhere I felt like giving him a hug.

'Rick. I've tried to explain… the reason I've struggled in particular is that I never signed up for this kind of trip.'

His brow furrowed. 'What do you mean?'

'My sister – she booked it as a treat after a lottery win. It was meant to be a luxury getaway. A top-notch hotel with spa treatments, five-star food, room service… but at the last minute she swapped it. I work in hotel management and she was worried that sort of holiday wouldn't be a true break from the nine 'til five. So instead…'

'You're telling me you had no idea? She lied?'

'I wouldn't call it that exactly… there are different kind of untruths.'

'Not in my book.' His brows knotted together. He caught me looking. 'Sorry. Ignore me. Amy's a great person, I can tell that already. I'm sure she had good reason.'

'Hence the long nails, the impractical clothes, the big hat… I was expecting… well… accommodation more like this home of yours. And lie-ins, not early starts. Bucks Fizz for breakfast instead of fish soup. Hot Jacuzzis, not cold showers…'

Rick looked intensely at me. 'I made a lot of assumptions. So your job is in the hospitality business?'

For a second I wanted to be honest but I couldn't mention my sacking in case it got back to Amy. It would have been good to talk about it. But like I'd said to him – there were different kinds of lies. 'I'm currently employed as an assistant manager,' I said. 'So I understand some of the challenges you're facing. I know what it's like to not have the whole of the team on board. It makes it difficult to achieve goals.'

'Then why stay?' he asked. 'No doubt you'll fit in fine after a few days of acclimatising,' he added quickly, 'but you have the perfect excuse to leave so why not just fly back home? I'm sure your sister would understand.'

'Amy really wanted me to enjoy this holiday; she said I needed a complete break. She was excited to treat me. It's been... a challenging few years. I haven't had a holiday since I left home.'

'When was that?'

'Nine years ago.'

'Wow.' Those dark eyebrows practically disappeared into his hairline.

I felt an urge to laugh out loud but was still bruised by the way he'd assumed the worst about me, ever since I got off the boat.

'It sounds like I'm giving you a sob story – but this isn't one. During that time I've really been able to focus on my career, but that's why Amy was thrilled to be able to afford to take me abroad. I don't want to spoil things for her.'

'Seagrass Island must be quite a let-down for you.' He gave a rueful smile.

There was something about Rick that made me want to open up, in a way I didn't with other people.

'Frivolous as it sounds, for once I wanted to be the one waited on hand and foot; to escape into some sort of fantasy life away from the stresses of reality.'

'I get it. Sometimes I feel like running away from it all.' He cleared his throat and swung those long legs off the bed and stood up. 'Maybe a positive can come out of all this. You can say no but I'd hugely appreciate it if you would look at the website. I've assumed it spells out plainly what life here is like but I'm clearly going wrong somehow, if people are leaving early, and it's really important to me... to my family... and to the island, that Seagrass Conservation is a success; that as many people as possible post photos and talk about us positively on social media and tell friends about us when they get back home.'

He wanted me to help? Having done nothing but criticise me since I'd arrived? Yet his earnestness was appealing and I noticed the tired lines around his eyes – lines I often saw reflected back when *I* looked in the mirror.

'It's a business I need to grow... and I forget that not everyone coming here will have studied the environment or have a formal interest in conservation or climate change.'

I followed him downstairs feeling more like myself every minute – and wondering, why, when it came to Seagrass Conservation, Rick exuded such a sense of urgency.

'The staff who used to work in our home don't start back for a couple of weeks. They'll get the place ready for my gran who's visiting in September.'

'Was everyone okay after the hurricane?'

We sat down on the sofa. 'Yes. This place has a strong cellar under the kitchen. Thank God everyone was able to take refuge in there. In fact, I'll just fetch us a couple of cold drinks. The kitchen equipment was unpacked and plugged in yesterday. I've stocked it with a few things from the canteen. Then I'll get my laptop...' He gazed at a large round clock, the hands set against a tropical beach scene. It was positioned on the far left-hand wall, next to an old-fashioned barometer. He palmed his forehead. 'What am I thinking? You must be exhausted. Thanks to those sand crickets you hardly slept last night. And thanks to you jumping around almost as much as them, neither did I.'

Tentatively we smiled at each other. I could tell he was as unsure as me about this friendlier atmosphere between us.

But it felt good to feel more like his equal, instead of a nuisance.

'It's okay. This cool, relaxing lounge has revived me.'

Rick came back first carrying a bandage and some antibiotic cream. He jerked his head towards my hands and sat down.

'May I? Those blisters need re-dressing.' Carefully he applied the ointment and wrapped bandages around my fingers. I hoped he couldn't hear my loud heartbeat. He disappeared again, this time bringing back two juices and his laptop, and turned on a radio that played cheerful steel band Caribbean calypso music. As he sat down and started to tap his feet, all I could focus on was him.

It was something I'd fought against, for years. If I felt my body responding to a man, I always took that as a warning, to remind me that a strong physical attraction sped things up, when time should be taken to really get to know someone – to spot a partner's potential faults before taking things further.

Because I was determined never to fall under the spell of someone like my father.

17

I wasn't expecting to meet the man of my dreams on Seagrass Island.

But now I realised it was true.

I absolutely had.

He wasn't my usual type. A bit hairier. Very talkative. I didn't understand what he said half the time – well, *all* the time, in fact – but actions spoke louder than words and he really was the cheekiest...

... monkey.

I smiled at Chatty, even though he couldn't see. He was next to me, in the Games Room, on Rick's shoulder, tickling his ear. Every time Rick groaned and pulled his paw away, it shot right back, as if Chatty knew that if he did it often enough, Rick would lift him onto his lap for a cuddle.

'I wish I had your energy,' I said to Chatty and stroked his head. His paws both clutched my hand and affectionately bared his teeth on my skin, not leaving marks, nor hurting me. I whistled his favourite tune. He froze and cocked his head, body swaying slightly. Everyone chuckled. It had become our thing.

'It's great, at last, to have someone appreciate my unmelodic whistles.'

'You are definitely two of a kind, on that score,' said Rick. 'It's a good thing Chatty can't understand you!'

The Games Room was busy. Amy and Benedikt sat in front of a chess board – Jonas watched them, playing a pensive tune on his harmonica. I was glad he'd managed to at least pack one instrument. Helga chatted to Jackie and the permanent staff. A couple of Italian volunteers played snooker. There was a queue for the darts board. Calypso music tinkled in the background, from a radio. It was already dark outside. A couple of moths had snuck in. One was as big as Chatty's head and pale purple with black patterns. I'd almost knocked my glass of water over when it flew near my face. Malik called it the black witch moth.

Chatty climbed back up onto Rick's shoulder and wrapped his tail and arms around his head. My hand followed him and he nestled his cheek in my palm.

'Thanks again for today,' Rick said. 'Your comments about the website were really useful. I've discussed them with Jackie and she agrees. I don't know why we've never had a page for volunteer stories.'

I'd decided to help him, thanks to the bereavement counselling I'd once had. Anabelle might not have been a great stepmother but I'd always be grateful to her for visiting me, those first years when I moved out, even though it was only a couple of times a year. She'd arrive with a food hamper. It was unsaid between us that Dad didn't know she was there. She'd suggested I get counselling, and told me that losing my mum at an early age was a traumatic thing.

I didn't consider it until my first Christmas on my own, alone in the bed and breakfast. Dad hadn't invited me to the celebration at his house. Loss, at many levels, hit me hard. I went to bed for two days and saw my doctor the following week. A month later I had my first session with Elaine.

The thing she taught me that resonated most was not to hold onto resentments. I hadn't realised how angry I was, deep down, that Mum had left me and Amy. And I was angry at Anabelle for not standing up more to Dad. Elaine helped me let go of that.

Over the years that perspective helped me cope with Prue. And in this instance, it helped me give assistance to Rick. Elaine taught me how holding onto grudges would harm me the most, in the end.

However, her advice would *never* change my view of Dad. He'd hurt Amy as well as me. I could never forgive him for that.

'It could also be useful for you, getting everyone to fill in a questionnaire before they leave, with honest opinions. Feedback is everything – in my opinion anyway.'

Rick raised an eyebrow.

'Prue. My boss. I suggested a feedback box at reception, for customers to write down their comments and submit anonymously. She dismissed the idea outright – said the only thing that mattered was the hotel meeting *her* exacting standards.'

'Well, I certainly appreciate your input. Jackie and I also both agree it is a good idea to extend the gallery of online photos.'

'Yes. To some crazy people, the outside of the shacks, on stilts, could look kind of cute…'

He smiled.

'For the browser to get a real feel for the accommodation you'll need a shot of the inside as well. And there are no photos of the compost toilets. They would impress real environmentalists but at the same time weed out potential volunteers who think this place is going to be more comfortable.'

'Same with the kit list,' he said. 'I think you're right. We need to explain why the items are important instead of just listing them. Like the long-sleeve shirts. One volunteer thought we just put that to keep off the sun so she ignored it because she was keen to get a tan. She hadn't realised those sleeves are actually to protect people from bites as well.'

I waved across the room to Amy. Her forehead looked burnt. I'd have to remind her, tomorrow, to make sure she wore her cap at all times. She placed her hands over her face, pretending to sob as she lost the game of chess. Benedikt laughed and pulled her fingers away, challenging her to another match. A humorous, sulky expression crossed her face, so he started singing 'Let It Go' from *Frozen*. For some reason it was Jonas who looked as if he'd been beaten.

'There is something else,' I said.

'You're not going to start charging me, are you?' said Rick and consulted his watch, 'because I'm timing you in case you do so by the minute.'

'Don't give me ideas – although I am something of an expert, having done a basic course in website design once.' I smiled. It was when I first lived on my own. I wasn't near my old neighbourhood or old friends. The evenings were lonely so, with the help of my counselling, I forced myself to be proactive and found a reasonably priced evening course that would add to my skillset. Recently I'd helped the vet's where Amy works set up a blog. 'First off, I'd say your website looks… complicated. You could do with simplifying the pages. Making them cleaner and more user-friendly. I'm happy to help.'

'That's really decent of you.'

I shrugged, wondering if he meant it or if he was only being nice because he needed my assistance. I wasn't going to hold a grudge, but that didn't mean I was going to jump straight into thinking we could suddenly be good friends.

Although I had to admit, his sincerity about conservation was kind of appealing. Of course his looks were striking – nothing like the men from my past. Take Callum – he had the neatest hair. A sedate demeanour. Was attractive in a wholesome way. I'd always considered myself lucky to be going out with him. He had the loveliest smile and treated me well but our kisses never set me alight. I liked that because he felt safe. However, in the end patient Callum accused me of *making do* with him.

It was a horrible accusation. I'd vehemently denied it, upset at the thought that I'd upset him. He'd be the perfect catch for someone. Just not me.

I wasn't interested in finding a seductive, six-pack, mesmerising Mr Perfect. On purpose I'd looked for a Mr Won't Sweep You Off Your Feet – but Callum proved that came with its own challenges.

However, Rick… Perhaps it was the carefree island vibe that weakened my guard. We were only a couple of days in but already the basic nature of the site made me feel that civilisation, the normal rules I lived by, were part of some other life.

'Your brand… it doesn't come across really strongly on the website,' I continued. 'You call this venture Seagrass Conservation and that title is all well and good – it's solid and serious and this is a trip for people determined to do their bit for the environment. But the website is missing something brighter and lighter to pull people in – and I might have the solution...'

'I'm all ears,' he said as Chatty had started tickling his ear again.

I jerked my head at the monkey. 'That little man there. Make him the face of your brand. Create a cartoon image and have him on the website with speech bubbles containing sound bites relevant to each page. Plus an actual video of the real him – perhaps with one of you showing the viewer the animal enclosures, with Chatty on your shoulder...'

Rick didn't respond but at least he didn't suck in his breath and frown like Prue used to.

'Sell simple merchandise. Key rings. Fridge magnets – maybe small plush monkeys wearing T-shirts saying Chatty. You could easily find a manufacturer of personalised toys on the internet. People go mad for buying mementos and gifts.'

He stared.

My mouth felt dry. 'You think it's a rubbish idea?'

He leant forward and gave me a tight hug, Chatty clinging on for dear life and squeaking his huffiness. The hairs stood up on the back of my neck. Warmth radiated down my body. I glanced at Amy who watched with the biggest grin on her face.

'I... I take it you approve then,' I stuttered.

'Sorry, yes...' His eyes crinkled. 'I've never even thought about doing something like that. Maybe this is what's been missing. The success of this venture is so important, I think I've lost my sense of humour.'

'I'm not sure about that,' I said. 'In the tent last night you wore orange socks covered in bananas.'

'Thanks, Sarah. Thanks so much for this.' His voice wavered. 'The last couple of months I've felt as if I've been wading through marshland, trying to think of ways to boost Seagrass Conservation. Jackie's been great but it's a relief to have someone on board with a fresh pair of eyes. It could be just what's needed.'

His appreciation felt warmer than sunshine and that was saying something, in the Virgin Islands.

It was soon nine o'clock and even though it was Saturday tomorrow, and we could lie in, everyone was shattered. I kissed Chatty on the head and Rick and Jackie headed off to take him back to his enclosure and to check on Wink the screech owl who had gone off her food. Laughter and singing carried across the night air as we headed towards the shacks, accompanied by harmonica playing. I still couldn't believe how clear the sky was, away from city lights. The ivory moon, the sprinkling of glitter across the ebony sky... it gave Seagrass Island a touch of the magical. Spending time with Rick today – explaining why I was finding life here so difficult... me helping him out and once again feeling useful... all of that gave everything a shinier dimension.

Amy and Benedikt passed me by, murdering 'Tonight' from *West Side Story*, Helga behind them attempting to join in, pulling a face as they drowned her out. I caught up with Jonas and linked arms. Benedikt shot me a look as he went by and quickly masked it with a smile.

What did he disapprove of?

18

Throughout the night my legs continued to itch, aggravated by hot air trapped by the sheets I was determined to stay under. Despite making sure the shack's door was closed, I still felt squeamish. I also had a nightmare about a giant moth landing on my face and woke up fighting the mosquito net. Thanks goodness it was Saturday and I could unwind. Helga sprung up at six and went off for a shower. Amy followed shortly after. Jackie had invited her to check on owl Wink, so they were meeting by the enclosure before breakfast – whereas I dozed until eight and then went to wash.

I took a glass that I'd borrowed from the canteen the previous night, to trap any adventurous tarantulas, annoyed with myself for feeling scared because I'd battled much bigger fears as an adult. My thoughts immediately turned to Mum, and how much I missed her, oh so much. Especially her hugs. I couldn't lose myself in Anabelle's arms, not in the same way. I had no memory of ever being physically close to Dad. Apart from my eighteenth birthday, nine months before I moved out; Anabelle had bought a ring bearing my birthstone. Dad had playfully given me a sideways hug.

He'd squeezed just that bit too hard and said to look after it as it might be the only ring anyone ever gave me. Then he'd pinched what he called my choochie cheeks and insisted I eat only a thin slice of birthday cake.

Yet he didn't like it when I lost weight after leaving home. It hadn't been intentional, but working so hard at the hotel meant that pounds dropped off and I didn't have much money for food back in those days.

It was obvious he preferred to feel superior wherever possible and my slimmer figure that he'd always told me I should aspire to, narrowed his range of insults.

Shower safely completed, I pulled on a pair of trousers that belonged to Amy, my pair that she'd secretly packed for me now beyond wearable. They were too short but luckily the waist was elasticated. I'd change into something smart later, when we went over to Tortola, after an early lunch as the shops started shutting at four o'clock. Today's trip was just to get our bearings but I was determined to come back to Seagrass Island with a sensible wardrobe of my own.

'Klopf, Klopf,' said a deep voice.

I opened the door to the shack and grinned. 'Knock, knock, to you too, Jonas.'

'Breakfast?'

'I can't wait for tomorrow's special Sunday one.' We walked in the direction of the canteen. 'Where's Benedikt?'

'He went with Amy to see Wink. I didn't like to tag along. I didn't want to… how do you say… play blackberry.'

'*Goose*berry,' I corrected and punched his arm. 'Amy and Benedikt? Nah. They're just mates. I don't see it.'

'Really?'

'Well… anything's possible, I suppose. I'll have to grill her later.'

'That sounds barbaric,' he said.

'It means to question someone intensely, in English.'

He smiled. 'I know. Okay. Tell me what you find out.'

I studied his features as he took out his harmonica and played it as we went to eat. Was Jonas jealous? Was it possible that he had a crush on my sister? I couldn't see much common ground between them whereas Benedikt and Amy certainly lit up a room when they sang their favourite musical tunes.

I'd had heaps in common with Callum. Like me he worked in hospitality. Loved baking. Was estranged from his parents. But in the end that wasn't enough without a physical pull.

Whereas Rick… I'd thought about him last night when I couldn't sleep. He was passionate about the outdoors. What with my hotel career, I was passionate about the opposite. He'd grown up surrounded by a family that worked together, holidaying blissfully with each other on a Caribbean island the grandmother had especially bought for them… whereas I…

Yet despite any differences there was something about him that demanded my attention.

I needed to calm down.

The words *all I ever think about is Gary* came into my head. It was Anabelle, in a soppy voice, talking on the phone to someone about Dad. Before they'd been married. Before she lost her happy-go-lucky laugh and self-assured stride.

A refreshing swim in the sea – that would shake off this Rick nonsense. Jonas was up for it. We just had time for a quick dip before lunch at eleven-thirty. Rick wanted us to be on the boat, ready to leave at twelve-thirty sharp. So Jonas and I left a note for Amy and Benedikt.

Talk about washing your worries away. Along with other volunteers, who'd come back from the messy morning task of preparing the animals' food, Jonas and I splashed around, ducking each other under the water and swimming underneath, pointing out flamboyant fish. Today I'd buy a snorkelling kit. I'd forgotten how healing the sea was. My bites were forgotten, along with the blisters. I relished tropical water lapping against my shoulders and soft sand between my toes along with a current tickling my belly. I wore a new pink polka dot bikini. It stood out from the others' functional one-pieces and I'd hurried into the sea as quickly as I could, my body feeling very conspicuous.

I'd never felt comfortable swimming. Imagining pairs of eyes scrutinising me. Boyfriends had helped dull the paranoia. Made me realise most men weren't as judgemental as Dad.

Jonas loved it and I said he could borrow it. He'd ducked me again in response.

He and I swam out and raced back. I couldn't stop laughing when I won and Jonas protested that his waterlogged dreadlocks had weighed him down. We both squealed when a shoal of silver fish surrounded us, weaving in and out of our legs. I felt a childish excitement as I dived down and found the prettiest shell. Jonas carefully stashed it in a pocket in his swimming trunks.

There wasn't a swim-up bar or lilos in the shape of flamingos but this was the first time I'd felt as if I'd truly escaped England for a better location. The sun beat down and we lay exhausted on the beach, letting waves lap deliciously over our bodies. We did sand angels, our arms and legs flailing as we lay horizontally. Other people joined in. Just as we started a piggyback race Amy and Benedikt appeared.

Jonas started to run faster.

Could he be trying to impress my sister?

Except he tripped. Staggered. We both went flying and landed flat on our faces, almost colliding with Amy. I turned my head to look at Jonas spitting out sand. He caught my eye. We both laughed hard. In fact, my stomach hurt so much I couldn't move.

'*Mein Gott*! You could have both broken your necks – and Amy's,' said Benedikt and glared at Jonas.

We got to our feet, Jonas checking I was okay. I pulled seaweed out of his hair. Someone shouted out it was lunchtime and Malik was serving a favourite – spicy beefburgers with chips and pineapple relish. I needed to change and tidy up my hair. Apply some makeup. After the last few days the idea of that sounded exciting! The men hurried off, Benedikt still berating Jonas for being so careless.

'Strange,' I said. 'They usually get on so well.'

'I think Benedikt is a little in awe of him,' replied Amy. 'He was talking about how Jonas wants a rock career. Benedikt regrets not following his heart and becoming a pianist. From what I can tell he finds his banking career… suffocating. Perhaps he's envious that Jonas is so laidback.'

'Or… have you really not noticed…?'

Amy turned to me.

'Perhaps those two are secretly competing for the same woman,' I said and grinned.

'What do you mean?' she asked.

We climbed the ladder into our shack. Helga wasn't there. We sat on Amy's low bed.

'Jonas reckons Benedikt fancies the pants off you – I think that's jealous thinking. Jonas looked so miserable watching you two play chess last night. And as soon as you appeared just now he acted all macho and started running faster and that's why he tripped. Ah. Of course. I bet Benedikt is telling him off because he is secretly annoyed that Jonas might have impressed you.'

'Benedikt fancy me?' Amy burst out laughing. 'Sarah. Leave the crush spotting to me. There is no chemistry whatsoever between us. Not even when we sing! Benedikt's more likely to be your type. He's got a thing for long hair, for a start, and mine couldn't be shorter. He told me he was growing his. I've never seen it out of his man bun but he says it's already down to his shoulders.'

'I don't think so… I've sensed that he really doesn't like me.'

'Rubbish,' she said in an assured tone. 'Only today he was asking me all about you. What your type of man was. And whether you liked music.'

I shrugged. 'So, how was the owl?'

'Wink is still off his food. I don't know how Jackie and Rick cope. They must get so attached to the animals they look after here. I'd fall to pieces if one died…'

'That's not true at all.'

She looked up from under her fringe. 'Isn't it? Remember how Dad sneered at me when my hamster fell ill? My eyes were swollen from crying at the dinner table. He told me to pull myself together; that I'd never make a good vet if I couldn't cope with the death of a rodent. I… I've never forgotten that.'

'As usual, he spoke complete nonsense,' I said briskly. 'Think of all the pets you've got to know – the regular clients at work – and how you've attended the procedure when they've been put to sleep. You've come home a little quiet. Perhaps shed a couple of tears. But it's always amazed me how you've sprung up for work the next day, determined to help the next sick pet. Jackie wouldn't let you near the zoo, to observe an animal in a fragile state, if she didn't respect your experience. You're a professional just like they are.'

'I guess… she did let me into the enclosure to offer Wink some beetles, but Benedikt had to wait outside.'

'There you go.'

Amy blushed.

'It's only natural you should worry. I bet the best vets are those who don't block off their emotions one hundred per cent.'

'Klopf, Klopf,' called a voice from outside. 'Burger and chips await. Benedikt and I leave in ten minutes.'

Amy and I looked at each other as a harmonica cheerfully played. 'I'm sure Jonas doesn't fancy me either,' she whispered. 'I'd have picked up a vibe by now. He's more likely to fancy you in that stunning bikini.'

I grinned. Despite feeling like the odd one out, my new bikini was comfortable and it had felt surprisingly liberating not to have a full-length mirror to scrutinise myself in.

'Come on. Let's stop worrying about the men,' she said. 'Us women need to get ready.'

I grabbed my makeup bag. 'Here's to finding the old Sarah and shopping and dance bars and…'

Amy grinned and passed me her hairbrush, not even chiding me for ringing home to once again check on Nelly.

19

Rick stood on the helm of the fishing boat, white shirt flapping in the breeze as we left Seagrass Island. The first few buttons were undone revealing a tanned chest. I tried not to look at the fitted linen trousers. Malik had insisted on steering us across to Tortola.

'Go, enjoy yourself, have a few cocktails,' Malik had said to Rick over lunch. 'You never take a break. My lovely Zina finishes work at the beauty salon at seven. I can cook dinner for her as a surprise. It suits me perfectly. We've missed seeing each other for a couple of weeks as she's been putting in so many hours lately, training to be a masseuse and Reiki healer as well.'

I breathed in the salty air. Rick clapped his hands. 'Right everyone… a bit of information about your new home. There are four main British Virgin Islands and fifty smaller ones, thirty-five of which are still uninhabited. Road Town is the capital of all of them, on Tortola where we are going today. The collective population of all the islands is around thirty thousand with twelve thousand of those people living in Road Town itself. Eighty-five per cent of inhabitants are African or of African descent and…'

I gazed across the ocean. Never had I felt such joy at

slipping into a pretty skirt and top, and strappy sandals. I felt like me again. Jonas had let out the longest wolf-whistle which was met with a frown from Benedikt.

I knew what Amy would say but surely I wasn't that out of practice at reading the opposite sex? There was no way Benedikt liked *me*. It was more likely that he saw Jonas as some sort of player who enjoyed flirting and had Amy on his radar next.

'… Hurricane Irma did a lot of damage to Tortola,' said Rick, 'destroying houses, yachts and cars. It looked barren and brown afterwards because the hurricane stripped the trees of their leaves. But as you can see, the lush tropical green landscape is back. In the first year alone after the devastation much of Road Town was rebuilt. There is still work to do but it's an up and running tourist centre once again and—'

A woman with black pigtails squealed and pointed to the left-hand side of the boat. Helga caught my eye and jabbed her finger at the ocean, grinning.

Oh my word.

A group of dolphins had decided to join us.

Everyone took out their phones, Benedikt pushing to the front with his. I didn't want to lose this moment worrying about how to take the best shot. I stood on tiptoe and admired the strong, curved forms that cut through the air in a perfect semi-circle, before diving, smiles first, back into the whipped cream white crests of water. One after the other the dolphins flew through the air, cleanly rising upwards before seamlessly entering the water again.

They followed the boat as if seeking out company. What

had I done to deserve such a precious moment? Tears came to my eyes. I couldn't help it.

Rick watched as I wiped my face, as if he'd never seen a person cry before.

Despite the tough start to this experience I stared at the dolphins. The sun, and waves sparkling underneath its rays. The lushness of Tortola in the distance. What a contrast to the grey of London and its urban outlook. I'd almost forgotten what a tonic it was to breathe in air flavoured by fresh brine and not car fumes… To be able to look into a never-ending horizon instead of a finite computer screen and feel a breeze lift my hair that was normally sprayed rigid.

'Why do they jump out of the water?' asked Jonas, slipping his arm around my shoulder.

Rick put a hand above his eyes to stop squinting. 'No one knows for sure. Some think it's to get rid of parasites – or just because they are happy. It might be to spot other pods. You're lucky today. Some volunteers never get to see these guys.'

'That's an amazing photo, Benedikt,' I said, looking at his phone. 'You've captured that jump just at the right moment.'

'Thanks,' he said in a flat tone.

If only Amy had heard. She'd realise I was the last person he was out to impress. But I wasn't going to let anything like that ruin my day. The dolphins moved on and I stared at rich green trailing clumps of seaweed happily bobbing past, like the discarded wigs of mermaids. Amy and Benedikt had the rest of the boat in tears of laughter with their exaggerated rendition of 'Under the Sea'. I went over to Rick.

'Thanks for the travel sickness tablet.'

'No problem. It should last eight hours so will just cover you tonight. Malik will sail us back around midnight.'

'Are you going shopping?'

'No. But I'll take you all to the retail area and point out the most reasonable stores. Some are a bit pricey. Malik and I will then visit his brother. It's always fascinating listening to him talk about his latest research or marine conservation project. Afterwards Malik will see his wife, Zina. I'll spend the evening with all of you. What are you hoping to find? A fashion boutique? Shoe shop?'

'A branch of Crocker & Crowley?' I asked.

His face fell. 'No... there was a plan for that but we had to shelve it.' Rick cleared his throat. 'There's a chemist that's great for makeup, I believe, and—'

I held up my hand. 'Functional clothes. Extra supplies of insect repellent. These are my new staples.'

He laughed. I cleared my throat and stepped back, feeling unnerved at our new camaraderie.

'I think you are going to fit in just fine,' he said. 'I have to be honest – I didn't think you'd last longer than a day, after you swore that you'd stay... but I've learnt that you can't judge a person by their hat, even if it's one more suited to *Breakfast at Tiffany's* than back-breaking work in a rainforest.'

I smiled and looked at my phone, a text from back home having come through. Perhaps we had misjudged each other. However, I still had reservations. The physical pull felt exciting but unnerved me as well.

I read the text and frowned.

'Everything okay?' he asked.

'Oh, it's nothing, just from work,' I said vaguely, wishing again that I could be more open about losing my job. Lynn from housekeeping had messaged saying she and the team were really upset about my dismissal and wanted to meet me for a goodbye drink when I got back.

I used the shopping trip to find souvenirs to buy them. Lynn was an avid fridge magnet collector and I found some lovely shell necklaces. We walked near the harbour and then visited the main street in Road Town. Before leaving us, Rick talked more about the construction work still underway. An Australian tourist who visited the British Virgin Islands regularly said several of his favourite specialised stores had been destroyed. Most of the ones now, in the form of colourful wooden huts, sold generic products and not all of them had been made locally.

But who could blame the vendors? Rick had mentioned that over eighty-five per cent of the houses on Tortola had been damaged or destroyed. Personally, I was thrilled with the choice of wares displayed outside shops on hooks and rails and in stacks, including straw hats and colourful sarongs, Caribbean dolls and the spices and jams Tortola was known for, pottery and art. It was still several weeks until I went home but who knew when I'd come shopping again. After a full week's volunteering I might want to do nothing but chill on the beach next Saturday. So I relished the sound of customers bartering, of clothes' hangers banging together and bag and purse zips undoing.

I bought pairs of cool linen trousers, along with cotton shirts, and found a chemist to stock up with plasters and creams.

Jonas shoved his sunglasses into his pocket and took out

his harmonica. Appropriately he played the Pina Colada song, as we headed to get a drink, several of us singing along about making love at midnight and singing in the rain. Eventually he ground to a halt as he shut his eyes and lost himself in the tune. Passers-by paused to listen. His body swayed. I marvelled at the different dynamics Jonas put in and the intensity of the playing.

Even Benedikt stopped to stare. His body rocked in time too. Amy held onto his arm but he hardly seemed to notice. But then he was a piano player. He must have missed music just like Jonas. A crowd formed and clapped, calling for more. Jonas blushed deeply, thanked everyone, put his sunglasses back on and continued walking.

Near the harbour we met Rick at a bar named Papaya Sunrise. He was waiting in the corner at a large table with several seats.

He took my breath away. His striking face. The solid frame. The humour that twitched across his mouth.

A stern-looking terrier sat on one of the seats. Six p.m. Saturday night and the place was already filled. Like Rick's family's house there were no windows, just shutters to pull down at night. Tables outside were filled with locals and tourists. Calypso music wafted across the room as if its notes were dancing with the air's atoms. Rum cocktails awaited us, dressed up with paper umbrellas and chunks of fruit.

'I know Maia, the manager of this place,' said Rick, beaming. 'We go a long way back. When we were little I used to throw spiders in her face. Amazingly she's still talking to me and asked her boss, Sultan, to save this table for us. We ought to thank him, really.'

We looked around for a man in charge and Rick started

laughing. He whistled and the terrier jumped off its seat and disappeared under the table. Rick bent down and emerged with the dog in his arms, licking his face.

'Sultan is very eager to please and excellent at guarding seats, as long as you order a lot of cocktails.'

We all grinned. Amy tickled Sultan's ears.

He put the dog back onto the floor and indicated to the chairs. 'I imagine you feel like sitting down after shopping.'

With relief I collapsed into a chair next to Rick and put down my bags. Carlotta looked disappointed – even more so when someone else sat the other side of him. It was rare for her to look anything but jovial. Amy sat next to me. Benedikt and Jonas were opposite. Jackie and Helga had stayed behind as part of the team that would do the evening animal feeds.

Rick had unbuttoned his white shirt further. He was a handsome man, no doubt about it.

Handsome sounded like an old-fashioned word these days. But Rick was kind of old-school attractive and despite the spiky slightly reckless hair he could have easily passed for a dapper Fifties hero like a racing driver or military officer, what with his broad shoulders and strong arms... with the humour he exuded and sensitivity he almost managed to conceal, and a secret story I could sense lurking in his shadow...

All these ingredients made up the kind of man I knew would bring nothing but heartache. The fact I was waxing lyrical about him was a bad sign. Therefore I held my gaze strictly above those undone buttons and took a large swig of the fruity cocktail – in the process almost poking my eye out with the umbrella. Rick grinned and removed it once

I'd put the glass back down onto the scratched mahogany table.

'You all right?' he asked. 'I've heard of vodka eyeballing but fruit juice might really mess with your sight.' He passed me a paper napkin.

'How was your chat with Malik's brother?'

'Fascinating,' he said. 'And sad. Worrying.' He sighed. 'Research has shown another effect of global warming on turtles. The sex of their eggs is determined by the incubation temperature – hotter ones produce female hatchlings. Therefore unless turtles start nesting at a cooler time of year, hotter summers will mean the sex ratio will be out and the turtle population will eventually be mostly female.' Deep lines appeared in his forehead.

I didn't know what to say, so rested a hand on his arm. He smiled and sparks ran up to my shoulder.

Rick's phone rang and he looked at the number and answered it. 'Hi Lee…'

His brother.

'What? Yes. Look, I told you, it's all under control. Mum and Dad said what?' He sighed. 'We've been through all this before. No, I'm not stressed. I just need a little time and… but… hold on…' He frowned and left the table.

Fifteen minutes he came back, rubbing his forehead.

'Everything okay?' I asked as he sat down again.

He nodded and picked up his glass. Slowly the frown disappeared as the calypso music got louder. Everyone ordered more drinks. Darkness fell. Moths fluttered inside the building. Pizzas arrived and we all insisted on paying for Rick's. Jonas had his beloved spicy sausage on his. Other customers jigged to the music in the middle of the bar, the imaginary dance floor extending outside. Amy grabbed Benedikt's hand and they got up. I held my arm out to Jonas. He gave a small shrug back and shook his head before staring at his phone.

'I'll have to do, then,' said Rick and took my hand.

Before I knew it we were on our feet. Sweaty bodies surrounded us. The music was now too loud to talk. My face was directly opposite his open shirt. Amy and Benedikt stood beside us laughing loudly as they did the dirtiest dirty dance. My sister lost herself in the music, caring little about whether or not she had an audience. The same could be said for people all around who shook their shoulders and twisted their bodies, stepping from side to side and clapping in time with the music.

Carlotta tried to cut in, with her pole dancer's figure. But Rick didn't seem to notice, and down in the mouth she turned her attention to one of the many men happy to replace him.

This boosted my confidence. Perhaps I wasn't such a bad dancer. My hips began to mirror Rick's as my confidence grew with the style of dance. Somehow it felt easy to mirror his moves. His shoulders shimmied at me. Mine shimmied too. It felt natural. Instinctive.

I fought the urge, really I did, to wrap my arms around his neck so that we could sway together, up close, our limbs and hearts guiding each other. But it was no good and my arms started to rise in the air…

Until I noticed Jonas. In the corner. Crying into his cocktail.

20

I made my excuses to Rick and headed over to Jonas. I pulled him up and led him outside to one side where a wooden table was covered with empty glasses, under a thatched palm leaf parasol. We sat down opposite each other.

'Why have you brought me out here?' asked Jonas and he stared at the harbour in the distance. Moonlight illuminated dappled sea water surrounding silhouettes of yachts and fishing boats, with bats diving to and fro. Nearby bushes smelt of vanilla. Chirps and whistles filled the air. I'd heard them on the turtle trip – Rick told us they came from the endangered coqui frog.

'What's the matter?' I asked gently.

'Nothing.'

'Jonas – I saw you crying.'

'You misunderstood. My cocktail, there was a piece of lemon, it was very bitter. That's all.'

'It's me. Sarah. We may have only known each other a few days but in this place it feels like a lifetime. I know that you hate banana. Have a second tattoo your parents don't know about. That if you ever have kids you'd name a boy

Bruce after Springsteen and that you love tea but go mad if anyone puts in the milk before water.'

'All of that qualifies you to know when I'm upset?'

'Absolutely.'

'Fair enough.' He gave a wry smile. 'I didn't realise I'd been talking about myself so much.'

'I'm a good listener. So spill.'

He looked puzzled.

'That means tell me – what's upset you? Or who? Is there any way I can help?'

I jumped as something furry rubbed against my legs. Sultan's soulful eyes stared upwards, into mine. I picked him up and put him next to me, on the bench.

'Sultan wants to hear too.' I tickled him behind his ears. 'Is it something to do with Amy?' The dirty dancing she was doing with Benedikt must have piqued his jealousy. Perhaps he was worried she really did fancy his shack mate.

But to cry? Something didn't add up. It had to be deeper than that. Jonas hadn't wanted to come to Seagrass Island but must have been made of strong stuff to go along with it.

No, those tears had to be about something really close to his heart.

'Is there someone you're missing back home?' Maybe he was yearning for the Maxi friend he'd mentioned. Perhaps he hadn't wanted the breakup and was hoping they'd get back together.

Jonas shook his head.

'You like someone here then, don't you?'

He met my eyes before groaning and holding his head in his hands, dreadlocks falling forwards across his face.

Sultan jumped under the table and bobbed up next to him. He whined. Jonas lifted his head and stroked the dog whose tail immediately wagged.

'I know you like Amy.' There. I'd blurted it out. Sometimes that was the best thing. Growing up with Dad had taught me that. As the teen years passed I noted how he'd use his charm to try to pass off insults and mean comments. As my confidence grew, I'd cut through that nonsense and call him out for the bully he was. He didn't know how to respond to me being blunt.

'You're jealous of Benedikt. It must be hard to watch them together – I know they are such good friends, but you've no reason to be, you see—'

'Whoa! What? No.'

'It's okay – you don't need to feel embarrassed.'

His eyes widened. 'What on earth makes you think I like your sister?'

'The looks you shoot her and Benedikt when they're together. It's obvious – to me anyway. That night, in the Games Room, when they were having fun playing chess you really didn't look happy. Then you and I did that piggyback race on the beach. As soon as Amy appeared you ran even faster as if trying to impress. I don't blame you,' I added hastily. 'We all do those things when we like someone. But Jonas – you're a great guy. There are lots of other women here and—'

'You don't understand,' he said quietly, and stroked Sultan again.

'Then talk to me.'

His shoulders bobbed up and down.

I reached across and squeezed his fingers that were resting

on the table. 'I won't push but I'm always here if you need a chat. I don't like seeing you unhappy.'

'Thanks. I mean, it's not as if you're used to seeing my miserable face because I've been *that* cheerful since having to empty compost toilets and eat rice three times a day, right?'

We exchanged smiles.

'Come on,' I said, briskly. 'Let's head back. The conga drums are calling us.'

We stood up. Sultan jumped down and scampered off towards the bar. Jonas hesitated. Sat down again. I joined him where Sultan had been, right by his side. Arms linked, we sat in silence.

'It's not Amy,' he muttered.

I didn't say anything.

'The moon's beautiful, isn't it?' he said. 'Think of everything it's looked down on over the centuries. Dinosaurs. Ancient Egyptians. Wars.' He smiled. 'Bruce Springsteen concerts. Yet night in, night out it stays the same, hanging in the sky, watching clouds waft past. I wish I was like that. I wish external factors didn't have such an effect on me.' He stared me straight in the face. 'The person I like. You're almost right. My sulkiness when they played chess. Me running my hardest on the beach. It was all to try and make an impression on…' He swallowed. 'Benedikt.'

I stared back at him, unblinking. Digesting his news.

'But Maxi… you said you'd broken up with *her*. I assumed…'

How could I have been so stupid? Of course. It made sense. That's why he gave Benedikt one of his precious chocolate bars for the turtle trip – and why he'd been surprisingly disappointed not to be going with us. I thought back to the rapt look on Jonas's face when he'd talked about the silly selfies Benedikt took with the moth on his head.

'I think I've been, what you'd call, a Dummkopf.' I paused. 'And you know what… with this fresh perspective I reckon Benedikt feels the same about you. Amy says he's into long hair. He often shoots me disapproving looks. And the way he told you off when you raced and fell in the sand – I thought it was because he was worried Amy could have got injured. Thinking back, he didn't check she was okay. It was you he focused on.'

Jonas shook his head. '*Nein*. He seems really into Amy. I hate to say it, but they look good together, especially when they sing their awful songs.'

'Haven't you picked up a vibe? Say at night, in the shack – don't you chat about stuff? Life back home? Previous partners?'

'Nope. There's lots of banter. Remember Alistair and Craig are in with us too. Alistair's in his fifties, so there's not as much talk about dating as there might have been if it was just us three younger ones.'

I unlinked our arms and slipped one of mine around his shoulder. I pulled him close.

'But why – if you don't mind me asking – why the tears? I get how you must feel as if you really know him already – like you and me do – but it has only been a few days. He hasn't rejected you. It hasn't got to that point yet…'

Years of supporting Amy through breakups and romance problems had taught me when to recognise I wasn't getting the full story. Like Sebastian. Rock star looks. Charisma in buckets. She'd fallen hard. I'd liked him a lot but inevitably, a man like that, he broke her heart – the day after her twenty-first birthday party as well. They split up. The two of them had looked so happy the night before. Amy had sobbed on my shoulder and just said they'd simply grown apart and it had been a mutual decision. But eventually I'd wheedled out more information – something about a stupid one-night stand.

I'd never felt so angry. But it hadn't surprised me. Sebastian's appealing looks and confident manner had always reminded me of Dad.

Ever since then I'd kept a close eye on her relationships and told her if I got a negative vibe. She'd get cross. Tell me heartache was all part of the risk of falling in love with people and she accepted that and dealt with it. I just couldn't bear to see her hurt; couldn't help giving my view.

Jonas's shoulders shuddered. I looked sideways. A tear rolled down his cheek.

'I only came out last summer,' he muttered. 'It's been a confusing few years. I used to date women as well but it never felt right... the physical stuff...' He squirmed in his seat. 'As the university years passed I knew for sure that I was gay but I still went out with my best friend there, Maxi, for a little while. That relationship – my last with a woman – meant I could no longer deny my sexuality to myself. She was – rightly – furious when she found out; felt she'd been used as some sort of guinea pig. We're only just getting our friendship back on track one year later and then I come over here...'

'Have you dated any guys?' I said, gently.

'I had a brief fling with a man I met at a rally against student cuts. That confirmed everything for me. But I avoided going public – because that would have meant being truthful with my parents.'

'Would that have been such a bad thing?'

'I thought so. They are so straight-laced. Conservative. They wouldn't admit it but I know they are concerned about my dreams to play music full time and would rather I use my degree and become a computer consultant. I thought me being gay wouldn't fit the neat little image they had of their son. But it came to the point where I just couldn't hold it in any longer.' He bit his lip. 'I was really scared, you know, when I finally told them? I couldn't stop shaking, bracing myself for rejection. I remember curling my fists as if arming myself, nails digging into my palms.'

'What happened?'

'I should have known better. Mum and Dad were brilliant. Said they'd known for a while – so had Helga. The three of them had been patiently waiting for me to announce it myself. I'll never forget the relief I felt – the fear draining out of me.' He gave a wry smile. 'You must think me a real drama queen.'

'Of course not. I can't imagine how big that must have felt – telling family something like that.' I asked again. 'So why exactly is this business with Benedikt so upsetting?'

His voice wavered. 'Shortly after that first fling with a man, I… I think I felt some sort of euphoria about finally being on the right path. It was such a relief. It made me a little reckless. I'd had virtually zero experience at approaching other men. I liked Friedrich, on my course. We were good friends. I'd always found him attractive and wishful thinking convinced me he was gay. I told him how I felt.' He covered his face with his hands. 'Friedrich made it clear he was straight. I've never felt like such a fool in my life. I still cringe... I still feel sick about it, looking back. And our friendship was never the same again.'

'Oh Jonas, I'm so sorry...'

'It was utterly humiliating – almost worse because Friedrich was kind about it.' Jonas's hands slid away from his face. 'I felt so stupid and it's really knocked my confidence. I don't think I'm ever going to meet the right man. I've felt so lonely over the years, struggling to come to terms with who I really am, and then once I finally do that happened...' He sniffed. 'I know it's early days. It all sounds ridiculous. But I've just got this feeling with Benedikt – that he... he's someone rather special. Yet he turns out to be straight too.'

'I kind of get it. Talking to men – getting it right, that's always been hard for me. Trusting, putting myself out there – it takes real guts to lay your feelings bare. I think you've been really brave.'

Jonas sat more upright and wiped his eyes.

His attraction to Benedikt didn't sound ridiculous because I'd felt that pull towards Rick and being thrust into the rainforest meant that connections developed at top speed.

'Look at me. Sniffling like a spoilt toddler. Sorry Sarah. I'll get over it. It must be the alcohol. I've got a supportive family and I'm grateful for that.' He sighed. 'Hopefully this month in the jungle will toughen me up.'

'Yes, I saw a tarantula and actually didn't scream earlier. I now feel I could conquer the world.'

'You must promise me, Sarah. *Promise* you won't mention this to anyone. Not even your sister. She might tell Benedikt.'

'I honestly reckon he fancies you. Amy said he was asking what sort of men I like. I reckon he's as worried about us getting together as you are about my sister and him.'

'Or you are his back-up plan if he doesn't get Amy.' He managed a smile.

'Thanks!'

'Promise,' he said. 'Not a single word.'

I promised, slipped my other arm around Jonas and gave him the tightest hug. He held on for a long time. I held him back. It felt good. At that moment Benedikt and Amy tumbled outside looking sweaty and tired. I caught his eye and before he could mask it Benedikt let slip the coldest stare.

There was no doubt in my mind. He liked Jonas as much as Jonas liked him.

But what could I do to bring them together?

21

'Which has been your most *enjoyable* task this week?' asked Rick, dark eyes twinkling.

We sprawled on a comfortable sofa in the Games Room. It was half past seven and we'd just arrived there after eating. Evening time spent here had become a daily habit. It was Friday. I'd actually survived six more days and had managed to control my urge to ring home and check up on Nelly – not that I would have had much time for phone chat.

Amy had more than survived – she'd thrived on helping out with the animals and her face was a picture when Wink's appetite returned. Also, she'd gone for a stroll early one morning after a swim and found an injured bird. She'd carefully placed it in her cap and covered the hat with the dry T-shirt she'd pulled over her swimming costume. Amy had known that being in the dark would cause the bird less stress. Jackie was very impressed, especially when she found out Amy already suspected it was suffering from a broken wing.

'There's no question that your sister has the knack of handling animals,' she told me later. 'Efficient but compassionate. And she has that extra quality – a great bedside manner. It's clear her job is driven by a true love of, and respect for, wildlife.'

Then one afternoon Rick had an urgent phone call. He, myself and Amy and two other volunteers were on the afternoon food preparation duties and he had to leave. She'd immediately offered to do his share and make sure the food shed was tidy before everyone went back to camp for dinner. He'd been happy to give her that responsibility.

'The most enjoyable task? Now that's a very hard question,' I said airily and sipped my beer. Amy and Benedikt were, as usual, playing chess. Jonas was in the middle of a card game with Jackie and Helga. He didn't look invested.

I'd kept my promise and not said anything to Benedikt – or my sister. As the days passed the clues about Benedikt's feelings became more obvious to me. He always poured Jonas a glass of water at the dinner table before anyone else and complimented his shirts featuring various bands. If he took a good photo he'd show it to Jonas before anyone else.

However, the biggest revelation this week had been how well Rick and I got on. Like me, he hated jogging and loved American TV comedies. Bizarrely, we both had the same drink fetish – milk and Coca Cola mixed together in equal quantities. I'd never be such a keen conservationist like him and he was beginning to understand that this volunteering experience was a huge challenge for me.

'But that's okay,' he'd said, very early last Monday morning, as we'd headed off to do bird counting. 'Because I can tell you don't give up once you've put your mind to something. We're similar like that. My driving is a joke in the family. It took me over fifty lessons back in London to pass my test, second time around, but I was determined. I'm not saying it's always a good trait – my brother often calls me stubborn – but it has its advantages.'

'I did a car maintenance course once. I stayed behind the week we were shown how to change a tyre, I found it so difficult. It took me so long to master what to do, I ended up taking the teacher for a late-night curry. But I got there in the end.'

He'd gazed at me. Muttered that I was made of stern stuff before changing the subject. I had, indeed, persevered this week, tended to my blisters that slowly healed and done my best to avoid more mosquito bites. I'd worn sensible clothes and my cap. I hadn't even bothered with my makeup, nor attempted to style my hair.

Which was an unexpected but surprisingly welcome change. Perhaps it was due to my new undomesticated surroundings. I liked to think myself body positive and was grateful I'd never become obsessed with chasing a slim figure like some of my friends. But being well-groomed... looking smart... like Mum, like Anabelle... I'd fought against the voices telling me I should be like them. But then there seemed little point once I gained employment as a receptionist. How refreshing it was, for the first time in my life, not to have easy access to a mirror.

Day in, day out, this trip was surprising me. And another thing that lifted my spirits was making the effort to keep Jonas cheerful.

Rick put his drink back on the floor by his feet. 'Perhaps an easier question might be which task has been the most bearable?'

I returned his wide smile and took another sip of the beer, feeling rejuvenated following an afternoon of trail clearing.

I said the word 'Chatty' to catch the monkey's attention and tickled his head. He was perched on Rick's shoulder, holding onto a leather pendant around Rick's neck. Without his sight perhaps he thought it was a piece of trailing ivy or a plant that might bear fruit. Chatty let go and curled his tiny hand around my wrist. I was used to this now. It meant he didn't want the tickling to stop. He bared his teeth on my skin just to emphasise his desire.

'The bird counting trips have been annoyingly interesting,' I said.

Overnight nets were left out in different locations – near the beach and in the forest. Then we'd get up really early and examine them. Jackie would identify the species of bird and tag one of their legs before we'd release them again. As the sun became brighter, we'd climb rope bridges to observation platforms in the trees and count more birds using binoculars. From the canopies I'd seen sandpipers with long beaks, a yellow-billed cuckoo, a variety of doves, a woodpecker and a green and yellow parakeet. But most beautiful of all, in the nets, was a delicate hummingbird with iridescent green and purple plumage. It looked as if it had flown straight out of one of Monet's water lily paintings.

Amy had wanted a budgie once, as a little girl, but Mum had firmly said no – keeping anything in a cage, and alone, was cruel. She only let Amy have a hamster as he had a plastic ball to run around in and research revealed they preferred to be solitary animals. Mum also preferred potted plants to cut flowers. Dad called her over-sensitive.

'I also… well, not sure I'd go so far as to say *enjoyed* but managed to endure my second turtle egg collecting trip with

Jackie . And the butterfly catching on Tuesday really taught me patience, sneaking up on ones that weren't in motion.' There were delicate white butterflies, yellow ones and a vibrant orange species too. 'As for cleaning the shower blocks and emptying the toilets...' I threw my hands in the air. 'What's not to adore about that?'

Rick grinned and gently lifted Chatty onto his lap, and took over head-scratching duties. However the monkey reached out. I put my hand between his paws. He held on tight. Rick passed me the lead handle and placed him on my lap instead. I whistled 'Daydream Believer'. Chatty sat still for a moment.

Rick's eyes crinkled. 'Chatty and you have really clicked.'

The little blond face reached up and he chewed my chin. Very gently I tapped him on the nose. He squeaked indignantly so I moved my finger behind his ears and began scratching.

'Seriously though...' I exhaled. 'I have liked parts of the experience so far. A spa break would have still suited me much better but I have to admit to feeling a degree of satisfaction over certain tasks. Like when it was my turn to bury the turtle eggs in the protected sandpit. And even though I needed a shower after cutting up all that juicy fruit for Chatty, for the birds, the bats and iguanas, it felt good to watch them devour their food.'

'You had a really shaky start. I've never seen anyone recover like that.'

And I wasn't expecting to like you, let alone seek out your company, I thought.

Take our evenings in the Games Room. It just felt right,

sitting with him. The chat was easy now. The humour frequent. Perhaps there wouldn't be a problem simply enjoying the company of a man like him.

As long as we were just friends.

Nothing more.

Because I knew how that would end.

When I first arrived on Seagrass Island Rick had made me feel like Dad used to.

Useless. Laughable. As if I didn't belong.

Oh, Rick had wrapped it up in a gentler way but his initial attitude still struck nerves I hadn't suffered from since I'd become independent.

Plus I couldn't let myself trust those warm sensations he aroused in me, that made me feel safe and happy in his presence. Because Mum and Anabelle would have never married Dad if they'd known what he was really like. He must have hidden it well, until it was too late. Whereas I'd already had a glimpse of the real critical, sullen Rick…

Are you sure asked a voice in my head? *He seems lovely now. Dad would have never been so compassionate over a little monkey, for a start… Perhaps this more easy-going version is the real Rick.*

I pursed my lips. No. I couldn't risk it.

'I don't think I'll ever get used to certain aspects like the lack of aircon at night. I'd like to say I didn't miss junk food but right at his minute I'd do almost anything for a Big Mac or family-sized chocolate bar.'

'Anything? Stay up all night with a newly found injured bird? Clean out the bat cage? Their droppings have a certain aroma.'

'Funnily enough, if I had to, neither of those things

would bother me. Oh, I don't like emptying the compost toilets, but that's simply because of the volume.' I shrugged. 'I'm pretty self-sufficient – and you'd be surprised at the disgusting habits of some hotel guests that I have to deal with.'

Rick stared intently at me, before nodding eventually.

'Still,' he continued, 'I've never had an unenthusiastic volunteer stick it out before. So, if you ever feel you need a break, the beach huts up at the house are practically finished. You're welcome to stay in one if you ever need a bit of respite.'

'Thanks,' I said. 'In fact… seeing as it's the weekend tomorrow… could I come over tonight? Not to stay,' I added quickly. 'But it would be great to cool off in a mosquito-free zone before heading to my sauna, I mean shack.' I gave a broad smile.

A smile I hoped would make him say yes because I had an ulterior motive. The guitar. The grand piano. Somehow I felt they could bring Benedikt and Jonas together. I wasn't sure how and hoped seeing them would give me inspiration.

'No problem. I was going to ask you to come over anyway, at some point this weekend – would you very much mind looking at the website again? I've been working on it late into the evenings all week and Jackie has added her input.'

'You didn't waste any time.'

'We can't afford to,' he said and for a moment the light left his eyes.

Seagrass Conservation must have needed more money to run than I'd ever imagined. The price he charged volunteers certainly wouldn't be all used up by the cheap accommodation and basic meals –although last Sunday's breakfast wouldn't have looked out of place on a luxury cruise liner with an array of pastries, fried eggs and toast.

Rick stood up. 'Shall we go there now? I'll just put Chatty back in his enclosure and then my grandmother wants to Skype quickly.'

'Is everything okay? It's rather late, isn't it, and a Friday night?'

He looked at his watch. 'It's just gone half past eleven in England,' he said, 'but Gran's always been a light sleeper and never goes to bed before midnight. She probably just wants to check that I'm going to simply whitewash the bedrooms. I threatened to paint them bright pink, her least favourite colour.'

Rick gave a smile yet it didn't reach his eyes. He rubbed a hand across his face, a weary expression clouding it. 'It'll only be a quick call – hopefully. Give me half an hour. Come straight in when you arrive, if I'm still on the computer. Right. Come on Chatty, Jackie is over at the enclosures checking on one of the lizards that has been looking off colour. It's an early bed for you, although I'm sure Jackie will want a cuddle.'

I bent down and nuzzled Chatty's head with my nose and lifted him over to Rick, with the lead. The two of them disappeared into the darkness.

Amy came over. 'You two looked deep in conversation.' I could tell she was trying not to grin. 'Bet you're really glad you stayed on Seagrass Island now.'

No. I'd rather be back home with Nelly and Netflix. Definitely. No doubt about it. With my duvet for one. And the task of finding a new job...

'I don't need to ask if *you're* enjoying it,' I said.

Her eyes shone. 'Oh Sarah, it's everything I thought it would be, and more – being up close to such exotic animals and their natural habitat… I'm so grateful for my lottery win. Handling some of these animals… it's brill dealing with the pets at Paws & Claws but I'm out of my comfort zone here and am loving it. I'm beginning to realise that… I am good at what I do. Does that sound big-headed?'

'No. It sounds wonderful. Some well-deserved self-belief.'

She gave an orangutan-sized yawn. 'But now it's time for bed. Helga wants me to get up and watch the sunrise with her. She's can't believe a week has passed already and it's not enough for her, seeing it when we do bird counting. I don't suppose you fancy join—'

'No,' I said decisively and she laughed. 'In any event, I'm going up to the house for a while, now, so tomorrow I might have a lie-in.'

Amy raised an eyebrow.

'To help Rick with the website. I gave him a few ideas,' I said in the most matter-of-fact voice I could muster.

'I'm saying nothing,' she said with a secret smile.

I went to ring home and check up on Nelly. Then I changed my mind and Amy looked surprised. She said she was glad and that I worried too much. We said good night to each other – but not until I'd pretended to tuck her up in bed.

'Get off me!' She wriggled under the covers on the lower bunk, laughing as I smoothed down her hair like I used to when she was a little girl.

'Now you get some sleep,' I called in my strictest parental tone as I climbed down the shack's ladder. 'No sneaky reading once lights are out.'

I was laughing too hard to hear her very impolite reply.

I made my way through the darkness, using my torch to avoid stones and tree roots that might cause me to trip. Deep in thought I walked straight into the Crowleys' house. It was only when I got inside that I realised Rick was in the middle of an argument. He sat on one of the long magnolia sofas, laptop on his knees. I stood trapped, not wanting to leave in case he saw me but feeling awkward about staying.

'For Christ's sake, you haven't got a clue what it's like here. It's just the same old, same old, thinking the worst from you, always wanting instant results and not trusting me to manage on my own. We'll get there. I just need a bit of time.'

Wow. He clearly had a plain-speaking relationship with his gran.

I didn't hear the muffled response but Rick shook his fist at the screen.

'No. I'm not letting things get on top of me. My blood pressure is fine. And I will not be calling it quits. There's more at stake here than just the house. Age doesn't always bring wisdom, you know.'

I turned away, not wanting to intrude.

'Naive and irresponsible? How dare you!'

A slamming noise made me turn around. A red-faced Rick stared at the closed lid of his laptop.

22

I wasn't sure where to look so pointed at the piano, sleek and black with the bird carving perched on its top. 'I was just admiring it. Did it survive the hurricane?'

'What? Oh. Yes... just about. In fact, we're forever grateful to this old lady. She saved the life of one of my young cousins who had legged it out of the basement to look for one of the cats. She was on holiday here with her parents. Trixie has always been something of an adventurer and didn't believe the wind would really be that bad.' The redness had faded from his cheeks. 'I got up to all sorts at her age. I once tried weed at a party in my late teens. Lee recognised the smell when I got home.' Rick shook his head. 'Even though he's only three years older than me he went mad. Threatened to tell Mum and Dad, despite it just being a one-off. For as long as I can remember Lee's been bossing me around...' He smiled. 'And with those words I realise I sound like a sulky teenager.'

'Sounds like he did you a favour! And that he cared.'

Rick thought for a moment. 'Possibly. It didn't feel like it at the time. That's the trouble at that age, I guess – you think you're invincible and can do what you want without repercussions.'

I didn't. When I left home at eighteen a secret voice in my head told me I was bound to fail. However, over time, I realised that wasn't really my voice, it was Dad's.

'Trixie didn't think she'd get back to the basement so hid under the piano, holding onto one of the legs. It had been blown against the wall and jammed there. It's a miracle she didn't lose her life. It's almost back in top condition although it makes a vibrating noise when played. I'll have to get that sorted otherwise it will be one more thing for Lee to complain about.' He gave a loud sigh.

'That was your brother just now? Sorry, I couldn't help but overhear. I thought you were due to have a call with your gran.'

Rick looked aghast. 'I would never speak to her like that. Lee used to take the lead when we were younger and still tries now. He thinks it's low-key and subtle but it's not.'

I sat down next to him. 'What do you mean?'

'He's always checking up on me under the guise of just wanting a chat or meeting for lunch. I moved flats a few years back. Lee insisted on coming to view it with me – pretended he was in the area and dropped in before I was due to leave to see the estate agent. I'm a grown man, for goodness' sake! Being a few years older can be a gulf when you are children – but that gap drastically narrows when you hit your twenties. Yet he still won't treat me as an equal.'

Something shifted uneasily inside me. I recalled the time our washing machine broke. I was working overtime, to cover a member of staff's illness, so Amy went window-shopping. She found a bargain replacement and was so excited. It was the last model in the shop. I'd insisted we hold off buying it until I could view it as well. We lost it to another customer.

Rick looked at me with tired eyes. 'He knows nothing about the environment and has only gone along with Seagrass Conservation because the island was in such a mess after the hurricane – he thought my venture would help get the place back into shape, plus create funds to rebuild our family home... but there he is, trying to advise me at every turn, telling me I'll have a heart attack if I keep putting in so many hours.'

I squirmed again. 'I have to admit my sister gets irritated with me, sometimes – checking if she's pumped up her bicycle's wheels or taken her vitamin tablets – so I suppose I get your brother.'

Rick listened intently.

'But I'd have thought Lee had enough to contend with back in England and would be happy to leave you to sort matters here.'

He put the laptop on the cushion next to him and sank back into the sofa. 'Trouble is, that's not the whole story... our family business... everything Gran and my granddad worked for...'

I raised an eyebrow.

'Crocker & Crowley...' He swallowed and held his head in his hands. 'The business has almost gone bust, Sarah.'

'*What?*'

'That's why, over recent years, we've had to close so many stores.'

'But Crocker & Crowley is everyone's go-to shop for kids' shoes. And Amy and her colleagues swear by it for getting comfortable, long-lasting shoes.'

'That's the problem – we realised, too late, that we hadn't moved with the times.' He looked up. 'We've lost our appeal to youngsters and, well, we just aren't fashionable. Nowadays the choice and competition is vast and there's the phenomenon of disposable fashion – designs that rapidly go from the catwalk to the high street and are only meant for what's called a micro season.'

'I suppose, these days, you can buy such cheap shoes from well-known clothes stores as well.'

'Exactly. Shoes are more affordable than ever. For many customers now it's the diversity and pricing of the product that counts above quality and longevity... Or it's the opposite in that they want designer labels, the top sports brands – shoes like the ones their favourite celebrities are wearing. We're kind of stuck in the middle. We still do well with small children but that income isn't enough to carry the whole business.'

'I'm so sorry to hear this.' No wonder the success of Seagrass Conservation had become so important. 'So that's why you charge the volunteers so much to take part? To save the family business?'

He looked up and shook his head vehemently. 'Good God, no. Absolutely not. Yes, some of the profits – there aren't many – have been used to help with the rebuild of our house. Crocker & Crowley couldn't afford to pay for that by itself. But every other penny is used for the project. People's wages. Food. Accommodation. Veterinary bills. Our breeding programmes. Specialist animal feed... Lee was keen for how my plans meant restoring the island to its former glory because... truth is...' His shoulders slumped. 'We might have to sell this place.'

'Oh no.'

'I'm really hoping it doesn't come to that – that we can

turn the shoe business around. Because someone might buy Seagrass Island who's only interested in having a luxurious pad for their free time – who isn't invested in animal welfare. If they aren't interested in wildlife then Seagrass Conservation will be dead in the water, along with my plans for what we are doing here to benefit the whole Caribbean region and for educating people about the challenges brought about by extreme weather, tourists and poachers…'

He sighed. 'Being more optimistic, though, another reason we've used some of the project's funds to rebuild is because if we do have to sell the island, we stand a much better chance of attracting a buyer – someone who might continue to run the conservation side – if there is accommodation with the wow factor that is ready to move into.'

'That makes sense.'

'Who knows how it will pan out, though…'

We sat in silence for a moment.

'I don't know about you but I need a shot of comfort. Milk and Coca Cola?'

I nodded.

Five minutes later he was back with two glasses. He leant over to the nest of sturdy mahogany tables, with carved animal feet, at his end of the sofa, dragged out the smallest and placed it in front of us. He put our drinks down and collapsed onto the sofa. I lifted mine and took a large mouthful. Delicious.

'So Crocker & Crowley isn't going to jump on the fast fashion bandwagon?'

'No. At least my family and I agree on that – even Lee. It goes against everything the company stands for in terms of high-quality products that last. Plus there are the environmental issues. It wouldn't sit well with us, as a family that also run a conservation project. People need to get back to a wear and repair mindset, instead of throwing items away at the first sign of deterioration. My gran, brother and parents may not want to save the world like I do...' He gave a small smile. 'But they've seen how the wildlife of the British Virgin Islands' alone has changed over recent decades.'

'I suppose you *could* justify using some of the money from volunteers to inject cash into Crocker & Crowley – and then, in return, the company might be in a position to give back to Seagrass Conservation.'

Rick glugged back his drink. He put the empty glass down on the table and wiped his mouth with the back of his hand. 'Seagrass Conservation doesn't earn nearly enough to make a difference. Crocker & Crowley has reached a crisis point and we can't kid ourselves any longer that, somehow, trade will pick up. I feel as if I've let everyone down. Perhaps I should have stayed in England and like my brother and parents, focused on rebuilding the shoe business – and supported everyone there.'

'Rick. No one can work miracles. It's still early days. Once we get that website ship-shape bookings might great increase and—'

'I don't know... What if I have to abandon the whole thing? If we are forced to sell and the new owner isn't interested in my mission? I'm worried about what will happen to the injured animals. Chatty. The turtle conservation... Crocker & Crowley, it's in my DNA. What hurts my family hurts me. The only way of saving it might be for me to go back into the oil industry. The salaries there are more than generous for someone with my degree and experience.' He turned to face me. 'But I hated my old job.'

'Apart from closing stores, what other measures are being taken?'

'Firstly – and most importantly – we've tailored our ambition. Lots of retail companies have struggled due to the rise of internet shopping and we accept that. Our goal is to be able to simply maintain trading from our four top stores in London, Manchester, Newcastle and Bournemouth. Then we'll expand the range within those shops. Introduce a slightly cheaper, more on trend line for young adults, yet still push our fitting service for children. We'd hire a marketing agency to help us refurbish the stores and modernise the whole brand – without alienating loyal customers.' He bit his lip. 'It won't be pleasant. Staff will have to go, including some of our longest-serving designers. But we recognise the need to bring in fresh blood.'

'It all sounds like a big ask – but I'm sure it can be done,' I added hastily. I sat more upright and studied this family man with such a big heart.

Sincere. Earnest. Driven by admirable qualities.

It's not what I expected. Not from someone with his looks and charm.

And that felt… uncomfortable.

'I've not got anything planned for tomorrow afternoon. Why don't you, me and Jackie have a brainstorming session and really revolutionise that website?' I said, wanting to help and loving a challenge. Prue rarely involved me with troubleshooting the big problems at Best Travel. I'd been really excited, once, when she'd asked me to help her reassess the publications we advertised in. I researched and showed her how we could target potential guests online as well. She took on some of my ideas, passing them off as her own. 'It's getting late now. I'll bring a fresh pair of eyes over with me, tomorrow after lunch.'

'You'd really do that?'

'Of course.'

His face brightened. 'Great. Jackie won't make it as she's taking a group on that boat trip we advertised in the canteen. Malik could go instead but she deserves a break.'

'Your brother… Will the argument pass?'

His lips pinched. 'No. The disagreements between us are ongoing and have been getting worse over the last twelve months. I try to remind myself he's under a lot of pressure too. We both worry about Mum and Dad. They should be thinking about retiring now instead of seeing their life's work, as well as Margot's, go down the drain.'

To change the subject away from his own family, he asked about mine. I told him I knew what it was like to have rifts, explaining a little about Dad. How difficult things had been when Mum died, without going into detail about how I'd had no choice but to leave home when I was eighteen. The detail would have meant talking about the terrible thing Dad said to me as I left. His accusation that made had me staring into the darkness, at night, for weeks.

We talked about Rick's old job in the oil industry. How he'd ended up using his degree to work in an office, something that had never been part of his dreams.

Rick was easy to talk to and quietly sympathetic. A good listener to boot. I ended up telling him more than I usually would to someone I'd only known for a week.

Perhaps it was because I was cocooned on a tropical island, away from reality.

Or maybe it's because you and Rick are a perfect fit, said a voice in my head that I immediately quashed.

Eventually we sat in silence again, on the sofa facing the back of the property, with the pool and Tiki-style beach huts. It looked like the front of a postcard one might send from a luxury holiday. I imagined the place with Rick's relatives milling around, the bar open, people in the pool, dance music playing.

It was a full moon tonight, creamy white and majestic – and thoroughly romantic.

Talking about my childhood. Rick talking about his. This connection, whatever it was, between us felt stronger than ever…

Perhaps that's why I did it.

Rick turned to pick up the glasses. I turned at the same time. Our faces came into close proximity. I breathed in a faint musky smell. I'd noticed it the other day. It offered a strange contradiction – that someone so down-to-earth would bother with aftershave. The urge overtook me. I leant forward and pressed my lips firmly against his.

His body stiffened briefly then his lips parted. Suddenly the air-conditioned room felt as hot and humid as outside. Forget the moon – in front of my closed eyes hundreds of stars sparkled as my nerve-endings fizzed. A fluttering noise brought me back to reality and we pulled apart.

Just over his shoulder a shadow swooped and almost hit his head. I yelped and jumped backwards. Rick scanned the room and bellowed with laughter.

'It's just a bat. That happens sometimes.'

What on earth had I just done?

'Sorry about… I don't know what I was thinking…'

'I'm irresistible, right?' Rick beamed. 'No need to apologise. I rather enjoyed it.'

That heartbreaking smile. There was no other word for it. I gave a nervous laugh.

'I must be dehydrated,' I said. 'Delirious, in fact.'

'You've just had a very refreshing, long drink,' he said, clearly enjoying my discomfort. 'I never knew coke and milk was an aphrodisiac.'

I got to my feet. Pronto. 'Right. Better go. Amy will wonder where I am. I'll see you here after lunch then?'

'If you can wait until then,' he teased and stood up.

'Don't flatter yourself,' I said sharply though I returned his smile.

Desperately I looked around the room to take us onto a different conversation. The piano. Of course. A plan popped into my head that could bring Benedikt and Jonas together.

'You said the piano's vibrating?' I said in as steady a voice as possible. 'Benedikt plays the piano. His dad is a tuner. I bet he's picked up some knowledge over the years and could sort it out for you – when the place is empty, of course, so that it's perfectly quiet for him to analyse the problem.'

'That would be great. One less thing to worry about. I'll mention it to him.'

'Maybe Jonas could come over at the same time. He's a musician.'

Rick was looking at his laptop again. 'Sure. Why not? Perhaps they could come over tomorrow after our computer brainstorming session, if they haven't got other plans. I'm going to spend my evening in the Games Room with the permanent volunteers, refining last minute arrangements for the sports day we've got planned on Sunday.'

'That sounds like fun.'

No, it didn't. I hadn't travelled four thousand miles to take part in a sports day. I'd come for massages and cocktails by the pool. But Rick looked so downhearted, bending the truth might cheer him up. I could think of a million other ways to lift his mood. They didn't involve talking. They didn't involve clothes.

'It should be,' he said as if only half-listening to me now.

'See you tomorrow, then,' I said. In my haste I left via the back entrance.

23

I sat in the canteen and yawned before pouring a glass of water. As Amy got older and came to live with me it was no longer worries about her that kept me awake at night. It was others about bills, broken boilers or stalling cars – but also ideas and brainstorming about how to improve Best Travel, hoping I could persuade Prue to let me make some changes.

Last night was one of those nights. A week on Seagrass Island and – slowly – the cloying humidity seemed more bearable and I didn't feel afraid if I heard a bird's screech. No, what kept me awake was, firstly, I had to admit, that kiss. The sort I'd never shared with any previous boyfriend. The type where time stood still – or rather galloped at a pace. A heavenly oblivion I'd not known existed away from a film reel.

Kiss was a simple word. It seemed inadequate to describe what happened between Rick and me. The electricity between us. The way it made my heart thump. It had blocked out all other thoughts; it made me feel as if I were living for the moment.

My life had become one of routine and responsibility – of

getting up and doing the same thing every day. Whereas this kiss made me feel reckless, spontaneous…

I couldn't remember the last time I'd felt so intensely alive.

And yet he'd laughed it off. So had I, thank goodness. Mistakes like that could be difficult and embarrassing to remedy. My heart warmed with gratitude as I recalled Rick's easy manner.

He made me feel relaxed yet ruffled at the same time.

It was a combination difficult to ignore.

I gazed around as people sat down with their lunch, forcing my thoughts to shift to the other things that kept me awake last night, triggered by my walk around Rick's outdoor pool after making my escape. I'd soaked up the sense of luxury and taken a peek inside the Tiki-style two-storey beach huts. Their top floors were the bedroom – downstairs, the lounge and bathroom. I'd spotted wicker furniture in greens and cream. The rooms boasted wooden features, Caribbean art and glossy green plants all around with discreet aircon units on the walls. Margot certainly wanted her visiting family and friends to feel as comfortable as possible, what with hammocks between nearby trees. With the similar decor these huts seemed almost like extensions of the big house.

As I'd left, the strong night-time scent of the pink propeller-shaped frangipani flower had wafted my way from nearby bushes. I now knew the name of several indigenous species. Near the bar stood a powder puff tree with its delicate fluffy pink blooms. I'd turned back to see a bat swoop across the pool. Moonlight lit up the bamboo bar and its palm leaf parasol.

All of this exotic, tropical, romantic ambiance… it gave

me the kernel of an idea that might help Rick with trying to raise money. After hearing that heated argument with his brother, it was obvious to me that the family's financial situation was heading towards a tipping point. Maybe I had the answer.

I thought back to my initial surprise about how a volunteering holiday could cost so much. But getting to know Rick and seeing his work in action made me understand why. It also made me realise that he had real integrity regarding how that money was used.

No, someone would have to come up with a completely new idea, to create cash to inject into Crocker & Crowley.

I'd got up with Amy early to help feed the animals. Jonas came along and tried to charm the tree boas by playing his harmonica. Benedikt joined us too – thank goodness. Alone, I thought Amy might quiz me about my evening at Rick's house and I wouldn't be able to keep it to myself that we'd got close. Not that I usually hid things from her but the last thing I needed was my teasing little sister Googling wedding dresses.

After feeding the animals, as it was Saturday, we enjoyed some chill time on the beach, lying in the warm tide, collecting shells to take back to England. Helga found the prettiest yellow and pink scallop and insisted I have it. We played volleyball in mixed teams. I'd suggested men versus women but only so that Jonas and Benedikt were together. Jonas cottoned on and shot me an angry glare.

It had been the same all week. Any hint that I was trying to pair them up had been met with indignation.

'You never stood a chance,' I said, and took a sip of

water. I smiled at Benedikt whose team lost. Amy and I sat opposite him and Jonas on one of the long white tables, tucking into fried fish sandwiches.

'The score was so close and it was pure luck than you won,' he replied and re-tied his hair bun. 'Your mischievous sister distracted me when she started singing "Summer Nights". Amy knows I'm a sucker for any song from *Grease* since starring as one of the T-birds.'

'Benedikt.' Amy's mouth twitched. 'You told me that was at school. You were thirteen and should have moved on by now.'

'I was voted best singer of the night and won a book voucher,' he protested before he and Amy dissolved into laughter.

Jonas forced a laugh and looked thoroughly miserable. He couldn't have noticed how Benedikt had gazed affectionately when he'd ducked under the water, out at sea, and surfaced with a clump of seaweed tangled in his dreadlocks. I wondered if Benedikt had noted how Jonas was the first to arrive at his side when he swallowed seawater and started choking.

Amy and Benedikt got up to help Malik wash up the plates. The volunteers did that at weekends.

'Volleyball was fun,' I said to Jonas and delved into my trouser pockets, a small part of me still missing my colourful shorts and tailored halter-neck tops, my cute sandals and Audrey Hepburn sunhat. I pulled out a handful of shells. 'Isn't this one gorgeous?' I passed him a shiny yellow, horn-shaped conch.

He ran a finger over the curves and ridges. 'This afternoon

I'm asking Rick if I can change shacks. Both Alistair and Craig snore. I'm not getting any sleep.'

'You've never mentioned the noise before.'

'You know me, I'm not a complainer,' he said and his mouth attempted to quirk upwards.

I reached out to take the conch and my hand lingered on his. 'It's Benedikt, isn't it?'

His eyes glistened. 'It's too hard – lying below him each night. Wishing he was next to me. Like during the day when I wish I could hold his hand. I'm sure Rick won't mind. Not all of the shacks are completely full.'

'If you just did some digging – casually ask Benedikt about past relationships, I'm sure you'd soon realise that—'

'No!' he hissed. 'I'm not risking being humiliated again, after what happened with Friedrich. And I won't risk losing Benedikt's friendship.'

'Then let me—'

'You promised.'

Amy came back. 'What's everyone doing this afternoon? Jackie's asked me to help clean out the tree boa enclosure. I'm so excited. We've had snakes come in at Paws & Claws but I've not handled one yet.'

'That's the kind of excitement I can do without,' I said and playfully punched her arm, about to ask if she was wearing insect repellent as there was a mark on her skin that looked like a bite. But then I thought back to the conversation with Rick about his brother Lee. Amy had needed my support as a child but had I really become a domineering older sister in adulthood?

'I'm helping Rick with his website again.'

Her eyes twinkled.

I looked at my watch. 'In fact, I'd better get going soon. Just one thing,' I said innocently as Benedikt joined us. 'You two men… would you mind popping up the house early this evening?'

'Why?' asked Benedikt.

Jonas's eyes narrowed. I held my nerve, making my voice sound as bored by the subject as possible.

'Rick wants everything to be perfect for when his grandmother next visits. The house is almost complete but the grand piano is a much-loved piece of furniture and has a problem – a vibration noise that wasn't there before. What with your family's experience with pianos, I thought you might be able to work out what the problem was.'

Benedikt shrugged. 'Happy to take a look but I'm only a piano *player*.'

'Great! And Jonas – there's a guitar. Rick hoped—' okay, bending the truth just a tiny bit '—you could give it the once-over? His family… they… they enjoy holding parties and musical evenings. It's important that the instruments are in tip-top condition.'

He folded his arms. Suddenly I became very interested in a tiny spider climbing over my hand.

'If either of you have anything on, or were going on Jackie's boat trip then, of course, don't worry, it can be done another time,' I said airily.

'I was only going to do my laundry and chill,' said Benedikt and drained his glass of water.

Jonas studied me for a while longer and then his shoulders relaxed. 'I suppose I could go. All I've got on is Helga teaching me chess. And I do miss strumming my guitar.'

Benedikt clapped him on the back. 'Great. Then you'll be able to play with me.'

'Thanks, guys,' I said and stood up. 'I'll find you both later.' I left the canteen. Footsteps sounded from behind and fingers curled around my arm. Desperately I tried to think of another good reason as to why the guitar needed attention. However, it was Amy.

'Let's walk,' she said. 'Your route to the house passes our cluster of shacks.'

'You don't mind me spending the afternoon with Rick, do you? After all you will be tied up with the tree boas – but not literally, I hope.'

'Of course not, but you can stop with the website charade – what's the real reason you're going over?'

'It's no charade, sis.'

Of course I'd be lying if I said I wasn't looking forward to seeing him. This morning, every time our paths crossed, we'd smiled at each other. He asked if I'd slept well. I told him about an especially beautiful butterfly I'd spotted by the showers. The usual conversation but somehow heightened by yesterday's physical contact between us that no one else knew about.

Up until today I'd thought secrets were bad, like when I'd discovered Dad had been dating Anabelle whilst Mum was dying or Amy used to borrow fake ID, in the sixth form, to get into clubs.

However, this secret felt good.

'He needs to bring in more business so I'm helping out.' And I needed to share with him the idea I'd had. I felt a burst of energy, inside, like I did back in England when I came up with a plan to improve Best Travel.

'But why you?'

'Remember that website design course I did? It was basic but—'

'Drat! I'd forgotten that. Guess that means your time with him is legit. I was hoping your relationship might have gone to the next level last night and you were just too shy to tell me. It was a big disappointment when you came back to our bunk beds.'

'Amy Sterling! This isn't Ibiza, you know! This is Seagrass Island, full of serious-minded people, wearing the most unsexy clothing, drinking mainly un-intoxicating water. The only romantic action here is between the birds and the bees.'

'I doubt that,' she said, laughing. Her face turned serious. 'But I'm glad you're having fun. That's all I wanted from this holiday.'

'And I'm glad you are too. It must be the perfect break for a veterinary nurse.'

Amy didn't say anything.

'You *are* loving it, aren't you?'

She looked up, from under her fringe. 'Is it bad of me to say it's going to make going back to Paws & Claws seem a little less appealing?'

I raised an eyebrow.

Her cheeks flushed. 'I... I always felt that I was kind of... well, lucky to be taken on there... as if they didn't know how, secretly, I wasn't up to the job. But helping Jackie, being hands-on with exotic creatures, feeling so at home talking to her and Rick about animal conservation... feeling like an equal, as if I am knowledgeable with skills to share... it's made me think that perhaps I'm capable of more than what I've been doing.' She swallowed. 'Does that make me sound delusional?'

I could have punched the air. For the first time, ever, could Amy be aware of her amazing potential? I mustered all my strength and managed not to squeal that I'd always told her that and she should have gone to university.

Because it looked as if my little Amy was working things out for herself.

My little Amy.

A lump rose in my throat.

Day by day, here, I watched her blossom like one of the beautiful Virgin Island flowers.

She wasn't little anymore. She wasn't mine. I'd known that for a while but couldn't deny that with the fresh eyes I'd been given, away from the hum drum.

I gave her a tight hug. 'No. It doesn't.' I took her by the shoulders. 'One thing Mum always used to say to us, "You can achieve anything you put your minds to." Do you remember?'

Amy nodded.

My fingers squeezed. 'She said that for a reason. Mum utterly believed in us. And I've always believed in you too.'

Amy gave a shy smile and we said our goodbyes.

I followed the path to the house feeling nervous at the prospect of meeting Rick – in a good way. There he was. Inside. On the sofa. Chatty on his shoulder. Thank goodness we had a chaperone, even if it was the furry kind. I didn't want to make a fool of myself. I knocked on the wooden door frame and went in.

Rick looked up, put Chatty down, next to him and came over.

'Thanks again for this, Sarah. You don't know how much it's appreciated.' He sounded jaded – a voice he never shared with the other volunteers. It felt special that he let me see that side of him. Rick reached out a tucked a loose strand of hair behind my ear. I wished he hadn't done that... yet was so glad that he had. He leant forward. So did I.

24

Rick fetched two milks mixed with Coca Cola. Forget an 'our tune', we had an 'our drink'. We sat on the sofa. He opened his laptop. Our shoulders brushed and again we kissed.

'That was… passable,' he said as we parted, eyes crinkling. I could have stared into them all day. They made me want to throw off the shackles of responsibility that had always tied me down. My skin flushed. My heart thumped against my chest as if telling me to wake up – as if it were rapping the following advice…

… this is what it should feel like when you're with a man. From the off you shouldn't be telling yourself to give it time or that all relationships need work. The chemistry should be there from the instant you meet – that first look, that first word, that first touch… you shouldn't be able to stop thinking about him any more easily than I should stop pumping blood…

'Yes. Very satisfactory,' I said and sipped my drink. I put it down and tightened my ponytail. 'I'm not sure Chatty would have been impressed though. If he could have seen he'd probably want to give you a few tips.' I took another mouthful.

He chuckled. I did too and my drink spluttered down my top. I wasn't bothered. I hadn't even smoothed down my hair before entering the house and after years of grooming it felt refreshing. They said the mirror didn't lie, but that wasn't true – depending on your mood it could make you stride like a catwalk model, or skulk, hiding your face under a hood. Reality came from the inside, not a sheet of mirror. Perhaps when I got back to England, I'd remove one or two of the mirrors around the flat.

Chatty hopped up and down excitedly before settling on my lap, leaning against my chest, his little face staring upwards even though he had no sight. I spoke to him for a few moments. Said how handsome he was. Scratched behind his ears. When I glanced up Rick was staring.

'I think I've got competition.'

Cue belly laughs again.

'Yes. Sorry. Unless you can learn to whistle out-of-tune, you stand no chance with him.'

Rick scribbled whilst I analysed each website page and how user-friendly it was; before I knew it the afternoon flew by.

'Your tips are amazing.' He consulted his notebook. 'It's obvious now – the amount of information on each page does need reducing, for clarity. I have to stop being afraid of white space. Plus there aren't nearly enough photos. I've been thinking about it since you first came up with the concept – I'll definitely incorporate an image of Chatty as the face of our brand. As for your idea of running a blog with all the latest news – I can't believe I never thought of that. Volunteers can guest post and keep former ones up to date with news of the new enclosures and benefits of the work they did. I could offer them a slight discount if they did.'

'That will build a community of people who have worked here in the past and keep them involved after they've left. You stand more of a chance, that way, of them continuing to talk about Seagrass Island with people they meet. In terms of advertising you can't beat word of mouth commendations. Customers at Best Travel often tell us they heard about us through a friend, business associate or relative. Perhaps you could reach out to influencers in the conservation space, inviting them to come out to the island. I'm sure that would pay dividends.'

Rick listened to every word.

'And don't forget what I said about the design being mobile phone friendly – your current model isn't quite. I can fix that. In fact, I can make all the changes I've suggested. It won't take long. Plus I'd suggest expanding, a little, on how exactly the money is spent. I understand, now, why staying here is so expensive but potential volunteers may not. I'd explain in more detail about how you hope your work will benefit other islands too.'

'Cheers, Sarah. I so appreciate all this.'

'I'm not totally selfless. Hopefully all this will mean I get to spend more time with Chatty.'

Rick yawned. Chatty heard, jumped over to him and slipped his paw into Rick's mouth. He pulled the monkey's hand away.

'Be careful what you wish for! It's a miracle that I'm still alive, what with all the germs Chatty must deposit on me each day doing his little tricks. Come on, little chap – let's go and see Jackie.'

'There is something, actually, I'd like to do that *is* selfless – and I need your help. Benedikt and Jonas – I'll go and get them now to take a look at your piano and guitar. I don't suppose… do you have a bottle of wine and any snacks?'

He shrugged. 'I've got beers. There's a family-sized packet of crisps. Malik comes over one evening a week and we need them to fuel compiling the weekly shopping list together – that's our excuse, anyway. Why?'

'I just thought the lads deserved a treat – seeing as they are doing you a favour.'

'Sarah. You just rubbed your nose. Don't you know, that's a classic giveaway for when someone's lying?' He pulled a comical face but his tone had sounded serious.

'Honesty's really important to you, isn't it? And of course it should be,' I added hastily.

Breaking eye contact, he stroked Chatty's dark back. 'Yes. I was let down once. Badly.'

Up and down his hand went. The monkey gave an appreciative squeak. Rick remained silent. I didn't like to pry.

'Just between us… I think they fancy each other. They just need a shove in the right direction.'

He looked up. 'Ah… I thought so! Now and then I've seen them stealing looks at each other and Benedikt doesn't seem to like you and Jonas getting friendly.'

'You've noticed too?'

'What else do they need? Candles, music…?' Rick smiled and pretended to play an air violin.

'No. With the piano and guitar they should be providing the latter themselves. Just some privacy, I guess. That's hard to find, amongst the shacks. And this house is a gorgeous setting.'

'No worries. We all need a hand in the romance department – unless you are totally enchanting, like me.'

'Don't kid yourself,' I said but nevertheless blushed.

Rick took my hand. His tone turned serious. 'This… this… whatever it is between us…'

'We don't need to label it, do we?'

'No.' He squeezed my fingers.

Thank goodness because I found the whole dating scene confusing. *Love Island* kept me reasonably up to date – along with Amy's input. There was casual dating, dating exclusively, officially being boyfriend and girlfriend… but it was best to keep this simple, especially as I'd been going home in three weeks.

'I just want you to know…' He cleared his throat. 'I'm not like some holiday rep who goes for a different woman out of every new bunch of arrivals. In fact, this is the first…'

'*Whatever it is,*' I chipped in helpfully.

'Yes. The first *whatever it is* with any volunteer. I like you Sarah. You've got guts. And family is important to you. I can tell by the way you've spoken about your late mum and it's obvious how much you care for Amy. It's like me. My brother, Lee, drives me to distraction but I'd be there for him, like a shot, if he had an emergency. And I've worked my guts out getting this house restored partly because I'll never forget the hurt on Gran's face, when she saw it crushed, and I'd do anything to make her happy. She's given my parents, Lee and me so much. I love her to bits.' He grinned. 'And there are other things about you I just can't ignore… such as coming to this conservation project with such a unique dress sense. You had me at that Audrey Hepburn hat.' He gave me a little push and went to stand up.

Before I could reply Chatty gave a series of impatient whistles and squeaks and bared his teeth against Rick's shirt. His dinner time was looming.

'Oh wait... I had another idea I wanted to run past you – about how you could raise more money to keep the island in your family. You see...'

But Rick was already on his feet. 'Can it wait? I bet it's great but...' He rolled his eyes. 'His lordship, here, is hungry.'

'It won't take long.' I clenched my hands together, adrenaline running through me. It was an ambitious project but could turn Seagrass Island around.

'Why rush?' he said. 'Time's a bit tight now. How about later? I really look forward to it.'

'Oh...' My face dropped. 'Okay...'

He glanced at me. Looked at his watch. 'Go on, then. I suppose I've got five minutes.'

I sat upright again, an adrenaline surge returning. 'I'll try to sum it up.' I shuffled to get more comfortable as he sat down again. 'I believe you should turn this place into a luxury getaway destination.'

Silence.

'You mean have *strangers* stay in our house?' he asked eventually.

'No.' I leant forwards. 'In the beach huts. Each can accommodate a couple. You could take individual bookings or small groups. This location is stunning. The beach wouldn't take long to tidy up. Malik could run weekly boat trips. Your family's chef could do the catering. Seagrass Conservation could still run and guests might like to visit the animal enclosures. That could be an added attraction.'

'That would mean never living in our home again.'

'You might not anyway, if you have to sell up. And actually, with this plan, not that much would change. You and your family would have your own bedrooms in the house and could cherry-pick guests. Plus once things are up and running you wouldn't need to rent out the huts all summer long. I've looked at luxury stays on other Virgin Islands. The amounts people are prepared to pay are astronomical and you'd soon be raking in thousands and—'

Rick held up his hand. 'Sarah. No. Loud guests upsetting the animals? Music at all hours? Litter? The whole thing would be an act of lunacy.'

I blinked several times. 'But Rick, this could be the answer to all your problems.'

'I'm sorry, Sarah. There's no point discussing it.' His face hardened as he stood up. 'I appreciate the thought you've put into this. It would probably suit anywhere else. But I've seen the damage tourists have done to the natural world.'

'It wouldn't be like that.'

'With all due respect, I think I know more about this subject than you.' He gave an exasperated sigh.

'Rick, it's just… I know about hotels and—'

'Let's not argue,' he said, voice tight. 'Bring Jonas and Benedikt up to the house at around six. I must Skype my gran, after finding Jackie to confirm that everything is in place for the sports day tomorrow. I'll see how that injured parrot is doing that your sister found and brought back.' His tone softened. 'Jackie's already said she'll be sorry to see her leave – she's become a real asset handling the animals if they need any medication.'

'Didn't she hold an iguana a couple of days ago?' I asked, going along with the game of forgetting we'd just had a disagreement.

'Yes. Jackie managed to get a syringe full of antibiotics into its mouth whilst your sister held it firmly, whispering to calm it and stroking the sides of its throat. They can get quite frantic under such situations but Jackie said Amy took it all in her stride. Right. See you later. And thanks again for your idea. I just don't think it would work.'

We both managed a smile, though I could tell we both forced them.

Dragging my feet, I headed back to the shacks. I told Amy what Jackie and Rick had said about her and the animals. Mum would have been so proud. She, too, had adored animals and plants. I imagined the chats they would have had and the trips to parks and zoos – whereas Mum and I would have gone shopping.

At five to six I found Benedikt and Jonas and we headed up to the house. Jonas teased me about being quiet for once. I muttered an excuse about feeling tired. When we got there, Rick rushed out, phone in his hand.

'Bit of an emergency. The ill iguana has taken a turn for the worse. I'm on my way there and am just dialling the vets... Could you do me a favour, Sarah? I've left my laptop in the beach hut nearest to the house, on the right. I thought my chat with Gran might overrun past six, so set myself up in there. Would you mind bringing it in? That way I'll remember to charge it overnight. Oh, and by the way, lads,' he called as he disappeared down the path. Us three went into the house. 'As a thanks for you looking at the instruments I've left out some beer and crisps. Take as long as you like. I've a feeling I'll be out most of the evening.'

He came back whilst Jonas and Benedikt eagerly went over to the drinks. I went outside again to meet him. His fingers brushed against my arm.

'Thanks again, Sarah… for all your help.'

'You really don't like the hotel idea?'

He pursed his lips.

'Okay. I know when I'm beaten,' I said.

'I… I'm really glad Amy swapped your holiday at the last minute. Your other thoughts, about the website, have been brilliant. It's ironic that, for someone not overly interested in conservation, your input might make a real difference.

I held his hand, feeling like a teenager, despite a note of wariness that had crept in, at the way he'd so quickly dismissed my hotel idea.

'Your boss is lucky to have you,' he said.

I cleared my throat, nodded and thanked Rick for the compliment, wishing I could tell him the truth. Instead I let him go, went into the house and crossed the living room.

'Have fun,' I said to Jonas and Benedikt and headed out the back. A noise attracted me to the beach hut on the right. I went over, walked onto its decking surround and climbed the wide staircase, swatting a fly out of my face. I pushed the door open after admiring a rust-coloured lizard clinging to the wood, above the door, as if it were a splat toy that had been thrown. A gust of cool air blew through the room. A door to my left was ajar and revealed the bathroom. I went to the right. The noise was a sharp voice coming from Rick's laptop, on top of a glass coffee table, in front of a wicker armchair.

'Rick? I can't hang on forever and we need to sort this out. I agree with Lee, it's now or never to make some big decisions and I won't be put off any longer.'

This didn't sound good. Perhaps I should let her know Rick had gone. I sat down, not sure what to do.

25

Tentatively I pulled up the screen. A tanned face stared back, distinct with its wrinkles and bright lipstick, and topped with a colourful turban. She looked rather like a fortune teller you might see at a fair. Large glasses with a leopard print frame jumped out at the screen. I envied her flamboyant dress sense.

'Um... hello... I'm a friend of Rick's... he's had to dash off.'

'Hello there, dear.' The voice lost its edge. 'I didn't catch everything he said.' She sighed. 'Oh, how very like Rick. And how annoying. Is he coming back soon?'

'I'm afraid not. One of the iguanas is ill. He must have thought you'd heard him say that.'

'I could recognise the style of a shoe by the sound of its heel on the pavement when I was younger.' She rolled her eyes. 'But whilst old age supposedly brings wisdom, it takes away your hearing and sight.' She fanned herself. 'What's the heat like, dear? It's been over thirty degrees here in London and great for topping up my tan.'

'Your climate is similar to here, then,' I said. 'Just without the mosquitoes and tarantulas.'

Her smile revealed perfect dentures. 'I'm Margot.' She

shuffled back comfortably into her seat, wearing a voluminous purple and green kaftan. 'Are you one of Rick's volunteers?'

His? That made it sound as if the conservation work wasn't a family project.

'I'm Sarah,' I said, still perched on the end of my seat, the tinkling of piano keys wafted towards me by the breeze. 'Yes. I've been here just over a week.'

'Are there many volunteers?' she asked. 'Rick said all the shacks were full and he was really pleased how things were going.'

'Um… yes,' I said in a high-pitched voice, sounding a bit like Chatty.

She studied me. Leant forwards. One painted eyebrow raised, her face filled the screen. 'Or is my grandson doing his usual and blurring the truth because he doesn't want to worry his old gran?'

'No… there are lots of keen volunteers about,' I said brightly.

'Is every shack full?'

'I haven't seen inside them all.'

'You say you're a friend of Rick's? If you are up at the house you must know each other quite well. I'm assuming he's told you about how… how it's proved to be quite a challenge, funding the rebuild of our home.' Margot slumped back into her chair, looking every one of her years for a second. She sipped a glass of water. Her voice broke. 'It's such a worry. Rick means well but these plans of his… what with the company struggling and unable to find any way out of…' She took another mouthful and sat more upright and readjusted her turban. 'Tell me about yourself. Where do you work back home?'

'In a hotel.'

She stared out of the screen for a moment. 'Your smooth skin suggests you cleanse well and usually wear makeup and though polish-free, your nails look strong and well looked-after. Your long hair – well, the end of your ponytail, draped forwards over one shoulder – hasn't a split end in sight, according to my glasses. I'm guessing you work on reception – or have done at some stage.'

'I'm impressed. Yes. Now I'm in management and looking to move upwards. I love Best Travel…'

'I sense a *but*.'

'But… it's not stretching me anymore.'

'Never spend one decade doing the same as the previous one – that's always been my motto. And have you got a five-year plan?' she asked.

'What? Um, no…'

'You should have. Draw one up tonight. Don't wait until you get back to England. And reassess at the end of each year how much progress you have made… Has your salary increased? Have you been given more responsibility? Set yourself targets and analyse why – if it's the case – you haven't met them.'

Oh.

This was new.

This felt nice.

Someone advising me on my career.

I'd never had that.

I had memories of Mum encouraging my hobbies and studies, but once she'd gone the only thing left was Dad's negativity and Anabelle doing her best but ending up pandering to his opinions.

I'd wanted to join to a meditation club, once, as a teenager, held at the local Buddhist centre. We'd had a talk about it at school. It sounded great for dealing with exam anxiety and a couple of my friends were going. One parent offered to take me each week. Anabelle was all for it and said she'd bring me and my friend back. My stepmum's favourite Instagram celebrities all practised it. But Dad immediately dismissed the idea. Said too much thinking was a bad thing – that people who gazed at their navels also couldn't see passed the end of their noses when it came to dealing with the real world. That life was stressful and I just needed to get on with it – like he'd had to. Anabelle tried to change his mind and mentioned the famous people who did it. He'd laughed in her face and she'd visibly shrunk into her cashmere jumper. I didn't mention it again.

'I was seventy-nine last month,' Margot continued, 'so I reckon it's time for a change and a new challenge – and Seagrass Island needs to change too. That's why I gave the go-ahead for Rick's conservation idea as I approached another decade. However…' She went to say something then closed her mouth. 'I'm sure you've got things to do, Sarah. Lovely talking to you. I'll catch my grandson tomorrow.'

The lines between her brows looked more due to stress than age.

'Goodbye, dear.' She went to stand up. 'It's a shame no one can magic up a way of solving my family's problems. I like to think I'm a good judge of character and you're an intelligent young woman. You haven't got an answer, have you?' There was a sad edge to her jokey tone as she got to her feet. 'Nice chatting to…' Her leant forward to the screen. Sat down. Peered at me. 'That look that just crossed your face.'

'What do you mean?'

'*Can* you see a way to make the island thrive?'

'No.' I forced a laugh. 'I don't know anything about conservation.'

'But you booked this stay on Seagrass Island.'

'Not really, you see my sister won—'

'Please. Don't hold back. If you've had the slightest spark of inspiration, I'd be so appreciative to hear it.'

'I just think the conservation project will falter if you don't somehow open it up to tourism as well. But then what do I know?' I added brightly.

Sharing my idea with Margot – wouldn't that be going behind Rick's back? He'd already quashed it and yet... I so desperately wanted to help. And I hadn't been given time to explain the detail to him. Perhaps I could tell his gran and then they could discuss it together. Maybe he'd listen to her.

My hands felt clammy as she adjusted her leopard print glasses.

'Carry on.'

'That's it, really.' I didn't know what to do for the best.

'Anything, Sarah. Really. Your tourism comment – you might be onto something.'

She looked so desperate. I took a deep breath. 'I work in a budget hotel but I want to make a step into the luxury side of hospitality. I've been researching that area of the industry for months.'

'I've been lucky enough to stay at some fantastic hotels over the years. My husband and I especially loved Ocean Allure in the South of France – a pink turreted villa surrounded by magnolia and lemon trees with a pool cut into rock, marbled floors and soundproofed walls.'

'Well, I've had an idea – about how your family could bring in more income,' I said, feeling awkward. 'I imagine it's a delicate subject but Rick did tell me a little about how—'

She held up her hand. 'You and I can speak as businessperson to businessperson, no?'

'Of course.' I sat a little taller. It felt good to be taken seriously – to be treated as an equal by such a successful entrepreneur as her.

'Then don't feel embarrassed – Crocker & Crowley *is* in trouble. Please. Share your thoughts. And thank you for spending your time on this.'

'The house and beach huts – your home is gorgeous. With the pool. Exotic surroundings. The table outside. Plus the cinema room. The gym. And piano.'

Talking of which, the music had stopped playing. Instead I heard laughter. Were Jonas and Benedikt drinking the beer? Were they getting closer?

'Yes. Family love staying there. We invite my sister's brood. My husband's relatives. My precious Caribbean paradise has nursed people through broken hearts, divorce and bereavements. Throughout the summer guests come and go. Evenings are the best, with fairy lights outside, rum cocktails flowing and card games under the stars. The youngsters enjoy a midnight swim. Malik sometimes mans the bar if we're having a party – I've made several friends in Tortola over the years.'

'How about… just until the shoe business gets back on its feet, or at least consolidates its position – Rick mentioned you'd decided to focus on trading from just four stores…'

She nodded.

I leant forward. What harm could it really do? With building enthusiasm, I told her all about my luxury hotel plan.

Margot didn't speak for a few moments. My pulse raced and I braced myself for rejection. A strained look contorted her friendly features and she took off her glasses and rubbed her eyes before slipping them back on.

'I'd completely understand if you didn't want to lose your privacy here,' I said. 'It's a real bolt hole from the strains of city life. And Rick's not keen. He's worried any tourists would impact on the island's nature.'

'But we have to be practical. And the build is almost complete…'

'You could trial the idea. If it didn't work out well, nothing lost. But if did… who knows about the future? You might build a few more beach huts. A venture like this could be good for the shoe company and Seagrass Conservation.'

'Yes… I can see that. Yet we are almost into the middle of July…'

For a moment I hardly listened. I swallowed. Stared at the screen.

Someone like Margot liked my idea?

'If I worked flat out this week, I could get a website up and running,' I gushed. 'You could offer a discounted rate to start – for guinea pig customers. You've got all the bedding. The beach huts are fully furnished. They have internet connection. Initial costs wouldn't be huge. Rick said the kitchen is almost finished.'

'But he's busy with his wildlife work. Lee and his parents are needed here in England. I'm not due to visit until

September. I could fly over earlier but these days I'm not completely confident I could manage all of—'

I took a deep breath. 'Let me help. I'll set it up. I've been itching to change direction for so long now. I'd be thrilled to be part of something like this… for the next three weeks until I go home, that is…'

'I couldn't ask you to…'

'Of course you could. Seriously. And I wouldn't need paying. If it got me out of cleaning the compost toilets, that's worth more than any fee.'

Margot smiled briefly.

'There is something special about Seagrass Island. It inspires such passion in Rick. If there's any way I can help boost his conservation project and protect the island's ecosystem… if there's any way I can help such a well-respected brand as Crocker & Crowley, well… I'm totally up for it.'

'How would we advertise?'

'I've already subscribed to a load of holiday magazines and websites for the research I've been doing, back home. I know exactly where to place ads. The ones online could go up quickly. It would all be a little haphazard for the rest of this season, but if things went reasonably well, you'd have the winter months to really pull the plan together.'

'Okay. Let me think about it. I can't get my head around the idea of strangers living there.'

'The conservation volunteers are already here. What's the difference? And… forgive me for saying this but—'

'Go on. Remember. This is business. I won't take it personally.'

A sense of worth infused my body. I used to enjoy that sensation when Amy was little and I could solve her problems.

'What choice have you got?' I said, firmly. 'You can't be precious about this. It's not as if Seagrass Island is your main home. Sometimes we all have to make decisions that are difficult in the short term but necessary for a shinier future.'

Life had taught me the right decisions often didn't bow to sentimentality.

'Have you set out this idea in writing?' she asked.

I nodded. Yes. It was in my nature. I'd already drawn up a plan on paper whilst brainstorming.

'Could you email it to Lee? Then he, myself and Rick can discuss it.'

Lee? Oh crap. What was Rick going to think about that?

'Of course, I mean, if you really think…'

She gave me the address and at her request I sent the file over straightaway.

'Thank you. Thank you. Thank you,' she said. 'This solution has great potential. Lately the family has suffered such difficult times… but I sense you know all about those, from personal experience.'

'Things… haven't been easy since my mum died.

'Has it been long?'

'I was eleven. Had just started high school. Amy, my younger sister, was seven.'

She gave an understanding nod.

'I soon realised I had to leave home as soon as I could and work towards providing a solid base for Amy. I was only eighteen. It meant leaving her behind, along with the precious memories of Mum in the house I grew up in.'

'It sounds as if you were very, very brave.'

My eyes pricked.

'Maybe I was brave – and that's what you need to be here.'

'Sarah!'

Rick. He was calling my name.

'Please excuse me for a minute – I think your grandson is back.'

I went outside and climbed down the steps. Rick stood by the pool – with Carlotta. She gave me a warm smile before placing her hand on Rick's arm and whispered something in his ear. He laughed.

A prick of something unpleasant pierced my chest. The whole scene reminded me of Dad and the way he'd been with other women. How that had made me determined never, ever again to seek approval from a man like him.

'Rick – your gran was still on your laptop when I found it. I've been chatting to her. She's waiting for you now.'

'That must have been quite a conversation, lasting this long,' he said and turned to Carlotta. 'How about we catch up tomorrow?' He winked at her.

Hadn't he said I was the only volunteer ever to make him feel anything? Yet I shouldn't assume. Rick probably had good reason for the flirtatious tone of his words.

Carlotta looked as if she were about to swoon. Humming, she disappeared into the house. Rick's phone pinged, he clicked on a notification. For some reason his face turned ugly and red. I hoped another animal wasn't ill. I waved goodbye to him and caught up with Carlotta. Benedikt and Jonas weren't to be seen. I looked at my watch. It was time to get back for dinner.

'Isn't Rick delectable?' said Carlotta. I thought how much more attractive her Italian accent must sound to Rick than my plain London tones. 'Fancy a jog back to camp?' she said and stretched.

'No thanks. It's too hot for me. I'll just walk.' She left the building and started running. No wonder she looked so lithe.

A loud, irritated voice caught my attention. I returned to the pool. Outside the beach hut, laptop closed and under his arm, Rick paced up and down.

26

'You've told Gran about your idea? And worse... gone behind my back and shared the idea with my brother? I just got an email from him enthusing about your plan. I told you... it's a non-starter.' Beads of perspiration glistened on his forehead. 'Gran's phone rang, so she had to go, but she wants to speak about it later.'

'Rick... don't be silly... I haven't deceived you! Margot sensed that I had an idea and—'

He snorted. '*Sensed?* You mean you took the opportunity to bombard her with your plans.'

'It wasn't like that. But you hadn't had time to hear the detail and she seemed desperate for a rescue plan. I'm so keen to help. I didn't see the harm. She asked me to email Lee. I thought three heads might be better than one.'

'You didn't trust my view?'

'I'm just trying to—'

'You've only been here five minutes! Whereas I've spent a couple of years thinking through the conservation venture. My gran and Lee know hardly anything about the work I do and how it needs time to grow. I just need another year to—'

'If I understand rightly, Margot doesn't feel you've got that long,' I said, quietly.

He flinched. 'But a hotel? Here? Guests who think nothing of throwing away drinks cans and disturbing turtle nests?'

'Guests who pay. Guests you could carefully select. It's all about advertising in the right places.'

Rick wiped his forehead with his arm. 'You aren't a conservationist – nor are Gran or Lee – so I wouldn't expect any of you to know all the risks from tourism, but the implications could be horrific. Small birds and reptiles might crawl into discarded plastic containers and glass jars, looking for food and getting stuck. The litter they might try to eat could be toxic and—'

'Just think about it for a second, Rick… there would be hardly any set-up costs. We aren't talking hundreds of guests. Ten at a time at the most.'

'And if it takes off the idea might expand. It will give my brother the perfect opportunity to try and take over. He'd bring the conservation work to an end. I can see it now – the shacks would be converted to more tourist accommodation. The animal enclosures into some kind of freak show. Lighting would go up. Parties held. The turtles wouldn't feel able to nest on our island. Birds would keep away from the noise. Litter would destroy wildlife and the careful balance needed to maintain their environment. He'd try to turn Chatty into some kind of entertainment.'

'Stop. You're not thinking straight. You're blowing this out of all proportion. There's no reason why—'

'You work in a hotel, Sarah. You didn't even want to stay at first. I don't think you're qualified to decide what is best for Seagrass Island.'

'This isn't just about your project though. It's about saving Crocker & Crowley. All I wanted to do was—'

'Avoid camp duties? A project like this would neatly fill your remaining three weeks, away from the dirt and heat and manual work, whilst filling my grandmother with false hope. She mentioned briefly how you'd offered to work on it full-time until you went home.' He sighed. 'I get it. Honestly, I do. You were tricked into coming here. If I was you, Sarah, I'd want to find a way out of all the physical work too, but…'

My hands locked into fists. 'You really think that's my motivation? That I'm only thinking about myself?'

Suddenly he looked even older than his gran. 'Why should you care about us?'

'You're right,' I said. 'Why indeed?' I strode through the house before marching out of the front door and out the other side.

Getting close to a man like Rick was always going to end badly.

It stopped right now.

What with Carlotta all over him.

The way women looked at him wherever he went, be that an airport or dance bar.

His laughing, teasing manner.

I sat down under a powder puff tree.

Oh Gary, yes, you're right, that's so funny.

Aren't you lucky to have Gary as your dad?

Isn't your dad handsome?

Oh Gary, you're such a tease – I know you didn't mean that insult.

Sorry Gary, I should have known better.

You're right, I can see now, it is my fault.

Whatever makes you happy, Gary – that's all I want.

I'd observed my dad's manipulation over the years. These days they called it gaslighting. Like a slow-working poison, he was toxic. Women never realised this until it was too late and they were totally hooked.

I couldn't help it, a passionate attraction made me vulnerable – made me feel as if I'd be opening myself to hurt.

I felt that right now: the pinch in my chest. It made me want to run back. To throw my arms around his neck and kiss the disagreement away. To apologise for getting involved.

That's why everything about strong sexual passion was so completely wrong.

It skewed reality.

I only had to look at him to find myself swept into a heady fantasy land.

I had only been trying to help. If anything, he owed *me* an apology. I shouldn't feel to blame.

This is what Dad did. *He'd* cause an argument but, somehow, it was always Mum who ended up saying sorry.

It always had to be about him. It was the same with Anabelle. I found no comfort in that. It would have been good if Mum's death made him reassess the way he treated women. But it didn't. He'd still flirt with the female neighbours – just like today when Rick had flirted with Carlotta.

Dad wasn't dark, like Rick, but had thick blond hair, wide shoulders and a strong face. He was tall. Clothes hung off him as if he were a model. Grey streaks made him look distinguished. As I got older, I noticed how women's eyes were drawn to him as he entered a room. How he relished the attention and used it to get what he wanted.

When I was younger, I'd sit on the stairs listening to dinner parties he'd persuaded Mum to hold. Even at that young age it struck me that I often heard him laughing and chatting with the female guests. Not with Mum. And any compliment would be directed at a stranger's dress or hairstyle – not hers.

Seeing Mum's love for my father, how she'd kiss him however mean he was, and then the same behaviour from Anabelle who often told him how lucky she was to be with a sought-after man like him, that gratitude – it frightened me. I didn't want to end up with someone like him.

I had to break free from Rick before things became more serious. For Mum's sake and what she'd made me promise on her death bed. I closed my eyes, unable to think of her passing. Instead I got up and brushed myself down. Pasted on a happy face. Forcing myself to hum, I walked back to camp. Amy couldn't stop talking about tomorrow's sports day.

'Guess what,' she said and grabbed my hand, swinging out arms as we walked towards the canteen. 'I helped Jackie organise the whole event and chose the teams. I've arranged it so that you and Rick are paired up for the three-legged race. Time's ticking if you're going to have a really memorable holiday romance!'

27

I sighed, sitting on my bed having returned from my early morning shower, rehearsing what I'd say to Amy. But it was no good. I couldn't spoil her dream holiday and leave because of my argument with Rick.

All night, in bed, I'd dissected the conversation I'd had with Margot. Her words rang in my ears about how the island was a paradise that healed relatives' broken hearts and that got me thinking about the type of client we could target…

I got up and stretched. I scraped my hair back into a ponytail. Yet what was the point of brainstorming?

'Klopf, klopf!' called a voice by the door. 'Hurry up. The amazing Sunday morning breakfast awaits. I've heard rumours that there are chocolate croissants this week – and my favourite spicy sausage.'

I pulled open the door. Climbed down the steps. Benedikt and Amy waved from ahead. They'd been for an early morning swim.

'You didn't fancy a dip in the sea?' I asked. Jonas shook his head. A big grin spread across his face. I pulled him up the ladder and onto my bed.

'Sarah, I'm flattered,' he protested, 'but really, you're not my type.'

'Idiot,' I said and tugged his arm so that he sat down next to me. 'Dish the gossip. Why do you look so happy and does it have anything to do with your Hamburger?'

'Maybe, it does, you Londoner,' he said airily.

I waited. Nothing.

'Jonas! Did you have a good time up at the house, last night? You'd gone by the time I came out of the beach hut. At least tell me if Benedikt found out what was wrong with the piano.'

'The vibration was caused by the wooden carving of the parrot on top. The base of that wasn't completely flat so it rocked every time a note was played.' He eyed me suspiciously. 'It's almost as if it was simply a silly excuse to get Benedikt and me up there, together.'

'I knew nothing about that parrot,' I protested.

'Anyway, Benedikt and I chatted. Do you know, he wasn't actually born in Hamburg but—'

'Did you kiss?'

His fingers traced his leather bracelet. A shy look crossed his face.

Success!

'Not that it's any of my business,' I said. 'Come on. I need that chocolate croissant if we're running around all day.'

'No. We didn't. But we talked. You were right. He's not interested in Amy, you or any woman. And we laughed – a lot. Eventually we headed over to the Games Room and taught each other card games. When we got back to the shack he hugged in a way that told me he might like me back.'

'Oh Jonas. I'm so happy for you.'

His eyes shone. 'I was beginning to give up hope that I'd ever meet a man to love – a man who might love me back.'

'It's amazing, really, isn't it, that any long-term relationship exists? What are the odds of meeting someone who feels the same, whom you can trust with your life, whom you respect, who is fun…' I squeezed his arm. 'You must be beginning to feel so… complete.'

'In a way that I never felt was possible,' he said hoarsely. 'It's very early days but is so great, after all this time, simply to feel I can just be me. I don't have to put on an act. Or question my feelings.'

I hugged him tight. Sure, I'd had problems finding the right partner but compared to Jonas… His stomach rumbled loudly.

He stood up. 'Come on. My sausage is calling.'

'You already have a pet name for him?'

'Sarah!'

We hurried over to the canteen and sat down at a table with Amy, Benedikt and Helga. Rick was in the corner with Chatty. As each day passed I'd become more fond of that little monkey. I knew exactly which spot to tickle on his head to stop his impatient squeaks as he relaxed with pure bliss. I loved his gentle, cheeky nature. How he played with Rick and me yet never scratched or bit. And nothing could ever look cuter than him tucking into a treat from Malik.

I didn't have much of an appetite until I smelt fried bacon. And eggs. The croissant melted in my mouth. As did the pancake and syrup. The steaming latte was divine. Comfort eating at its best. The morning hygge heat made me feel as if I were strapped against a comforting hot water bottle.

'I can't move,' declared Amy and her eyes twinkled. 'That was *almost* as good as the Sunday fry-ups you make me back home.'

'I'll need to enter a lot of races later on, to burn that lot off.'

'I can easily arrange that,' she said and winked.

When we finally felt like moving, Amy went with Jackie to the animal enclosures. Jonas stood by the food counter, telling Malik about his favourite sausage recipe with sauerkraut. Benedikt stood right beside him, his arm casually around Jonas's shoulder. I'd caught Helga watching the two of them, whilst we all ate, with the biggest smile I'd ever seen grace her face.

'The sports day will start in one hour, at eleven o'clock,' announced Rick as he stood up.

He didn't look at me. It hurt. Right in the middle of my chest.

'We'll meet on the beach. If things get a bit boisterous it's better to fall on the sand than hard ground.'

It felt odd having free time during the day. Normally we'd have just returned from a turtle trip, bird counting or trail clearing and would be heading to bed for a short nap before lunch and the afternoon's activity. Last weekend, when we'd gone into Tortola, I'd bought a handful of postcards. Maybe I'd go back to my shack and write them. Mrs Chips, my next-door neighbour, would be waiting for hers. I liked her almost as much as her surname. She'd become widowed five years ago and we often swapped news as we met, walking into our block of flats. This last year I'd helped her with cleaning and shopping after a fall she had, followed by a bad cold – or just to talk. In return she baked me the most amazing cakes.

I didn't have many people to write to. The only things of importance to me, back in England, were inhuman ones like Nelly, my career and my flat.

I had no partner.

No mum or dad.

Dad didn't count. He'd alienated his relatives over the years, making it clear he thought he was better than them. Even his own parents.

Same with Mum's. He'd isolated her. I could see that as I became older. He did the same with Anabelle. I caught her crying, one day.

'Cherish your younger sister, Sarah,' she'd said. 'I really miss mine.'

'But she only lives in Nottingham, doesn't she? That's not the other side of the world.'

She'd dabbed her eyes. 'Your dad says it's too far. He works so hard to provide for us he needs the weekend to relax. And, he's right, of course,' she'd added in a shaky voice. 'We should all be grateful to him for the comfortable life we have.'

'Well, I'm never letting a man get in between me and Amy,' I'd declared hotly.

'I hope not,' she'd said in a low voice, even though he wasn't in the house. 'Although... it's not always as easy as that; not when you fall in love.'

I'd grimaced and hadn't understood at the time. But as I got older, I learnt more about domestic abuse. Anabelle's bruises were emotional ones. Ones I'd never have seen as a child.

Amy and I hadn't got to know aunts and uncles. I'd never seen my cousins. If I owned an island like this one, I didn't know who I'd invite over to stay. And there was nothing wrong with that, I told myself briskly and stood up. Relying on other people was dangerous. It was much better to be completely independent. My chair scraped the basic tiled floor. Jonas had cleared the plates. I squinted as I headed out into the sunshine. I needed to clear my head.

First, I'd take a stroll along the beach. My cap was on. I'd applied sun cream first thing – I'd taken on a new morning regime that was far simpler than cosmetic one back in England. The bites and blisters still annoyed me but I'd slowly acclimatised to the heat. Without realising it the camp was becoming a home, just like the basic bed and breakfast had when I first moved out. Perhaps that's why the human species had survived so well. It was good at adapting.

I smiled and listened to myself coming over all biological since living on Seagrass Island. I arrived at the beach and pulled off my trainers and socks. I left them in a pile and headed to the water's edge, bent down and rolled up my trousers. Gentle waves welcomed my toes, like old friends. I whistled a tune, determined to shake off any negativity. A squeak joined in. I turned around and looked up to see Rick and Chatty.

I whistled 'Daydream Believer', ignoring Rick's gaze. He crouched as I reached up to Chatty who crossed onto me.

'He recognises that tune of yours better than any voice,'

said Rick. 'It normally takes him longer to take to a new person. His tail wrapped around your neck is the ultimate accolade. He doesn't even do that with Jackie.'

Its furriness tickled the skin below my ears. With one arm raised so that I could scratch the monkey's head, I turned back to the horizon. In the distance, yachts skimmed the water's surface. Further along, to the right, shouts and screams led me to notice Carlotta and her friends played ball in the sea. She spotted Rick and strode out of the ocean in a white bikini, like Ursula Andress in that Bond movie. All that was missing was a knife strapped to her bottoms. She ran up to Rick and on tiptoe put a hand on his shoulder.

'Is it still okay to come around to yours later, bello?'

Bello?

'Sure thing.'

She grinned at me before running off.

'Carlotta... her and me... it's...'

'None of my business,' I said.

Rick moved forwards and stood by my side. His fingers intertwined with mine. For a moment I forgot myself and squeezed his back. Then I stepped away and glared.

'No. I'm sorry. After saying I'm ignorant about the needs here and only out for myself? Believing that I went purposefully behind your back? All of this...' I batted the air between our hands. 'I don't think so.' Gently I unwound Chatty's tail, lifted him down, kissed him on the head and placed him back on Rick's shoulder, even though he stretched out his little furry arms to come back. 'You and me... whatever it was... it's over now. I've helped you with your website. Passed on my luxury hotel proposal to you and your family. I'm done. You can easily find another manager if my idea does go ahead. Let's leave it at that.'

I ran across the sand as fast as I could, as if the sports day had already started.

28

Amy tied my left leg tightly to Rick's right whilst Jackie stood to one side with her whistle. Across the beach ten couples were lined up. Others stood at the sides to cheer us on, having already had their go in a previous round. Jonas and Benedikt were together and neither had looked so happy since they'd arrived. On the other side of them were their Scottish roommates Alistair and Greg who'd be leaving at the end of this week. Helga had teamed up with Carlotta who'd been standing close to Rick until the pairings were announced. Her chin had practically touched the sand when she'd discovered she wasn't to be his partner.

Out of necessity Rick and I had an arm around each other's waists. I'd managed to avoid him during the event so far. The tug of war had been easy, with the staff – permanent volunteers, Rick, Jackie and Malik – playing against a team made up from the rest of us. I hadn't taken part in the one hundred metres dash. Nor had Rick. Jackie whispered that it was because he always won and felt bad about that.

Why did he have to have such attractive qualities? I knew from crushes on famous people that if someone had an ugly personality their hotness soon diminished. Like the soap star with entrancing green eyes and a snappy dress sense.

He'd been caught stealing from a charity he supported and instantly loss his gloss.

Rick's allure simply increased the more I saw him interact with any living thing. He even gave up his banana for the fruit and spoon race, knowing it would be one of the easiest fruits to balance because of its shape and less smooth texture. He persuaded one of the shyer volunteers, Dario from Spain, to swap with him – told some story about the smell of bananas making him gag. Dario had been given a round, shiny passion fruit that would have easily toppled off. Sure enough, a beaming Dario came first.

We'd had a clothes relay and sack race after one Amy secretly called the starfruit snog. It involved dividing everyone into six big teams. They lined up and then had to pass a starfruit between their necks to win, without using hands. If anyone dropped it on the ground the team had to start again. There was a real knack to pinning the fruit to your chest, with your neck, whilst turning around from one team member to the next. The fruit's ridged sides helped. Unsurprisingly Amy positioned me not only in the same team, but right next to Rick – even though he'd offered to stand in for Amy several times and let her take part. However, Jackie had insisted Amy had fantastic organisational and leadership skills and was key to the sports day's success. So we'd got up close. I'd smelt his subtle aftershave. Briefly our skin had touched and I'd tried to ignore the flare of heat in my stomach.

Compared to that, the last race didn't seem so bad.

'Everyone ready?' called Jackie.

I stared straight ahead.

'Shall we start with our outside foot?' Rick asked.

'Sure,' I said politely.

I didn't like falling out with anyone. I hated sounding anything like my dad. That's how he'd sulk with Amy and me, and with his wives – after issuing blatant insults in a matter of fact way, as if there was no doubt his opinion was right, the passive aggressive tone would kick in. He'd be super polite and distant, bearing an unjustified aura of disappointment. This could go on for days. As a result, Anabelle would become more subservient by the hour, cooking his favourite meal, wearing more makeup and even smarter clothes than usual.

It would make me feel sick - and when the ice finally broke and she gratefully fawned over him.

'Three... two... one...' Jackie blew her whistle.

I moved forward with my outside leg. Slowly we got into a rhythm and built up pace. The couple on our right shrieked as they tumbled to the ground. I lost my balance halfway along and almost fell but Rick pulled me up. Then he tripped and I righted him. I started counting out loud so that we knew on which beat to move the next leg.

'Go, Sarah!' shouted Amy.

Suddenly I wanted to win. I couldn't be the most knowledgeable conservationist here, or the bravest. Tarantulas still sent shivers down my spine. And Rick clearly thought my hotel proposal was ignorant. But the three-legged race, this small triumph – maybe I could do this.

I counted louder and built up speed. My chest heaved, my pulse raced, my ponytail flicked sharply from side to side. We overtook two couples and I spotted Jackie at the finishing line. The sand felt uneven beneath my feet and we had to steer around a piece of driftwood.

'Almost there, Sarah, you're doing brill!' hollered Amy.

Sure of victory, I pushed forwards even more, spurred on by my little sister. It reminded me of when, about a year after Mum died, I started baking. Anabelle had moved in with us and was always on a diet. Yet she never forced me and Amy to eat more healthily. In fact, she'd send me sympathetic looks when Dad made one of his unkind comments. I saw an old photo of her once. I'd been snooping through her things when she first moved in and found an old album. Anabelle had caught me. Yet she didn't get angry and let me flick through until I came to some photos of her at high school, with curves and fuller cheeks. She looked great. But at that point she'd taken the album away.

Anyway, her calorie counting meant it was down to me to re-create the comforting snacks Mum had provided. Amy would always be the first to taste my offerings and insist on second helpings, even when I shredded the carrot too thickly and it stayed crunchy in the carrot cake, and when my peppermint biscuits turned out so strong they tasted of mouthwash.

She cheered me again and I ended up running faster than Rick. In the excitement I'd stopped counting.

'Hold up, Sarah,' he said. 'We're no longer in sync.'

You said it, I almost replied. 'Try to keep up.'

Rick and I were neck and neck with another couple. We only had a few metres to go. I leant forward, hoping that would help and… Oh no! The front of my toes caught a clump of dried up seaweed and I shot forward. Due to the speed I pulled Rick with me. We both hurtled downwards. His chin ended up in my stomach.

'Get off!' I hissed.

He sat up. We looked at each other, his hair spikier than ever. We both spat out sand. The other couple flew past us to the finishing line. Rick reached forward and pulled something from my hair – a vibrant clump of lime green seaweed. Trying to catch my breath, I smoothed down my ponytail. Rick caught my eye, paused and then placed the seaweed on his head. Seawater dripped down his face.

'That's a vast improvement,' I muttered.

Amy came over. 'Oh, what bad luck! You two almost won.'

She helped me up. Carlotta helped up Rick and, laughing, she took off the seaweed. I couldn't help bristling at the easy manner between them. We untied our legs and strolled over to water's edge, whilst everyone else congratulated Amy and Jackie on a brilliant day and headed off to the canteen for cold drinks. I told Amy I'd catch her up. Rick and I started to walk.

'Sarah, about...'

I waited for it – for what Dad would have said. How a superficial charm would explain to me how the argument about the hotel had been my fault; how he'd forgive me, just this once.

We came to a fallen tree trunk and sat down, facing out to sea.

He turned to me. 'Sorry.'

My brow knotted.

'For being an absolute idiot. I should never have spoken to you like that yesterday. You were only trying to help. I guess I'm over-sensitive. This conservation project is so close to my heart.'

My fingers uncurled. 'All right. It's your family. Your business. Let's just forget it,' I said warily.

Wow. He seemed to mean it.

'But it's not all right. I accused you of being selfish – you who have helped me so much. If I'm honest, my brother, the way he likes to take over… well, you emailing him was my worst nightmare. Although you weren't to know that,' he added hastily.

'And if *I'm* honest, the way you dismissed my plan… it hit a nerve too. Dad used to do that – and my boss at Best Travel.'

We looked at each other. Waves broke on the sand. I mirrored the understanding that flowed into his face.

'I do hugely admire your passion for Seagrass Island and the wonderful wildlife here.'

He sighed. 'But perhaps that blinds me. It all seems kind of hopeless sometimes. The iguana died. That put me on edge as well.'

'Oh Rick – I'm so sorry. I didn't know that. But look… I'm not the enemy – and nor is this hotel idea. I honestly believe both projects could be run side by side. Things can't go on as they are. Action needs to be taken now,' I added softly.

He hesitated before taking my hand. He raised it to his mouth. Reluctantly I took it away.

'I've no bad feelings towards you – quite the opposite. But last night, it did make me think. I'm only here for three weeks. Perhaps it's better to stop things now. We're both too old for a holiday romance.'

And I'm too old to get hurt, especially by someone like Rick, someone who I actually really like.

They didn't feel safe, the feelings I had for him. Already I was falling, falling for those earnest eyes; for the drive; for the man who could make everyone laugh and who has won the complete trust of a vulnerable monkey he loved.

He'd apologised, but what if that was a one-off? Anabelle mumbled something once after a disagreement with Dad.

'He wasn't like this before we got married. It's all about him now. Planet Gary.'

Rick stared into my eyes. His shoulders drooped very slightly. 'Whatever you want.'

We stood up and his phone rang. I moved away to give him privacy but the sea breeze soon blew an angry tone over.

'This is totally unacceptable, Lee,' I heard Rick say eventually. 'We haven't even agreed on... no, it doesn't save me any work. Hey! Don't cut me off.'

Cue an eerie silence filled only by the cry of seagulls. Rick marched over.

'A mate of Lee's has been let down at the last minute. He and five friends had booked a fancy hotel in Jamaica, for five nights, but it suffered a fire last week. So Lee's offered them the beach huts. Explained to them that they'd be our guinea pig guests and therefore gave them a really cheap rate. He reckons he's saved me the bother of finding our first customers.'

'How could he do that – you haven't set your prices? In fact, you and Margot haven't even agreed this hotel idea is actually going ahead.'

'I know. The whole thing is crazy. Gran won't be pleased that he's organised this without consulting her. Lee doesn't even know this guy well anymore. They met at university and he saw about the cancelled booking on his Facebook page and contacted him – Jason, he's called. Honestly...' He exhaled. 'When we were kids, I worshipped him. Lee was my cool older brother. I'd try to wear clothes like his and would sneak a squirt of his aftershave...'

I smiled. Amy had been the same. I went through a phase of defiantly wearing Goth-like thick black eye liner to annoy my dad. Amy drew black felt tip around her eyes. It took a couple of days to wash off properly.

'... but these days he's just bossy. Interfering. Superior.' His neck flushed. 'Sorry. I probably sound as if I'm still at primary school. You and Amy seem to get on so well.'

'It's hard not to want to help her,' I said, the words sticking in my throat that I was probably a lot like Lee. 'I care about her. Deeply. Maybe that comes across as interference. I'm sure part of your brother's motivation is the same – it's because he loves you. Not because he assumes you'll fail.'

Rick tilted his head slightly.

'He looked out for you when you were younger as well?'

'Yes. The older boy next door punched me once. I was at junior school. He was at high school with Lee. He said I'd looked at him in the wrong way. My brother went mad. I don't know what he said or did but that boy never bothered me again. And I had a car accident when I was eleven. Almost didn't make it. Lee visited me every day in hospital after school, missing his favourite clubs and getting into trouble for not doing homework. I remember his red eyes. I was asleep one day and heard him whisper that he loved me. After that he was a like a shadow when I went out – like a bodyguard, looking out for me more than ever.'

'He probably doesn't want to see you hurt in any way again – trauma like that can be hard to shake off.'

'You sound as if you speak from experience.'

'Our... messy childhood is a long time ago, but when I look at Amy, often I still see that young girl who used to get hurt. Perhaps Lee still thinks about the time he almost lost you and pictures his younger brother in that hospital bed, recalling the sense of helplessness he must have felt.'

I'd never forget seeing Mum in hospital at the end. How I sat, holding her hand. Dad wouldn't let me stay long. He was more clinical than the doctors. I'd studied her petite, slim fingers. The ruby ring that had belonged to her mum. The immaculate nails – I'd never seen them chipped before. The small wrists. She'd longed to get a bracelet tattoo with meaningful charms attached. A cake because she loved baking. A bird due to her love of wildlife. A book because I loved reading. Amy wanted her to get a cat or a dog to represent her. But Dad had scorned the idea and declared she must have been going through an early midlife crisis. I wasn't sure what that was, at the time, but reckoned he must have been wrong. I thought the tattoo idea was all about Mum's love for things and people and sounded ace.

I understood Lee. I'd always done whatever I could do protect Amy. It has become an ingrained habit.

I stared at Rick, each of us in an opposite position – older sibling, younger sibling... either way it was complicated.

'But inviting people over for almost a week to a hotel that hasn't even been set up yet?' Rick grimaced. 'They've managed to get their flights refunded. Lee's got a friend in the travel industry and she found them last minute cheap ones to Tortola. Lee said I was making a fuss over nothing and needed to pull my head out of the sand; that they'd be the perfect guests to test our hospitality skills on, that it would easier for me and that five nights wasn't long.'

'Hospitality skills? What even are they without a firm team in place to change beds, make meals, to take them out on excursions and…?'

'And guess what?' Rick ran an arm across his brow. 'They arrive this Thursday. That gives me just three days to prepare.'

29

'Sarah, wake up.'

The words sounded muffled. I opened my eyes and sat up, focusing on uniformly coloured turquoise waves. Rick's pool did look inviting. I lay on a wooden beach bed. A lap top snoozed on the floor next to me. I gazed across to the other bed. Rick was stretched out there, head propped up on one hand, stubble beard thicker than usual, shirt ruffled, eyes half-open.

'I can't believe we fell asleep out here,' he said. 'Brandon and Nia just woke me up.'

They were a married couple who worked for the Crowley family before the hurricane. She cooked and maintained the gardens. Brandon did the housekeeping duties and tended the pool.

'They've been brilliant this week, helping you get this place ready for guests.' With a yawn I adjusted the bed so that I could sit up.

'We were sorry to see them leave after the storm but they promised they'd come back when the building work was done and have been working in a hotel on Tortola in the meantime. Lucky for us they weren't happy there and didn't have to give notice to leave.'

'Don't they mind the extra hours this hospitality venture is going to involve?'

Rick and I had been too busy for chit-chat this week. Both of us had barely slept. Troubleshooting. Cleaning. Panicking. Telling ourselves it was all for the greater good. Jackie managing the conservation volunteers, which was where Rick would much rather have been.

'No. They haven't got children and they lived here anyway, with Gran. The gardens need tending all year round and she has a lot of guests – mostly family members but they still need food and beds changing. They just see it as one job – whatever is involved doesn't seem to bother them.'

'Brandon's done well, emptying the pool, cleaning and refilling it.'

'Yes, and I couldn't have got the kitchen ship-shape without the two of them, him fitting all the appliances and Nia giving the walls a lick of paint. It's a bit makeshift but will have to do until these guests have left.'

I yawned again. It was Thursday morning. I couldn't believe Lee's friends would be arriving in… I gazed at my watch. Eight o'clock. Their plane landed at Beef Island airport in nine hours.

'Talking of people being brilliant…' Rick sat up too and reached out his hand. I slipped my fingers into his, ignoring the electric buzz.

I'd seen a programme, once, about falling in love. The high people felt during those initial months of a love affair was because the brain released chemicals similar to morphine. You soon became addicted. It was nature's way of guaranteeing our species formed relationships. The pain of a broken heart was a real biological thing caused by the withdrawal of those chemicals once a romance ended. It was finally my turn to experience it.

To help cover his absence Jackie had given Amy responsibilities like supervising the animal feeding. My sister couldn't have been happier. The long-term volunteers were able to look after the new arrivals. Only a couple had trickled in on Monday. A larger number would be arriving next weekend, coinciding with a group leaving so the overall head count wouldn't change much.

'You know me,' I said. 'I'll do anything to avoid the dreaded trail clearing and—'

'Don't do that. Don't put yourself down. You've been magnificent.'

Out of nowhere a sob rose up my throat. For that single moment he couldn't have been less like Dad whose ego had relished the low self-esteem of anyone around him, family included.

'Not only have you helped give the beach huts a spring clean and changed all the sheets, you've worked into the night on the website. Creating an online platform for this... that's massive. You've researched activities on Tortola and talked to Malik about him taking the group on a shopping trip and boat tour, plus dropping them off for a dolphin-sightseeing trip – don't think I haven't noticed.'

I'd also been working on an idea, in private, for the longer term – a way to make Seagrass Island even more appealing. However, I wasn't sure what Rick would think.

I withdrew my hand and brushed hair out of my face. 'It's not just me. Jonas and Benedikt led that team of volunteers to clear up the beach where the boats come in. There's not a scrap of seaweed on the sand now. And Malik bought those sunbeds at cost price from that friend of his who supplies hotels. I love Nia's idea to provide a beach waiter service. You tell me she's great at making rum cocktails?'

'Second to none.' Rick stood up. 'Did you just deflect a compliment?'

'Might have. But let's see how good you are at accepting one because I've been truly impressed. I know your heart isn't in this scheme. But you've put your opinion to one side – for the moment anyway – and totally invested in getting ready for these guests.'

'Come on. Brandon's making us his famous fried chicken and waffles,' he said gruffly.

'For breakfast?' His cheeks had flushed. That was enough to tell me he'd taken on board the compliment.

'You complaining?'

'Nope. I might just have to come on holiday here myself.'

'Don't wait for me. I'm just going to see Jackie for a moment.' Deep lines formed in his forehead. 'To check that—'

'No. You must eat. Jackie will be fine. She's the expert on animals and Amy is helping. Even you aren't indispensable,' I said, remembering what Amy had said to me when I'd worried about coming away.

In silence we entered the house and I stretched my back before we collapsed onto the sofa. Brandon brought out two plates on trays.

'At least the cinema room is ready, if we happen to have a bad night's weather,' said Rick in between mouthfuls of crunchy chicken and the lightest of waffles. 'They can download movies and watch in luxury.'

'There's the gym for early birds and if the guests have an

empty afternoon I wondered if Nia might be prepared to a cocktail-making session. Or a cookery lesson and teach guests how to make an authentic Virgin Island dish? It needn't be complicated and could be something they could eat in the evening, so it wouldn't cost you any extra money. If it was a success you could add that activity onto the website. The cooking ties into another idea I've had.'

Rick shook his head.

My spirits sank. 'Of course, you may think that wouldn't appeal and Nia—'

'Sarah – you're a superstar. I love it and will ask Nia as soon as she has a free moment. No, I was shaking my head in amazement. You must drink from a secret fountain of inspiration.'

Reenergised by his positive attitude and the comforting food, I got up and followed him outside again. We sat down on our respective benches.

'How do you come up with all these things?'

'At some point in the future—' right now, in fact, but for Amy's sake I'd keep that to myself '—I aspire to move into the luxury side of the hospitality industry. I've spent many hours surfing the websites of high-end hotels across the world.'

'How is our website coming along? I mean the bones of it – I don't expect you to have—'

'I put the finishing touches to it last night. Obviously this is a temporary site that will need refining if this business takes off… do you want to take a look?' I added, cautiously and picked up the laptop.

Rick shuffled up nearer to me. A dragonfly hovered in front of us. I admired the iridescent body and fragile-looking wings. I flipped open the laptop and pressed the power button. Moments later Rick was studying my design. It reminded me of Mum and my first weeks at High School before she died. She always took enormous interest in my homework, never doing it for me but pointing out areas where 'I might want to look at that again'. She'd ask questions about my lessons and knew all my teachers' names – and their nicknames.

At first, I was going to edge the pages of the website with green and turquoise, to give it a fresh, island feel. However, that would have made it more like the Seagrass Conservation website, instead of a look that shouted luxury. Therefore, I'd used a colour in between beige and mustard that provided a sumptuous gold theme. The background was white. Each page was headed with a shot of the front of the house, which had powder puff trees either side. Yesterday I'd taken photos for the gallery including several of Chatty on Rick's shoulder, plus the animal enclosures, getting beautiful shots of Wink, the snakes and seabirds. Since Monday I'd photographed meals Malik or Nia had made – apart from the fish soup – and, importantly, the beach huts inside and out, plus the pool.

Rick gasped. 'I have no idea how you put this together in a matter of days – even the reservations page.'

'That was tricky. The last time I looked at my watch, last night, it was 3 a.m. I messaged a friend from the web design course I went on. We've kept in touch on social media. Fortunately, thanks to the time difference, she was up, back in England, and more than happy to help me out.' I rubbed my eyes. 'In fact, she took a quick look at the whole website and on the back of that I improved several elements. The bookings process is basic at the moment but that can be altered in time.'

'It's bloody fantastic, that's what it is.'

'Once search engines pick up the site you'll be in business, so to speak. I've connected with Margot on LinkedIn. I hope you don't mind. I messaged her before falling asleep and sent her the link to take a look.'

'And Lee?'

'I… thought I'd leave that email to you and your gran.'

'Don't feel you can't contact him. I can't be an arse over this venture anymore. Like it or not guests are imminent, so it makes sense to keep him in the loop.'

I gave a thumbs-up.

'Gran will certainly want to be involved at every level.' He paused. 'I'm just a little worried about the evenings. We can run trips into Tortola, but it isn't as if we have bars here or—'

'Rick – that's the point. The island's remoteness, that's its selling point. That doesn't mean it's dull here, more that it's exclusive, away from the general public.'

'We'll still need to occupy visitors after dinner. However, this week I'm going to need that time to catch up with Jackie, paperwork and be at the Games Room. I can't abandon the volunteers completely, they've spent good money to be here. I've also got to have an in depth talk with Lee and Gran about exact pricing.'

'Why don't we Skype her this afternoon before going to the airport? Then she can discuss our views with your brother. This Jason has paid an all-inclusive price, hasn't he, for everything that takes place on the island, so we'll just charge for excursions, and he and his friends will pay for their own entertainment on Tortola. That might be the way to proceed.'

'Yes, that could work.' He sighed. 'Then there's Chatty... I've missed the little chap these last few days. I haven't spent nearly as much time with him – and I bet he's missing you.'

I smiled at the thought of his cheeky blond face. Eyes were so important for connecting with people – and even my cat Nelly. But I still felt close to blind Chatty through his whistles and squeaks, through his expressions and playful actions. 'How about I sit with Lee's friend and his party? I'm used to schmoozing clients at the hotel. I can help Nia serve the food and drink. It's only for a few nights.'

'I... I can't thank you enough,' he said and put his empty plate on the side table.

'What about Jonas and Benedikt? They could play the guitar and piano together. And Jonas is really ace on the harmonica.' This would be the perfect opportunity for them to spend time sharing their love of music. I really had to see Jonas and catch up on any gossip! 'I'll pop into the canteen at lunchtime to ask them. They might want to come over this afternoon to practise.'

'More beer and crisps required I suppose.' He grinned.

'So there are six guests – are they made up of couples?'

'Presumably,' said Rick. 'My brother is going to text me their names and exact flight details this morning.' He frowned. 'You said a few moments ago that Nia teaching guests to cook tied into another idea you'd had.'

I closed the laptop, put it back on the ground and turned to face Rick. This might be difficult but profits were profits and he had to start bringing them in.

'It's purely from a business point of view. We could run

it past Margot this afternoon. There's a chance you may not like it as it's not wholly authentic. It will mean some last-minute tweaks to the website and a sign making, plus gardening work and...' I swallowed, anxious yet excited about explaining more.

'I'm all ears.'

'People, men and women, the world over... everyone loves chocolate. I felt a real buzz when I saw the cacao trees on the turtle trip. You've practically got a whole orchard of them. Can't you see? It's a USP – a unique selling point – for Seagrass Island. You and your family haven't ever given this house a name, have you?'

He looked puzzled. 'No.'

'I think you should call it Cacao House. Get a sign made. We need to dig up a few cacao trees and replant them in the front, perhaps replacing some of the powder puff ones. Then I'll re-take the photo that tops each page on the website.' I was rambling now. 'I've looked it up online – I believe, on a very small scale, you could produce your own brand of chocolate just for the family and visitors. The pods are ready for harvest and they mature several times a year. Think how much that would appeal to guests – to make their own bars? You could cordon off the trees and turn that area into an orchard, so that it doesn't overrun the indigenous species – I know that was a concern of yours.'

'Chocolate? *Cacao House*? But this is our home. That name doesn't mean anything to us.'

'No, but... whatever it takes, right?'

Reluctantly, he nodded.

'Cacao isn't a common word back home – I'd mention on the website that it's pronounced Ka-Cow. There must be a sign-maker on Tortola who could fix you up with one and perhaps illustrate it with, say, a bean pod.'

He rubbed the stubble on his chin that was looking more like a beard after not having time to shave for a few days. 'It sounds complicated.'

'It wouldn't have to be ready – obviously – for this week's impromptu guests. But I can't see it taking long to set up. Visitors could pick their own beans – that's another activity open to us, a trek over to the orchard.'

'Chocolate-making?' He shook his head. 'What about equipment?'

I raised the palm of my hand. 'Hold on.' I got YouTube up on the screen and found the clip I'd watched yesterday. Rick studied it until the end.

'We'd probably need a proofer,' he said. 'And a sous vide. We've already got a coffee grinder.'

'Yes, I checked with Nia. I reckon, tops, it means investing a few hundred pounds – which, in the bigger picture, isn't that much for the traction I think this will give us when it comes to bookings.' I was smiling and talking at the same time. It ached! 'It will be a steep learning experience, no doubt about it, and it may not work – guests making chocolate out the pods they've actually picked – due to the fermentation process in the proofer taking around five days to get the slime off the beans. But we can have a stock all ready for roasting and grinding.'

'Cacao House. I think we should go for it.' Rick looked sideways at me. 'By the sounds of it your talents are wasted in Best Travel. How much longer will you stay there?'

'Who knows?' I said, brightly. 'It pays the bills. There's no rush for me to take my career in a different direction.

With a mortgage to pay I'd need to think very carefully about change.'

I'd eat plain toast for a year if I had to, to have a job where my input was valued. But I had to keep that to myself for now.

Rick got to his feet, extended a hand and pulled me up. His phone made a vibration noise and he took it out of his pocket and read a text.

His brow tightened and he angrily swiped the message away. 'Chocolate-making, cookery lessons… we certainly won't have to worry about those for the next few days…' His nostrils flared as he retrieved the text and turned the phone's screen to me.

Rick. Think I forgot to mention. My mate, Jason… This trip is his stag party. Make sure you've got plenty of booze in. I've done a bit of research. There are a couple of strip clubs on Tortola. If Jason's Facebook page is anything to go by that might be their sort of thing. We're probably talking extreme sports. Pub crawls. I trust you'll get it sorted. Should be fun! Cheers. Lee

30

A stag party? In an exhausted daze I went back to camp. Strip clubs and pub crawls? You couldn't get further away from what Seagrass Island was about.

But this is business, said a voice in my head and I tightened my ponytail. Part of me understood why Lee had grabbed the opportunity to get a booking.

I'd done my best to calm Rick. Brandon turned up. Said he'd seen stag party holiday at the hotel he and Nia had been working at, on Tortola, so could draw up a list of suitable bars and excursions. It was almost lunchtime by the time the three of us had talked everything through. I left Rick to Skype his gran. I needed to ask Jonas and Benedikt about playing to the guests over dinner, and to tell Malik about the possible rowdiness of the guests he'd offered to take out and how they weren't actually couples. I quickened my pace.

'Sarah!'

I lifted the brim of my cap and stared into the distance. Amy stood waving her hand, a towel wrapped around her head. I hurried over and joined her in the shade, by our shack. We hugged.

'I've hardly seen you all week. Here's you pulling

over-nighters up at the house...' Playfully she shook her finger. 'I do hope you took precautions.'

'Did you really just say that?' I raised an eyebrow, trying not to laugh. 'I told you, I had a website to design. I've hardly slept – and not for the reasons you think. The only viruses I could have come into contact with would have been computer ones.'

'You haven't even shared a kiss?'

I cleared my throat. 'Amy, I'm sorry, but I've got to go, you see I need to find Malik to—'

'Oh. My. Goodness. Things have at least progressed.' She jumped up and down and punched the air as the towel unfurled like a huge snake and fell onto the ground. 'I'm so happy for you! He's compassionate. Intelligent. As for those Calypso hips...'

'And he lives four thousand miles away from me in England. So don't get too carried away.' I picked up the towel and gently whipped her with it, before handing it back.

Amy stuck out her tongue and we both grinned. It was something she'd do to me as a small child if I insisted on holding her hand when we went shopping – or reminded her to wash her hands after using the bathroom. Mum used to do things like that. Anabelle wasn't clued up at first. I'd understood that, even though I was young. She didn't have kids of her own. But Dad didn't get it. I'd found her crying a few weeks after the honeymoon. She muttered something about being a useless stepmum after failing to keep us both supplied with clean school shirts and neither of us much liking her cooking. So Amy helped me bake her a cake. It was wonky and the buttercream ran but it made her cry again. She even ate a big slice, knowing Dad wouldn't have approved. He made it clear he liked his wife slim.

'How are things going with Jackie?'

Amy dragged a brush through her knotted hair and talked about cleaning out the animal enclosures. She hung her towel on a line we'd hooked up, leading from our shack to a nearby tree. We walked to the canteen.

'I found a frog near the boa enclosure,' she said. 'It moved slowly and its eye looked odd. I reckon it's been bitten by something – a mongoose perhaps. It was lucky not to have been eaten. One was brought into the surgery once. It had been bitten by a dog. Like that frog, its eye had become infected, so I asked Jackie if there was a suitable tank we could keep it in and if she stocked the relevant eye drops.' She stopped for a moment. 'It felt good, you know? Realising I could help this creature without anyone telling me what to do…' Her cheeks pinked up.

Yes, you're a vet in the making, I said – but only to myself. Observing Rick's relationship with his brother was giving me a deeper understanding of my relationship with Amy and how I hadn't fully let it evolve. I needed to let her make her own decisions – and hard as it was, mistakes too.

Lunch was Fungi, a common dish in the Virgin Islands made from cornmeal and okra and served with fish. Not my favourite. I caught Jonas's eyes and we both wrinkled our noses. We had a form of communicating that didn't involve words. Right from the first day, we'd felt exactly the same about so many aspects of the island. When I thought back to our arrival, I was amazed at how we'd now settled in. Jonas looked radiant and beckoned me over to where he sat. I hesitated but Benedikt gave me a warm smile. I got my food and headed over whilst Amy sat down next to Helga.

'I've missed you, Schatzi,' said Jonas. 'How is the website going?'

Benedikt stacked his and Jonas's plates and took them away.

'Never mind my website,' I whispered. 'Tell me the latest about you and your favourite Hamburger.'

'Nothing to tell,' he said coyly and pushed his dreadlocks away from his face.

'Have you spoken about your feelings to him?'

He broke eye contact. 'Not exactly. But Alistair and Greg return to Scotland this weekend so we'll have more private time.'

'Goodness me. Your cheeks look hotter than the sun at midday.' I leant forward and grinned. 'Come on. There's something you aren't telling me.'

'We might have... the other night... outside the shack, just before we went in... he took me by surprise...'

'Jonas! Hurry up!'

A joyous expression looked back at me. 'We kissed.'

I grabbed both his hands and squeezed the gently, letting go as Benedikt returned. I asked the two of them about playing music for this week's guests. Jackie said she was happy for them to miss bird observation whilst they practised this afternoon. Jonas got up to fill the water jug and came back before going over to Rick who'd just come in with Chatty, saying he'd find out what time Rick wanted him and Benedikt to be ready for tonight. Benedikt poured me a fresh glassful and offered to get me a piece of fruit. He came back with a fragrant mango that he proceeded to slice. He pushed it my way with a fork neatly positioned on the side of the plate. I sensed he knew I was no longer a threat to what he might have with Jonas. I offered him a slice. His shoulders relaxed and I asked him to show me his latest Instagram pictures.

Being in love, it made people do out of character things – like amiable Benedikt becoming unfriendly. That's what frightened me about my feelings for Rick. At Mum's funeral I'd got talking to one of her university friends, Carol. She was interested in my school studies. Carol was a lawyer. She told me how Mum had dropped out in the final year because she met Dad and their relationship became serious. He'd been doing well at work and bought a big house. He'd wanted Mum to turn it into a home and become his wife. Carol spoke about how, before that, it had been Mum's dream to become fluent in French and work as a translator – how she and my mum had spent a whole summer getting the train around Europe. I wondered if that was why we'd often holiday abroad. Mum must have missed travelling.

Carol never said anything negative about Dad; never indicated she thought Mum had made the wrong decision. In fact, I remembered her saying how happy Mum looked on her wedding day and how much she'd loved me and Amy. But Carol did say that following your own dreams was very important. That life was short and you didn't always get a second chance.

What if Rick was my chance? What if this was my opportunity to find true happiness?

Or what if being with him ruined my future aspirations?

I finished my fruit and went over to him. He was thanking Chatty for searching his hair for ticks. He almost pulled off the jokey tone but I could tell it was forced. He sounded stressed. I whistled 'Daydream Believer' and the monkey reached out and clambered onto my shoulder and wrapped his tail around my neck. I squashed his body against my head as a way of hugging him and an appreciative squeak filled the air.

'I could do with this scarf back in chilly England.'

Rick barely smiled. He beckoned to me to follow him outside. 'I've spoken to Gran. She's not happy about the stag party but agrees with Lee that we don't have much choice.' I squinted in the sunshine. He took my elbow and moved me into the shade. 'If Gran can accept these changes to the home she created, then who am I to disagree?'

'She'll go with Cacao House?'

'The news about the stag party distracted me and I've yet to explain the whole chocolate-making idea. But I've put out feelers to Malik. One of his friends is a woodworker. Apparently, he's developed a particular skill for sign-making after demand shot up during the months of rebuilding after the hurricane.'

'How about I check over the beach huts this afternoon and make sure everything is ready for the arrival of Jason and his friends?'

'Sure,' said Rick in a resigned tone. He'd put on his Indiana Jones hat. It was pulled down at the front as if he were hiding from the reality of the next few days.

I pulled it up. 'What is it?'

Chatty left my shoulder and felt his way over to Rick. True to form he grabbed the hat and dropped it on the floor. Rick gave a genuine chuckle and picked it up.

'Nothing. Ignore me. I need to shake myself out of this pity party. Seagrass Island survived a life-threatening storm. It can survive the high jinx of a few holidaymakers.'

'Why don't I come with you to meet the guests? Let's Skype Margot and prime Nia to be ready with cocktails. I'm used to greeting customers on a daily basis back home – although I know you've had your fair share of experience of that here so—'

'Really? That would be great!'

Twenty minutes later we sat on the sofa up at the house, Rick's laptop on his knees. Margot came into view, wearing the familiar leopard print glasses and a matching turban this time.

'Sarah. Lovely to see you again. Rick, you're looking tired.'

'Don't worry, everything's in hand,' he said, sounding more sure than I knew he was.

'You pick up Lee's friend later?'

'If you can call him that. They only know each other on Facebook now.'

'All the better,' she said. 'If this stay doesn't pan out well there will be no personal repercussions for your brother.'

I admired her objective stance.

'Sarah and I have been talking about pricing.'

'As have Lee and I,' she said. 'We think the way to move forwards is as you are now – charging an inclusive price for everything on the island and guests paying extra for excursions they book, and food and drink if they visit other islands...' She leant forward. 'And can I take this opportunity to say how much we appreciate you helping out, Sarah, and lending us your expertise free of charge. You're clearly a go-getting person. I'll be interested to see where you are, five years from now.'

My chest glowed.

'Actually, Sarah has another idea to help attract business to the island,' said Rick. He nodded at me.

I took a deep breath. 'Do you like chocolate, Margot?'

The wrinkles in her face deepened. 'If I could comfortably carry a secret stash around in this turban all day, I'd be tempted.'

This was a good start. Not that her face so much as flickered as I set out my idea. Calling the family home Cacao House. Harvesting the trees all year around. Producing a boutique brand of chocolate tourists could take home. Margot listened intently.

'I could get a sign made,' said Rick. 'Put it up before the first proper guests arrived.'

'USPs. You're good at them, Sarah. Rick told me about your idea to have a cartoon version of Chatty lead browsers through Seagrass Conservation's website. This is the same. The chocolate – it's something that's unique to this hotel venture. Along with the nearby conservation project, it's the thing that could make us stand out from local competition.'

'You like the idea?' I asked, tentatively.

Margot leant back into her armchair and folded her arms.

'I'm not entirely heartless when it comes to business. It jars, simply giving our beloved home a name to make money. But...' She smiled. 'As Rick knows, his granddad loved chocolate more than anyone. He'd certainly approve. That makes the idea feel more personal.'

'I'd forgotten that. He would buy a large family bar for himself every Friday, and you were lucky to get a look in, he would eat it that fast.' Rick glanced at his watch. 'Right, we need to get going to the airport soon. Sarah? A cup of tea before we leave?'

He passed me the laptop and headed towards the kitchen. Margot asked me again to explain the chocolate-making process. We discussed the equipment the Crowleys would need to invest in. She grabbed a notepad.

'I'm good friends with a restaurant owner on Tortola. He might be able to put me in touch with suitable suppliers. I'll email him as soon as this call is over.' She put down her pen. 'So, Sarah... have you drawn up that five-year plan we talked about last time?'

She'd remembered.

I'd asked Dad to help me draw up a revision timetable once, for my GCSEs. I was in a major panic. He was always going on about how his projections at work paid off. I thought he'd help if for no other reason than to impress me with his organisational skills.

It was the last time I asked him for anything. He'd waved me away and said not to disturb him the football was on – muttered that if I couldn't put together a timetable on my own then there was no point even sitting the exams. He did his usual thing and made it sound as if that last comment were a joke. But I always knew with Dad that was just a cover. The only time he hadn't done that was when he'd made the terrible accusation against me on the day I'd left.

'I did. Thank you. Suggesting that has really made me focus.'

'What's the first thing on your agenda, when you get

home?' she asked. 'A bright woman like you – you said that Best Travel wasn't stretching you anymore…'

Margot even remembered the name of my last employer. My eyes pricked. Anabelle had done her best over the years to recall the details of my life, but never really took on board who were my best friends or which were my favourite foods – not like Mum had.

'I've learnt an awful lot there,' I began.

'I like that,' interjected Margot. 'Loyalty. Gratitude gets you a long way in life – but not if you take it too far. If you've worked hard, that's your debt paid, so you needn't feel you owe this Best Travel employer anything if your gut is telling you it's time to move on.'

'That's what your suggestion has made me realise – I have no time to lose. Not if, in five years I want to be at least assistant manager somewhere spectacular, with an income that means I no longer have to ask myself if this month's earnings will pay all the bills.'

'Don't forget your personal aspirations,' she pushed. 'I've always been ambitious but never forgotten that my career is only one part of my life. Do you want to travel? Get married? Have children? Learn how to cook Thai food? Run marathons? Because if so, those dreams also need to be factored in.'

At that point Rick came back. He passed me a mug of tea. Sat down again. He told Margot about the mini bar we'd put in each room – effectively a shelf of small bottles of alcoholic and soft drinks, plus packets of nuts. She said how impressed she was with the hotel website and had a few ideas of her own. She'd email a family photo taken there just before the hurricane. She thought the personal touch – a photo of the Crowley family – would help attract the right kind of clientele.

I was sorry to end the call. Margot was so easygoing. She made me feel valued and gave me faith that being forced to leave Best Travel earlier than I'd wanted would turn out to be a positive thing.

At five o'clock Rick and I stood side by side, over on Tortola, at the arrivals gate in Beef Island airport. He was holding a sign that said Jason Elliot.

Raucous laughter bellowed across as passengers started to appear.

My palms felt sweaty. None of this would be happening if I hadn't come up with the concept of renting out the beach huts. I didn't want to let down lovely Margot, Rick – or myself.

31

It'll be fine, I told myself. They are mature businessmen – not eighteen-year-olds who don't know their own limits. Shouts and whoops caught my attention and I focused on the crowd of people coming into view. There was a young man soothing a crying baby. Grandparents. Loved up couples. And… a group of men in their thirties and forties creating most of the noise, wearing red T-shirts that said in large capitals *STAGS LOVE A VIRGIN* followed by the world *island* in really small letters.

Scrub my earlier comment.

Adrenaline pumped throughout my body. I always got a high from checking in new guests. Each one was an adventure. You never knew whether you'd be glad to see them leave or hope one day they'd come back.

A tall man with short blond hair and wearing an expensive watch and tailored shorts strode over. He clapped Rick on the back. Grabbed my hand and kissed it.

'I'm Jason Elliot.' His words slurred slightly. 'You must be Rick Crowley and you…?'

Clearly they'd started their holiday on the plane.

'Sarah,' I said, in a polite voice. 'Welcome to the Virgin Islands. I believe congratulations are in order…'

The other men crowded around and the smell of whiskey rudely filled the air. Rick and I shook hands with them all before heading outside to the people carrier taxi. He asked the group about their flight. I talked to Jason about his upcoming nuptials.

Okay. We could do this. Rick and I were in control. Or at least I thought so until we passed a small supermarket and Steve, a portly man in luminous lime green shorts, took off his cap to scratch his bald head and ordered the taxi to stop.

'Quick booze stop, mate,' he said to the driver, ignoring Rick and me. They all piled out, returning shortly afterwards carrying bags full of beer and vodka and stuffing crisps into their mouths, rogue ones tumbling onto the taxi's floor as they got back in. The car continued down to the dock. Twice, Steve stuck his head out of the window to wolf whistle loudly. Rick did his best to engage the men in conversation but they weren't interested.

It was the same on the boat and they opened beer cans as soon as they boarded. Rick pointed out aspects of the coast and a seal but the men were too busy sharing jokes and rolling up their sleeves to get a tan to show off back in the office. One winked and asked if I had a boyfriend whilst the others shared lurid jokes and banter that became more outrageous as the alcohol flowed. A short man in Hawaiian shorts burped and lobbed an empty crisp packet over the side.

'Please don't do that,' I said as warmly as I could. 'Plastic pollution is bad enough as it is. It's not good for the seagulls or—'

'Spare us the lecture love,' said Steve and laughed. 'Jeez, the amount we're paying we can do what we want.'

'Hey. Steady on, Steve. Show some respect, mate,' slurred Jason.

'Just a little joke,' he said and looked sheepish, swaying unsteadily. 'It was decent of you to fit us in at such late notice. Sorry. You're right of course. It won't happen again.'

'No problem.' I smiled.

'The ex's brother is big on recycling,' he continued. 'God knows he talked about it enough to me during the miserable five years I was married.'

'Are you all single?' asked Rick, brightly.

'Me, Jack and Tony are happily divorced,' said Steve. 'Jase, as you know, is about to sign his life away. Pete and Chris are single and looking for action.'

Only the groom-to-be was in a relationship. Oh God.

'As best man it's down to me to make sure we all get the most out of this week,' continued Steve. 'What has Seagrass Island got to offer six red-blooded men in their prime?'

'Plenty of trail-clearing if you want it,' said Rick. His grin looked false. 'Lee will have told you about our conservation project.'

Steve swigged his beer. 'Nice try mate. I run my own landscaping business so I do enough of that back home. I was thinking more of hands-on action with the lay-deez if you know what I mean.'

'Brandon, who works on Seagrass Island – he knows Tortola well and has helped us plan several trips you'll enjoy. A bar crawl. The best nightclub in the British Virgin Islands. During the day there's a dolphin spotting trip and snorkelling for those of you up for that. Or you can relax on our very own beach with waiter service. Lovely

Nia – Brandon's wife,' I hastily added, 'makes the best rum cocktails.'

A couple of the men turned to listen.

'There's fishing as well,' said Rick. 'And a tour of Seagrass Conservation for those who want it…'

'I wouldn't mind a photo with your monkey we've heard about,' said Steve. 'A photo of me with that on my shoulder is bound to be a hit when I'm trying to woo the ladies.'

A wave of protective feelings rushed over me. A glazed smile crossed Rick's face. Chatty was sociable for sure, but a gentle creature. Any meeting with these party people would have to be handled carefully.

I sidled over to Rick as the group spotted a shoal of large fish under the surface and took photos, challenging themselves to see who could identify them first once they picked up an internet signal.

'The key is going to be to keep this group busy,' I said.

Rick took his eye off the horizon for a second. 'Still sure you want to be involved?'

I rubbed my hands together. 'I'm loving the challenge.'

'Glad one of us is.'

'I've dealt with pre-wedding parties at work numerous times over the years. We're talking sick on the carpets, broken lampshades, noise into the early hours that I've had to quash. Once a girl even got handcuffed to the bathroom pipes for a joke. I think I can cope with this lot.'

'Talking about vomit…'

On cue one of the party had thrown up over the side. I hurried over with tissues and offered my bottle of water but they glugged back more beer instead. Rick headed towards the jetty and parked up. Finding it hard to walk in a straight line, the men disembarked. They rapidly found their feet when Nia appeared holding a trayful of cocktails.

'Cool. A private beach. Means we can do what we want,' said Steve. 'Which one of us is first in, lads? Get your kit off.'

Drinks were downed. Empty glasses clumsily returned. Shorts came off. I spun around and looked at Nia. The two of us hurried towards the boat to grab the men's luggage, leaving Rick gaping. The three of us carried cases across the sand and planted them on the pathway that led to the camp and up to the house.

'Right, gentlemen,' Rick shouted. 'We'll start taking your bags up to your accommodation. Please follow as soon as you are ready.'

Nia went ahead to organise arrival snacks.

'I can't believe this crowd,' said Rick. 'Gran would be horrified.'

'Would she?' I countered. 'It's business. The island is private. And whilst they've booked under a discounted rate, they are paying your family to stay here and have a perfect right to enjoy themselves. They're just a bit boisterous, that's all.'

Rick put his hands on my shoulders. 'Thank God you're here,' he said. 'How can you do that? Kind of switch off your personal feelings?'

We walked on and eventually I broke the silence. 'Like I say, I've had years of dealing with customers.'

'It's not just that, is it?' he said. 'I've seen you during the last couple of weeks, switch into a sort of... harder mode when faced with doing something you aren't keen on. It's as if you've got a reserve of toughness at your core. I admire that. Where's it come from?'

We stared into each other's eyes.

'It didn't always pay to be myself when I was younger. If I showed my vulnerability Dad would take advantage – he'd do anything to make himself look like the better person.'

An arm slipped around my shoulder. 'Then he's missed out, because the glimpses I've seen of the Sarah behind the mask are pretty special.'

A lump formed in my throat and gratefully I heard footsteps sound behind us.

Jonas and Benedikt were playing a jazz tune when we arrived, in the smart clothes they'd worn one night when we'd had drinks and music to celebrate Carlotta's birthday. The men caught up and tucked into Nia's canapés with gusto. Rick showed them to their beach huts. Jonas and Benedikt left for the canteen, saying they'd come back at eight when Nia would serve the guests dinner.

Rock music suddenly cut through the air. Steve stood, in swimming trunks, outside his beach hut, a boom box on the steps. He rubbed his stomach fondly and belched before lobbing his lit cigarette into nearby bushes. Rick and I hurried outside. He stamped on the cigarette. Oblivious, Steve crouched down and suddenly sprang into the air. Clutching his knees tightly he flew into the water, bombing the surface. Seconds later Rick and I stood dripping with water as Jason and his friends surfaced from their huts and shouts of laughter resounded around the pool.

32

Saturday morning. It felt good to be asleep in someone's arms. Warm. Safe. Cocooned from the realities of life, like redundancy and the prospect of struggling to pay bills... Snuggling under the covers I contemplated the last couple of days. Thursday night, after Jason and his friends had arrived, we'd all sat up until 1 a.m. talking. Rick and I finally left them drinking cocktails in the pool. They'd asked for a full English breakfast Friday morning and wanted Malik to take them snorkelling in the afternoon. Rick had accompanied them whilst I'd stayed behind to help Brandon and Nia clear up the villa. There were cigarette butts everywhere and spilt drinks on beds. The mini fridges we'd put in had already been emptied.

Being part of something, right at the beginning, learning by mistakes, trying out new ideas – it exhilarated me.

Brandon and I had also replanted several chocolate trees either side of the house. We chose younger ones as they were easier to dig up. The established powder puff trees we wanted to remove were harder and a couple of the volunteers helped out with the back-breaking work. After a shower, I took a new shot of the house and uploaded it to the website. Whilst looking after Lee's old university friend was important, we still needed to push forwards with the bigger plan. Search engines had now picked up the website and that the number of views was growing.

I felt like skipping! Holding hands with Amy and circling round and round as fast as we could! We'd had plenty of moments like that when we were little, with Mum. She had the most infectious laugh and put fun into the most boring things. Like when I'd have my fringe cut. She'd secretly pull silly faces at me from behind that I saw in the mirror. I'd almost burst from trying to control the urge to laugh.

Jason and his friends had returned from the snorkelling remarkably dry. Rick said the wettest part of them had been their throats. They'd been keen to go out last night and we'd taken them on a bar crawl. Steve almost got punched by a man whose girlfriend he'd tried to chat up. One bar manager ordered them out after a shouting match about Brexit – Steve and two of the others had been firmly Remain. Jason and the rest Leave. Insults had started to fly. We'd got back to Seagrass Island at around 3 a.m. and plodded up to the house, the men now laughing about their argument. A vague memory returned of Steve serenading me with a slurred version of 'Ain't No Mountain High Enough' as we ascended.

I yawned again, pressing myself comfortably into the warm body behind me. It has been so long since a strong pair of arms had held me tight. This pair felt like a perfect fit. They felt right.

Crap.

Heart racing, I ran my hand down my body. Thank God I was dressed. Nervously my eyes fluttered open. Please don't let me be in one of the beach huts with one of the stag party. I took in the mahogany ceiling and vase of flowers, the whitewashed walls and tropical paintings. Relief gushed through me. I was in the spare room, at the house. I'd more or less lived there since working on the website. I shuffled and turned around and gazed at Rick, looking adorable whilst asleep.

The tanned face and inky hair contrasted the white pillows. For the first time I noticed the faint hairs on his muscular forearms and how long his eyelashes were. His breath touched my face and felt sweeter than any sea breeze. Our mouths were mere inches apart. Heat spread through my limbs and pooled in my pelvis as they yearned to wrap themselves around him. I longed to lose myself in the warmth... in him.

I remembered now. He'd come into my room when we got back. I'd shown him the new photo on the website. With the men laughing loudly outside and splashing in the pool, even though it was late, I'd taken Rick once more through the process of treating the cacao beans. We decided that the fermentation stage to remove the slime off the beans would definitely take too long for some short-stay guests to be able to use beans they'd actually picked. Therefore, in the optimistic spirit of preparing for bookings, we would harvest a starter batch of pods ourselves and get a supply of beans ready for roasting and grinding. Margot had already emailed to say she'd been in touch with her restaurant friend on Tortola and heard back with details of a reliable company that could supply us with a proofer and sous vide. We could take delivery of the equipment as early as next week if we got our order in on Monday morning.

'The volunteers will help us,' I'd said.

'I feel guilty asking,' Rick had replied. 'They aren't here to pick beans. And they've really rallied around this week, keeping the beach tidy and covering your, Jonas and Benedikt's duties. They're a great bunch of people.'

'That's because they respect you so much.'

'I'm not sure about that,' he'd muttered.

'It's true.' I'd punched his arm. 'Somehow the camp has got wind of Crocker & Crowley's financial problems. They want to help. And apart from their fondness for you, none of them want to see Seagrass Conservation close.'

Rick snuffled, rubbed his eyes and I moved backwards as he woke up. He'd never know that we'd been cuddling.

'Morning,' I said and sat up.

He yawned. Looked around. 'We're making a habit of crashing out in each other's company.'

'Do you think that's because we're both crashing bores?'

'Speak for yourself,' he said haughtily and we laughed. 'I didn't sleep well. I've a nasty feeling Jason and his friends went exploring. I woke up in the middle of the night and heard laughter that faded away, and then distant shouts. I was too tired to get up and just hoped they wouldn't get far without torches. I woke up again later. It was still dark. More laughter and then silence.'

'I must have slept through. They could have used the torch app on their phones. I wonder what they were doing.'

'I'll have to have a word with them. The forest is a dangerous place at night, with hidden tree stumps to fall over and creatures like scorpions and snakes that might act in defence if they feel they are being attacked by clumsy feet.'

I got out of bed and stretched. 'I'll fetch two juices then I need to head over to the shacks, shower and get some fresh clothes – I've used all the ones I brought here.'

Rick grinned.

'What?'

'You've come a long way. The Sarah who first arrived here would have jumped at the chance of washing at the house. Now it doesn't bother you. You're choosing bath time with tarantulas over our brand-new guest en-suite.'

Borrowing Amy's habit, I stuck my tongue out at him and left the room. Urgent voices sounded from downstairs. Surely the guests weren't already up after their late night?

'Rick!' called a voice.

It was Jackie. Amy was there too. The door behind me creaked open. We both hurried downstairs.

'What's the matter?' he said.

Jackie wrung her hands together. 'I don't know how this has happened, but Chatty isn't in his enclosure this morning.'

'What?' Rick's face paled.

I felt sick.

'I'm sure I locked it last night, after putting him to bed,' said Amy. 'It's the first time Jackie's asked me to do that on my own. This is my fault.'

'No. I trust you completely,' said Jackie, firmly. 'There must be another explanation.'

'Perhaps he somehow opened the unlocked gate and escaped,' I said.

'I've just been so busy this last week. As his main carer I should have made sure I freed up more time to spend with him. What if he managed to somehow get out and went looking for me...?' Rick's voice wavered. 'I've let the little fella down big time.'

'Nonsense,' I said, even though the well of nausea inside me was growing. 'I'm sure there will be a rational reason. Now let's think. What time did you put him in there, Amy?'

What if he'd got injured? He must be feeling so lonely, feeling his way in darkness.

'Nine o'clock, as usual, after a night in the Games Room. He settled on his favourite branch, at the back on the left. The one he likes swinging on.'

'Did the door look forced open this morning?' I asked.

'It's not that kind of lock,' said Jackie.

'Ah yes. It's a large, heavy bolt.'

She nodded. 'We've never needed to bother with anything else because this is a private island and the only visitors we have are into conservation and would only want the best for him.'

Rick stopped walking up and down. 'Until recently. Oh my God...' He rushed upstairs and came back with his laptop. He sat on the sofa and logged in. We stood behind as he went onto Facebook and typed in Jason Elliot.

'What are you doing?' I asked.

'Following a hunch,' he said, his voice tinged with anger.

Jason's page came up. He scrolled down. First up was a photo taken last night – of a grinning Jason holding Chatty firmly in his arms.

Chatty was baring his teeth and cowering.

33

Rick's laptop fell onto the sofa as he stood up. Barefoot, he strode outside towards the pool, across decking and damp morning grass.

'Rick, just wait!' called Jackie.

But he walked straight up to Jason's beach hut. He rapped on it loudly. He tried again, this time using his whole fist.

'All right, all right,' called a tired voice. Jason appeared with tousled hair, wearing nothing but his shorts from last night. 'Rick, do you know what time it is? I feel as if I've only just gone to bed.'

'Where's the monkey?' asked Rick, face the colour of the nearby flame tree flowers.

Jason scratched his head and then a sheepish look came over his face. 'Look, mate...'

'Don't call me mate,' he said in a measured voice. 'You broke into one of the animal enclosures. You scared one of our animals.'

'Scared?' Jason snorted. 'He was grinning. We reckoned that was a trick you taught him, right?'

'That wasn't grinning, you imbecile,' said Rick.

I put a hand on his arm but he shook me off.

'He was frightened to death – baring his teeth, that's

what monkeys do in situations like that. He was ready to fight for his life if he had to.'

Steve came out of his hut, rubbing his bare belly. 'What's going on?'

'Where's the monkey?' I asked.

Steve screwed up his eyes in the sunshine that promptly disappeared behind a rare cloud. 'Ah yes. That. Sorry guys.' He cleared his throat. 'No harm meant. Although he was probably glad to get out of his cage. We were just having a laugh.'

'A laugh? Chatty's blind. He must have wondered what the hell was happening.' Rick moved forwards. 'Is he in your hut, Jason?'

'Blind?' Jason gaped, as did Steve. 'Mate, sorry, we had no idea... it was dark... look, we put him back in his cage straight afterwards. He was only out for a few minutes.'

Steve shook his head. 'Jeez, I mean... we'd never have touched the little chap if we'd known he couldn't see.'

Rick threw his hands in the air. 'He's not a pet. You shouldn't have touched him at all, sight or no sight. He's not in his enclosure this morning. Did you lock it afterwards?'

Jason and Steve looked at each other.

'Can't remember,' mumbled Jason.

'I'm sure we turned the key,' said Steve uncertainly.

'It was a bolt,' said Jackie.

'A heavy one. You'd remember pulling it across,' said Amy.

'Come on,' I said to Rick. 'Let's get our shoes on and go and look. He can't have gone far.'

Nothing else mattered at this moment. Not the success of this week. Not the bigger vision for the hotel venture. Not my unemployment back home.

'We'll come. Just let me get dressed,' said Jason and turned to go inside.

'You've done enough already,' snapped Rick and he hurried back into the house.

'Just leave it,' I muttered to Jason and Steve. 'I'm sure Chatty will be all right.'

But I was far from sure. He couldn't see. That made him the perfect prey. What if he'd crossed a snake or fallen into a stream? I shivered, partly due to the temperature that was unusually lower today – but mostly because I felt fearful for Chatty.

I followed Rick in. Amy and Jackie stayed to get more details from the two men.

'It'll be all right. We'll find him,' I said as he picked up a pair of trainers he'd discarded near the piano last night.

Rick shook his head. 'I should have never listened to you.'

'What do you mean?'

'This stupid hotel idea. I should never have let my gran be persuaded.'

'I don't think your gran *lets* herself be persuaded by anyone,' I stuttered.

'What was I thinking?' he continued. 'Allowing total strangers, who aren't interested in conservation, onto our precious island – an intoxicated stag party at that? I know you want to move into luxury hospitality at some point in the future, Sarah, but using us to test out what it's like…'

'Now, just wait a minute, that's not fair,' I said as he bent down and slipped on his trainers. 'You and I, Lee and your gran – we all talked this venture through.'

'I got carried away with your enthusiasm. And why the

hurry to change direction, anyway? Is your job back in England really that bad?'

'It's okay...' I broke eye contact.

'Sarah? What aren't you telling me?'

I met his gaze. I couldn't hide the truth any longer. Not in the face of what had happened. 'It's just that technically, it's not my job anymore. The manager let me go. She never took on my new ideas and—'

His jaw dropped. 'What? You've been lying all this time...' He swallowed and muttered something about thinking I was different. 'I'm all for ambition but this is taking things too far...'

'What on earth are you talking about?'

'You... creating your own job, here. What was your next step? To convince my gran that you'd be the perfect person to run this place permanently? Has that been the real motive? Pretending you still have a job back in England so that we wouldn't suspect that your motives were less about helping us and more about your career?' He shook his head. 'Lee would consider your drive admirable but me... why not come clean instead of deceiving me?'

I gasped. 'No, of course that wasn't my motive! I just wanted to help. None of that ever even crossed my mind.'

In silence he walked past. I grabbed his arm.

'You really think I'm just out for number one?'

'I don't want to, Sarah.' His shoulders bobbed up and down. 'But why not tell me you'd been sacked, right from the start? We've talked about your job several times yet you never let on. What am I supposed to think?'

'I... I didn't want to worry Amy. That's why I didn't

mention my sacking right from the beginning. It only happened just before we came here and—'

His brow furrowed. 'Amy seems pretty rock solid to me. She's not a child. Why would you keep something like that from her? No. That doesn't make sense. There has to be another reason.'

I stepped back and, in that instant, realised that all along my sister had been right. Before coming here, I was still treating her like a little girl. Rick wouldn't even entertain the idea that I'd feel the need to protect an adult, like that.

A heavy, cloying sensation constricted my chest.

'If you'd been upfront about your aspirations, who knows, maybe I'd have given your ambition a chance – but the way you've fooled me and used my family...' He shook his head. 'Is that why you suddenly ended things between us? Because you realised this project might actually take off? Had getting close to me just been part of that scheme? You said you thought we should halt any romance because you'd be going home soon. Was it really because you felt the opposite might happen and you weren't actually that into me after all?'

I pursed my lips. 'First you thought I came up with this hotel idea to get out of doing conservation work. We got over that misunderstanding. But now you accuse me of coldly trying to forge a career here, instead of genuinely trying to help you and your family?'

'Sarah...' His voice faltered. 'I really don't want to think...'

'Why should I be surprised? Men like you always try to shift the blame.' My voice choked. 'You're just like my father. It was never his fault that Mum died, it was always *mine*,' I spat those last words through anger.

There.

I'd said it.

The awful accusation Dad threw at me when I left home at eighteen.

The comment that tortured me for years afterwards.

I was shaking. My throat hurt. Confusion crossed Rick's face.

Footsteps sounded. Amy appeared. 'Sarah, are you all right? Did you mention Mum? What's this all about?'

'No... you... you misheard. We... we were just disagreeing about the best plan for searching for Chatty. Look.... let's just get going...'

Rick left the house and started to run. Amy, Jackie and I followed. As fast as we could we went down to the camp, past the shower block and up to the animal enclosure. Chatty's space stood empty. My stomach was in knots as I pictured him alone and frightened in the forest.

Pushing the argument with Rick out of my mind, along with the others I searched under every bush within a twenty-metre radius but didn't spot anything. Not even monkey droppings. Rick called his name. We listened for the familiar whistles and squeaks but only heard the call of sea birds and distant merry shouts of volunteers no doubt taking an early swim as a start to their weekend.

Jackie examined the bolt. Amy searched his enclosure for the hundredth time. Rick stared in despair at the surrounding foliage.

'What's his favourite food?' I asked.

'He likes eggs,' said Jackie.

'He loved those cashew nuts I prepared for him, the other day,' said Amy.

Rick looked at Jackie. 'But his ultimate treat...'

So now he wasn't talking to me.

I was upset. And angry. I thought we'd become friends at the very least.

Jackie's face brightened. 'I'll see if we've got any.' She turned and ran down the path that led to the canteen.

'What is she fetching?' asked Amy.

'Freeze-dried fruit. Strawberry and banana are his absolute favourite,' muttered Rick. 'Sometimes Malik orders them in to put in packed dinners, for the overnight turtle trips – they are lighter than carrying fresh fruit. Chatty played with one of the bags, once. Worked out how to open it, not knowing there was food inside. His face, when he tried a slice of freeze-dried strawberry, it was a picture...' Rick almost smiled. 'Ever since then the rustle of a bag gets him so excited. You should see him when we all eat crisps. I often wonder, as well, if it reminds him of all the junk food his was fed before being rescued. It was a hard job to wean him off that fat and sugar.'

We continued to search under nearby frangipani bushes and called out Chatty's name until Jackie got back, arms full of small bags. A few clouds moved in. At least the monkey wouldn't get too hot, if he was far from water.

'Let's make a pile of them,' I said. 'With a couple of bags open.'

'In fact, we could sprinkle the contents of one on top, so that the smell spreads,' said Amy.

'And rustle the plastic in our hands to attract his attention,' said Jackie, none of us voicing the option that Chatty might be nowhere near or had suffered something worse than getting lost.

Five minutes later we stood together, looking at the pyramid of treats on the ground, by a group of palm trees. We scrunched the packets in our hands. The concentrated sugary smell wafted through the air. I hardly dared breathe. An insect landed on my head. Rick brushed it off. We looked at each other. Frustration hung in the air between us. Despite our harsh words, I hated seeing the worry etched across his face. Those dark eyebrows knotted. Despite everything I wanted so much to give him a tight hug.

But I wasn't like Mum. I wasn't like Anabelle. Rick had hurt me. I wouldn't go back so he could do that again.

'Where *is* he?' said Jackie.

He didn't appear. We waited in silence. And waited. And waited some more.

Eventually Jackie looked at her watch. Said we might have to accept the obvious – that Chatty had suffered an accident such as drowning, or fallen victim to a more violent outcome.

My throat hurt. Tears hung in Amy's eyes. Shoulders hunched, Rick turned away. Eventually he faced us again.

'He's got to come back,' he muttered. 'We'll wait a bit longer.' He gave a wry smile. 'Who else is going to appreciate Sarah's godawful whistling?'

'That's it!' I said and everyone looked me. I took a deep breath and started to whistle 'Daydream Believer'.

As usual it was out of tune and I missed a few notes, but the sharp sound carried high and wide. Amy couldn't help wincing.

Eventually I stopped. 'Did you all hear that?' I whispered. There was another squeak.

'Chatty?' Rick called. 'Come here little fella…' He walked forwards.

The squeak sounded again. It came from above. I looked up into the tallest palm tree, just behind the pyramid of fruit packets.

I exhaled. My eyes felt wet. 'Up there,' I said and pointed before whistling again.

Rick lifted his head and hurried forwards. He reached up towards Chatty who sat on a branch, clinging to the trunk.

'Pass me an open packet of fruit,' he murmured.

Amy darted forward and obliged.

Rick lifted it as high as he could and rustled it. Chatty's head twitched. Slowly he slid down the tree and touched Rick's hand. On tiptoe he reached up and lifted him down. He held him close, burying his face in the fur.

'Sorry, little fella. So sorry. I've neglected you this last week,' he murmured, eyes shining when he looked up. My heart swelled as he gently scratched Chatty's head.

Familiar whistles and squeaks came from Chatty who cautiously climbed onto Rick's shoulder, as if he were telling him all about his overnight adventures. I mumbled his name and reached out my hand. He bared his teeth on it gently and clutched it with his paws. Then he wrapped his tail tightly around Rick's neck and started to groom his hair, showing little interest in the food.

Rick sank to the ground at the base of the tree. The three of us joined him quietly. Rick ate one of the strawberry pieces. The sweet smell became stronger as he chewed. Chatty stopped grooming him and slid down onto his lap and ate one too. Then he crawled in my direction when he heard me talk. I settled him on my knees and stroked the wiry limbs. Jackie passed him an unopened packet and he excitedly proceeded to open it, look more like his old self, especially when another piece of the dried fruit was in his mouth. I tickled behind his head as he ate.

Amy noticed a cut on his ear. Jackie phoned the vet who agreed to come over to the island and give Chatty the once-over. Whilst she discussed the appointment with Rick, I kissed Chatty before making my way back to the shacks with Amy.

Rick's accusations. My recent realisation that I wanted more than ever to move my career forwards. Margot's talk of a five-year plan that I'd already drawn up. It was time.

Time to go home.

34

We sat on my bed in the shack. The air wasn't as humid as usual. It was almost time for lunch but I didn't feel hungry.

'Now that we're alone… is… is everything all right?' asked Amy. 'Why the icy atmosphere between you and Rick?'

'We've had a row.' I sighed. 'He's angry about Chatty and blames me for the whole hotel idea and these troublesome guests.'

'What an idiot.' She put an arm around me.

'To be fair… I lied to him about something and that's made him think I have an ulterior motive for the whole plan.'

She took her arm away and shrugged. 'A lie? That's not like you. I bet there was good reason. He's lucky to have had access to your expertise, if you ask me, all the research you've done these last months.'

I stared into my lap. 'I lied to you as well – or at least, I didn't tell you. I thought it was for the best but I realise now… you'll always be my younger sister but it's time I started treating you like an adult.' I looked up. 'Sorry if I haven't. I'm so used to looking out for you.'

She tilted her head and raised an eyebrow. I took a deep breath.

'Rick thought my ulterior motive was to create a job here for myself because… just before this holiday Prue sacked me because I'd made a decision without consulting her and—'

'*What?*'

'I've lost my job.'

She paused. I waited for the look of anguish on her face – concern for me and how we'd pay bills.

Instead, she folded her arms and smiled. 'Good riddance, I say. It's been a long time coming, sis. This could be a positive thing.'

'It could?'

'Maybe this is the push you need to take the next step with your career. So why is Rick so upset?'

'I didn't tell him either – pretended I was still employed, in case you got wind of it. Now he thinks that all along I've been planning some sort of takeover with my hotel idea – that trying to help him was more about me creating a job for myself here.'

She placed her hand on mine. 'Rick's a decent guy. He was just upset about Chatty. You're no liar. He knows that deep down.'

'The thing is… I… I do lie occasionally. To you. I did when we arrived. Because sometimes I worry that the truth might hurt. But this trip has opened my eyes. I won't do that anymore.'

'What was that lie about?'

'Fancying Rick.'

A puzzled look crossed her face. 'But you do?'

I sighed. 'Yes. That pretence came true. But it wasn't the case at the start. I told you he was the reason I was staying on this island because otherwise I knew you'd work out I was only doing it to keep you happy – and you wouldn't have allowed that. But Amy… I am going home now – it's time I sorted out my future. Sent off applications. Also, the way things are, I can't stay here near Rick. Tomorrow I'll head over to the airport and see if I can change my flight. You finish the month here.'

'But that's only seven days away! Don't go. Just avoid him. Move back to the camp.'

I shook my head vigorously.

Amy stared. 'Perhaps this growing up malarkey is about respecting each other's decisions,' she said, softly. 'It doesn't mean we don't care.'

She really had grown up. How had I not seen this before?

'How about making the most of our last day here? Have you got anything planned?'

'I was going to hang around with Jackie. I've learnt so much, these last three weeks. I assumed you'd be busy helping Rick with the stag party. But Jackie must be sick of my company, to be honest, and all my questions about bird species, reptiles and insects. Did you know that spiders eat tons of mosquitoes? Respect.'

'I still don't much like them,' I said and managed a smile. 'How about… I know! How about a picnic? Just you and me. Somewhere quiet. I'd love to visit the turtle beach, again. It was so secluded, so beautiful… We'd keep our distance of course – avoid the stretch of sand where they are nesting. It's going to be hectic once I get back to England. I'd love one last tranquil afternoon.'

Amy jumped at the chance. She disappeared to let Jackie know. I went to the canteen to ask Malik if there was any chance of a packed tea. He was more than happy to provide cheese sandwiches, mangoes and slices of his famous coconut tart that he made every weekend.

I caught Jonas's eye. He and Benedikt were having lunch with their shack mates who'd be heading back to Scotland later this afternoon.

He stood up and wrapped his arms around me. 'It feels as if we haven't chatted for ages.'

'Why, have you got something to tell me?'

Jonas smiled shyly and stepped back. 'Let's just say,' he whispered, 'the way things are going, I may not be single by the end of my stay here. Me and Benedikt… my gut feeling about him was right – we just seem to click. And before you ask for all the details, don't – Helga worked it out and has just interrogated me. I think she's almost as excited as me!'

'Oh Jonas, I'm so happy for you.'

'I can't stop thinking about him. It's torture – in a good way. And I don't even mind the fact that he's never read a *Harry Potter* book or watched a Marvel comic movie.'

We both grinned.

'I like it when he teases me about my South German accent. Love is weird, right?'

I wasn't sure. I realised now I'd never had it with Callum.

'I'll miss our little chats. You see… I'm going home tomorrow, all being well. I've got to get a new job. I can't put it off any longer. I hope you'll send me updates about everything, on Facebook.'

'You've lost your old one?' His face fell. 'I'm sorry to hear that. Although I'm not sure how I'll manage without you.'

'Really?' I glanced over at Benedikt and then looked back at Jonas, raising an eyebrow.

He shrugged and laughed.

'You aren't on your own anymore. Not that you need Benedikt's support. You've fitted in here brilliantly all by yourself.'

'You'll visit me in Germany? Remember what we talked about? Me taking you for coffee and my favourite apple cake?'

'Of course – as long as you keep your word and come to London. Don't forget I promised you afternoon tea and a trip to Buckingham Palace.' I playfully pulled the end of one of his dreadlocks. 'Thanks, Jonas. I couldn't have done this without you – my buddy for emptying the compost toilet. You kept me sane, knowing that I wasn't the only one struggling.'

'Same here,' he said. 'I'm proud of you, Sarah; proud of us both. I thought this place was hell on earth when we arrived, but now…'

'It's actually a little bit of heaven,' I said softly.

He nodded.

I sat down with Amy and Helga to eat lunch – the dreaded fish soup. Except now that I was leaving it didn't seem nearly so bad.

Who'd have thought I would ever miss this place?

But I would.

The apricot sunrises.

Dusky pink sunsets.

Dear, dear Chatty's tail wrapped around my neck.

The fragrant frangipani flowers.

Volunteers' camaraderie.

Jonas's harmonica playing.

Even… well, no. I'd never miss the eight-legged shower companions.

Amy collected up our crockery and went ahead to visit the toilets before we left. I smiled my thanks at Malik as I collected our packed teas, barely hearing him say something about incoming cloud.

Tomorrow I'd return to England.

I shivered as I walked outside.

35

We took it in turns to carry a rucksack that held our food, bottles of water and a rug. I'd hesitated over whether to bring waterproofs. Malik had to be wrong. There were no signs of bad weather approaching. Sunlight still broke through the clouds and we hadn't had a single drop of rain in three weeks. I doubted it was going to start now.

We passed the animal enclosures and headed up hill. The breeze became stronger and offered welcome relief from the afternoon heat that whilst cooler than normal, still made me yearn for a siesta after lunch. We passed the flame trees that only had a few flowers left now. I'd never cease to admire the delicate, fluffy blooms of the powder puff trees and felt quite sad this could be one of the last times I saw them. When we passed the cacao pods, I told Amy about my idea for chocolate production. She chuckled at first, thinking it was a joke.

'I'm deadly serious,' I said as we stopped to examine a pod that had fallen onto the ground. I picked up a stone and smashed it several times in the middle before prising the tough skin apart.

'Wow,' said Amy. 'The inside looks like a white, slimey pine cone.'

Carefully I took that part out and we both breathed in.

Amy pulled a face. 'It has a chemical smell.'

I sniffed again. 'Yes, but also a fruity fragrance. Apparently the white flesh covering the beans is edible.'

'No way am I eating that!'

I pulled out a clump, counted to three and put it in my mouth.

Slimy, slippery and not completely unpleasant, but nowhere near as delicious as chocolate… I swilled it around in my mouth and finally pulled out a recognisable bean.

'That's amazing,' said Amy.

I slipped it in my pocket and we continued our walk, passing sugar apple trees. Just before the top of the hill I tripped over a root and landed in a face full of soil. Laughing, Amy helped me to my feet. I brushed down my trousers and winced before joining in.

'Everything okay?' she asked.

I leant against a palm tree. We both drank out of our water bottles. No, it wasn't. I was thinking about Dad. I didn't often mention him to Amy, for fear of bringing back bad memories. But she was strong, I was realising that. Maybe I'd been wrong. Perhaps it would help her – both of us – to talk more about our childhood.

'Remember when we went out for that meal for Dad's birthday? I was fourteen,' I said tentatively. 'You'd have been ten. We were meeting an important client of his, with their family. He used his big day as an excuse to take them out for a posh meal and claim it all on expenses.'

Amy thought for a moment. 'The restaurant with swings for chairs? And a waterfall in the middle? Yes, it was unforgettably lush and I also remember because beforehand...' She looked at me.

'I tripped and fell outside and laddered my tights,' I said. 'Dad was absolutely furious. He didn't even ask if I was all right. I couldn't help crying. It was a bad graze, full of gravel.'

'I went with you to the toilets and helped wash it out. He wanted Anabelle to stay with him.'

'His only concern was presenting the image of an idyllic family, with his slicked back hair and Italian cut suits and that stupid, oh so highbrow accent he'd put on when talking to anyone related to business. I commented on that once. I thought it was funny. But he shouted so loudly. Told me to never make fun of him again. I thought he was going to hit me. Fortunately, Anabelle stepped in.'

I waited for Amy to tear up at the memory.

Instead she surprised me.

'But just look at how we turned out,' she said. 'It hasn't defined us. We've both had relationships – some good, some bad – that's normal. He didn't put us off men for life. He just made it clear what we don't want in a relationship. I'd say that makes us winners.'

Normally I would have nodded and changed the subject. But me and Amy – our relationship was heading towards a more open territory...

'But aren't you wary of his type? You know, good-looking, charismatic...'

'Like Rick?' She smiled.

'To be honest, Amy, I've always steered clear of anyone remotely like him.'

'You mean sexy as hell?' She pushed my shoulder.

'I'm serious.' I took another swig. It was as if the water was alcohol and loosening my tongue. 'That's why all of my previous boyfriends have been more...'

'Like friends? Really?' The humour left her face.

'It's been scary, meeting Rick and feeling such a strong attraction.'

'Sarah... Rick isn't Dad. He was a one-off. Just because a guy's good-looking and confident doesn't mean he shares Dad's crap qualities as well.'

'But Rick's hurt me, all the same. He's accused me of—'

'You lied to him, Sarah. What was he supposed to think?' Her shoulders bobbed up and down. 'He's nothing like Dad. Trust me, if he was, I'd be the first to chase him away, but you've seen his passion for the environment, his love for Chatty – our dad never put anything or anyone before himself.'

Something stirred inside me. It didn't feel good. 'But... but what about Sebastian who broke your heart and split up with you the day after your twenty-first birthday? He was a smooth charmer, just like Dad. You were so upset afterwards.'

Amy's face blushed a deep pink.

'Sorry. You probably don't want to talk about it.' I put away my drink.

We started to walk down the hill.

'I don't want to discuss it, Sarah, but not because of what you're thinking. The truth is... I'm not proud but it was *me* that cheated on *him*. A friend of mine got drunk at the party and let slip that I'd had a one-night stand. It was someone I met in a nightclub. A stupid mistake. To be honest I was getting bored with the relationship but didn't have the guts to tell Sebastian. He was a good guy, Sarah. A perfect gent. Fun. Loyal. Honest.'

I spotted an iguana but didn't even point it out to Amy. Sebastian was in the clear? It was Amy who'd cheated on him? So... when it came to romance had I been playing unnecessarily safe? Amy and I should have talked about all this years ago.

'You must be ashamed of me,' she muttered.

'No. We've all made mistakes. You'll have learnt from it.'

'God, yes. I've never cheated since and wouldn't again.'

We continued through the forest. The chirp of crickets drowned out our silence. That was one thing I liked about Rick – our friendship felt comfortable. I never felt the need to fill any gaps in our conversation with small talk. Finally, we reached the beach and took off our shoes. The fluid wet sand felt blissful.

'We'll stay here, well away from the nesting site,' said Amy.

'Agreed.' I threw down the rucksack, rolled up my trousers and headed into the waves.

I shivered and looked up. More clouds had appeared and huddled together. The strong breeze had built into a wind. Amy sat on the beach and examined a shell. I turned back to the water and stared at the horizon. The swell of the waves looked steeper than normal.

'When the clouds have moved off and the wind has died, let's go for a swim,' I called.

'Sounds like a plan,' said Amy and stood up. 'I'm going to collect shells. This is the last free weekend. Next Saturday it'll all be over.'

I looked down into the shallow water as clear as a tear drop and bent down to pick up a piece of bright green pottery, shifting up and down with the ebb of the waves. I ran over to Amy and gave it to her.

'Isn't it pretty? Remember how we used to dig in the garden for pottery fragments, thinking they were treasure?'

'Yes. Mum would help us wash them. Later, Anabelle wasn't interested so you'd do it with me.' She put the ceramic triangle into her pocket. 'The pieces we found reminded me of our family, once Mum died. Broken. Scattered. Never to be whole again.' She looked at me. 'I blamed Dad for smashing it up, with his cruel words. Mum did a good job of acting like the glue and keeping us together, smoothing over arguments, making sure you and I were mostly seen but not heard.'

I'd tried so hard to make her childhood happy; hoped that most of the sadness swerved by her. It hadn't.

'However, I used to think it might have been better if Mum wasn't the glue,' she continued. 'If instead she left the fragments of our family behind and took you and me away, the three of us to build something new.'

'Me too.' I slipped my arms around her shoulders. We stood for a while until goose bumps appeared on our arms. 'I wish I'd brought a fleece. It doesn't look as if this weather is shifting. Perhaps Malik was right. He mentioned a storm. I didn't think it likely.'

Amy studied the sky. 'Look how dark those ones have become. We haven't got protective clothing either. I hate to say it, but perhaps we should head back.'

A speck of rain fell onto my skin and overhead a flock of sea birds left the island.

'Let's take refuge in the forest until it blows over,' I said.

Amy picked up the rucksack and I followed her off the sand, jumping as a clap of thunder sounded. Large globules of rain pelted down. We ran the last few steps and stood under the canopy of leaves. Then everything became much worse, very quickly. Lightning jabbed the horizon. Huge waves threw themselves onto the beach instead of gently stroking the sand. Palm trees leant from side to side. The tall rainforest canopy parted. Torrents of rain fell down. We lifted large glossy leaves above our heads but the weight of water meant that they didn't say horizontal.

Thanks goodness we'd managed to rescue Chatty before this weather hit.

For half an hour we sat underneath a tree, soaking, teeth chattering. Cracks of lightning punctuated the steady beat of rain like an out of place exclamation mark in a sentence. I forced a smile when Amy looked at me. She didn't smile back.

'You don't think... a hurricane... it couldn't be another, could it?' she asked.

My instincts compelled me to say automatically that no, don't be silly, this is just a freak rain shower.

But Amy and I were equals and looked after each other now.

'I hope not. Surely Rick would have warned us? It must have been forecast for several days. I feel so stupid for not taking in exactly what Malik was saying about the weather. What do you think we should do?' I asked instead of thinking I had to do the fixing myself. 'Stay or try to make our way back? I'm not sure which is best.'

She glanced at the sea. 'Perhaps we should move. I don't like the height of those waves. If there was a tsunami…'

I wanted to tell her to stop catastrophising but she had a point – we were out in the wilds, in the middle of the Atlantic ocean, not nestling in a cosy bar near the river Thames.

I yanked Amy to her feet. Heart racing, I pulled the rucksack onto my back. Amy hurried through the rainforest. I ran to keep up. The ground had become muddy and I lost my balance. I tried my best to right myself. My back ricked. Lightning cracked as I slipped and tumbled to the ground.

Pain shot across my forehead as it hit a tree root.

36

Despite the throbbing pain, I managed to open my eyes. Footsteps pounded above the rain and Amy appeared. She knelt by my side.

'You're bleeding,' she said loudly, above the storm. Her voice wavered. 'You're all right, aren't you?'

I wiped my hand across the wound and flinched. As I sat up, I looked at my fingers, smeared with red.

'I'm okay.'

'What?'

'I'm okay,' I said louder, even though it hurt my head. 'Just give me a minute.' My teeth chattered uncontrollably. Another clap of thunder made us both jump. It had been a strain to walk against the force of the wind but we *had* to get back to the camp and proper shelter. Aside from the raging weather, everything else in the forest was quiet. There was no bird call. No chirp of insects. And the fragrance of flowers had disappeared. All I could smell was damp bark and woody soil.

'We need to get away from these tall trees,' I said. 'They could be blown down on top of us.'

Amy shook her head. 'Near those tall trees is exactly where we should stay. They will attract lightning first. If we stand in an open space, we'll be the target. For the same reason we need to avoid the top of the hill. In retrospect I think we're just going to have to crouch down until...'

'Until help comes or the storm passes,' I said firmly.

'Exactly.' An unspoken understanding ignited between us. We would get through this. Amy took my arm and we sat at the base of a nearby sugar apple tree. Rain stung my face.

Unpleasant questions popped into my head. What if this weather actually did turn extreme? We should be inside a building or underground.

What if I never had the chance to say sorry to Rick for lying about my job? For backing off even though I could hardly spend one minute without him in my thoughts?

I'd always imagined Amy and me growing old together. Perhaps we'd travel or both have kids and they'd be friends...

Nelly... Suddenly I missed our cat so much.

And what about Chatty?

My heart ached as I recalled my last proper conversation with Mum, before the end came, a moment of lucidity amongst her growing incoherence.

'Look after Amy,' she'd said, under her ever-weakening breath. 'And look after yourself, Sarah. Live life for me. One day have the retirement I'm going to miss out on, with friends, family and hobbies, all against the backdrop of a job you've loved. You deserve that, my darling, and so much more. Never forget how much I love you. I'll be watching. I'll be your own shiny star.'

I'd held her hand tight, trying to will my life into her, with an unblinking gaze, not wanting to miss a single second of her last moments. Then Dad had come in. Told me my time was up. I wouldn't beg for more time. That would have upset Mum. So I bent over her. Kissed her cold cheek. Smoothed her hair neatly like she used to when she said goodnight to me. I whispered that she looked lovely. It was hard. I was only eleven. I told her she'd been the best mum a girl could ever want. Mum was mumbling by now. Something about me being a good little girl. Dad pulled at my arm.

I didn't want to let go.

I left that room looking over my shoulder, part of me understanding that I'd never see my mother again.

Amy was waiting outside, playing with her favourite doll. I'd smiled brightly and told her Mum sent her love. She wanted to see her. Dad had picked us both up at school. She didn't understand why she couldn't go in. I told her the room smelt of yukky cleaning products and that Mum was practically asleep anyway.

A tear ran down my face. I'd tried so hard not to cry in front of Amy over the years but maybe I should have. I gulped. Sat upright. Amy and I could deal with this.

'Come on,' I shouted. 'We'll freeze to death at this rate. We need to build a shelter. We can do it, Amy. You and me.'

We found a clear space of ground, behind a cluster of wide trees and searched frantically for fallen branches. When we finally had enough, we stood them up in circle and pushed them together at their highest points, wedging the rough ends in between each other. Amy pulled the belt out of her trousers and reached it to me as I was the tallest. As best I could, I tied the branches together, at the top. Then we draped glossy leaves around the sides, fighting the wind to weave them clumsily in between the poles of wood.

One large gust would knock it sideways but the surrounding trees offered protection from the worst of the wind – for the moment anyway. Exhausted, we crawled into the small enclosure. Every time the sides shook, we expected the wigwam to collapse. Thirstily we drank and left our water bottles outside to refill the natural way.

Minutes feeling damp turned to hours shivering. Amy leant her head against my shoulder. Outside it began to turn dark.

I cried now and again, thinking about Mum. Amy saw. We talked about the past. She cried too. We sat holding hands. Amy thanked me for stepping into Mum's shoes. I thanked her for giving me the motivation to stand up to Dad.

For just a second it felt as if Mum were in there with us too, keeping us warm, telling us everything would be all right. I started to whistle Daydream Believer. Amy joined in singing. We got louder and louder, tears streaming down our faces as we finished.

'If we get out of this, both of us must follow our dreams,' I said.

Amy nodded. 'For us. For Mum.'

Eventually the tears stopped. To my surprise, I felt better for them. Stronger somehow, as if sharing our grief bonded us even more closely.

I cocked my head. The wind had eased. The rain sounded lighter.

We were going to be okay.

I'd go home. Give Nelly a big hug. Apply for jobs. But before all of that I needed to speak to Rick. The storm reminded me of how quickly life can be snatched away. Mum had passed only two months after her diagnosis.

'Sarah! Amy!'

I strained my ears and shook my sister.

She held fists in the air. 'Who's there?'

I almost felt like laughing. 'It's all right. I don't think we'll need to fight. They know our names.' I put an index finger to my lips. 'Listen.'

Someone shouted out again.

I scrabbled out of the makeshift tent, knocking the sides. They fell apart. I pulled Amy out, behind me.

'Over here!' I hollered as rain now fell more like confetti.

'This way,' shouted Amy and jumped up and down.

Rustling preceded bushes swaying not because of the storm, but due to people pushing their way through foliage and emerging in the dusk. An Indiana Jones hat. Two other men – one of them bald. A woman with bobbed curly hair. I narrowed my eyes and gazed through the approaching darkness. Rick, Jason, Steve and Jackie.

'We made it,' Amy whispered. 'At one stage I wasn't sure we'd…'

'Me neither,' I said, my throat feeling full. 'But we are two strong women who've been through a lot in our lives, and that will always help us get through future ordeals. We've inherited that strength from Mum.'

I'd never stop looking out for Amy, like Mum had wanted me to, but I now knew part of that meant being strong enough to take a step back, to let her look out for herself too.

Rick ran over. Jackie as well. She hugged Amy. Rick threw his hat to the ground and took me by the shoulders.

'What happened? Your head…'

Briefly I explained. He reached into a big rucksack Jason

passed him and handed Amy and myself a waterproof coat each. Gratefully we pulled them on – or tried to. Suddenly my limbs felt too heavy to lift. Rick helped whilst Jackie poured steaming coffees out of a flask. Jason and Steve didn't say much whilst we munched the packed teas we'd not had a chance to eat.

'We thought it was another hurricane,' I said, in between mouthfuls of coconut tart, crumbs tumbling out as I spoke. I bit hungrily again. 'I should have listened to Malik. He warned me. But my mind was so full of Chatty and... other stuff.'

'What hit today was just the tailwinds of a hurricane that, thankfully, stayed out at sea,' said Rick. 'It surprised the forecasters. Yet normally we track the weather a few times a day. The guests... looking for our favourite monkey... all of that distracted us as well.'

'This is our fault,' muttered Steve, and ran a hand over his bald head.

'We've been a bunch of first-class idiots,' said Jason.

They talked to Jackie about Chatty and she told them his story. Amy chipped in with tales of the other animals the conservation project looked after. Steve took the flask from Jackie and topped up my cup. He and I chatted.

'Seriously,' said Steve and stared at the ground. 'The way me and the guys have behaved – well, mainly me. I just didn't think about how the monkey felt. And the loud behaviour... the litter... I... I've kind of lost the plot, the last year or two. The divorce with the wife hit me hard.' He shook his head and looked up. 'I've been egging my friends on to make this into a real lads' weekend, as if we're twenty years younger. We'd like to apologise.'

'It's not your fault my sister and I went on a picnic,' I said.

He shrugged. 'I saw the panic on Rick's face when he ran back to the house to get waterproofs for you both. He muttered something about an argument about Chatty. How he'd said something stupid. I brought all that on and I'm truly sorry.' Steve left to fill up Amy's cup.

Rick caught my eye and came over.

37

'How do you feel?' he asked.

'Fine, thanks. Sorry for all the trouble.'

'If anyone's to blame, it's me. How did you manage?'

'We built a tent, out of leaves and branches.' Tentatively I took his hand and led him around to the back of nearby trees. 'It doesn't look much now but it did the job.'

He didn't let go of my fingers. 'Sarah, I'm sorry, the things I said… I was frantic with worry about Chatty and took it out on you. I know you've helped out through the goodness of your heart. All the hours you've put in… You've been incredible. I just didn't understand why you kept losing your job a secret and… I can't bear being lied to.' A cloud darker than the ones we'd run from this afternoon crept over his face.

'Do you want to talk about it?'

He bit his bottom lip.

'You don't have to.'

'I do. I owe you an explanation.' He reached up for Amy's belt and held the two ends in each of his hands, pulling them hard. 'Three years ago, just before I jacked in my job and moved over here to set up Seagrass Conservation… I was engaged. We met at work. She was an oil spill response advisor.'

'Sounds impressive.'

'Yes. Gabby loved her job. Loved the money. She seemed so confident with her bright red lipstick and professional reputation that was second to none. But she told lie after lie. Big ones. Small ones. When I found out she called off the wedding, a week before it was due to take place.'

'Oh Rick... that must have been such a shock. Was... was there someone else?'

'Everyone thought one of us must have cheated. But no. Nothing like that but it was complicated to explain to people, you see. When we first met, at my desk, a friend had left a packet of cigarettes there. She thought they were mine. Told me she smoked too. When she found out I didn't, she stopped – said I'd inspired her. Made a big thing of it. Every time that conversation came up during the relationship, she told me how I'd transformed her life. But the truth was she never used to smoke at all.'

'Why make up something like that?'

'Gabby lied over money as well. She was always buying me presents but secretly ran up huge debts. It turned out she wasn't well. Gabby had an eating disorder. Despite her incredible success at work and looks that were always earning her appreciative looks, she didn't feel good enough. She was the first in her family to go to university and felt anything but leading a perfect life would let her proud parents down. She'd lied to me about so many things to cover up her problem... made up all sorts of food intolerances. Got out of big family food events with my family, like Christmas, by pretending her gran had died. That particular lie became so elaborate. She even took a day off work for the supposed funeral.'

'Gosh. I'm sorry. Sorry for her. Sorry for you.'

'I can see now that it wasn't *her* lying – it was the illness. I hope she's doing okay. But… it left me with all sorts of questions, such as didn't she think I'd want to help? But then I did my own research… began to understand just how she must have struggled with such a big secret. My heart broke when I thought about how she'd been suffering on her own.' He pulled the belt tighter. 'It broke even more when she pushed me away. I felt so helpless. And then all of her lies that we became entangled in… it just got too much. I really loved her. Thought we had a future together. It took about a year to get over the fact that I thought I'd known a person so well when, in fact, I hardly knew them at all. I told her none of the past mattered and that we'd get her treatment, together. But she was too embarrassed and broke it off a couple of days after admitting the truth. Ghosted me everywhere on social media. Did her best to avoid me at work.'

'I can't imagine how that must have felt.'

'I'm over it now and some good came out of it – the breakup made it easier for me to decide to give up my career and move here.' He rolled up the belt and put it in his pocket.

'I *should* have told you about my unemployment. There was opportunity enough. I can see how it looked odd. It's just… you know the way Lee is with you – the brother who thinks he knows best?'

Rick nodded.

'I've always wanted to protect Amy – like Lee after your

accident. I know she's grown up and it seems ridiculous but I hate the thought of her ever being upset. It makes me feel sick inside. A sickness I used to feel as a child. Dad could be so vindictive – in a sly way. If Amy got hurt, it hurt me too.'

He took my hand again and his grip tightened.

'I don't blame you for your outburst,' I continued. 'If our cat, Nelly, was ever taken my head would be all over the place. The truth is, today, it's made me... What I mean is... how we've been together these last weeks... you and me... you see...' I draped both my arms around his neck and stood on tiptoe. I pressed my lips firmly against his, heat glowing through my body as if it was midday and the clouds had parted. He kissed back, gently at first, then stronger, harder.

'Does it sound strange,' he said in a husky voice, 'worrying you've lost something before even knowing if you've really had it?' Our faces were inches apart. He held my waist tightly. Finally we parted.

Gently he ran a finger across my bruised head. 'I was so convinced Gabby was *the one*. But then you and Amy got lost in this storm. The thought of something happening to you... the overwhelming sense of panic inside...' He swallowed. 'Whilst I felt deeply for Gabby, I never felt like I have the last couple of weeks.'

Once more we shared a kiss. It ignited a storm inside me. An exhilarating, breathless, sensual storm I never wanted to end.

'I suppose we'd better make our way back,' he said eventually. 'Get you and Amy checked out.' He went to say something else but turned to go instead.

'What?'

'It's nothing.'

I raised an eyebrow. 'No secrets.'

'The comment you made about me being like your dad; about him holding you responsible for your mother's death...'

I'd never repeated his hateful words to anyone. Dad had spat them out of Amy's earshot and Anabelle had simply stood there in horror. I'd buried his spite into my memory, as deep as I could. But now and again his words crept out and crowded my mind, like a parasitic weed.

'I was only told about how ill Mum was a few weeks before her death, when she became confined to bed.'

We sat down on a nearby log.

'I denied it to myself. Refused to believe it was happening. Until Mum...' My voice caught. 'She confirmed my worst fears one day, after school. I was sitting on her bed. She took my hands. Hers felt so fragile. She started rambling about when she'd be gone. Muttered stuff about how I'd always have Amy. That I was a sensible, resilient little girl and had a great life ahead of me.'

'I didn't sleep that night. I felt so alone. And frightened.' I stared blankly into the distance. Rick held my hand so tight. 'But that didn't stop me leaving home as soon as I could. Dad was a malicious man.'

'You said I was just like him...'

'His charisma – that's how you remind me of him. He got away with his behaviour because of that and his good looks. My mum and stepmother both lived their lives to keep him happy. The way I feel about you...'

'I'm not him. And you're not them,' he said gently.

'It just struck a nerve – you doubting me and my motives for helping out. You see Dad *never* believed in me. He just wasn't interested. He's always too worried about what other people thought. You know, he changed his surname by deed poll.'

'It's Sterling, right?'

'Didn't used to be. He was born Gary Smith but wanted a name that sounded rich. That was the reasoning behind what he called the cat that came to live with me and Amy.'

'Nelly?'

'He called her Chanel. I guess with the names Amy and Sarah my sister and I got off lucky.'

'But blaming you for your mother's death…? What happened right at the end, then? An accident?'

I snorted. 'Dad had a way of twisting things to put people down – even his daughters – but especially his wives. I don't think he'd genuinely believed I'd move out. He didn't care about me – just how it would look to his friends and business colleagues. He told me I'd never manage. As an angry parting shot said Mum's breast cancer…' My voice wavered. 'It was because I pushed her over when I was a child.'

'*What*?'

I felt shaky. 'We were messing around. I was about eight. Mum was tickling me. We were in the lounge. I laughed and shoved her as hard as I could. You think parents are all powerful when you're small. I never thought she'd fall over. I must have caught her off-balance. She twisted and fell down, catching her right breast on the corner of this low mantelpiece, in front of the fire. She screamed out. We couldn't hug her for days because of the swelling and pain. She'd laughed about it over the years. Said her breast had been wonky ever since. I hadn't thought about it for ages until Dad threw that accusation at me.'

'What a ridiculous thing to say.'

'It didn't seem so. The cancer came on the right side. I felt sure I'd read something, over the years, about breast trauma causing cancer. His accusation still hurts. I wish it didn't.'

Rick enveloped me in an embrace.

'Then a couple of years ago I got talking to the husband of one of the vets where Amy works. We got talking about my Mum. I kept the subject vague but moved it onto the causes of breast cancer. He said studies had been done and there were no links proved between cancer and breast injuries.' My throat ached. 'I felt such relief – and was so angry at Dad for having let me blame myself all that time.'

I closed my eyes and exhaled deeply. It felt good to share this with someone – and for that person to confirm that Dad was speaking nonsense, even though the rational part of me knew that. It was something I'd not even felt able to share with the therapist Anabelle encouraged me to see, all those years ago when I first left home. Eventually Rick took me by the shoulders. Held me firmly. Look me straight in the face.

'He should never have blamed you, even if it had been true. It was an accident and apart from anything else, you were a child.' He shook his head. 'I'd never hurt you, Sarah. Not intentionally. I hope you know that.'

'I do.' A tear rolled down my cheek. 'That's what cuts most about Dad. There were no excuses I could make for him. He always knew exactly what he was doing. I doubt he even believed the accusation himself. Whereas you and me... I suppose sometimes, when people are hurting they say things they don't mean; then regret it and say sorry.'

'Perhaps we should talk less,' he said.

'Sounds good to me.'

We looked at each other and smiled. Rick's phone buzzed.

'You should answer that.'

Rick pulled a face and tapped his finger onto the screen. Both his eyebrows raised. He scrolled up and down, reading it again.

'It's a text from Malik. About Gran. She's just landed in Antigua and will be catching the plane to Tortola once this weather has completely died down.' He beamed. 'So much for not coming until September. She'll be here tomorrow. I can't wait to introduce you.'

38

After our ordeal Rick offered both Amy and me a bed at the house. But now that I was about to organise an early flight home, I felt an odd affinity with the shack – in the same way I looked back on that first bed and breakfast I moved into, all those years ago. Not with fondness but... a kind of gratitude. It had made me what I am – in the same way this shack had taught me that I could still survive hard times.

I sat on my bunk bed and gazed at my cracked, unpolished nails. Part of me was looking forward to returning to the executive life. Smart suits. High heels. However maybe, in the future, I'd chill more about the way I looked at weekends. I hadn't thought much about my appearance, with Rick – unlike how I'd been with previous boyfriends. And with Chatty around there had been little point in styling my hair.

I'd hardly slept, thinking about my departure.

Perhaps I'd visit Rick here.

Maybe he'd come to London.

Or was this just a fling?

Whatever the outcome, in lots of ways, I owed this trip a lot.

Who'd have thought I'd ever be thankful for this island swap?

Amy returned from the showers, rubbing her hair with a towel. She threw it onto my bed. I lifted it up and lobbed it on hers. We smiled at each other.

'What time does this Margot get into the airport?' she asked.

'Just before lunch. I'm going over to meet her with Rick.' It would also give me a chance to sort out my early ticket back to London. I lifted up my phone. 'Guess who I got an email from this morning?' I asked as we headed outside and sat on the steps of the shack, soaking up the early morning sun. 'Prue.'

Amy tidied her hair with her hands. 'What did she want?'

'Me to go back. Apparently the last three weeks have been hell with regular customers asking where I am and her having to sort out the housekeeping problems herself. She's even offered me a pay rise and said something about her nephew having a lot to learn.'

'You aren't considering her offer?'

'You see this finger?' I said and lifted one up. I jabbed it at the screen and deleted the Best Travel email.

Amy grinned. 'Great, because our return to England is going to herald a new beginning for both of us.'

'What do you mean?'

'Promise not to say I told you so?' She took a deep breath. 'I'm going to apply to university to study veterinary science. Next year. So I have a couple of months of research ahead of me too, to choose a course and get my application in this autumn. My grades weren't quite high enough for all the courses but I'm hoping my years of experience, working as a nurse at Paws & Claws – and the stay here – will act in my favour.'

I gaped. 'Amy... that's brilliant. What's changed your mind?'

'Helping Jackie. Being given responsibility in the way I'm not as a nurse back in London. It's boosted my confidence. Made me realise that...' She looked at me. '... Dad was wrong. I *have* got what it takes. I've been thinking since our chat yesterday. His attitude towards us – it affected your view of men. Now I can see how it affected my view of my career prospects. I suspected as much over the years and wished I'd ignored him and trained as a vet – but always told myself it was too late. I don't believe that now.'

'What changed?'

'Look at Rick, leaving his oil job and starting up Seagrass Conservation – despite a geology degree not giving him exactly the right know-how. His passion has carried him through, along with Jackie's expertise on animals. And then there's his gran – she sounds as if she's never stopped aiming for goals. Jackie changed direction and moved here to help Rick... I reckon age is irrelevant if you've got the drive.' She sat up straighter. 'It's time we both stepped completely out of Dad's shadow.'

We sat there holding hands like we used when we were little, sitting on the stairs at night, listening to our dad pick an argument with Mum or Anabelle.

'We'll still send him a Christmas card, and one for his birthday,' I said.

'But that's all. No more visits where we do our best to ignore his insults and sit through him talking about nothing but the latest deal he's closed.'

I nodded.

'What about Rick?' asked Amy. 'How is your relationship going to work? Are you sure you won't stay just one more week, now that you and Rick are hitting it off?'

'No. Not unless I can't exchange my ticket. I'm worried about the bills. You'll need every remaining penny of your lottery win for university. The longer I'm out of the job, the bigger the threat that we'll lose the flat we've both worked so hard for. I'd love to stay here for a few more days. The island has really grown on me.'

'Say that again?' she said and a smug look crossed her face.

I smiled. 'I guess we could both say *I told you so*, in different ways. I am glad you swapped our holidays. Apart from anything else, it's bolstered my gut feeling that it's time to move on and challenge myself.'

'That's how I feel,' said Amy. 'Dealing with the injured parrot and helping get the medication down the iguana and so many other things... Jackie's trust in me has made me realise I'm more capable than I thought - and yes, just like *you* always thought.' She kissed my cheek and smiled. 'Veterinary nursing is challenging and I love looking after the animals that stay overnight, but I've always wanted to be more hands on; to replace the reception and nursing work with diagnosing or even surgery.'

'I'm so proud of you,' I said quietly. 'So impressed at the way you've taken on extra responsibilities here and helped tidy the enclosures and feed the animals, even though you haven't been rostered in. I imagine Jackie's really going to miss you.'

Amy blushed. 'I'm already thinking that if I save really

hard, I could afford to come over next summer. I told Jackie about my plans. I hope you don't mind me discussing it with her first.'

Was this what it felt like to be a parent? Sad that you are no longer number one when it came to hearing big news and dishing out advice – yet at the same time so happy that your child is capable and independent?

'Of course not. We've both made new friends – you've confided in Jackie. I've had Jonas.'

'You get on with him so well. I thought he might be a toy boy for you at first. I sure got that wrong! Anyway, Jackie said I might be able to work as an assistant to her, next summer. Seagrass Conservation probably couldn't pay me but might cover the cost of my flight and I'd have a shack and free meals here like the volunteers.'

'Look at us. Moving forwards with our lives. When you won that lottery, we won much more than pounds and coins.' With a bursting heart I hugged her tight before leaving to meet Rick up at the house. I had some really exciting news to tell him. Piano and harmonica notes drifted along the breeze. Jonas and Benedikt must have been practising. I stopped for a moment, by one of the cacao trees, and caught Rick's eye as he stood in the lounge clapping, as they finished a jazz tune. He spoke to the pair before they came out of the house.

'That sounded fantastic,' I said.

Jonas kissed me on the cheek before putting his arm around Benedikt's shoulder. Benedikt grinned at me.

'Thanks. In fact, playing together has given Benedikt and me an idea,' said Jonas. 'Both of us feel we are at a crossroads in our life. We love music. On our own we've

never found the courage to take that love further. But...'
He looked at Benedikt who nodded. 'I'm going to move
back to Hamburg where I studied. I'm familiar with the
city and the music scene is great there. Benedikt needs a
flat mate to help with the rent as he's going to resign from
his job at the bank. I'll get a part-time job. We'll work on
our first set. To start with we'll try to get gigs in small bars
and to pay the bills working as waiters or shop assistants –
whatever it takes.'

'Wow. That's really great and... what a step. I'm pleased
for you... if you're sure.'

I seemed to be wired with a maternal gene when it came
to anyone younger than me.

'I know what you are thinking,' said Benedikt. 'That we
haven't known each other long. What if things don't work
out – between us? But we have thought about that...'

Jonas nodded. 'First and foremost we're friends. That's
what the music career will be built on if it takes off – and
everything signed in black and white if we ever get that far.
If we don't follow our dreams, we'll always be wondering
what if...'

'And a life full of *what ifs* is no life at all,' said Benedikt.
'Things could get complicated – we know that – but an
artistic life, one way or another, was never going to be
simple.'

I stared at them and darted forwards, embracing them
both at the same time.

'I hope you'll still talk to me when you're both famous.'

'We are expecting you at our first gig,' said Jonas.

'Amy as well. We need someone to look after my dog,'
said Benedikt and we all laughed.

I hurried indoors and told Rick about their impressive plans. But he hardly listened. Instead he came over, gently took my hand and led me to the sofa. We sat down. Deep lines were etched in his brow.

'Rick? What's wrong? Is your gran all right?'

'Sarah, I was chatting to Jonas... What's all this about you going home early?'

39

Part of me yearned to stay near Rick. Jonas and Benedikt were moving in together after just a matter of weeks – but it was to follow their hearts musically as well. I couldn't justify any more time here – not when I had a career to forge back home.

Mum left university for Dad. Anabelle gave up her job and own earnings. Looking back, I could see how that allowed him to isolate them from their friends.

I hadn't fully understood the extent of his abuse at the time.

Because it was abuse.

I was growing up. Reading online news articles. Surfing social media. I came across similar stories. They gave me strength. Made me understand just how selfish and controlling my father was. When I was small, I didn't think I would ever understand adult relationships. Mum veered between being so happy and so sad, navigating her way around Dad's anger, saying his moods were due to him working so hard and that we should all try to make his life easier.

Sometimes I thought that I was to blame. Perhaps I was especially naughty. Maybe I was born bad and causing problems between Mum and Dad. My self-esteem recovered a little when I read those articles in my teens. It wasn't me. It wasn't Mum or Amy. Nor Anabelle.

The only person to blame was him.

As my twenties passed, I chose my partners carefully and realised there were other types of men to Dad. Yet I could never shake off a deep urgency, within, to remain completely independent.

'I'm sorry you heard it from him first, Rick. Everything has happened so fast. The thing is... I need to pursue my career. Luxury hotel management is competitive and I stand the best chance of landing a position back in London. I can't afford to be out of work for long.' I told him about the offer from Best Travel that I'd turned down and the luxury hotels I'd already got in mind, to apply to, and talked about how I was going to restructure my CV.

'I understand. And I respect you so much. Perhaps we can visit each other.'

'Yes,' I said and glanced away, knowing, as he probably did, that in time the distance, cost of travelling and work obligations would prove too much.

Suddenly I remembered the exciting news. 'Talking of work, have you looked at the new website today?'

Rick shook his head.

'There's an email. This could be your first proper booking! And it sounds much more suitable. It's a mixed group of retired people. Just eight. Good friends by the sounds of it. Four of the partners used to work for the same publishing company and left work at around the same time. They formed a book club to stay in touch. They all happen to be animal lovers as well and fancy a trip together. One of the couples recently suffered bad news and I get the sense that the others have rallied around and suggested a getaway last-minute trip away – somewhere secluded. That's what is most important to them.'

'It sounds like that enquiry told you quite a story!'

'The email signature belongs to a well-known author. Perhaps that explains it. I've seen her on a television chat show. That might be another reason that the privacy of Cacao House appeals.'

I smiled. To think I'd once thought this trip was going to mean a month in the company of Richard Branson and other famous people.

'They are interested in visiting the animal enclosures. Learning about local wildlife. Sampling authentic Virgin Island cooking.' I punched his arm. 'Brilliant, isn't it? You must reply today. They have a few questions before going ahead such as how bad are the mosquitoes and can you cater for food allergies.'

'Would you mind casting an eye over my response? This is completely new territory.'

'Of course.'

'I'm going to miss you – purely from a professional point of view, of course.'

I loved how his frequent humour made those mocha eyes even warmer.

'You'll soon get the hang of it but can always message me with questions. Or we can Skype.'

We stood up and headed down to the jetty with Jason and his friends. We'd assumed they'd be eating at the house this evening, as usual, but they'd insisted on going across to Tortola for a 'quiet meal'. A friend of Rick's over there offered to drop them back. Nia said they'd been quiet all day, in the pool or playing cards on the sun beds. Brandon had told them about Tortola's botanical gardens and they'd decided to visit there tomorrow.

We didn't say much, in the boat, as Rick steered. I searched the waves for dolphins already feeling homesick – homesick for the island I'd be leaving. How was that possible? I'd only been here for three weeks but felt so different from the woman who'd turned up here with her impractical clothes and matching attitude.

Seagrass Island had changed me, I thought, as I stepped onto dry land. I'd never felt homesick before. Aged eighteen I'd been glad to leave Dad. It hurt not living with Amy. I still missed Mum. But I felt no attachment to the life I'd led with him and Anabelle.

'Can we go in here, quickly?' I said to Rick as he searched for a taxi. I pointed to a gift shop.

'Don't worry about us – we'll sort ourselves out,' said Jason.

'Right. Well there's a great rum bar by—'

'We won't be overdoing it,' said Steve and he gave a rueful smile. 'So no need to worry about locking the monkey up.'

'We all make mistakes,' I said.

'How about Nia cooks you all her delicious stewed oxtail, tomorrow night, and I persuade my grandmother to take you through her legendary collection of rums?' added Rick. 'Miraculously they were one of the few things not wrecked by the storm. She's got cherry rum, a chocolate one, lime and black spiced. A reserve blended for Christmas. Another that's 151 proof.'

The men's faces brightened immeasurably. 'That's decent of you,' said Jason. 'It sounds like a plan.'

'It is a stag holiday after all,' said Rick, as the men climbed into a nearby taxi in an orderly fashion. 'They messed up but helped put things right. I can't ask for more than that.'

I slipped an arm around his waist. Gratefully I escaped the hot, sticky air and entered the shop. I wanted to buy presents for my friends in housekeeping at Best Travel, and my neighbour, Mrs Chips. She and her late husband had taken me under their wing when I'd first bought the flat and was still learning to manage on my own and work out how to turn off the water supply or wire a plug. I decided on a selection of spices and jams that the islands were famous for as she loved cooking.

Shopping meant I didn't have time to find out about changing my ticket home, when we arrived at Beef Island airport, before meeting Margot.

'I'll do it after we've met her,' I said. Side by side Rick and I stood behind the barrier at the arrival gate. His hand slid into mine. I looked up and we kissed.

He took off his Indiana Jones hat and placed it on my head. 'Suits you, Calamity Jane.'

'I tell you, it felt like a calamity when I first met you, rostering me to clean the toilets.'

'But I won you around. Clearly the way to a woman's heart is to give her housework.'

'Jeez. There's no trouble in working out why you're still single.'

We stood laughing.

'Now I understand the modern phrase *to feel like a third wheel*.'

'Gran!' said Rick.

In front of us stood a slim woman with a slash of red lipstick and iguana green turban, wearing a loose kaftan.

'Lovely to meet you,' I said when she reluctantly extracted herself from Rick's hug.

We paused for a moment and then she leant forwards and embraced me. Margot was taller than I'd expected – taller than me. I loved her floral perfume. I hadn't been brave enough to wear scent since arriving in case insects considered it an invitation to bite. Her face bore wrinkles but her supple movements could have belonged to a woman half her age.

'I'll take your luggage,' said Rick and reached for her pull along case.

'I can manage very well, thank you,' she said sharply and he shot me a smile.

'Oh well, if you are that capable, you won't need a coffee to wake you up after such long flights.'

'Now you are talking nonsense,' she said and chuckled.

I looked for a coffee shop but instead we headed to an empty row of chairs and sat down. Rick, in the middle, reached into his rucksack and pulled out a flask. He handed me and Margot a cup each, wedged a third in between his legs which I took and held in my other hand, and he poured three drinks.

'No one makes coffee like Nia. I've been craving this for weeks. She uses my favourite brand of Caribbean Mountain Coffee.' Margot took a sip and sighed.

'I thought the coffee tasted different when I was up at the house,' I said.

She took another sip. 'If beans are roasted too little, the

coffee hasn't got enough flavour. Too much and it tastes smoky. This drink is made from beans that are just spot on.'

'You are quite a connoisseur,' I said. 'Like your rum – I've heard about your collection.'

Margot's eyes crinkled. 'Yes. I like specialist products. I find if something is niche more love and care has gone into its production. That's why, the more I've thought about it, I love your idea of naming our home Cacao House and us becoming a boutique chocolate-maker.'

She asked me more about the chocolate-making process. Rick waved to a local bar owner he knew well and went over for a chat.

Margot drained her cup and put it on the chair next to her. 'So, tell me… how long have you and Rick been dating?'

'What? Oh… um… we're not…'

She rolled her eyes. 'Forgive me. I'm in my eighth decade. No doubt I've got the terminology wrong. I can't keep up with all of the terms youngsters use these days…'

'Me neither,' I said and we smiled at each other.

'It's clear to me you two are more than just friends. When a woman wears a man's item of clothing—' she glanced at the hat '—it's her being territorial.'

'He gave it to me,' I protested. 'And Rick and me… it's not been that long.'

'Well, I'm pleased. His last relationship didn't end well.'

'He explained.'

She patted my knee. 'Then you must be close. It's not something he talks about now – not even with me.'

She took out her compact and re-applied her lipstick. I looked over at Rick. He caught my gaze, winked and came back.

Margot stood up. 'Let's get going. It's super to be met by my grandson, but there's only one real man in my life.'

'I know my place,' said Rick. 'Honestly. Never thought family would put me second to a monkey.'

'Is he okay?' she asked. 'Enjoying meeting the volunteers?'

Rick couldn't have told her about the stag party's escapade.

'He's fine. And will be glad to see you. He's become quite attached to Sarah. Having you around will soften the blow when she returns to England.'

'Talking of which, I almost forgot to enquire about getting my ticket changed,' I said and rummaged in my handbag. Margot spoke urgently to Rick; I heard her say something about an idea. He expressed surprise first and then what sounded like approval. I turned to go when a hand curled around my elbow.

'Don't be silly,' said Margot. 'Why would you go back to England when we're about to offer you a job here?'

40

I gaped. 'But you haven't even decided… this business is still in the fledgling stage and—'

'Let's get on the boat. I'll explain as we head over to Seagrass Island. Surely an extra day or two here won't make too much of a difference whilst you think it over? And if you still want to go back early, I'll personally pay for a ticket, so that you aren't out of pocket if it's too late to change your old one.'

'Chatty would appreciate any extra time with you,' said Rick. His whole face had lifted.

'That's low.' I tried to take on a scolding tone but failed. 'But Margot… I've drawn up that five-year plan you talked about. I'm itching to get back to England and put it into action.'

'My – our – offer isn't going to hold you back, dear. Right. Rick. Let's find a taxi. Now tell me about this stag party.'

Rick and I exchanged looks. By the time we'd reached the harbour I realised Margot was a persistent and perceptive person. She'd sensed something was afoot and quickly deducted it was to do with Chatty.

'They did *what*?' she said and stepped onto the boat. Rick carried on her luggage and his gran and I sat near the front, as Rick took his position at the steering wheel. 'They didn't realise he's blind? Why didn't you tell me about this?' she said to Rick in a sharp tone, as we slowly pulled away from the jetty. 'Is Chatty full recovered? Did you call the vet? Is he more shy with the volunteers now? Do you think we should—'

'This is exactly why I kept it to myself,' said Rick. 'I didn't want to worry you as you lived thousands of miles away. It would be different if you were closer.'

'I hope so, young man. I'm not made of feathers, you know.'

'Don't I know it.' He groaned. 'Titanium wings, more like.'

'So, this job offer, Sarah,' she said and smiled warmly. 'It's the position of hotel manager. Our venture is small – the perfect size for you to start out with. Your ideas so far have been completely on point.'

'Manager? But I live in England.'

'I was as surprised at first, when Gran mentioned it to me,' said Rick, 'but it makes perfect sense.'

'How so? I have bills to pay. A flat to maintain for – I mean, with – Amy... and our cat.'

Rick took his eye off the horizon for a second. 'Only Gran would have the audacity to ask someone to give up their London life!'

Margot snorted. 'What, give up pollution and noise, the hustle and bustle, for tranquillity, blue seas and sunshine? It wouldn't be much of a sacrifice.' She paused. 'Or would it? What's your gut reaction, dear?'

'No one has ever...' I swallowed. 'Your confidence in me... it means a lot. I can't help worrying, though, that it's misjudged.'

Her face softened. 'You remind me of myself, you know. I doubted myself a lot when I was younger.'

'Seymour?' asked Rick, as he waved to a passing fishing boat.

'Yes. Husband number one – but only in the numerical sense. I was eighteen. We got married at the end of the first year when I was studying fashion at university. We thought it was wild and exciting. My parents were furious. They'd never liked him – told me he was jealous of my talent.' She pulled down the sleeves of her colourful kaftan. 'Turns out they were right. By the end of the second year he never wasted an opportunity to put me down. I learnt quickly not to show him my ideas in their early stages and it killed my creativity for a while. Mum and Dad were brilliant. They gave me the strength to divorce him in my early twenties. It took a while for me to shake off the doubt he'd planted inside of me.' She took my other hand. 'Sarah, look at everything you've achieved – go-getting. A hard worker. A person with aspirations. Responsible. And, from what my grandson says, not someone to be messed with.'

'I never said anything like that,' he protested and glared at his gran.

She grinned. For all her sharp edges and feistiness, Margot was a very jovial person. 'It's because of *all* those reasons that I see myself in you.'

'But you've got so much business know-how, Margot. Why do you need me?'

'I know nothing about hotels. You're the expert. That goes for your computer skills as well. Plus you are someone I can trust.'

'Gran's an excellent judge of character,' said Rick.

'Granddad told her not to employ Nia and Brandon all those years ago – he didn't feel they had enough experience in housekeeping. She certainly proved him wrong.'

'A gut's a great thing. One should always follow it. Not your heart – or at least when it comes to business,' she said. 'It will be a challenge. Bringing in bookings will be the number one priority. I imagine looking after the guests, once they are here, will be easy compared to that.'

'Never assume anything,' I said and laughed. 'I once had a male guest ring down to reception on his mobile phone – Best Travel doesn't have room service. He said there was a problem with the television and the kettle. He wasn't happy and wanted to see the assistant manager or manager about it. In retrospect he knew we were both women. When he answered the door, the man was wearing nothing but a smile.'

'Goodness me!' Margot's jaw dropped.

'Then there was the hen party that came back drunk. They congregated in one room and played Truth or Dare until the early hours, despite several warnings. The man next door to them eventually knocked and complained. The woman who answered was dared to kiss him by her friends. He was furious and almost got her charged with sexual assault. His wife was even more angry and threw a punch.'

'See. You've got the knowledge I need. Clearly I have a naive idea of the hotel industry.'

'Still sure you want to go ahead?'

'There must be pleasant guests as well!'

'Yes. One regular knits egg cosies. She brings me a different one each time she stays. And many guests always leave their room as tidy as they found it. They're polite. Grateful for any assistance and take the time to give us good reviews online.' I bit my lip. 'On the one hand I feel excited about your offer – seeing the chocolate production through, for example. And looking after guests on a much more personal level than I've been able to at Best Travel...'

'I sense a *but*...' she said.

'Amy. Our flat.' I shrugged. 'I can't just drop the life I have. And there's the salary. I know Crocker & Crowley is struggling but I'd at least need what I earned at Best Travel to pay the mortgage, building insurance, council tax... It's our home. I wouldn't sell up – certainly not until Amy and I saw how things panned out for both of us.'

'I've thought about that,' said Margot. 'Done my own research. Looked at the figures. I was flabbergasted at how much other Virgin Island hotels charge. Like you say, I agree, if done properly, this venture could soon rake in thousands. And once the shoe company has reduced its number of stores... and as Seagrass Conservation continues to expand...'

Rick looked more relaxed than I'd ever seen him.

'We'd be short-sighted not to invest some of that money into a decent salary for you. My first rule of business – you have to put in, to get out. You've already shown me just how hard-working and innovative you are.'

I pictured myself living alongside Rick. And Margot. Nia and Brandon. And, of course, Chatty. Golden sunrises instead of London smog. A morning dip in the sea instead of a musty commute.

Margot let go of my hands. 'You must make your own decision, my dear. I'm here for any questions. I'll support whatever you decide.'

She leant forward and gave me a hug. Her embrace

reminded me of Mum. It felt comforting, being so close to a person who genuinely appeared to care. A person I really seemed to click with. Someone who could advise me and offer life experience.

I had no parental figures. Prue was purely professional. The neighbours were friendly but had their own children.

I'd managed. I'd had to. There were plenty of people worse off.

But now and then I cried at night, wishing there was someone I could ring who would tell me everything would be all right. Of course, after the last few weeks I realised that person, now, could also be Amy.

I stood up by Rick's side and watched as Seagrass Island became closer. He kissed the top of my head. Margot began humming.

The three of us on this boat.

It was almost as if I were part of a happy family.

I relished a sense of... of belonging.

As we stepped off the boat Amy and Jackie came into view. Margot disembarked, keen to cuddle her favourite monkey. She neared Jackie and as soon as Margot spoke his name, Chatty reached out and moved onto her shoulder. Amy gave me a hug and introduced herself to Rick's gran. Without thinking about Chatty, I whistled Mum's favourite song. He stopped moving and turned his head in my direction. With a surprised look, Margot beckoned me closer. I reached out my arm and Chatty clambered across. His tail wrapped around my neck and he began grooming my hair.

'It seems to me you belong here, Sarah,' said Margot.

There was that unfamiliar word again.

'Now that would be funny...' said Amy and she laughed. 'If me swapping a holiday resulted in my sister swapping her whole life. I guess it would serve me right though – losing my best buddy. I'd end up a sad crazy cat lady, living alone with Nelly.'

41

'What was that all about? The looks Rick and Margot exchanged,' Amy said as we walked up to the house, Chatty batting my ear.

What could I say? It's actually *me* who's considering moving out – not only of our home, but our home country as well.

'When I talked about living on my own I sensed… I don't know. Have I somehow put my foot in it? Don't tell me Margot lives back in England with a load of cats.'

'Not as far as I know.'

Jackie, Rick and his gran overtook us. I heard a piano and harmonica. Chatty stopped playing with my ear for a second.

'Nia and Brandon thought a small welcoming party might be nice,' said Amy. 'So stop slowing down, sis. Let's get ourselves a rum cocktail. Nia's baked the tastiest looking peach cobbler muffins and mini banana fritters and—'

'Margot's offered me a job.'

Amy stopped in her tracks. We stood under the shade of a palm tree.

'With Crocker & Crowley? In retail? But what about your luxury hotel plans?' Her face turned serious. 'Well done, that's really great, but just because you've lost your job don't rush into something you'll regret. We can use some of my lottery money, for a while, to—'

'No. Here on Seagrass Island…'

Amy's eyes widened.

'… As manager of the new luxury complex. She really thinks her family should give my idea a good go. I've got the experience they need. I'd be in charge of the website as well and…' My excitement fluttered through the air like the butterflies in my stomach that became apparent every time I thought about Margot's offer. Just imagine, me starting this business from scratch? But I couldn't do it to Amy. What if she fell ill or suffered a broken heart or… We had no close relatives – there was no one else for her to turn to, back in England. 'It's ridiculous, right? Come on. Those cocktails sound good. It'll probably be my last shot of rum for a while.'

Amy didn't move.

'What?'

Chatty squeaked as if to echo my question.

'I recognise that tone,' she said. 'It's the one you use if I suggest a film at the cinema that I'm desperate to see and you don't want to but pretend you do.' She stared at me. 'So… you moving to Seagrass Island… living here with Rick…'

'That wouldn't be the reason,' I said firmly. 'It would be a bonus but taking Margot up on her offer would be about me and my future.'

'So you *are* thinking about it.'

We stood in silence for a few moments.

'Yes. No. Of course not.'

Amy exhaled and paced up and down.

'You and I, we're a team, Amy. Us together forever. That's the way it's always been and always will be. And Nelly is a fantastic cat but she couldn't argue with you about which Netflix series is best or…'

Amy stopped walking around and faced me. 'I think you should do it.' She folded her arms. 'I was joking back there, about cats and me going crazy. You'll never get another opportunity like this. To set up a luxury hotel from its very beginning – how would you get on board a project like that in London, with no direct experience? And if you aren't happy living on Seagrass Island eventually, just think what your input here will look like on your CV back in England. It will really set you up to get a high-end job anywhere in the country.'

'What about you, living on your own? Then there's university next year…'

'Financially, in terms of the mortgage, I'm guessing things probably wouldn't change much, depending on your wage here, right? Unless you thought we should sell up and—'

'No, it's our home, Amy, and I've already discussed that with Margot. I'd not consider her offer for a second if I wasn't earning at least as much as I was at Best Travel. And with your studies next year I could help out as, on this island, my living expenses aren't going to be nearly as high as back in London. Not that I'm seriously mulling over moving abroad,' I added quickly. 'I mean me, living amongst tarantulas and scorpions?'

Amy raised an eyebrow. 'What, exactly, is stopping you?'

You. Us. Me worrying.

'Sarah,' she said gently,' I'm a big girl now. I could study in London. Find a student who'd like to move in with me for the company, and to help with costs. I'm hoping Paws & Claws will give me some casual hours, to fit in with my studies once I've started.' Her mouth upturned. 'Nelly would love having someone new around to pet her – or rather new servants. Plus I'd visit when I could. You could come back to England. We've got Skype. Social media. The phone. As you know, next summer I'm hoping to come over here to help Jackie again. I can forward your belongings on when I get back at the end of next week.'

'I don't know.'

'Then there's you and Rick,' she said. 'You can't pretend that's not a factor.'

'What if it didn't work out?'

'No point projecting into the future. What will be will be. There's no way of knowing but that's no reason not to give it a chance.'

I shook my head. 'How come you're so wise?'

She took my hand. 'I learnt from the best. You deserve this, sis. Yes, I'll miss you but I've got my life to lead. You trust me, don't you? To live my own life? To look after Nelly? To make this work?'

I looked down at our hands, fingers intertwined. Petite and slim, hers reminded me of Mum's.

I lifted my head. 'I do trust you, completely Amy. I know you'll manage. More than that – you'll thrive. And if you don't… if *either* of us are struggling, we're still there for each other. The miles in between us won't matter – right?'

Beaming, she nodded.

'I should feel insulted – you seem almost pleased to see the back of me.' I smiled, a tiny, needy, unsure part of me left over from my childhood wondering if that was the case.

She cupped both of her hands around one of mine. Her voice sounded thick when she replied. 'Part of me is. I've always felt as if I've held you back, even though I know you would never see it like that. It feels liberating for me to see you break free from the responsibilities you had to take on. I'm going to miss you so much – but in a good way, knowing that you are following your dreams… as I will be. And the thought of some independence… it's nothing against you, but that does sound exciting. Does all of that make sense?'

I couldn't speak and simply kissed her cheek.

'You really like Margot, don't you?'

'She's so easy to talk to. We just seem to click.'

Footsteps sounded. We both turned towards the house.

Long legs. Broad shoulders. Spiked hair.

'Are you coming in?' called Rick as he stopped by one of the cacao trees.

Rick and chocolate-making – that was one irresistible combination. Amy was happy. Nelly would be looked after. I clicked with Margot and felt that friendship would grow. The island had found a way into my heart with its unassuming, natural beauty – as had dear, sweet Chatty with that cheeky blond face.

I reached up my hand and ruffled his fur.

'Talk to Rick, Sarah. Tell him you're staying. I'll see you inside.' Amy strode into the house.

He came over. 'Everything all right?'

'Yes… Amy and me… we were just talking about the future. How… I need to let go.'

Rick lifted my chin. 'She's lucky to have you.'

'But talking to you, about Lee – it's made me realise I've

been that domineering, interfering older sibling. Thanks for giving me that perspective. It's helped me see Amy's position.'

'Thanks to you too,' he said. 'You've helped me understand my brother better. I think his continual concerns does stem from that accident I had as a child. Thinking about it, when he tries to take charge here there is often a comment about me working too hard and worries about my blood pressure or stress... what I see as a lack of trust is actually a big brother caring. In fact... you've inspired me to tackle him about it.'

He took my hand and led me around the far side of the house to a log, positioned in front of a small pond. Eye-catching Ginger Thomas plants surrounded it. Nia had pointed out a cluster near one of the beach huts. I admired the vibrant yellow flowers. Delicate water lilies bobbed up and down, in the middle of the pond.

'I used to bring girlfriends here, as a teenager,' said Rick and reached up for Chatty sensing that the monkey was tired. I passed him the handle to the lead and the monkey settled on his lap.

'How on earth did you meet girls, holidaying on Seagrass Island?'

'Gran has always had friends on Tortola who came over for dinner – with their partners and children. To be honest they were more just holiday affairs.'

'Is that what this is?'

His face became serious. 'I don't know. What do you think?'

'I'd like to stay and find out, whilst I take Margot up on her offer. I'm ready to step out of my comfort zone and let my sister step out of hers too.'

'That's fantastic.' He leant forward and my heart pumped

furiously as I smelt his aftershave. However, I pressed my palm against his chest. A puzzled look crossed his face.

'First, I have to be honest – my career aspirations have driven this decision. I… I'm so happy it means getting to know you better. You've opened up a part of me I've been too scared to unleash with any other guy. However, I can't build my life around a man. I have to carve out a life that is all mine. That doesn't mean I don't want to find a partner. Just that…'

'Your needs have to come first. I get that, Sarah. I could never give up my conservation work or move back to London. Some things are just as important as finding love. I don't think that's a bad thing. In my opinion, you and me, we're on the same page.'

'Fancy writing a few more chapters together, then?' I asked shyly.

'You betcha,' he said with no hesitation and leant even closer for the longest kiss ever.

Well, it would have been if it weren't for the indignant squeak from Chatty who must have felt excluded by the sudden silence.

I pulled away. 'Oh, dearie me. I'm not sure it's going to work with three in this relationship.'

'Me and Chatty – we come as a package, I'm afraid,' he said and chuckled.

'I wasn't talking about *him* being the third wheel.'

We both laughed.

I ran a finger over Rick's soft, inviting mouth. 'You, me and Chatty surfing the ups and downs of our daydreams together? I wouldn't swap that for the world…'

Epilogue

One Year Later

'You look beautiful,' Rick whispered.

I stood on the sand, in bare feet, by the jetty, surrounded by friends and Amy – and current guests. Cacao House, as a holiday destination, was growing from strength to strength.

The sun beat down on my arms. I wore a floor-length ivory crochet lace dress with wide shoulder straps and a flowing skirt beneath a tighter bodice. Rick stood in front of me in a cream linen suit and pink tie, accentuating his tanned skin and those dark, seductive eyes.

Was this really happening? Was I really getting married?

Yes. To a man whose love, loyalty and integrity had won my heart. He respected my view when we argued. He supported my dreams. But most of all, he made me feel like the centre of his world and not as if I was merely some accessory.

During the last twelve months I'd sensed the scars, from my childhood, slowly begin to heal. Rick had taken our relationship gently, until an uncontrollable passion overwhelmed us both.

Margot had helped me too. We'd spoken a lot. Really spoken – about my past and hers. Before long, it was as if we'd been friends forever. I treasured her advice and the experience of her years.

She talked about Seymour, the first husband who controlled her. Years after the divorce, through a mutual university friend she discovered that he'd had a breakdown and undergone counselling. To her surprise it turned out that he'd suffered a traumatic and abusive childhood.

'Everyone has a story, Sarah,' she'd said to me one night. We'd been sitting by the pool, Rick taking a midnight swim, she and I keenly trying out a new star constellation recognition app on my phone. 'School bullies often come from neglectful homes. Addicts use substances due to low self-esteem. Seymour controlled me, I suspect, because he'd finally been given love and was afraid of losing it. It's no excuse for his terrible behaviour, but I wish he'd felt able to talk to me. Your father will have a story, too. One day, perhaps, you'll discover it.'

It gave me a degree of peace, thinking of my father like that – that maybe Amy and I were unloved not because we were somehow lacking... that, instead, that there was another reason that had nothing to do with us.

We didn't invite him to the wedding. But Margot had planted an idea. Maybe one day – I didn't know when... I still didn't know if... I might instigate a conversation with him about his childhood.

I caught Amy's eye and she winked. Like me, she wore a garland of island flowers in her hair. She was over for the summer, helping out Rachel. Her new housemate, a colleague from work, was looking after a very spoilt Nelly. She was off to university in September. I'd visited her at Christmas. Admired the changes she'd made to the flat, repainting and adding her own personal touches. I missed her, yet my heart swelled at watching her bloom.

Jonas gave me a small wave. He stood with an arm around Benedikt. I'd Skyped him every few weeks and they both visited London for a festive weekend when I went to see Amy. The two of them had settled well together, in Hamburg, and started to get a few gigs. They'd been songwriting furiously since leaving Seagrass Island and were going to play at the wedding breakfast.

Lee gave Rick a thumbs-up. Rick gave one back. He'd had a chat with Lee the first time his brother visited after I decided to stay. I could tell straightaway, by how he'd hugged Rick that the sibling love ran deep. They discussed the childhood accident. Lee admitted he was over-protective. Rick promised to take it easy and to ask Lee before anyone else if he needed help on the island. Then both brothers went back to teasing each other and indulging their competitive streak with swimming races and chess tournaments. Slowly things improved. Angry phone calls between them became something of the past. They still had their disagreements but now were able to talk them through.

Margot walked over, Chatty in her arms. He held a small box in his paws. Rick took it and kissed him on the head, as I did after whistling for a few seconds. He opened it to reveal two simple, silver rings. We hadn't wanted a fuss and tomorrow we'd be back at work. Although Nia had produced a mouth-watering table of food along with magnificent chocolate cake, made with our very own cacao beans...

At first the chocolate-making process had been hit and miss. We still had a lot to learn. But guests seem to enjoy the experience even if the results didn't always taste delicious! As time passed we'd instinctively tailored the holiday we offered by making it more of an eco-destination – that suited a growing market – heavily promoting recycling and sourcing food from local suppliers. Also we were thinking about investing in solar panels. Visitors got a tour of the animal enclosures and for an additional fee could take part in the turtle trips and bird observation. Those activities were proving to be very popular. And Margot had recently come up with the idea of Malik's wife, Zina, setting up a small beauty salon of her own here, for guests. Her new Reiki and massage skills suited our target market. The couple had responded enthusiastically.

Rick was busier than ever, running Seagrass Conservation. The number of volunteers was growing due to the revamped website and word slowly spreading, thanks to us getting conservation influencers involved on social media. His work had even been covered in a couple of magazines.

'Sarah,' he murmured huskily, 'are you ready for this?'

I gazed at the congregation and then back at his gorgeous, mesmerising face. The under-eye bags that testified to his hard work. The appealing lines that proved how much he laughed.

Me? Ready for the marriage I used to swear I'd never have? Ready for the daydream I never used to believe in?

Oh yes.

Because Rick wasn't a man who had changed my life.

Far more importantly, he was a man who'd supported me changing it myself.

Dear Reader,

The Summer Island Swap was inspired my son's trip to the Peruvian rainforest, when he was seventeen. Oh, it was hard waving him off at the airport! The long journey involved three flights and a boat and being a mother I, of course, imagined all the worst scenarios. On top of that there was to be no phone nor internet contact for two weeks.

However, there comes a time when every parent must let go. And I was also so proud of his desire to travel the world and take part in a volunteering trip. When he returned I listened in awe to his descriptions of the conservation work, all of which are reflected in this story - the bird counting and butterfly catching; the turtle egg collecting and trail-clearing. My son gave me a real insight into what it is like to take part in one of these demanding projects. This was helped by the photographs he brought back. My favourite was of a spider monkey wrapping his arms around my son's head, and this inspired the character of dear little Chatty.

In recent times we've seen the catastrophic effects of climate change – flooding around the world and the devastating Australian bush fires. The wondrous wildlife that lives alongside us has never been more at risk, with this to contend with as well as the ongoing challenges of, for example, logging and hunting. The natural world needs our help and support more than ever, for its own sake and ours. I hope my story shows that just one person, like Rick, can make a difference. A couple of years ago I stopped drinking bottled water after a twenty year habit. It's a tiny contribution but I firmly believe that all of us fighting the little battles will help win the overall war.

I hope you've enjoyed this novel that was written from the heart. We live on such a beautiful planet. Let's hope future generations can say the same.

Best wishes,

Sam X

Acknowledgements

Huge thanks to Clare Wallace, my supportive, tenacious, efficient agent at the Darley Anderson Agency. Thanks for helping me steer this author boat of mine across the choppy waters of publishing.

Thank you to my great editor Hannah Smith and digital marketing manager Vicky Joss at Aria Fiction – along with the rest of the brilliant team. I'm immensely grateful for all your enthusiasm, expertise and hard work.

As always, massive, heartfelt thanks to all the bloggers out there who support and review my writing. I'm continually in awe of your generosity and passion for books.

I'm so appreciative of my family – Martin, Immy and Jay – for their continuing love and support. Special thanks to Jay for his input into this story and putting up with my hundreds of questions!

And to my lovely readers – thank you so much for continuing to show an interest in my stories. Your feedback means the world and I'm so grateful for the support that allows me to do a job I love.

About the Author

SAMANTHA TONGE lives in Manchester UK with her husband and children. She studied German and French at university and has worked abroad, including a stint at Disneyland Paris. She has travelled widely. When not writing she passes her days cycling, baking and drinking coffee. Samantha has sold many dozens of short stories to women's magazines.

She is represented by the Darley Anderson Literary Agency. In 2013 she landed a publishing deal with HQDigital, at HarperCollins, for her debut novel Doubting Abbey. In 2015 her summer story, Game of Scones, hit #5 in the UK Kindle chart and won the Love Stories Awards Best Romantic Ebook category. In 2020 her dark women's fiction novel Knowing You, published by Canelo, won the first ever RNA Jackie Collins Romantic Thriller Award.

Hello from Aria

We hope you enjoyed this book! If you did let us know, we'd love to hear from you.

We are Aria, a dynamic digital-first fiction imprint from award-winning independent publishers Head of Zeus. At heart, we're committed to publishing fantastic commercial fiction – from romance and sagas to crime, thrillers and historical fiction. Visit us online and discover a community of like-minded fiction fans!

We're also on the look out for tomorrow's superstar authors. So, if you're a budding writer looking for a publisher, we'd love to hear from you. You can submit your book online at ariafiction.com/we-want-read-your-book

You can find us at:
Email: aria@headofzeus.com
Website: www.ariafiction.com
Submissions: www.ariafiction.com/we-want-read-your-book

𝗳 @ariafiction
𝕏 @Aria_Fiction
📷 @ariafiction

Printed in Great Britain
by Amazon